HIDDEN AGENDA

HIDDEN AGENDA

Anna Porter

FELONY & MAYHEM PRESS • NEW YORK

All the characters and events portrayed in this work are fictitious.

HIDDEN AGENDA

A Felony & Mayhem mystery

PRINTING HISTORY
First Canadian edition (Irwin): 1985
First U.S. edition (Dutton): 1985

Felony & Mayhem edition: 2018

ISBN: 978-1-63194-115-3

Manufactured in the United States of America

Library of Congress Cataloging-in-Publication Data

Names: Porter, Anna, author.
Title: Hidden agenda / Anna Porter.
Description: Felony & Mayhem edition. | New York : Felony & Mayhem
Press,
   2018. | Series: Judith Hayes ; 1 | "A Felony & Mayhem mystery."
Identifiers: LCCN 2017034180| ISBN 9781631941153 (softcover) | ISBN
   9781631941160 (ebook)
Subjects: LCSH: Women journalists--Fiction. | Murder--Investigation-
-Fiction.
   | GSAFD: Mystery fiction.
Classification: LCC PR9199.3.P624 H5 2018 | DDC 813/.54--dc23
LC record available at https://lccn.loc.gov/2017034180

For Cathy and Julia

Acknowledgments

My thanks to John Pearce who thought it could be done, Peter Worthington who planted the idea, Sam Vaughan who edited the first pages, Sylvia Fraser who still doesn't think mysteries are silly, Jack McClelland who taught me about publishing, Ken Lefolii who read two previous drafts without complaints, Marjorie Harris who might have written this book, and Julian for surviving the whole process.

CONTENTS

The icon above says you're holding a copy of a book in the Felony & Mayhem "Traditional" category. We think of these books as classy cozies, with little gunplay or gore but often a fair amount of humor and, usually, an intrepid amateur sleuth. If you enjoy this book, you may well like other "Traditional" titles from Felony & Mayhem Press.

For more about these books, and other Felony & Mayhem titles, or to place an order, please visit our website at

www.FelonyAndMayhem.com

Other "Traditional" titles from

FEL♀NY&MAYHEM

NATHAN ALDYNE
Vermilion
Cobalt
Slate
Canary

JOHN NORMAN HARRIS
The Weird World of Wes Beattie
Hair of the Dog

MARISSA PIESMAN
Unorthodox Practices
Personal Effects
Heading Uptown

ANNA PORTER
Mortal Sins

DANIEL STASHOWER
Elephants in the Distance

HIDDEN AGENDA

PART ONE

Judith

One

NO ONE LIKES TO think about suicides. Least of all, the men who run the subways.

On the night of April 8, 1985, at 11:05 p.m., as his train was rounding the bend in the tunnel just before Summerhill, it was the last thing motorman John Hogg wished to think about. On the downtown run Summerhill and Rosedale are the last of the suburban stations and on a week night almost no one gets on. The yellow lights make the platforms seem unreal. He could slow the train, slide into a fast stop, open and close the doors in almost the same movement, and start again as fast, for sport. Something to keep his mind off that other time. As he pulled out of Summerhill, Hogg began to unwrap his chicken sandwich.

When approaching the next stop, Rosedale, late at night, Hogg always had that same nightmare feeling, fear gripping his jaws tight and catching in his throat. His first suicide had been at Rosedale Station. In the heart of chic, residential old-world Toronto, where he sometimes took the kids for a Sunday drive to show them the palatial, Georgian homes.

Then, also, it had been late at night. The girl in front of the train no more than a blur of movement...

He had to stop thinking about it.

Most drivers didn't like the late shift, it cut into their family lives, but Hogg had asked for it. And got it. There were a few privileges to be had for twenty-three years on the trains. The kids were grown now, the wife was taking some damn-fool course at Ryerson, and he could get the day to himself. Peaceful. And some nights there were parties. Tonight should be a great one. One of his pals was retiring from the "service" (that's what they called it, like the army), and they were all getting together. No wives. Just the boys. And he'd heard a rumor someone had lined up a couple of strippers—for laughs.

He was running a few minutes behind schedule, the lights were green all the way, so he moved the speed lever to 75 and took another bite of the sandwich. A little dry. He was coming in fast, past that infernal cut-off where the platform starts...

He felt it before he saw it. A heavy thump-crunch. A shudder as it smashed into the front. Train slowed by the impact. A shoe hit the window at eye level. Brown. Brown spray splattered the glass. He ducked involuntarily before starting to apply the air-brakes. Somebody screamed. Oh god, no, it can't be. *Not here.*

"For chrissakes, John, stop the fucking car," he heard the guard yell into the microphone.

It was only then that he slammed on the emergency brakes, and pulled the train up, wheels shrieking, halfway down the platform. He jerked open his door.

There were three passengers in the front car. A young man, scrambling from the floor. A young woman, white-faced, holding onto the vertical bar with both hands. She looked at him, eyes wide, her mouth sagging open. Another woman was screaming, hiccuping for breath, her head thrown back. Hogg muttered something at the young woman. *Regulation: calm the passengers so as to prevent panic. They must stay inside the car until the police arrive.*

He reached back into his cubicle and pressed the alarm button, then walked to the first door, withdrew the emergency pass key from his breast pocket and opened it.

"Please, everybody, stay calm. Stay seated. The police will be here in a few minutes," he said to the man who was moving toward him.

He ran to the emergency alarm station at the end of the platform, broke the glass protection strip, pressed the trip lever down to cut rail power. Then he picked up the red phone, and dialed Transit Control. *Dial 555 for suicides.*

"It's a 555 at Rosedale. This is 2454—Hogg," he added unnecessarily. They would know anyway, as soon as he dialed, where he was and what had happened. They would also notify Police Communications who would direct police officers, ambulance and CIB personnel to the scene.

When Hogg turned, Jake Moore, the guard, was already at the front, bending to look under the train. Hogg jumped down to join him.

"Jeesus, what a lot of blood," he said. One of the two front fenders was bent and twisted out of shape. "That's where he must have hit." Blood splattered all over both fenders, and the lower half of the window. "There he is." Jake was on his hands and knees, pointing down under the belly of the car. There was an arm sticking out over the inside rail. An arm in a raincoat-sleeve, wrist wearing a gold watchstrap. "He's got to be dead," Jake said.

Hogg didn't say anything, he just nodded. No one could have survived that.

"Didn't you have another one here a couple of years back?" Jake asked.

"Yeah. A girl... She was just gone fifteen."

"What foul luck. Twice in the same place." Jake crouched down again to get a better look under the train.

"Did you see him jump?" he asked.

"No. I mean, yes, I must have. It all happened so fast."

"I thought you'd never stop the car," Jake said quietly.

Hogg became aware of other people on the platform, a small cluster with their feet at Hogg's shoulder level. Silent. Staring.

"Would all passengers please clear the platform," said the loudspeaker.

"Shit. I had to slow down first, didn't I? People get hurt if you stop too suddenly," Hogg blurted out, angry. "Your first one this, isn't it?"

Jake nodded.

"You'll learn."

They climbed back onto the platform.

"There's been an accident. Everybody please go upstairs," Hogg said.

"Everybody please clear the platform," the loudspeaker tuned in.

The spectators backed away, slowly. They made no move toward the stairs.

"Did you see what happened?" one of them asked.

"I saw him when he came down. Such a nice-looking man."

"Do you suppose he jumped?"

Hogg checked his watch. They were, as ever, efficient, he thought with some pride. The line supervisor was coming along the platform, waving people upstairs. Sensing the authority of the gesture, they began to move. It was 11:18.

Behind the supervisor's gray uniform, Hogg could see four other men in brown—Equipment Department and Track Patrol.

"You're Hogg?" the supervisor asked. "Where did it happen?"

"As I was entering the station. He came at me from the side. There was no way...hell, I couldn't even see him."

The supervisor scanned the side of the train for pieces of clothing, or body. Two of the other men were down on the tracks looking under the train. None of them were first-timers on the "jumper squad."

"Under car one. About in line with door one," a Track Patrol man shouted at the approaching police officers.

"Ambulance here yet?"

"On the way."

One of the policemen pulled out the emergency wooden box from the south end of the platform, broke the seal and pulled out the basket stretcher, a rubber sheet, and the chalk for marking the location of the body.

The doctor and two St. John's Ambulance men in white uniforms crawled under the train to determine whether the man was dead. Not that there was any real doubt. Still, one has to follow regulations; it's what makes the job bearable.

"He's dead all right," the doctor said, emerging from under the car. He wiped his hands on his white coat, leaving black and brown smears alongside the pockets. His face was flushed and damp as a policeman helped him up onto the platform.

"OK, everybody off the track. We'll have to move the train to get it out," said the officer in charge. "You the motorman?" he asked Hogg.

Hogg nodded.

In five more minutes they had the body on the stretcher. Most of the body. One arm arrived separately. It had been thrown across the meridian divide toward the Northbound lane.

The back of the head had been smashed. Some soft gray jelly lay beside the face. Blood caked over the forehead, across the neck and down the length of his fur-lined trench coat. The first impact must have broken bones in every part of the man's body, though all you could see was where his chest had caved in. He was covered in dirt, mud and black tar from the undercarriage. Still, he had been a handsome man. Maybe mid-fifties, hair brown to beginning white, face lined by too many smiles, gray-blue eyes staring up at the doctor's hand as he closed the lids, firmly.

Sergeant Levine was jotting in his notebook, policeman's shorthand, while he waited for the CIB photographer. Hogg let him into the first car so he could talk to the passengers. None of them had seen anything, so Levine let them go. The two women were going to take cabs home.

Levine returned to take stock of the man's personal belongings. The doctor, because regulations said he was the one to do it, had removed the blood-soaked wallet and some credit cards from the breast pocket and a cluster of keys, a pair of kid-leather gloves, gold-rimmed reflector-lens sunglasses, some business cards and a checkbook from the other pockets.

As soon as Levine saw that his partner had finished outlining the position of the body, he turned to Hogg who was waiting beside him.

"How did it happen?" he asked, pencil at the ready, not looking up from his notebook.

"I was coming into the station when he jumped. Must have been standing right by the wall. Couldn't really see much. Just a blur. Then his shoe hit the window."

"How fast were you traveling?"

"About 65 and slowing for the station," said Hogg, a little uncertainly, but who would know anyway?

Levine looked up at the line supervisor: "May as well get your show back on the road. I'll talk to the other witnesses upstairs."

"You'd better let Jake Moore take over at the controls," the supervisor said to Hogg.

"We'll have a relief crew waiting at Bloor. You guys take what's left of the night off." Then he jogged to the end of the platform to call Transit Control and ask them to restore traction power.

The two men with the stretcher were already climbing the stairs.

Hogg went into the guard's cubicle. Nobody asked any questions. At 11:31 the train was on its way again. Twenty-one to twenty-two minutes, Hogg thought: they've got it down to a fine art.

Detective Inspector David Parr arrived as the stretcher was leaving. As the officer in charge at Jarvis Street Station on Monday nights he should have been there earlier, but he was in the middle of questioning a particularly hostile assault and battery witness, and gaining momentum, when the call came. The case was coming up for trial within the week, so Parr had decided it wouldn't matter if he was a little late. Not a hell of a lot you can do for a suicide anyway.

Moving past the stretcher, he flicked the white sheet aside, looked briefly into the dead man's face, and continued on with a nod to the ambulance men.

"Bloody mess, eh?" he said to the constable who was bringing up the rear. "You'll notify the coroner?"

"Yes, sir," the constable said. "Sergeant Levine was taking inventory."

Parr waved him on and went to stand beside Levine at the edge of the platform.

"All over?" he asked cheerfully.

"It is now," Levine said, as one of the men in brown overalls scrambled up over the lip of the platform and handed him a highly polished tan leather shoe. Levine turned it over; it had hardly been worn. "Good as new," he said. "Look at that." He pointed to the gold printed label inside the shoe. "A Gucci, yet. Why anyone with a pair of brand new Guccis would want to throw himself at a moving train, I'll never know."

The supervisor came over to tell them he was letting people through at the top again. The two policemen fell in line behind him as he started up the stairs.

"Who was he?" Parr asked.

Levine shrugged. He handed over the plastic bag with the contents of the pockets, holding it between thumb and fore-finger as if it were some nasty insect.

"Here," he said. "You can have the shoe too. Pick up its mate over at the morgue. He won't need them. Not where he's going."

"Perks go with the job, eh?" Parr smiled as he rummaged through the contents. "Here we are." He pulled a driver's license out of the wallet. "George Harris, sixty years old. Lived at 24 Rose Hill Drive. That's not far from here."

"You'll be going over there tonight?" Levine asked.

"Yes. Soon as this is over."

"Don't you ever do it by phone?"

"Not if I can help it," Parr said quietly. "I sure as hell wouldn't like to be told on the phone. Would you?"

The supervisor interrupted them, opening the door to a small staff room near the Yonge Street exit.

"There were only six people on the platform," he said. "They're all in here."

"Good evening." Parr smiled encouragement as he entered. "We won't want to keep you long. Just a few questions and you can all be on your way again."

Six faces glared at him, silent. In shock, Parr thought. Suicides are damned unsettling.

In the corner, a kid about twenty with short-cropped, greased brown hair, leather jacket, tight blue jeans, scuffed leather boots, not quite punk but thinking about it. He held hands with a girl, same age, long damp hair, pale pinched skin. She huddled close to him, touching his body with hers. She seemed docile and needy. He was defiant. At his age, that was fashionable.

By the window there was a black woman, late fifties, soft felt hat pulled down low over her nose, worn khaki raincoat too narrow and too short, orange Dacron dress. She was holding a white supermarket shopping bag, her arms wrapped around it. She looked scared. Might have weathered some bad times with the law; more likely, she was an illegal.

A man, about thirty-five, sat uncomfortably straight-backed at the narrow table, an ashtray in front of him, his briefcase tucked between his navy-blue lace-ups. He wore a three-piece negotiating-blue suit, tinted rimless glasses, and was smoking his third cigarette. He had an exceptionally thin long neck with a jumpy Adam's apple tucked into his tight white collar.

The other end of the table was occupied by a man in his forties—balding, red-faced—and a pinched, matronly woman, possibly English. Clearly they were not together. They were a study in contrasts. She had half-turned away from him, balancing her outsize monogrammed handbag against the table leg. She wore a black mink coat, casually unbuttoned, her elegant knees composed over each other, foot tapping in anticipation. The man was sweating. He took a crumpled Kleenex from his lumberjack shirt pocket, shook it out, and wiped his forehead.

Levine flicked open his notebook.

"Could we please have your names and addresses. Police procedure, I'm afraid," he said deferentially. "Perhaps you'd like to get the ball rolling." He turned to the executive type, who was closest.

"Joseph Muller, 27 Roseborough," he said, shaking another cigarette out of the package. "Do we get called for an inquest or something?"

"I don't think that will be necessary," Parr said. "Phone number?"

Levine wrote down both the home and business numbers. A stockbroker going home late. Edgy.

"When did you arrive on the platform?" Parr asked.

"Couple of minutes before the train. I wasn't even near him when he jumped..."

"Did you see him jump?" Parr asked quickly.

"Well... I sort of saw a movement, out of the corner of my eye really. Then there was this awful thud."

"Was he already on the platform when you came down?"

"I don't know, really. I don't remember. I was reading the paper." He waved his rolled-up *Star* at Parr.

Parr thanked him and opened the door to let him out before turning to the others.

The apprentice punk hadn't seen anything. Nor had the girl. It was the thud she remembered. Her lower lip trembled when she spoke. While Parr questioned them the boy was pumping her hand, his eyes steady with hostility.

"Get them out of here," Parr murmured to Levine.

The man in the lumberjack shirt said he was a cab driver named Jenkins, taking a day off. "Teach me to take the gawd-damned train," he grumbled. He had seen Harris march to the edge of the platform, lean out to look up the track when they heard the train coming, then back up as if to get out of the way. But he didn't. He had sort of lurched forward again and fallen in front of it. Somebody screamed.

"Who?" Parr asked, but none of the remaining passengers admitted to screaming, so he went on with the questions.

The black woman, not unexpectedly, had heard nothing and seen nothing. She was so eager to get away Parr could feel her vibrating toward the door. He hoped they wouldn't have to call her or that she had given a false address. He wasn't going to harass her for identification. Rotten luck for her to be in the wrong place at the wrong time.

They had left the gray-haired woman to last. She seemed content sipping her tea, listening with grave interest, like a schoolteacher watching the class take turns at reading. That is what she turned out to be: Mrs. W.A. Hall, a retired school-teacher. The husband must have made the money.

She had seen Harris coming onto the platform. His right hand had been in his trouser pocket. His raincoat was open, loose, the belt swinging as he walked. Such a distinguished-looking man, graying at the temples. Couldn't have been much more than fifty. He had hurried to the end of the platform—the north end.

"To think now what his purpose was!" she said with a sigh. "What a horrible waste. And why would anyone choose such a messy way?"

"Did you actually see him jump?"

"No. I heard him hit, though. Sounded like a ripe pumpkin hitting the pavement. It was the black woman who screamed.

She kept screaming afterward too. Very emotional they are, on the islands. Though I daresay they see more violent deaths than we do. She wasn't so far from where I was. I saw she had her mouth open. She'd dropped her bag." She was quite certain the black woman must have seen the man jump.

Parr offered to drive Mrs. Hall home. It was more or less on his way.

She obviously enjoyed the idea of sitting in a police car. Her one regret was that Detective Inspector Parr would not tell her the name of the deceased. He couldn't, before notifying the next-of-kin.

TWO

JUDITH DECIDED IT was time for her to draw up a will.
Nothing fancy, mind you, no heavy legalese, just the basics, in
her own words. At age thirty-eight, a responsible person must
have a will. Even if she wasn't consistently responsible. A will is
something like a stocktaking.

> *I, Judith Hayes, being of sound mind* (mostly) *and body*
> (still holding on), *do on this day, April 9, 1985, leave
> all my clothes to my daughter Anne. My new sling back
> sandals can be held in trust for her until she is old enough
> to wear them. She's certainly big enough to wear them.
> My son, Jimmy, can have the typewriter, and the two of
> them can wrangle over the couch, the chairs and all the*

stuff in the kitchen. They can have their own beds. They can split the insurance dough. Their father had better take over the mortgage payments on the house. For all I care, he can even move in with them. I don't wish to have my kids move to Chicago and live with him.

She wondered if she could be quite as specific in a will and whether her instructions would be followed because they were in a will. Could James just declare himself legal guardian, or next-of-kin, or whatever, sell off the house (all the blood-sweat-and-tears to keep it these past seven years) and move the kids to that glass and chrome tower he called home in Chicago? She should probably postpone all thoughts of dying until she had ascertained what her rights would be afterward.

She climbed out of bed and padded down to the kitchen to make herself a cup of coffee. Naturally there was no milk in the fridge. Anne drank about a quart a day, and all those brilliant plans for the kids to keep an up-to-date shopping list on the little blackboard Judith had bought for the purpose had long been abandoned. The idea had been that when you finished something, you wrote it on the board.

No bread either. She didn't care so much about that, but the kids would notice when they got out the jar of peanut butter for their early morning treat. Serve them right.

The black coffee tasted stale, but it would wake her up and might get rid of the pounding in her head. There was a time when she could stay up till 4:00 a.m. drinking, talking and smoking cigarettes. Now, just a few drinks and she had a thumping hangover. Still, she was entitled to one the day after her thirty-eighth birthday. Fair way on the downhill slope. What gets you is knowing all the things you will never be when you grow up. For example, she would never be a great dramatic actress, or a ballet star, or a famous inventor. She'd never even be rich, damn it. Not even the editor of the lousy *Toronto Star*, let alone *The New Yorker*. Self-pity, Marsha had said...on your thirty-eighth birthday you are entitled to indulge in some self-pity. And double martinis on the rocks—hang your diet—and chain-smoking that last package of Rothmans Specials, and staying up until you're ready to drop—alone, or otherwise. She had had a few friends over for a late dinner, but had never quite found the courage to tell them what the occasion was. Allan Goodman had come with two bottles of Asti Spumante, a poor substitute for champagne, and barely enough to go around, but OK for toasting an evening if you weren't having a birthday. And it hadn't been Allan's fault; he didn't know. After they left, she had brought out the cake with all thirty-eight pink candles, all her wishes ready before she blew them out. Then she had finished the entire pitcher of martinis. She vaguely remembered having had a discreet little cry on the expedition up the stairs to her bedroom.

After a thorough search, she located the Alka Seltzer and managed to drink about half a glassful without gagging. The rest of it had stopped fizzing anyway. She took her coffee mug upstairs. In turn, as she passed, she banged on the kids' doors and opened them slightly.

"Time for another fun day at school."

She had got the idea of banging before she opened the door about a year ago when she found Jimmy examining his balls in the mirror. He had been furious at the intrusion. And she had been a little startled herself.

Anne was pulling her jeans on already. Amazing how that kid never had any trouble waking up.

"Hey, Mum," she said over one bony shoulder, "had quite a night last night, didn't you? How is the happy birthday girl this morning?"

"Don't ask," said Judith plaintively. "I doubt if I shall survive the day, let alone the next year."

"Why don't you go back to bed? We'll make our own breakfast."

"Can you get Jimmy out of the sack for me?"

As Judith crawled in between the cooling sheets she heard Anne's familiar hollering at her brother and the equally familiar grumbling reply. Then the phone rang.

"May I speak to Mrs. Hayes?" a polite male voice enquired. "I think so," said Judith cautiously. "Who shall I say is calling?"

"Detective Inspector Parr, of the Toronto Police Department." A pause. *My god, they're on to me. Parking tickets...those parking tickets I haven't paid. They're going to put me in jail.* She was still trying to clear her throat when the polite voice came back on the line.

"Hello. Is this Judith Hayes speaking?"

"Yes. This is she," Judith said firmly and grammatically, remembering to show no weakness in front of the police or they'll suspect you of more than you've committed. An armed robber she had once interviewed in the Kingston pen had given her that piece of advice. Why was it that policemen always made her feel guilty, even now that most of them were younger than she was?

"Mrs. Hayes, I'm afraid I have rather bad news for you," said Parr, in the soft, modulated tone he had developed for such occasions. "Mr. George Harris died late last night. It was a... sudden...death." He let that sink in, then went on quickly, "I was told by Mrs. Harris that you were with her husband yesterday. I wondered if I might come around and ask you a few questions."

Oh god.

Parr waited a while, then asked: "You did see him yesterday?"

"How did he...?" Judith choked on the last word. She was going to call him today. He had looked so well. Happy, really.

"It happened on the subway," Parr said not very helpfully. "You *did* see him yesterday?"

"Yes, we spent a couple of hours together. Did he have a heart attack? Did you say on the subway?"

"We haven't determined the cause of death yet," Parr interrupted. "May I come over this morning? It will only take a few minutes."

"Well, I had planned to..." Oh, what the hell. The day lay about her in ruins already. "Why?"

"It would appear you may have been the last person to talk to Mr. Harris. Routine questions, Mrs. Hayes. It's what we do."

"OK," she said, hesitating.

"Fine. I'll be there in ten minutes."

"Now, wait a minute. I've only just..." but the line was already dead. Damn him. Inconsiderate bastard.

She jumped out of bed, yanked her nightgown over her head, threw it back onto the pillow in almost the same movement and grabbed some underwear from the top drawer of her dresser.

"There's no bread," Jimmy said accusingly. He was leaning against the open door wearing torn jeans, a stretched sweater and his best tough-male pose. Cute.

"I have no time for that now, Jimmy. If you want bread, you can write it on the blackboard, or you can get it yourself." She took out a bulky black sweater. Like Jimmy's, it was guaranteed to hide all imperfections. Color appropriate too. What the hell did George have to go and die for anyway?

"Something wrong, Mum?" Jimmy's voice rose a little and he abandoned the hunched-shoulders-forward segment of the macho stance.

"Somebody I know just died." No tears. Swallow hard.

"Who?"

"George Harris, the publisher. You met him. He was a friend." She pulled on a pair of tailored slacks. They were new, with razor-sharp seams, and made her feel a little less like falling over.

"Hey, Anne," Jimmy yelled. "Can you put the kettle on? Mum would like another cup of coffee."

If Judith had had time, she would have gone over and hugged him. As it was, she just smiled at him in the mirror.

"You should see yourself," Jimmy said helpfully. "Must have had quite a night of it."

"You should see *yourself*," growled Judith. "I still remember when you liked to have your pants in one piece. Takes some asshole in the East End of London to start it, and all you kids think it's cool to have more holes than pants. Cool all right. Specially in the middle of April." Jimmy shuffled his feet for a second. Then he must have decided to let it go. She loved him for it.

Judith examined her face in the bathroom mirror. Even in this dim light it looked dreadful. Dark patches under the eyes, slight sag where the lines were etching themselves further in. She breathed in deeply to make sure her lungs were both still there, then alternated splashing hot water and cold water on her face.

"Jimmy just told me about Mr. Harris dying," Anne said as she deposited a cup of coffee on the cracked toilet lid. "Terrible. He was such a nice man." Anne sat on the rim of the bathtub.

"He wasn't that old, was he?" Jimmy asked.

"Look you two, I'd love to have your company for the rest of the day, but you have school and I have a policeman coming around in about five minutes. So please..."

They left, reluctantly.

"Are you going to be all right?" Anne asked from the stairs.

"Yes. I'll be fine, thank you. I mean I'll be OK." Judith coated her face with darker-than-skintone, cover-all, pan-stick make-up. It smoothed over the creases and added a touch of color.

"Not much of a birthday, is it?" Anne yelled.

"Your presents were good. Jimmy, where did you find that chime?"

"Chinatown. I wanted silk slippers but didn't know your size."

"Marsha's coming today, isn't she?"

"I sure hope so."

Judith outlined her eyelids in gray. It was a good color to lift up the green of her eyes, which needed all the help they could get. She picked a smoke-black mascara and pale lipstick.

"Are you kids still down there?" she shouted, feeling a little stronger. She never knew what to say or how to behave, other than busy, when people died—she had never been a good weeper. Must be a fear of losing control—that was Marsha's theory, at any rate. Marsha had endless theories about human behavior, and she had majored in Judith's special fears.

"Mum, I'll get the bread," Jimmy called, "and milk. OK? You can pay me back later."

Fabulous kids.

"Great. Thanks. Listen, tell you what, I'll make you guys a sumptuous dinner if you come home in time. We can all eat together."

Detective Inspector Parr was at the door. Judith grabbed for her hairbrush and whipped it through her long auburn hair. It needed washing, but even so, it was her best feature.

Anne opened the door and she and Jimmy left, making room for Parr to enter.

Detective Parr was not the type. The last time she had talked to a police detective, he had been ex-army, sturdy and square-shouldered. This one was thin and angular, fortyish, tall enough to have to duck at the door. His eyes squinted under heavy eyebrows. He wore a tweed jacket with oversize brown buttons, dark gray pants, a creased white shirt open at the neck and a stained blue-gray tie that had slipped askew.

"Mrs. Hayes?"

"Yes. Detective Inspector Parr, I assume. Come on in," Judith said coolly since he was already progressing toward the living room. He threw his raincoat over the back of a chair and scanned the room quickly. "Must have had a bit of a party here last night," he smiled.

"A birthday party. Sort of. Do sit down."

He chose a straight-backed chair by the dining room table and pushed aside a few of last night's dishes, all business.

"We'll make it as brief as possible." He flicked open his notebook. "I understand you were interviewing Mr. Harris yesterday."

"Yes, I was commissioned by *Saturday Night* magazine to write a profile of George Harris and his publishing house. Yesterday was our second interview."

"You've known him for some time?" Parr said.

"Yes. I worked for him once. Briefly. In the editorial department. Of course, I've seen him since. Parties and that. Lunch sometimes. I liked him—a lot. I think everybody liked him. He was that kind of man." That's another thing about talking to policemen—they make you prattle on like an idiot.

"Yesterday, how did he seem to you?"

"Perfectly normal, I thought. He did complain a bit about his financial problems, but that's par for the course. You can't run a good publishing house in Canada without having financial problems. He seemed very healthy."

"Did you think he was at all depressed?"

"Depressed? No. Why?... You're not suggesting he committed suicide...?"

"I'm afraid it's possible he may have," Parr said gravely.

"I don't believe it!" Judith gasped. "He just wouldn't have." She stood up and turned her back to the policeman, swallowed hard, smoothed over her face and her voice. "Would you like a cup of coffee? The kettle just boiled."

"Please. If it's not too much trouble." He was grateful she had gone into the kitchen. There had been more than enough tears already. The wife had had a hysterical screaming fit, then fainted. That was while he was standing at the door. The son was there, visiting, a fortunate coincidence that saved Parr from having to lug the unconscious Mrs. Harris into her house. Besides, he could not have left Mrs. Harris on her own. Harris Jr. had accompanied him to the hospital to identify the body.

Judith came back with a tray.

"How did it happen?" she asked.

"He fell or jumped in front of a subway train at Rosedale. We don't know for sure which."

Judith sighed and took a long sip of hot coffee. He wouldn't have jumped—not George. He was such a fastidious man. Even if he had intended to kill himself, he would have chosen a much more genteel way. Pills, for example.

"And you're sure he didn't seem at all unusual yesterday? What did he talk about?"

"Himself, mostly. And books. He had great hopes that he could pull Fitzgibbon & Harris out of debt by the end of the year. He had a very good list coming up this Fall. He knew he had a big winner. There had been some lean years, but he thought they were now behind him. Of course he knew the company would never get rich, but being out of debt would have meant a lot to him."

"Would mean a lot to anybody," Parr said, mostly to himself. "Harris Jr. gave me the impression that the lean years were very lean indeed. Wasn't he into the bank for a couple of million or more?"

"About two. But George was hanging in. And, as I said, he was optimistic. He seemed sure of himself."

"Would it have been realistic for him to think that one good list—how many books is that?"

"I don't know. Maybe thirty-five..."

"Well, could those books alone have got him out of debt?"

"Point is *he* believed it. While he believed it, he had something to fight for, and while he had something to fight for, he would not have given up. Not George."

Parr didn't mind her getting angry. As long as she didn't cry. He sipped his coffee and nodded reassuringly.

"What time did you leave his office?"

"Around 9:30. We were going to continue the interview next week. I was to call him today and set up a time. He thought he would have a drink with Marsha Hillier and me this afternoon."

"Who?"

"Marsha Hillier—a publisher in New York. She's coming because it's my birthday." That's the second time she had brought up the birthday in less than half an hour. Last night she hadn't told her friends, now she insisted on telling the policeman. Perhaps early senility?

"I'm sorry."

Why was *he* sorry? It wasn't his birthday.

"Did you and Harris leave his office together?"

"No. He said he had some work to finish and phone calls to make. He had a lot to do still. He couldn't have been planning to kill himself."

Once Parr had collected his raincoat and she was alone, Judith lit her first cigarette of the day and poured herself a generous Bloody Mary.

"That's for you, George," she said as she took a sip. "You never liked long faces or dreary people and you were a firm believer in Bloody Marys before noon."

She tidied up the kitchen and the living room, then took out the two frozen Quiches Lorraine she had been saving for a special occasion. They would defrost slightly by late afternoon.

It might be wise to invest in a dishwasher, she thought. Kids didn't like washing dishes any more than she did. If only she could get a big enough assignment, she might even prevail on the plumber to come and they'd have two working toilets again. You couldn't revel in such luxuries on $1,500 a month— when the going was good—and two growing kids. That's another thing: at fourteen and sixteen, respectively, shouldn't they stop growing soon? It would make a hell of a difference to the clothes budget. Even if Jimmy enjoyed having his jeans in tatters, he did like them to reach his ankles.

Hard as she tried to fill it with trivia, her mind kept returning to George Harris. What in heaven's name would he have been doing on the subway late at night? What, now that she thought of it, would he be doing on the subway at any time? George drove a car. His office was nowhere near the subway line. He never traveled by subway. Not even in dire straits. Hell, when the company was almost bankrupt, he still took first-class air tickets. Always a man with a sense of style. If he couldn't drive, he'd get a cab. He'd walk, for chrissakes! Worst came to the worst, he'd stay where he was. Let them come to him. Strange how the failure of his business to make money had affected George. The poorer the firm became, the more style he got.

She took out her interview notes which, as usual, were copious. Out of two hours with George Harris, she had recorded over thirty pages of tightly packed shorthand.

She had read through the first twenty when the managing editor of *Saturday Night* called. Had she heard the news, and could she get the story in by the end of the week? Now that George had died, there would be a number of stories. Hers was farthest ahead and they wanted it for the next issue. She said she would try, though she didn't think she could pull it together so quickly, at least not while there was any question of suicide.

The managing editor was quite convinced that they shouldn't probe into the suicide theory. The family wouldn't want that to be a topic of public discussion. They were entitled to *some* privacy.

After she had hung up, Judith finished reading her notes. Just as she remembered, George had been positively ebullient, really enthusiastic about the future. A few years ago he had had to restrain the publishing list, but those had been hard times in all spheres of business. Now he felt his debts were manageable. He anticipated that the whole industry would benefit from the federal government's new policy paper, and his firm, strong in its history of support for Canadian talent, would undoubtedly benefit the most. He planned to go to the American Booksellers' Association convention this year, for the first time in seven, because he had some important properties to discuss with American publishers. And he had just accepted an invitation to be the luncheon speaker at the annual meeting of the Canadian Authors' Association in Vancouver. He was going to talk about the importance of publicity for the success of a book and had a number of jokes and personal anecdotes already sketched out.

Would a man who was about to kill himself be inventing jokes?

Three

NOW THAT SHE SAW how miserable Judith looked, Marsha wished she'd been able to come last night, but Jelinek had staged an auction for Reginald Montgomery's new multi-generational saga, and Marsha had to be in on the bidding. It had opened at 4:00 p.m. with a floor price of $50,000, not an unhealthy start by Morrow (she guessed it was Morrow; the agent would sooner have sat on a hot griddle than reveal any names) and risen to $88,000 by 5:30. At 6:00 Jelinek had suggested she stop screwing around, which was his way of saying that the bidding was not going as high as he had in mind, but he noted her offer of $5,000 up anyway. The second round took over an hour. Marsha was ready with $100,000 when Jelinek called again, but they were at $120,000 already.

She had been obliged to call in Marketing for help. That meant giving young Markham a chance to parade his opinions while she forced herself to listen. She knew he had been waiting to be consulted because he had two sheets of statistics clutched to his chest, including sales figures for books she had never encountered. It was 6:30 and he had been waiting in his office for the phone to ring. Ambition without talent is a terrible thing, Marsha thought, but Larry Shapiro had insisted she call Markham if the price went over $100,000, and she had so much wanted to land Montgomery.

It wasn't over until 9:00. She'd lost the bidding and her temper at $150,000, Markham was still talking strategy, and it was too late to catch the last flight to Toronto.

She picked up the flowers on the way to La Guardia this morning, having guessed Judith would deny it was her birthday, so that there wouldn't have been any flowers yesterday. They were only daffodils, a perky glowing yellow, but they would brighten Judith's living room gloom. Marsha could never understand why Judith had stayed in this house after her divorce. Surely, she could have found something less dreary, even if she believed remaining in the neighborhood was essential for the kids. Too many changes would unsettle their delicate minds, Judith's mother had insisted. Marsha knew what the little lady really wanted was a restoration of the marriage. Even though it was James who had walked out, Mrs. DeLisle concluded Judith had been at fault. That was mostly what she decided about everything.

Marsha held Judith at arm's length, grinning, the daffodils between them. "How is the big girl today? Don't look a day over thirty, if you ask me. Not that it matters. Older is better. It's gentler, they say, more understanding. You'll love it."

"I hate it," Judith mumbled into Marsha's shoulder as they hugged each other.

"Did you ever think we'd make forty?" Marsha laughed. "Did you? No? That means you're doing better than you thought. Not even halfway through if you discount the years you're trying to forget..."

"I'm trying to forget last night and this morning."

"Too much celebration?"

"Too many martinis..."

"You're entitled."

"... and then George Harris died." Now Judith was crying into Marsha's shoulder.

"George Harris died?"

"Last night. Jeez, I'm getting your blouse wet. Come on in. I'm afraid I won't be much fun today..." She wiped her eyes on the back of her hand, exactly as she had used to when they were growing up together at Bishop Strachan School for girls, and told Marsha about her interview with Harris and about the policeman.

Marsha had known George for years, not closely. She had admired his enthusiasm, his willingness to take chances, and to push his authors with the Americans, who remained breezily unreceptive. She had made time for him when he came to New York and called on him when she was in Toronto. She had even allowed herself to be talked into publishing some of his authors, not because she always agreed with his assessment of their unsurpassed talents but because she had decided to back his judgment. He had often been right.

"Shit. He could have chosen a better time to do it." Marsha tried to snap Judith out of her gloom. "But I'm not going to let him ruin the whole day. Let's go to that ritzy restaurant you promised me, I want to treat you to something sumptuous—like carpaccio and zabaglione, and linguini with cream. You said it was Italian, didn't you?"

Marsha selected the dress and the shoes. She brushed Judith's hair and distracted her with David Markham and the auction.

"He actually believes in five-year strategic planning and comparative financial analysis, he refers to books as units and authors as elements, and he only laughs when he doesn't mean to. He whinnies if you ask him a question he hasn't anticipated."

"Why do you put up with him?"

"Larry hired him. He thinks we need some fresh thinking about marketing. He's fresh all right, wet-behind-the-ears fresh... I think he's angling for VP by next year."

In the event they had linguini with red wine and radicchio salad, and Judith told Marsha it wasn't going to work out with Allan Goodman, after all. OK for occasional companionship, but no point fooling herself there was any magic.

"Magic is fine for a month, kid, but it has no staying power. It's whether you can joke about making love when you wake up in the morning, and both laugh. *That's* the real magic."

"Allan is scientific about making love, and he doesn't think that's funny."

"I don't think my mother and father ever laughed together. About anything. He probably wore his vest to bed to make damned sure she wasn't going to touch him. I don't know how they managed to produce me; in those days there was no artificial insemination. I can't imagine them in bed together."

"You never could," Judith said. "Some thoughts we are never old enough for."

"Like what?"

"Understanding our parents."

They both had zabaglione, and Marsha gave Judith her birthday present: a round-trip ticket to New York for the coming weekend.

"It's what you wanted. We'll go to the theater. Have brunch at the Sherry-Netherland. We'll go back to the Frick."

"I have to finish my George Harris story. Now he's dead they want it in a week. You know, Marsha, he *couldn't* have planned to kill himself."

"Then get an extension and find out why he changed his mind. It'll make for a better story. But give it a rest for the weekend. You write better after a rest. Remember your group therapy story? It was fabulous."

"Yeah. I got sued."

"Nobody sues over boring stories."

"I don't know. It's hard to get away—with the kids..."

"Come on, they'd be glad to be alone for the weekend and you know it. Let your mother loose on them for mealtimes. They'll forgive you by the time they're thirty-eight."

"I still have the Nuclear Madness story to finish..."

"The one about closing the plant in Pickering?"

"And Whitby. It's $1,500. For the *Globe Magazine*."

"Not enough. Besides, it'll wait, and I can't. I'm in London the weekend after."

In the afternoon Marsha was going to visit M & A's Canadian subsidiary in Don Mills. She had to review the upcoming summer promotions and be back in New York in the evening. There was a reception for a British expert on contemporary papal diplomacy and its role in maintaining world peace. The event promised to be dreary but she had given Peter Burnett her word that she would attend. The expert was one of Peter's touring authors.

Judith was glad she hadn't asked Marsha about Jerry. Why spoil a perfectly pleasant lunch?

Four

FITZGIBBON & HARRIS seemed like the best place to start. On the way there, Judith picked up a copy of the *Star*. Next to a vivid description of the stray Russian warhead discovered in Norway, Harris, not unexpectedly, had made the front page. He occupied the bottom right-hand corner, with a suitably restrained headline, an old, but not altogether unflattering, photograph, and a few comments from a variety of celebrity authors who had known him. There was no hint of suicide but the copy made much of the company's financial problems. They were giving themselves an I-told-you-so comeback should the police conclude it was suicide. Nice.

Judith still felt a pang of nostalgia every time she drove into the Fitzgibbon & Harris parking lot. It had been good working here, even though she hadn't lasted long. All the executive parking spots were filled, except for Harris's. His name was painted on a white board at the head of his space—like a tombstone. She drove to the end and parked by the back entrance that led to the editorial department.

She found them all huddled together in Alice Roy's office, drinking Scotch out of paper cups. There was not much conversation and a great deal of cigarette smoke. Judith didn't want to go all the way in.

"Alice, may I speak with you for a minute?" she asked tentatively from the doorway. A couple of the older editors who knew her waved, but nobody smiled.

Alice's cheeks were puffy, her eyes red. With her narrow, thin shoulders pulled forward, long slender arms crossed over her chest, she looked like a bird caught in the rain. She came out slowly and closed the door behind her.

"You're not working on your story *today*," she said quietly, with only a hint of threat.

"Look, Alice, I know how you all must feel and I don't like barging in like this, but I do have to finish the story and dammit, I liked him too. A lot. You know that." A little petulant?

"So?" Alice leaned back defiantly against the hospital-green wall.

"So, I want to find out how and why he died. *Because* I care."

"We all care. That's why we won't have journalists snooping around today," Alice said, hostile. "Not even you," she added for old times' sake.

"Come on, Alice, don't you want to know why he committed suicide?"

"Isn't it obvious?"

"No."

Alice straightened up and fished a cigarette out of her mangled pack of Gauloises.

"When I left him at 9:30, or thereabouts, he was in the very pink of health, he was cheerful and optimistic."

"I take it you have your own theory?" Suddenly Alice was belligerently interested.

"No theory. Just a need to find out."

"Me too." Abruptly Alice took Judith by the arm. "Let's go up to the cafeteria and talk. There's nobody there now."

On the way up they passed the executive boardroom. Judging by the hubbub of voices, a meeting was in full swing.

"Deciding how we carry on till young Harris sells." Alice nodded toward the boardroom. "He's a jerk."

The rest of the building was mostly deserted.

"They let everybody off as soon as the news was announced," Alice explained. She got them both coffee and they sat overlooking the parking lot. One thing about the publisher's suburb in Toronto: they hadn't cluttered it with trees.

"The police claim somebody saw him jump," Alice said. "I was with him yesterday. We had an editorial meeting. The whole team: editorial, design, production. Mainly, we were tying down the schedules, since we'd already closed down the Fall list. George seemed pleased about the way it was going."

"Have you been harassed by the suppliers?"

"No." Alice pursed her lips as if to say none of your damned business, then she relented. "We've been paying at about a hundred and fifty days. Regular, reliable. They've learned to live with it. So had George. Cash flow is better now than it had been for the past several months and George was congratulating me on the success of last Fall's titles. Three are still on the bestseller list. In April." Alice smiled proudly for just a second.

"How much do you think he owed the bank?"

"Maybe $2 million. Hell, if we could carry it at 17 percent, it's no problem at 13. And if he was going to kill himself over the debt load, he should have done it in 1982—we were carrying $5 million then."

"When I left," said Judith, "he was waiting for some phone calls. Do you know who?"

"Could have been anybody. He'd stay late to finish reading some massive manuscript or work out a complicated deal, but then he'd tell everybody where he was. The phone never stopped ringing. He was the worst manager of his own time." Alice lit another cigarette. "Comes from not putting enough value on it, I suppose."

"Do you have any idea whom he might have talked to after I left?"

"No. None. Gladys says he had no more appointments. He'd told Jennifer Harris not to expect him home before midnight." Alice leaned forward. "You want a theory? I've got one for you: some nasty discovery he made between 9:30 and 11:00. Something to do with that pampered little bastard downstairs."

"Francis?"

"The same. He's always hated the firm. Ever since the old man planted him here as a summer student in '68. He confessed he was meant for better things than reading through the slush pile. He hates reading. He wanted to be a stockbroker and 'make an honest living'—his words. Didn't have a lot of choice though. George was determined he'd be a publisher. You know, grandfather, father, son. Generation to generation. Like Scribner's."

"So you figure he told George he was leaving and George got so depressed..."

"That's stupid. I've no idea what depressed him, but if I were you I'd start with Francis. He is the most depressing thing around here."

"Have you looked in George's office today?"

Alice shook her head.

"There wasn't a suicide note?"

"I don't know." Alice stood up so fast her chair toppled over. "Let's go have a look. We might even find his list of phone calls for the day."

Judith half expected George's office to be locked and guarded by a policeman, but it wasn't. Gladys wasn't sitting at her usual place either. "She's taken the day off," said Alice.

"How *is* Gladys?"

"Well. She's taking it all in her stride. As ever. She rather fancies Francis, I think. If you can believe Gladys liking anybody. Couple of times last year, I saw her laugh at his jokes. They have the same sense of humor. None."

Nothing had changed since yesterday. Harris kept a remarkably tidy office—it looked as though he had just stepped out for a minute. There were no final gestures apparent. His desk, imported Spanish oak on fancy cast-iron legs, was bare except for the two neat piles of incoming and outgoing mail and his correspondence file. His old-fashioned Stenocord dictaphone sat on the small cabinet next to his desk. On the opposite wall there was a floor-to-ceiling bookcase on which someone, maybe George himself, had lovingly arranged his best books for the past year. There were a couple of worn canvas-back armchairs. A blue-sky, rolling-wheat, all-Canadian landscape occupied the side wall.

Alice went behind the desk and pulled out the top drawer. "Here it is." She shoved a sheet of paper toward Judith. The list was typed, complete with phone numbers. Most had been lightly ticked in pencil. Some were bracketed with familiar company names, like The Royal Bank, Ashton Potter, *The Globe and Mail*, Axel Books. At the top, the date: April 8.

"Every morning, Gladys prepared a new list, starting with the calls George hadn't ticked off," Alice explained, leaning her cigarette into the clean ashtray. "Almost like sacrilege," she said. "He hated the smell of my cigarettes. Uncivilized, he called them." She started going through the other drawers. "You can make a copy of the list, if you like. I suppose you'll want to know what they all said to him?"

While Judith copied the names and numbers, Alice made a half-hearted attempt to riffle through George's papers. Then she sat in his chair and started to cry softly. She covered her eyes with one hand, lit another cigarette off the damp butt of the first.

"Are you finished?" she asked in a small voice.

Judith stroked Alice's hair, swallowing her own tears. "Let's get out of here," she said.

The next day Judith got up at 5:00 a.m., circled her typewriter for an hour or so, made two pots of coffee, rearranged her papers, re-read her notes twice, and finally when she had exhausted all plausible excuses, typed five reasonably clean pages of the George Harris story. At 9:00 she took a phone break and started on Harris's list. The first number belonged to a local politician who recalled clearly that George had phoned at 10:45 a.m., because he was then late leaving for his 11:00 a.m. meeting. They were discussing whether the politician should start an autobiography now, while he was still in power, or wait until his planned retirement. George had been both very circumspect and very discouraging in either eventuality. Despite that, the politician deeply regretted George's unfortunate death. *Pompous bastard.*

The second call was more difficult—an old woman in Smith's Falls whose husband had known George's father. She had written what sounded like a love story. She had not heard of George's death and she was somewhat deaf. It took Judith at least five minutes to convince her that she was not calling to arrange for the pick-up of her manuscript. Judith tried to imagine George shouting to be heard by the old lady and her heart went out to him, even now. Ah—the glamour of publishing!

The next few calls were uneventful. One was George's dentist—would a man about to kill himself make a dental appointment? Then there were two calls to printers about late deliveries of George's books. The problem hadn't been solved by the phone calls, which was bad news for George, but hardly bad enough to kill himself.

He had called a Toronto literary agent and made an offer for a new manuscript by a not-so-new author. It was not much of an offer, but the agent had not had a better one; she was running out of options and time, so she had accepted. Now she worried if the offer would hold, with George gone. That was around 5:30.

Between 2:00 p.m. and 4:00 p.m. George had called five of his authors. He arranged to have lunch with one, dinner with another, breakfast, separately, with two more and agreed to advance some urgently needed money to the last, even though the contract had already been paid up. At 3:00 he had talked to the editor of *The Globe*. Judith left messages for several more people on George's list, made herself a salami and lettuce sandwich, brushed her hair, put on some make-up and returned to her typewriter.

By 3:00 when the phone started ringing, she had finished a first draft of ten more pages. She had decided not to use the word suicide. She would talk about "the mysterious death of George Harris."

All of the people who returned her calls sounded shocked by his death, and slightly embarrassed. That meant the suicide theory was catching on.

There were two calls to bookstores who were cutting prices on George's books (bad enough, but...) and one call to Winston's confirming dinner reservations for Wednesday night.

There was a long-distance call to Max Grafstein, president of Axel Books in New York. Judith had met him once, when she was still working as an editor at Fitzgibbon & Harris. She had gone to New York to squire around one of George's young authors who was looking for an American publisher. George had been particularly insistent on her going to Max, because George admired him. He believed Max was the archetypal American success story.

They had had drinks in a bar on 52nd Street, where in semidarkness, with the music blaring, Max had actually affected to read about a third of the manuscript, suggested a title change, some cuts, a new first chapter, and then explained with great warmth, gazing deeply into the young author's eyes, why the book was not for Axel. It was a superb routine.

Marsha had later told Judith that Max had perfected it many years ago, and now used it only on newcomers because the act lost much of its pizazz the second time around.

Max, his secretary said, had already left for Toronto. He was going to attend Mr. Harris's funeral. Yes, Mr. Harris had phoned Monday. At about 5:00. She thought it might have been about a manuscript Mr. Harris had sent them. Mr. Grafstein had seemed quite excited. She added the last bit as if to say that it was mighty unusual for Max to show any excitement over George's manuscripts.

The branch manager at The Royal Bank could not divulge information about Mr. Harris or the nature of the conversation on the specified date, but he did not mind revealing that the call took place before noon.

Finally, there was a lawyer whom George had hired to defend Fitzgibbon & Harris in a recently launched libel action. He was confident they were going to win, though of course there was always the possibility...in any case, the amount involved would have been no more than three or four thousand dollars.

Judith slumped back exhausted. Then, impulsively, she picked up the phone again.

"May I speak to Detective Parr, please?"

"Just a moment."

"Hello."

"Hello. This is Judith Hayes. You remember, you came to see me yesterday morning? About George Harris's death?"

"Yes, Mrs. Hayes..."

"Well, I was just wondering if you've made any progress on the case?"

"What case?"

"About how he died."

"There is no case, Mrs. Hayes. The cause of death has been determined. There is no more for us to do."

"Won't there be an inquest?"

"No. Why *would* there be an inquest?"

"I thought...well, isn't that normal?"

"Not in a situation like this. It would only add to the family's grief. Were you going to tell me something?"

"I...no, I don't suppose you'd be interested now. What about the coroner?"

"What *about* the coroner?"

"Did he find anything?"

"Nothing to find. Why are you asking these questions? You're still working on your story?"

"I'm still looking for answers."

"What are the questions?"

"Mainly: Why?"

"That, Mrs. Hayes, is rather outside my area of concern and I do have to deal with a few other pressing problems. Look, I am sorry about Mr. Harris, but..."

"Sure. Thanks."

Judith slammed down the receiver a little more forcefully than she had intended. Certainly more forcefully than her parting line warranted. But she felt Parr had let a policeman's natural dislike of journalists show. Stupid of him. Damned shame, too. He was really a good-looking guy. She cut that thought short. A policeman, yet. And probably married to his first wife with 2.5 lovely children. All in Don Mills. That would be standard for a policeman.

At 5:00 the kids came home. They both sniffed around the kitchen for treats, Anne turned on the downstairs TV, and Jimmy turned on his upstairs stereophonic tape deck. It seemed pointless to go on with the story, so Judith shoved the cheap Wednesday's special roast into the oven and sliced up some onions and carrots... "Great for their eyes, Judith. When they're studying they must have carrots every day. Even one carrot is better than no carrot." "Mum, you don't still believe that old wives' tale about carrots giving you night vision..." "I know what I know. If you don't care about how they grow up...(sigh)"

Both kids hated carrots, but they would eat a few stoically. It had become a habit. She had started the carrot routine shortly after their first day at school, and though she didn't believe in it, some hidden guilt made her carry on. Maybe it was the same for the kids. They knew Granny was the power behind the carrots and that Judith was, once more, being squeezed. If eating a few of the tasteless things kept her together, what the hell?

Judith sat down next to Anne on the couch. Anne hadn't taken her Hudson's Bay winter-down sports parka off yet. She was leaning forward, elbows on her knees. Intent.

"How did it go today?" Judith asked.

"Hrumph."

"School. How did it go?"

"Oh. OK." Anne continued to stare at the TV set.

Anne did reasonably well at school, though she rarely seemed to work at it. Judith thought she took pride in appearing not to work. Before exams her light would stay on most of the night, but no one was allowed to notice, let alone remark on it.

Judith made one more stab at conversation.

"You want to hear about the story I'm writing?"

"About Harris?"

"About his death. 'Mysterious,' I am going to call it."

Anne reluctantly tore her eyes away from the TV set.

"You mean he was murdered?" she asked matter-of-factly.

That's what too much television does for you.

Five

JUDITH LIKED TO arrive early at funerals. If she came late, there was a good chance she would be caught standing just inside the door or, worse, in the center aisle where she might become a direct target of the minister's attention. It was also useful to have a prayerbook or missal to hide behind, or to mouth the right words when the time came. Hangover from a regimented childhood: better to have all the "amens" ready when everyone else did.

George Harris's funeral was held at the Chapel of St. James the Less, at 12:00 p.m. on Thursday, April 11. By a quarter of twelve the parking spaces were all taken and the black-suited man directing traffic for the funeral home was waving everybody on, up the path into the cemetery. There Judith had to make an excruciating U-turn on the narrow driveway among the ornate gravestones and squeeze her small Renault in behind a custom Rolls. The chauffeur watched anxiously in his rearview mirror. She smiled when she got out of the car and he tipped his blue cap as she went by. She knew his eyes were following her all the way down the path. *Great legs. Still.*

The entrance to the chapel was crowded and noisy. There were TV crews with hand-held cameras and newsmen with microphones. Judith wondered whether Jennifer Harris had issued an invitation or if the press felt it was fair game to accompany one of their own on his "final journey." Bet anyone a wreathful of white azaleas, two out of the three Toronto papers would use that phrase in their write-ups tomorrow.

Inside the chapel it was quiet. The coffin, draped in blue velvet, surrounded by enormous vases of white lilies-of-the-valley, stood to the left of the minister's wooden platform. The original architects had taken pains to work out where the coffin should be placed. Sunlight, turned yellow and intense blue by the stained-glass window, lit up the velvet and the flowers, moving them center-stage.

The front of the church was already packed. To the left there were two rows of honorary pallbearers, all Fitzgibbon & Harris authors. This was the closest they had ever sat to one another, an experience few of them would relish. Too many jealousies over who enjoyed the most attention and whose advertising budget had been canceled. Though most of them hated public speaking they fought for their right to a cross-country publicity tour every time a new book surfaced, each trying to outperform the others, each wanting to be asked back again.

Jennifer Harris, her small black pillbox hat and veil pushed forward, sat erect and uncompromising to the right of the pallbearers. Francis and his wife, their backs as rigid as hers, flanked her on either side.

Judith hoped to spot Max Grafstein early, so chose a pew not far from the door. It was already occupied by a *Sun* columnist and two fidgeting teenagers. Judith still remembered vividly the desperation children experience when they are hemmed in for a long, still time. For her father's funeral she had taken the extra precaution of putting Heathcliff, Marsha's pet gerbil, into her pocket for something soft and warm to run her fingers around. Midway he had escaped and scurried off under the seats, up the aisle, around the coffin, and disappeared from sight. Judith's tears when she thought about telling Marsha afterward had been genuine. She had received a disapproving stare from her mother, who hadn't known about Heathcliff and thought she was showing an improper amount of emotion in front of the other mourners. Such things should remain private.

The chapel filled quickly. A few whispered greetings were exchanged. Very low-key. The Premier of Ontario came, accompanied by his chief advisor and several members of his cabinet. Some MPs had flown in from Ottawa. There was an assortment of municipal politicians, the mayors of Toronto, East York and Mississauga. Judith recognized the publishers and editors of several daily papers, the Toronto-based magazines, the now under-employed Canadian bureau chief for *Time*, and a *Reader's Digest* vice-president, on the creative side, from Pleasantville. Naturally, most of George's rivals in the Canadian book trade showed up, from board chairmen to editorial directors, including two publishers from the West Coast. There was a smattering of literary agents, book manufacturers, booksellers, some of George's old air force buddies, most of his staff, and enough authors to start a convention of the Writers' Union of Canada.

The organist improvised a final cadence. The minister welcomed everybody and enjoined them to pray for George's soul, while turning to page 12 in their hymnbooks. Clearly, no one knew the words or tunes for this or any of the other hymns that followed. The minister admitted defeat at the end of verse 3 of "God cares about you" and asked them all to bend their heads in prayer. Saved from the necessity to sing, everyone prayed vigorously, with a strong crescendo on "For Thine is the Kingdom…"

Max Grafstein, arriving late, was nonetheless ushered into a pew near the front. The minister cleared his throat and looked around the chapel.

"We have come here today to say good-bye to a very special person. This is a tragic day for all of us, indeed a deeply tragic day for Canada. For George Harris was a man much loved and venerated by all those whose lives he touched. We have lost one of our heroes, one of our great cultural figures.

"George Harris was a fortunate man. Fortunate in a long and rewarding public life, and, as well, in a long and rewarding private life: in his wife of nearly forty years, in a family that surrounded him with affection and understanding..."

Judith wondered how George would enjoy his own funeral eulogy. She thought what a pity it was that more people did not think of writing theirs in advance. George's own version of his life would have been a damned sight less decorous.

Would he have thought of himself as fortunate? Probably. Though he complained frequently about the tribulations of the book business, there was little doubt that he had delighted in it. She thought of their last few hours together. George in his shirtsleeves, leaning far back in his chair, legs crossed at the ankles, heels propped up on his desk, relaxed and expansive. He had laughed when she asked whether he might consider selling the firm and retiring soon. It had been an incredulous laugh—the laugh of a man immersed in pursuing his goals, who had given no thought to abandoning them. He was leafing through a new manuscript when she left: perhaps another rabbit-out-of-the-hat trick, another piece of late Fall sleight of hand for the best-seller lists.

"His generosity," the minister said, "was second to no man's. You have come to bear witness to that today. He gave of himself to all of you. His judgment, his support, his unstinting, uncomplaining willingness to give of his time..."

Time was what he had most regretted. He had squandered too much of it in too many ways. His dream, he had told Judith, was to buy himself a house on a Georgian Bay island where he would spend a week every month. That would allow him the luxury of thinking about his problems before having to solve them—a luxury he had never been able to afford.

She didn't join in the final words for George's soul. He would have gagged at the thought of people praying over, of all things, his soul.

The organ began a sprightly Bach fugue. Jennifer Harris stood and floated, head up, back straight, down the center aisle and out the double doors.

Judith joined the throng pushing toward the exit. She would wait for Max Grafstein outside. The Canadian Broadcasting Corporation crew was still there, apparently interviewing some of the guests about George. The rest of the press had packed it in. The politicians were sliding into their chauffeur-driven limousines. The other mourners gathered in small groups, talking, as they waited to pass by the Harrises. Jennifer stood stiff and unyielding, at the foot of the steps, shaking hands with everyone and thanking them for coming.

Alice left a cluster of F & H employees, adjusted her brown felt hat and came over to Judith.

"George would have liked the turnout," she smiled. "A man doesn't know how many friends he's got until it's too late to do him any good. Any luck with the phone list?"

"Not so far. How is it at F & H?"

"Depressing. We're trying to figure out whom he'll sell to. If he merges with one of the big houses we'll all be out of work. Economies of scale, it's called." She fingered her string of white pearls.

Judith saw Max coming through the doors. He was slimmer than she had remembered, and though he hunched forward slightly as he walked, he was inches taller than anyone around him. His dark hair was peppered with gray and cut perfectly, strand by minute strand. He squinted into the sunlight as he came outside. His eyebrows pulled together in a grimace that ended around the corners of his mouth, showing a glimpse of teeth. He was fishing for his glasses in the breast pocket of his black-and-gray pinstripe. When he put them on, he looked a little like Richard Nixon, with hints of Cary Grant in his prime. Striking combination.

Judith waited for him.

"Mr. Grafstein? Max? You remember..." she asked tentatively.

"Why, sure. How are you?" He smiled uncertainly, and she now saw why his teeth had looked so white. He had a beige to golden tropical tan. No fifty-dollar sunlamp could give you all that glow.

"A lot of people here," he said, and started to move on.

"Max, I was wondering..." Judith said hurriedly, "are you flying right back?"

"Not until 4:00. Why?" They joined the line to shake hands with the Harrises.

"I'd like to talk to you about George," Judith said quietly. "It's for a magazine piece," she added as he edged forward again.

Jennifer Harris extended a plump, short-fingered hand toward Max.

"Thank you for coming," she said. "George would have appreciated it." She even smiled a little. Perfect decorum, Judith thought as she mumbled something incoherent about being very sorry. Jennifer looked straight over Judith's left shoulder. Her plum-red mouth was fixed in a tight line. Her soft hand rested, like a dead mouse, in Judith's palm for just a moment, then she said: "I hope you are going to write a fitting story about George." She put the emphasis on "fitting."

"Yes...of course," Judith said, then collected herself. "He was a great man."

"You know what I mean," Jennifer Harris said, her voice rising a little.

"So good of you to come," Francis said, bending to reach around his mother. "Judith, I *would* like to talk to you sometime."

"Yes," Judith mumbled. "Thank you." *Stupid*, why had she said that?

"What's your deadline?"

"They've asked for Friday, but..."

"Doesn't leave you much time." He shook his head as if in sympathy. "Could you make it this afternoon? My office?"

"Of course." *Amazing.*

"Would 4:00 be a problem?"

"Not at all," Judith said, a little too enthusiastically for the occasion.

They were past the Harrises, and Max turned to Judith.

"Whatever was all that about? The 'fitting' part?"

"I think she's worried I'm going to write about the suicide. We're supposed to believe that George killed himself, but we're not supposed to talk about it. It's not polite."

"He killed himself?" Max whispered, surprised.

"That's the prevailing opinion. I guess if it's good enough for the police and the family, it should be good enough for the rest of us. I think Jennifer Harris wants me to leave it alone."

"Will you?"

"No."

"Oh." Max was looking at her, waiting. "Why?"

"Because I care about what happened to him, and I'm not sure anyone else gives a damn. They just want to bury the dead. Fast." Judith hadn't realized until now that she was angry. "Maybe it's just the stubborn Irish streak I got from my father, but I want to find out what happened in the last few hours of his life."

Max nodded. He started to move toward the cab line.

"I still want to talk to you about George," Judith said quickly.

"I haven't seen him in several weeks, and, even if I had, I doubt he would have confided in me about personal matters," Max said quietly. "We drank together, talked a lot about books and ideas for how to publish them. I didn't even know he had problems—other than the ones we all have."

Francis suddenly appeared at Max's shoulder.

"You have a moment?" he asked with a sideways glance at Judith, and began to steer Max toward the parking lot.

"Sure," Max said.

Judith walked toward the cemetery. Most of the cars were leaving. Jennifer Harris sat in a black limousine, dim behind gray glass with a bunch of white lilies in her arms.

The CBC crew had pulled out. Good of them, Judith thought, not to come in for close-ups of the cremation. She preferred old-fashioned burials, the coffin lowered into the grave and covered slowly with earth. The whole dust-to-dust feeling the living could all share. She would write that into her will—a traditional funeral, just as she had wanted a traditional wedding. She and James walking down the aisle, James smiling encouragement. Here comes the bride. Forever and ever, amen. No second chances.

Max came back from the parking lot. His hands dug into his pockets for his gloves.

"I'd better be going," he said.

"Just a few questions," Judith pleaded.

Max pulled on his gloves, adjusting each finger and squeezing down on it, to fit snugly between the joints.

"I could drive down to the Park Plaza. We'll have a drink and it's easy to get a cab from there to the airport."

Max checked his watch. "All right. A drink would be nice."

He smiled when he saw the old Renault. He carefully repositioned Judith's notepads and pencils on the dashboard, stuck her full Dominion Stores shopping bag on the back seat beside Jimmy's muddy football gear and hockey gloves and dusted off the passenger seat before sitting down. He held his gold-monogrammed, black leather briefcase on his knees. Fussy and somewhat domesticated, Judith thought.

"Your husband is a sportsman, I see," Max said with a smile.

"That's my son," Judith said. "Big for his age." She was angry with herself immediately. Why did she still feel it was so important to be young? Stupid old-time conditioning. To prove to herself that she was beating it, she added: "He's fourteen." She maneuvered a risky left turn on Sherbourne and drew the car into the line of traffic on Bloor Street. Max didn't seem to have noticed her discomfort, so she went on: "I'm not married now. Haven't been for a while."

"I'm sorry," Max said.

Judith laughed. "I'm not—any more. Are you married?"

"Second time lucky," Max said absently. "I'm not much of a loner."

They reached the Roof Lounge at the Park Plaza a little after one. Judith took a table in the corner. It was a bright day outside, but here the tinted windowpanes and the soft red lights in the ceiling created an impression of early evening. It was the right atmosphere for a martini with olives. She didn't even have to ask Heinz for the extra olives. Max ordered a martini too, twist of lemon, on the rocks, double.

"About George," Judith said. "Drinking buddies do get to know each other, and you've known him for..."

"Twenty-nine years, I figured this morning."

"What kind of person do you think he was?"

"For the magazine?"

Judith took out her notebook.

"*Saturday Night*," she said.

"Significant. A great publisher. There are few of us left now in a world of MBAs and word processors. With books and authors the shortest route is not necessarily the best. There is no one tried-and-true method. Authors specialize in being different and George understood that better than most. That's why he was successful." Max leaned closer. "It's hard to believe he killed himself."

"Did he seem depressed when you talked to him?"

"No. When?"

"Yesterday. What was that about?"

"How do you know I talked to him yesterday?"

"George kept a running record of his phone calls."

"Amazing." Max shook his head slowly from side to side as if to shake off an unpleasant thought. "George wasn't the type of man who would keep meticulous notes of telephone calls. He had too much grace for that sort of petty bookkeeping." Max sighed and stared out the window.

Judith took a long slow sip of her martini, touching her lip to a chunk of ice. It felt comfortingly sensuous.

"So what did you talk about?" she persisted.

"Business."

"Can you elaborate?"

"Of course. But..." Max paused to brush a stray bit of fluff from his neatly crossed knee, "...I see no possible connection between that conversation and his apparent suicide. None. We talked about money. Percentages and advances. That sort of thing."

"For anything specific?"

Max looked at her as if she had just asked the dumbest question he had ever heard.

"For an author."

"Anyone I know?"

"I doubt it," Max said. "Anyway. It was the sort of conversation George and I have had about a dozen times every year since I've known him. We were going to work out a joint venture. Share costs. Split the royalty advance."

"You're not going to tell me who the author is," Judith guessed.

"You're right."

"Why not?"

"The deal is still going ahead, I hope. Once I'm ready to unwrap it, I could let you know. Give you a Canadian exclusive." He put just the right amount of emphasis on "Canadian" and grinned patronizingly.

"Did it involve a lot of money?" Judith persisted.

Max pondered that for a moment. "Depends on your point of view. Not too much for this book, too much for some others I've seen."

"More than $100,000?"

"What sort of question is that?"

"Curious."

Max chuckled.

"Maybe." He waved at Heinz for a couple of refills.

"That's all you talked about?"

"That's all."

Judith changed direction.

"You've met Francis Harris before?"

Max nodded.

"Not a patch on the old man, but don't quote me on that. He doesn't have the grace."

"There is talk he might sell the company. Did George ever talk to you about selling F & H?"

"Never. He was married to the business. You know that. I hope you're wrong about Francis. He could hire the right sort of people and hang on to the firm. Maybe *his* son will inherit the talent."

What about his daughter? Never mind.

"Do you always have so many olives?" Max was gazing at Judith's drink with apparent disbelief.

"Only in the Spring. Good for the digestion."

The bar was starting to fill up. Two men came in and sat at the next table. One wore a green raincoat and carried a large brown attaché case. The other had papers in a blue folder, wore a cashmere turtleneck and a brown wool jacket with patches. His face was crumpled, friendly and vaguely familiar, tanned so that the creases showed up pale by contrast. He smiled at Judith. She smiled back.

"Has anybody considered the possibility that George simply fell in front of that subway train?" Max asked.

"No, that's New York. The police say he jumped."

Max checked his watch absentmindedly, then waved for the bill.

"I take it they have more to the theory?" he asked.

"They think he was depressed. That he owed too much money."

"Ridiculous. He always owed too much money. That's the nature of the business up here. Not enough people, too many American books. The Swedes have it easy. So do we. One best-seller on the list in the States, that's 200,000 copies hardcover and maybe a million dollars in subsidiary rights—paperback, bookclub, excerpts. And movies…we option more books in a month than the Canadian movie industry would in its lifetime. It's still tough to survive, but not as tough as George had it. What's a best-seller here? Ten thousand?"

"Sometimes. We had a couple close to a hundred thousand."

"George said the most he'd had for a paperback deal was $50,000. Point is, up here, you can't ever get really lucky... But George loved it anyhow. Back in '62 I asked him if he'd come to New York and work with me. That's when I went to Axel. He could have had anything he wanted. Editorial control, big office, profit-sharing, eventually maybe a spot on the board. He didn't even consider it."

"Why?"

"I don't think he cared about money. He cared about books. And his authors. He wasn't about to leave them."

"Wouldn't he have taken them with him? I mean, couldn't he have still published them in the States?"

"Most of that stuff doesn't travel. Too Canadian."

Heinz deposited the bill on a small silver platter, exactly midway between them. Judith reached for it, but Max was quicker.

"I know about free-lancers," he said.

On the way to the elevator, Max put an arm around her shoulders—a friendly gesture, hardly touching before it dropped.

"Good luck with the story," he said. "Let me know what you find out."

Judith left him in the lobby digging for change in his pockets, a fast phone call before he went to the airport.

She had retrieved the Renault from the underground parking lot and nosed it onto Avenue Road when a cab pulled out with Max in the back seat. His briefcase was open on his knees, he was writing in a book. She waved but he didn't see her.

The southbound traffic cleared and, as Max's cab passed, she saw the man with the creased face and patched jacket get into another cab.

Six

BY THE TIME Judith made it to Fitzgibbon & Harris, the sun had quit. It was 4:10 p.m. but it had begun to turn dark. Judging by the slate-gray clouds, Torontonians would be given their usual punishment for thinking too soon of Spring—an April snowstorm.

She decided not to bypass protocol and went in by the main entrance. The young woman at reception invited her to find a seat in the hospital-like waiting room while Gladys Whitaker was paged.

Judith had never felt comfortable in this chrome and glass room. The only concession to its surroundings was a black-painted, steel, free-standing bookcase a few inches from the wall on which someone had meticulously arranged Fitzgibbon & Harris's latest offerings to the world of literature.

52

Judith had sat in this room only once, thirteen years ago, waiting for a job interview. Her kids were still babies, Jimmy just beginning to walk. They had moved into a new house in Leaside, ten miles and a hundred social strata from the one-bedroom apartment they had lived in on Spadina while James finished college. The new house had big bay windows and four bedrooms upstairs. James had opened his veterinary surgery downstairs, the family lived on the second floor. James used to bring some of the sick animals up to show Anne and Jimmy. They came in all shapes and sizes and ailments: broken wings and fractured legs, crushed, mangled, bitten, beaten, torn, with gashes in their stomachs and backs, with needles in their sides, with eyes missing; some just came to die. Even these James liked to hold and pet for a while. He believed it helped them relax. They were always quiet—the animals. Judith wondered why they became so still when they were in pain.

James would sit holding one on his lap for hours. In the evenings while he read his paper, watched television, wrote his reports and recommendations, he liked to cradle an animal in his arm. He was happy then. Maybe they all were. Much of the time Judith had been bored, though she didn't know that at the time. She had thought she was going through a middle-class phase of liberation and a little bit of uninvited self-discovery. That, at any rate, had been palatable to James and boredom would not have been. She had been encouraged to go and find herself—and while she was searching anyway, why not look for a job?

Then, as now, it had been a gray day. George, who for all his sensitivity to human needs had never liked the idea of being on time, had kept her waiting here for about half an hour. She had bought herself a powder-blue floral-pattern wool dress, a beige silk scarf and a pair of gloves she had been determined to wear until the last possible moment. Her hands were chapped and red, her nails chewed beneath the carefully applied pink polish. She remembered her relief when Gladys Whitaker had finally come to usher her into George Harris's office and George hadn't wanted to shake her hand.

"Mr. Harris will see you now."

Same voice. Same place. Time turned back a full thirteen years. Judith shuddered as she swung around. Gladys stood in the doorway, her back to the receptionist, her hands in front of her waist as if she were holding a bouquet. Her nails were perfectly shaped and painted carnation red to match her lipstick. Her brown eyes stared steadily at Judith. Waiting.

"Mr. Harris..." Judith trailed off uncertainly.

"Mr. Francis Harris," Gladys said, impatiently.

Francis Harris, of course. Judith breathed in deeply. No time warp. She wasn't losing her mind after all.

She had never liked Gladys, though they had exchanged only politeness. Gladys kept to herself. She was exacting about her secretarial duties and had wrapped herself in George's mantle of power, assumed but never stated. She drank soda water at the interminable Christmas parties and the men from the warehouse never asked her to dance. She was too porcelain beautiful, and too much George's secretary.

"Mr. Harris and Miss Roy are both expecting you. Together." With that she turned to walk down the main corridor. She didn't glance back to see if Judith was following. Her dark-brown hair bounced up and down above her shoulders, each strand knowing its place.

Gladys's office faced George's across the corridor and through the glass partition Judith could see that she had been busy since yesterday. There were papers piled high on the floor, folders of various colors (George liked to keep different folders for different subject areas—yellow for accounting, pink for financial, brown for production) littered her desk. Their contents were arranged in mountainous layers next to the typewriter. Two of the filing cabinets were open, all their drawers pulled out. There were other drawers on the floor, lined up for easy access in front of the door.

Alice Roy and Francis Harris were sitting in George's office at the low coffee table under the blue and gold painting of the prairies. Between them, a metallic green ashtray was overloaded with cigarette butts. The air was heavy with Gauloise smoke.

Francis stood with his hand outstretched.

"We were afraid you wouldn't be able to make it," he said, motioning toward the window. It had started to snow. The wind shook the windowpane with fierce gusts, throwing wet flakes and frozen rain at the glass.

Judith took his hand: long thin white fingers, cold and dry. She shook involuntarily as she held them, then drew her hand away quickly. Francis pulled up a third chair for her with its back to George's desk. There were papers all over that too, files, folders and a couple of tall piles of manuscripts, some in cardboard boxes, some held together with rubber bands.

"It was good of you to come to my father's funeral," Francis said, folding himself into the low-slung canvas armchair.

"I wouldn't have missed it," Judith said. "I thought very highly of him." *What an inflated way of putting it...yech.* "I mean he was a very special person." She wasn't making it better.

"I was hoping you would feel that way. We all know that you cared for him." He included Alice in the "we all." "That is why I wanted to talk to you today." He took a deep breath. "First of all, I am going to have to ask you to accept that I, too, cared very much for my father. You and I never came to know each other while you worked here, and I haven't moved in your circles since. So you can't know much about me. Yet surely you will believe me when I tell you that my father's memory means more to me than it could possibly mean to you." Francis talked at a calm, measured pace, his words carefully chosen.

"I know he considered your story about him to be important because he made notes in preparation for his meeting with you." Francis tried a small smile. "I'm sure you're aware my father hardly needed to make notes for a run-of-the mill interview. But this one was different."

"He seemed relaxed..." Judith muttered.

"We have had a few bad years, as you know," Francis went on. "Business has been slow, and there was little hope that he could keep his creditors on the extended payments schedule they had previously accepted. Heavy bank interest payments have continued to be too great a burden. My father could no longer cope."

"That wasn't the impression he gave me," Judith said and looked at Alice for confirmation. Alice was studying her cigarette—her second since Judith had arrived.

"Of course not," Francis resumed. "You know my father... he had great pride. But there have been some damaging stories recently. Stories that he was making deals with his authors for delayed royalties, rumors that he was about to default at the bank. He was going to use the opportunity your interview afforded him to redress the negative impression." Francis poured himself a glass of water from the jug on the coffee table. "I believe he was planning to go out in a blaze of glory. He wanted you to write his epitaph. One that would leave his heirs with the appearance of a viable business, at least as far as the creditors were concerned, so they would not put us under when he died. He picked you because he trusted you and because he knew you would not betray him."

Francis leaned forward slightly, his elbow resting on one knee, his right hand dangling loosely from the cuff. The nails were manicured, like Gladys's.

"I think you will agree that he had gone to a lot of trouble to make his death appear accidental. That he didn't entirely succeed was not for lack of trying. Many still believe that he fell rather than jumped. The police and the newspapers have been gallant enough not to express their doubts. But it would appear *you* are planning to draw attention to his suicide. Because he misled you into thinking that things here were in great shape, you are unwilling to accept the facts. But there is nothing that your digging will uncover. There is no mystery. All that you would achieve is to cause pain to all those my father most wanted to protect: his family, his authors and his employees." Francis took a deep breath. "Now, I know you would not want to do that."

Alice, who had barely moved until now, bent over the ashtray, stubbed out her cigarette and stood up. Slowly she walked over to the window and stayed there, her back to the room, looking out at the storm. Francis stretched out in his chair. The pale light from the overhead lamp caught his sharp angular features and made them even sharper. His thin nose, slightly hooked over the bridge, his pale hands hanging like talons at the ends of the long bony arms made him seem vulture-like. Only his eyes reminded Judith of his father. They were the same pale blue, deep-set in concentration, and had the same calculating yet ingenuous look.

When Judith finally spoke, her voice came out in a whisper. "It's very hard to believe."

Francis nodded.

"I know how you feel." He clinched his advantage by sympathizing with her. "That's why I hoped I would have a chance to talk with you. The fact I want to impress upon you, Judith, is that what happened had been a long time coming. He had planned every detail. He preferred this to handing the firm over."

"To a buyer," Alice said from the window. She sounded unusually timid.

"I suppose you are wondering why Alice is here with me?" Francis asked.

Judith had been.

"Sheer coincidence, really," Francis said. "I came upon her in here, searching through my father's office. For your story, I think."

"I have every right to be here," Alice said.

"Of course you do," Francis said placatingly. "And it gave us a chance to have our little chat. Most fortunate, wasn't it?"

Alice nodded. Slowly.

"We have compared notes on a couple of things and found, I think, that we have a lot more in common than we had thought. For one thing both of us care deeply about the survival of this company. And that's what the issue is, Judith. The real issue." Once again Francis leaned forward, his elbows on his knees. "We have had an offer for the firm. It's the kind of offer that would allow for a steady, calm transition to the new owner. It would give the company the necessary cash-flow to resume business as it should be. It would take the banks off our backs and newspapers out of our backyard. It's simple, secure and realistic."

"Who is the buyer?" Judith asked.

"You can't expect me to tell you *that*. Not yet, anyway. It's taken months of planning, and it's the only way we can ensure a continuation of jobs here and security for the people my father cared about the most."

"His authors."

"His family." Francis smiled sadly. "Though he never could tell the difference."

"It *is* a generous offer," Alice said, without conviction.

"Judith," Francis said firmly, "my father picked you as a friend. I ask you to treat him as one. Write the story of his life, his work, his contribution to this country. Do not meddle in his financial affairs. Do not mention his suicide. Let's keep the old man's memory clean..."

Judith nodded a lot. She promised to think about it.

Alice saw her out. Both women were silent all the way down the corridor. Alice helped wind Judith's long striped scarf around her neck.

"He makes me feel completely uncomfortable," she said. "And there is something about all this that stinks."

"Do you know who the buyer is?"

"No. But I think it's some Brits. Couple of weeks ago Francis was dining with a bunch of them at Winston's. George wasn't there."

"You don't think Francis would want to sell the place without telling his *father*?"

"Who's to say?" Alice whispered. "He had the police in here today. They haven't found George's briefcase. The one he always carried. Not here, not at home. Francis has turned the place upside down. He was yelling at the detectives, accusing them of incompetence."

Judith pulled on her mittens. It would be a grim drive home.

Seven

MARSHA WAS BREATHING hard when she reached the fourth floor. Briefly, she had considered letting herself off that last test of endurance, but she had some energy left after her early-morning run and she needed to push her body sometimes. She unlocked the door, unhooked the chain, picked up the paper. Once inside, she leaned back against the door and waited for her temples to stop pounding. Then she peeled off her Roots suit and cotton underpants, threw them into the corner, plugged in the coffee maker and headed for the shower. She closed her eyes and let the water cascade through her hair and down her face, her muscles tingled with exhaustion.

She wrapped her hair in a towel, her body in a terrycloth kimono, and went to check if Jerry was awake. He wasn't. He was lying on his stomach, his face half-buried in the pillow, clutching it as though afraid someone might take it away from him. Marsha watched him for a moment, wondering if he knew how he revealed himself in his sleep. So much need and such great fear of losing.

She sat on the edge of the bed and gently stroked his neck and ear, brushed the hair off his forehead.

"It's time, Jerry."

He stirred once, groaned and buried his face deeper. Jerry had given her these pillows last Christmas, wrapped in Bloomingdale's best festive paper, red ribbons. Top-quality goosefeather. He had arrived on Christmas Eve bearing boxes of gifts, champagne, caviar, poinsettias, and apologies he couldn't stay. The family was expecting him early. He could not disappoint them again. The dinner had been planned in advance, cooked by the girls. It was all to be a surprise. Marsha had given him a fur-lined jacket, and cuff-links. They were gold, engraved with the Chinese characters for luck.

Once more she tousled his hair and ran her fingers down his neck to his shoulders, into the hollow between the muscles.

"Coffee's waiting."

"I'll be right out," he grumbled.

"Really?"

"For sure. Have I ever lied to you before?"

Jezebel wound herself around Marsha's legs and meowed plaintively.

"OK, I've got the message," Marsha told the cat and headed for the kitchen and the chicken chunks. Then she poured herself a cup of black coffee and padded into the dining room with the newspaper. Page one was busy with Pakistan's supply of 90 percent of the US heroin trade and the Senate inquiry into the Administration's aid to Zia's repressive, mob-assisted military clique. With Pakistan primed to invade the Punjab, was there any certainty the President would intervene on behalf of India?

As soon as she unfolded the second page, she saw the picture. Instinctively, before she had even glanced at the headline above or the cutline below, she knew what the story would be. The photograph was of Max Grafstein, at least five or six years ago. He had not yet acquired the distinctive white streaks in his hair. Somebody must have dug this up in the archives.

The headline read: "Publisher Murdered."

Max's body had been found on 54th Street between Lexington and Park. His pockets were empty except for a used Air Canada ticket that identified him. He had arrived at La Guardia Airport on the 4:00 p.m. flight from Toronto. His body was found at 7:00 p.m. The medical examiner concluded Max could not have been dead more than an hour.

He had died of a steel blade through the heart. The murder weapon had been discarded at the scene. The police didn't have much to go on, but were looking for a cab driver who might have picked him up at La Guardia. The *Times* literary people had compiled a hasty obit. Otherwise there would have been more auspicious mention of Max's brilliant career.

For a long time Marsha stared at the picture, motionless. She tried to remember Max as she had last seen him, tall, proud, self-assured. Max joking with agents at the ABA, talking big numbers, laughing when caught in an exaggeration. Axel had occupied five booths on each side of the aisle. They had brought man-size posters of their leading authors, a complete outer-space environment for the science fiction list they were launching in the Fall and a crateful of white doves they had let go at noon to celebrate *The Year of the Dove*, their Big Book of the season. Max had loved the action, the press gathering around him, the young bookstore clerks from Wisconsin who asked for his autograph. He had enjoyed being the center of attention, generating gossip, proud of his successes.

There were times Marsha had envied his style, the ease with which he made his presence felt. He had seemed indestructible. *A steel blade through the heart...*

"One piece of toast or two?" Jerry called from the kitchen. When she didn't reply, he came in. He had wrapped himself in a big white towel and was still dripping from the shower.

"Up bright and early as usual." He stroked Marsha's hair, then looked at her face more closely. "And already you're worried about something."

"Somebody I knew died last night."

"Who?"

She pushed the paper toward him.

"Max Grafstein?" Jerry let out a sigh and settled into a chair. He modestly crossed his legs. "City's turning into a goddamn hellhole. Nowhere's safe anymore. No one..."

"On the 4:00 p.m. flight from Toronto," Marsha read over his shoulder. So he would have been coming back from George Harris's funeral. George Harris. Now Max. She reached for the phone. "He's the second publisher I know died this week," she said.

"Starting a count, are you?" said Jerry.

"Don't be so flippant. I'm in the same business. Max was almost a friend."

She watched Jerry unfold the paper, marveling at how he could speed-read several columns at one time.

She dialed Judith's number.

The voice in Toronto was grouchy but awake. Judith had been up for a while, sitting in bed contemplating her George Harris assignment. She had finished the body of the story, but had no idea how to end it.

"Judith! You awake?" Marsha asked.

"More or less. I've been hoping you'd call. I'm having trouble with the story. It's Francis Harris. He told me yesterday..."

"Judith, Max Grafstein has been murdered," Marsha cut in.

"No! Max? When? How?"

"It's in this morning's *Times*. He was robbed and killed an hour or two after he came back from Toronto. Did you see him there? At the funeral?"

"Sure I saw him. We had drinks after the funeral. I asked him about George..." Judith paused. "Do they know who did it?"

"No. It seems to be just another run-of-the-mill downtown mugging."

"But that's terrible." Judith let out a long sigh. The awful finality of one more death. Tall, elegant Max looking at her over the bill, patronizing.

There was a long silence and Jerry poured more coffee.

"Judith, are you still there?"

"Uhum. I'm thinking."

"You're coming down tonight?"

"Yes. I think I'll shelve the ending. I can't handle it now anyway."

"You'll be here for dinner?"

"Yes. You knew him well, didn't you?"

"Nobody knew Max well. Not even his wives. I worked with him before he went to Axel. He was one hell of a publisher. I don't remember when he last made a wrong move."

"Last night," Jerry suggested, but Marsha wasn't listening. She had put the receiver back, but kept her hand on it, staring out the window.

Jerry folded the paper and pushed his chair back.

"I'm sure you won't want to know about it, but Nicaragua has been left to the Sandinistas after all. The Democratic Force has just folded its tents. Looks like the State Department is bailing out. Power of public opinion." He'd tried. "Well, is Judith coming?"

Marsha said yes.

"She doesn't like me much, does she?"

"No. She doesn't. But she doesn't know you much."

"You think she'd change her mind if she got to know me better?"

"She'd find you irresistible." She'd like him even less, Marsha thought, but their taste in men differed. Judith loved strong men who could, should the need arise, protect her. Luckily, the need hadn't arisen. Marsha was sure none of them would have been equal to the challenge. Marsha looked for men she could talk to. She needed companionship more than romance. At least, that's what she had come to believe from observing her parents' marriage. With Jerry there was no danger of running out of conversation, and he needed her for comfort.

"He's too needy," Judith had said. "Now he's got his expensive downtown analyst, and he's got you for free. He's laying the burdens of his lousy marriage on you, trying to share the guilt." But Marsha hadn't shared the guilt. Kate had never seemed real to her—she was part of Jerry's pattern of fears and self-doubt; part of his delusion of the beautiful home and adoring wife who busied herself with a variety of good works in Connecticut and rarely embarrassed him by asking questions about his life away from home. Sometimes Marsha wondered how his daughters viewed him. He had such a distant, appraising sense of them, as if he had nurtured a houseful of strangers. Not that he didn't like them, but they weren't part of him.

Perhaps she had chosen him because he was married. It meant they were not accountable to each other. No legal paraphernalia, no chance of messy divorces, no battles over property, no burning passion. Marsha felt no jealousy, no need to declare any sense of togetherness. Indeed she had a fear of belonging. Maybe that, too, was rooted in her childhood; knowing that she could never quite count on her parents being there when she needed them. For her father, the Service had come first. For her mother, possibly, beautiful things and important people.

"You won't have dinner with me, then," Jerry said, a little hurt creeping into his voice.

Marsha slipped behind him and wrapped her arms around his neck, her face lowered into the crevice between his neck and shoulder, her hands brushing the rough, curly hairs on his chest. Her fingers settled and tugged, gently.

"I guess I'll just have to make do with another woman," Jerry whispered and held onto her hands for a minute, squeezing them in against his body. Then he reached up over his shoulder and cupped one of her breasts. It felt smooth and cool inside the kimono, and fitted the palm of his hand perfectly. Marsha kissed the side of his neck in that soft warm place just under the ear, came around and lowered herself onto his knees. Her hands slid to the back of his head and she held him tight, pulling down toward her as his arms encircled her.

Eight

JUDITH DRESSED QUICKLY and carefully. Today would be fashionable but restrained: a beige-and-navy-print light wool suit, tie belt, a maroon silk scarf, navy high-heeled boots. For her face a thin layer of beige foundation, a touch of rouge—gray-shade eyeshadow, emphasis on the eyes. Jungle-cat eyes, James had called them. But in the end, it had been she who needed shelter.

As Judith entered police headquarters on Jarvis, south of Bloor, she took a deep breath to settle the tremor in her belly and smiled quietly to herself. She felt unaccountably confident.

The constable at the reception desk was impressed. He bristled with showy efficiency as he dialed David Parr's extension.

"Mrs. Hayes is here, sir," he announced cheerfully, his eyes grazing on Judith's bright auburn hair and the front of her navy-beige suit. It had not occurred to him that she had no appointment.

"Mrs. Judith Hayes." He listened to a few words from Parr, straightened his back, pulled his shoulders up and adjusted his collar with a curled finger. "Yes, sir," he said, then "yes, sir," and "yes, sir," as he replaced the receiver and swallowed before looking at Judith.

"He *is* here?" Judith spoke gently to help him cover his embarrassment.

"Yes. He'll see you now, Mrs. Hayes. 410. Take the elevator to the fourth floor."

As the elevator doors opened, Judith turned to wave at the young constable and was gratified to see that his eyes had followed her.

Parr's office was sparse, his desk black metal, his chair a matching straight-back with wheels. On the left, a large corkboard littered with pinned paper. Otherwise bare white walls. The papers on the desk were arranged in four neat piles. There were in- and out-baskets; the "in" was empty. Sole concession to the personal, a small picture-frame stood near an old-fashioned black telephone, facing him.

Parr came to his feet as Judith entered.

"Mrs. Hayes, you're becoming quite a detective. How *did* you know I would be here this morning?" he asked.

"I didn't. I took a chance. I could hardly have phoned for an appointment because you wouldn't have seen me." As a matter of fact, Judith had phoned to make sure Parr was in his office, but had hung up before she was connected.

"Don't be so hard on yourself," Parr said, and motioned toward the second chair. "I'm sorry if I was a little short with you the last time. It's traditional police behavior. Once a case is over, it's over, and if it's solved as well as over, we tend to shelve it gratefully and move on."

Parr sat tilting his chair back as far as it would go. He crossed his arms over his stomach. Relaxed. His furry-thick eyebrows rose toward the crinkled forehead. He wore a gently indulgent expression and the same tweed jacket he had worn when they first met. He looked more like a college professor than a policeman—a professor about to humor one of his errant students by listening to some outlandish theory.

"So what brings you here, Mrs. Hayes?"

Judith attempted to return his benign smile. "I thought you deserved another chance."

"Thank you."

"After the funeral yesterday, I went to see Francis Harris, at Fitzgibbon & Harris. He was anxious for me not to mention his father's...suicide in the article I'm writing. He said it would hurt his father's memory."

"That seems reasonable."

"Well, I've thought about it a great deal, and I don't think it *is* reasonable. Francis has been planning to sell Fitzgibbon & Harris for some time. That's no secret. He's never been interested in running a publishing house. Well, one hypothesis is that Francis found a buyer, told George—and George said 'No deal.' Francis threatened him, they had a showdown last Monday night, and, in despair, George killed himself."

Parr was nodding.

"Possible," he said. He had been careful not to say anything until after Judith had finished.

"He's been looking for George's briefcase. Right?"

"Right."

"He wants to find it because he's worried there may be some incriminating evidence in it. Maybe even a suicide note pointing to Francis. You haven't found it, have you?"

"No. It will probably show up though. They haven't been through all his personal effects yet."

"Have you asked the other people on the platform when he was killed whether he was carrying a briefcase?"

"We didn't think he had a briefcase with him."

"But Francis thinks he did?"

"He seems to."

Judith dug out a cigarette and looked for an ashtray. When she couldn't find one, she asked, "Is smoking allowed?"

"If you must," Parr said and pulled out a plain plastic ashtray from the top drawer of his desk. He pushed it toward her. "It's so unnecessary."

The worst kind of nonsmoker. Preachy.

"Can you reopen a case like this?" Judith asked.

"Probably. But there would have to be new evidence. Causing someone to despair and commit suicide is, oddly enough, not a crime. It's a rotten thing to do, and having met young Harris I wouldn't put it past him, but even if it were true, I'd have no reason to reopen the case."

"Right. But if you were to find the briefcase, and if there was something in it that proved I'm right, I could use the information in my story. Wouldn't that be justice?"

Parr thought for a moment.

"Yes," he agreed. "That would be just. However, if you're suggesting what I think you're suggesting, I would lose my job. And I don't think that's particularly just. Do you?"

"No one would find out. We'd call it privileged information. Journalists don't rat on their unidentified sources, some have even gone to jail..."

"I've heard about it," Parr said, "but I wouldn't want to take the chance."

"I'm serious," Judith insisted, seeing the grin on Parr's face. "If you find the briefcase, you could let me take a fast look at what's in it. Or you could look for yourself and tell me. If I'm right, you could tell me?"

"I'll think about it."

He saw Judith to the elevator.

"I don't suppose there is a chance you'd give me the names and addresses of the witnesses to George's death?" Judith asked from the doorway.

"Whatever for?"

"In case one of them saw something."

"No chance. But I'll let you know if we find the briefcase."

Judith took that to be a minor victory

In the elevator she wondered whose photograph he had on his desk.

Nine

JUDITH'S MOTHER HAD always lived in the same house on Park Drive, off Rosedale Road. Her father had bought it in 1909 and she had been born there. When she was twenty, she had married Judith's father in a simple Methodist ceremony in the parlor. When Judith was growing up her room on the third floor was the same one her mother had occupied as a child, and it remained very much as it had been during her mother's childhood, with the old illustrations from *The Wind in the Willows* and the black and white etchings from *Hansel and Gretel* still on the wall. The somber blue drapes and matching bedcovers remained, both hand-embroidered with tiny blue and white birds. Two hundred altogether, eighty on the bedspread, the rest on the drapes. Judith had counted them when she was ill with pneumonia. She had not been an enthusiastic reader then, and her mother did not believe in toys. Especially not in dolls. She had discouraged everyone from giving Judith dolls for her birthdays and when Judith did receive a pink-cheeked, dark-haired doll for her sixth Christmas, her mother tried to include it in their annual parcels for the poor. But Judith had already named the doll Christina and wouldn't give her up. She didn't care that she had become a lesser human being for keeping it. Her mother knew how to make guilt gnaw at the pit of Judith's stomach.

As she approached her mother's house, Judith felt the customary unease of her childhood. She rolled down the car windows. The air cooled her face. She would not stay long.

Her mother was wearing her oversized white apron.

"Come on in, stranger," she said. "I'll make you a cup of tea." She bustled ahead through the long hall and the dark, oak-paneled dining room into the kitchen.

Judith put on the old iron kettle and perched on one of several tall stools. "I would have been here yesterday, but I'm working on a story with a deadline."

Judith's mother resumed peeling potatoes with a thin-bladed knife. She disliked labor-saving devices like potato peelers. Judith knew how her mother felt about her free-lancing, and about journalists in general, so she went on quickly before the disapproving pursed lips opened.

"The children send their love. They would like to come for dinner on Saturday night, if that invitation still stands."

"Good. Good." Her mother smiled. "They're well?"

"Yes. Both fine. Anne's top of her class in English and History."

"She's given up that foolish theater stuff?" The potato skins went flying into the sink as the knife slipped under them.

"It was only the one play. She was very good in it. Really, Mom, you would have liked it. Her voice covers three octaves easily, and carries. They picked her for the lead in *My Fair Lady* over some two hundred other kids."

"Her voice is God-given. She certainly doesn't get it from you. You never had one." Snip, snip went the knife. "What about Jimmy?"

"He's great. Just fine."

"You're not mentioning his marks." Sharp as always, Judith thought, but she wasn't going to reply because she knew what would come next. "That boy needs a father. Boys have to have men they can talk to," her mother continued.

"James is living in Chicago now," Judith said lamely.

"I know; he called," her mother said and stopped for a moment to look at Judith.

"I don't want to talk about him now," Judith said. "I have to go downtown. I just stopped by for a few minutes."

Her mother looked up again from the bowl of stripped white potatoes.

Judith was determined not to give her an opening.

"Can I get you something at the supermarket? It'll save you a trip."

"No, thank you," her mother said primly. "If the children are coming tomorrow night I'll want to pick up a roast somewhere. That's what they like."

Encouraged by her success at sidetracking the conversation, Judith plowed ahead recklessly.

"Could they stay over Saturday night? I have to go out of town on a business trip. A couple of days only. I could leave them alone in the house, but it's for the weekend and I thought maybe you wouldn't mind."

"Where to this time?" her mother asked, as if Judith were in the habit of taking frequent trips.

"New York. I'm on an assignment," she lied.

"This evening?" her mother asked, staring at her with those cold pale blue eyes.

"They'll be fine this evening. They have friends coming over and they'll be listening to music. They've been alone the odd evening before."

"Yes. I know," her mother said in the same tone of voice she had used when Judith had admitted to sneaking a cookie between meals, or turning her light on after 10:00 p.m.

"I'll be home on Sunday night." Judith knew she had lost her momentum now, but she had to complete the duel in order to leave. Her mother, as usual, would have the victory. "Couldn't I help with some of the shopping now?"

"I'm sure you have more important things to do. I can handle it. Tell the children to come over about 7:00, bring their clothes for overnight. You can pick them up when you come back."

She followed Judith out.

"Strange you should have to work on a weekend," she said in the doorway.

"Thanks, Mum." Judith pecked her on the cheek. The skin on her face felt dry and warm. In the past few years the wrinkles had become deeper and her hair had turned almost completely white. Judith slipped her hand quickly over the narrow shoulders and gave them a gentle squeeze. Then she hurried off toward the Renault. Her mother stood small and erect in the doorway. She did not wave.

On her way, Judith had to go by the Rosedale subway station. On an impulse, she parked the car and went in.

She knocked on the ticket booth window. Both men inside looked up. One of them opened the door.

Judith told him she was working on a story about George Harris, who had died here on Monday night. She had a few questions.

"Well, you're in luck," the man said, nudged his colleague and came outside.

"I was on duty Monday night. This is off the record, though, as they say. I wouldn't want to have my tits caught in the wringer. Know what I mean? They don't like us talking about that sort of thing here. Head Office, that is. No good encouraging more of the poor bastards to jump. Right?" He smiled. "My name is Bob, by the way. Bob Myers."

Judith explained that she didn't work for either of the scurrilous newspapers which had recently taken runs at the TTC for a variety of inefficiencies, and reassured him that everything would be off the record.

They went over to a narrow red-painted bench the TTC had installed for senior citizens.

"I'm trying to write the story of George Harris's last day," Judith told him. "That's why everything you can remember is important. Everything. Like how many people there were on the platform? Were they all interviewed by the police? Was there anything unusual about them?"

Judith flicked open her notebook.

"Well, that night," Bob said, "jeez, everything got screwed up. Listen. I came on duty at 9:00 to relieve Szabo. Had my tea an hour later and settled in for a quiet Monday night. And then all hell breaks loose. First, there's a fight, couple of teenage punks going at it right here on top of the stairs. Bastards knew I could see them, but I'm damned if I'm going out there and get both of them on my back. So I sit in the booth pretending I don't see nothing. Then two passengers, a couple, come in and they're scared. So the guy knocks on my window and points at the punks—as if I hadn't seen them, for chrissakes. It's the uniform. They think you're some kind of a hero." He sighed as he settled back on the bench. "I did all that stuff in the war."

Judith waited for the memories to pass, then leaned forward. "What did you do?"

"I was in the bloody army."

Judith cursed herself for not having made the question more specific.

"In Holland."

Judith nodded. Then Bob saved the situation himself.

"Not like these bloody punks. Back then kids that age were sent off to fight for their country. Bit of flak up the ass would'ave done it for those two, I tell you." He chuckled. "Anyways, this guy keeps knocking on my window, so what can I do? I come out of the booth and I'm shouting at the punks, polite but loud, calm, the way we're told, but they ain't stopping. One of them's bleeding from the nose. He pulls a knife just as I come up. I thought he was going to rush me, but then he just took off and the other after him. Jumped these here bars and ran. Chicken bastards." Bob Myers grinned. "Felt kind of good though. They must'ave thought I had something to take off like that, eh?"

"Must have figured you had something up your sleeve."

"It's the attitude that counts. If people didn't get so damn scared they'd be all right, I reckon. Nine out of ten."

"Then what happened?"

"Then? That's the crazy thing. Just as I went toward them, I heard the commotion downstairs. The brakes shrieking. The screaming. You know. That's when your friend must'ave got his." Bob Myers shook his head. "Guy had it all. Business. Wife. Kids. Money. Famous even. Why would he do it to himself? Crazy."

"How many people were there on the platform?"

"No more than five or six, I think. Slow night, and what with the fight a few people were stuck up here when it happened."

"The police talked to them all?"

"They always do. Well, mostly. I didn't see the people on the platform, but you can check with Andy Frieze. He was the supervisor that evening. Good guy. He'd usually sit in if the fuzz are asking questions."

Bob Myers was getting restless, so Judith folded her notebook. "Thank you."

"Always happy to help a pretty lady." Bob stood up and grinned. "Any time." Then he walked rapidly toward the turnstile. A heavy-built blond dog was squatting on the inside, wearing the expression of divine beatitude characteristic of dogs in mid-shit. A woman with a blue hat and matching feathers was attached to the dog by a leash. The last Judith saw of Bob Myers, he was yelling at the blond fur and blue feathers.

Detective Inspector David Parr had left a message with Judith's answering service. That's how he had left his name: "David Parr." He said he would call again.

There was also a message from Alice. When Judith called her, she said she couldn't talk now, but how about lunch? Judith had arranged lunch with Allan Goodman some two weeks ago. They had specially picked Friday because neither of them would have to rush off to anything. In the evening he was flying back to Ottawa. Too late to catch him and cancel.

"No problem," said Alice. "Let me just switch to another phone."

She came back on the line a minute later.

"It's about Max Grafstein," she said. "He's been killed. In New York..."

Judith said she knew.

"But you don't know how Francis took the news. We were in George's office going through the files. I've been helping him. I have no choice you know. Then Gladys came and told us. Francis dropped everything onto the floor. He froze. He stared at Gladys as though she'd announced the Third World War. He looked like he was going to have a stroke. And I thought Francis and Max hardly knew each other. Then *Gladys* asked me to leave."

"He knew Max. They talked together after the funeral."

"They did? What about?"

"No idea."

Now Alice was really agitated.

"Did you find out what George phoned Max about last Monday?"

Judith told her.

"Doesn't add up," Alice said. "But then, Max would hardly tell you if *he* was about to buy Fitzgibbon & Harris, would he?"

"I thought Francis was supposed to be flirting with some British buyers."

"Max would make more sense."

"Why wouldn't George have told him to forget it?"

"Seems he'd given over controlling interest to Francis and Jennifer last year. He had only 35 percent. Francis probably persuaded him it was a good move, in case George died suddenly."

"And now the deal may be off."

"Right. That would explain why Francis took Max's death so hard. After a while, he sent Gladys to fetch me and told me it was imperative we go through all George's papers immediately. Even if it took all night. He said I should even search the manuscripts and folders in the editorial department and make lists of everything. That's crazy with about two hundred unsolicited manuscripts in there, but he insisted."

"What do you think he's looking for?"

"I'll tell you when I find it. Maybe some papers to do with an offer to buy."

Judith arrived at the Provençal late, as usual, and out of breath. Allan was used to both. The federal Department of the Secretary of State seemed to give him ample reason for frequent visits to Toronto.

Initially, Judith had found Allan attractive. There was a sense of steady power about him, something she thought could only come from unquestioning confidence in himself. The kind of confidence Judith had always aspired to and now, on the threshold of her thirty-ninth year, knew it was too late to acquire.

Allan was sitting at a corner table, drinking the last drops of what would have been a double martini. He was a man of habits. After hanging her handbag on the arm of her chair, Judith bent down and kissed him, lightly, on the lips.

"You look terrific," she said. "Have you been on another vacation?" She hadn't noticed his tan the night of her birthday party.

"Working at State is vacation enough," Allan said. "Drink?"

Judith chose white wine—a nod to her ongoing diet. He ordered a bottle of Montrachet, which was about four glasses and $27 more than she had planned for. She hoped he would insist on paying. He could easily bury her in a series of meetings to "interface with the private sector."

"You look harassed," Allan said. "What's up?"

"I'm working on an unusual sort of story, and I've been chasing my tail all week."

Allan leaned back in his chair, adjusted his neat tub-shaped, rimless glasses and raised his eyebrows in anticipation. "Well?" He waited.

"I don't want to talk about it much yet." And when she saw his expression, she added, "It's not ready for the telling. How have you been?"

"Traveling mostly. Just back from Sweden, Venice before that, and London. Bonn wants us to join the Europeans in banning the Cruise, and even though I'm doubtful we can go for it, there's a lot of pressure to keep our skies safe. I'm sure you've been reading about it. The Prime Minister thinks we should at least appear to follow Trudeau's peace initiative. He's become quite a hero over there. Next week it's Washington. Haven't had time to unpack. Another conference on cooperation. As if we weren't cooperating enough already. The Americans are never quite happy unless they have us peeking out of their hip pockets."

Judith was not entirely sure what it was that had earned Allan his formidable salary and reputation. While he enjoyed discussing the peripheries of his work, anecdotes about the famous and foreign dignitaries with long pedigrees, little secrets about who had had a hair transplant, or elevator shoes, or chipped china, he never discussed what he really did. All she knew was that he moved effortlessly through the upper echelons of government.

"What are we cooperating on this time?"

"Security, mainly," Allan whispered, so that it came out as more of a hiss than a word. But Judith didn't blame him. Silly as it may seem, one should not discuss national security at the Provençal.

She ordered the Filet of Sole Amandine; he had fresh salmon with dill sauce and told her of his travels, the problems he had been having with the twins—nineteen—his ex-wife's hysterical outburst at a Spanish embassy party when she saw him with the PM's press secretary. He told her of his meeting with the King of Belgium and what they ate at the state dinner, and about his own skiing accident in Austria. He would show her the knee injury later.

Judith congratulated herself on drinking all of the Montrachet without Allan's assistance and decided she would not examine his knees this afternoon.

She left him looking fragile and forlorn at the corner of Bloor and St. Thomas. His neat, tailored dark suit seemed more like a schoolboy's than a federal mandarin's. He looked so vulnerable, Judith felt a sudden surge of affection for him. Another sign the romance was over.

It wasn't until she made it to the Renault in the Colonnade parking garage that Judith discovered how effective the Montrachet had been: she was trying to find the keyhole on the car door with one eye closed.

Instead, she found her way back up the elevator and to a taxi.

Ten

DETECTIVE INSPECTOR David Parr was sitting on the top step of Judith's small trellised front porch, reading *The Sun*. The two squat pine trees James had planted when they had first moved to Brunswick Avenue almost hid him from view. All Judith could see at first was an arm of the tweed jacket, part of a newspaper and a Sixties brown loafer, but she knew right away it was Parr. Maybe it was the wine, but she felt strangely thrilled when she saw him. And pleased. He fitted into the surroundings. The sun was shining directly through the bare branches of the neighbor's oak and onto his light brown hair, making it softer and brighter than she had remembered.

"I was beginning to worry about your answering service," Parr said, folding up *The Sun*. "They said you'd be back around 2:00."

"I was at a luncheon," Judith said very formally. "Perhaps you would like to come in?" She was hoping that some coffee would counter the effects of the wine. Meanwhile she was enunciating carefully. Too carefully? James had always known when she had had too much to drink from the way her speech became private-school precise.

"Thanks. I like it out here. Don't see much of the sun any more."

"You've found the briefcase?" Judith tried hopefully.

"Not yet," he said, "we're still working on it. You thought I'd come to rat on Francis?" he grinned. "Not yet. I need to ask you some questions about the last interview with Harris."

"Oh. Perhaps you'd like coffee?"

"No, thank you."

"I would." She maneuvered into the kitchen, plugged in the kettle and waited. She made two mugs, black, double strength, carried them back to the porch and sat next to Parr on the top step.

"Well," she said, "what would you like to know?"

"Did he talk to you about a manuscript he was going to publish this year? Something special?"

"They were all special—to George. He had a big line-up for the Fall. I told you."

"Could you check your notes, in case he said one of them was…unusually special?"

"I'm absolutely sure he didn't. I don't need to check. But maybe if you told me why…"

"It's Francis Harris. He thinks he's lost a valuable 'property'—his word—his father was planning to publish. He says it was worth well over $100,000 and that it may be the only copy they had. That would be rather unusual, wouldn't it?"

"That they didn't have another copy?"

"No. The $100,000."

Judith nodded. Vigorously.

"Are you OK?" Parr asked, leaning forward and examining her closely.

Judith would have nodded again except she suddenly had a vision of her head bobbing up and down like a yo-yo.

"I'm fine. Just fine," she said, but Parr was still studying her face.

"Why doesn't he ask the author for a copy? Authors usually keep copies of their manuscripts."

"It seems he doesn't know who wrote the thing."

"He doesn't? Now, that's extraordinary. So how does he know what it's worth? No manuscript, no author—"

"From another publisher. They had, apparently, offered to buy it."

"They don't do that sort of thing without seeing a manuscript."

"They got a copy."

"Well?"

"Francis says they lost it."

"Oh."

Such beautiful blue eyes, she thought; she was going to have to pull herself together. She took several big gulps of coffee.

"Does this mean you're reopening the case?" she asked.

"This means that Francis Harris is convinced we have overlooked his old man's briefcase, and he's making a dreadful fuss about us finding it. Fast. He thinks the manuscript's in it."

"How are you doing?"

"Not so well." Judith could relax for a while. Parr had his own problems.

"Can I have that coffee now, Judith?" He stopped. "Mrs. Hayes, of course. I'm sorry."

"Judith is good. I like Judith better. Haven't cared for the Hayes part for a long time. It used to be DeLisle. Maybe I should change it back..." Babbling. That's what it was: babbling. Judith kicked herself on the ankle. There, dummy.

"David," he said placatingly. She thought he must have seen her wince. Then he reached over and touched her hand.

Judith believed hands revealed a lot about their owners. David Parr had a strong, warm hand with a broad palm and long fingers.

She brought out more coffee.

"We're having trouble locating some of the witnesses," he said. "The first two we checked, they're not at the addresses they gave. Muller—and that's probably not his name either—looked like the type who doesn't want to get involved. Jenkins, he was a cabdriver, relief, lived in a rooming house. He's moved since. Didn't leave a forwarding address."

"What about the others?"

Judith was wondering whether he had felt anything when their hands touched.

"We're trying to locate them." He rolled the newspaper and shoved it under his arm.

"I have to get back now." He started toward the front gate. Judith followed. "Thanks for your help."

"I wasn't much help."

When they were almost at the gate, he turned. It was so sudden that Judith fell against him. He caught her shoulders in his hands and held her for a moment, so briefly she wasn't sure afterward whether it had been accidental, whether he had been trying to steady her. But she was almost certain his mouth brushed the top of her head.

"I'll call you if something comes up," he said.

"Great."

As an afterthought, Judith asked: "Who's the other publisher who made the big offer for that manuscript?"

"Some outfit called Axel Books," Parr called back over his shoulder.

PART TWO

Marsha

Eleven

MARSHA'S MORNING never recovered from her reading of the *New York Times*. Her first appointment was with a visiting Australian publisher who had written several weeks ago. She had reluctantly agreed to Friday morning at 9:00, breakfast at the Plaza. Ever since Patrick White's Nobel Prize and the publication of *The Thorn Birds* one had to take Australian publishers seriously.

She tried hard to evince some interest in his list, but it was full of children's titles with robust Australian settings and down-home cookbooks like *Chinese Food the Australian Way*. She agreed to look at a big novel by a young writer and a book of baby-food recipes because she wanted to make him feel he had achieved something. It's a long way to come to be rejected.

Afterward, because she hadn't wanted breakfast, she stopped at the Oyster Bar and treated herself to half a dozen oysters and a Rémy Martin.

It was after eleven when she reached M & A. On the way from the elevator to her office six people asked if she had read about Max. The managing editor, Lynda Manning, stumbled in, slumped on the couch and announced: "I'm going to start taking cabs at night. This damned city is like a minefield."

"I know," Marsha said. "I can't get it out of my mind."

"Max wasn't the victim type."

"Nor was George Harris." Marsha stared out at the Fifth Avenue sunshine. "Maybe we should have picked another profession. This one's deceptively unsafe."

Lynda had once worked for Max and admired him for choosing to stay with the editorial people after he became president, rather than move up to the administration floor. Even though he had developed a keen sense of finance he liked to be where the action was, and the real action for him stayed around manuscripts and authors.

When Lynda left, Marsha wandered over to her desk. Margaret Stanley had, as usual, rearranged the papers to suit her own vision of an efficient executive's place of work. In-tray to the left with new mail and everything Marsha had left in disarray; out-tray to the right, empty. Directly in front of her chair the freshly typed letters, ready for signing. Next to the phone, a spike on which Margaret had carefully impaled Marsha's small yellow messages. It never ceased to amaze Marsha how Margaret managed to run all the message slips exactly through the center, so that they lined up one on top of the other.

She pulled them off and spread them out on the desk, ready for another game of solitaire. There were two urgents from agents demanding offers for their authors' new manuscripts today, or Marsha could kiss her options good-bye; confirmations of appointments in London with Pan and Michael Joseph next week; Geraldine Brunner asking if she had finally read the new chapters; invitations to book launchings; and a request to make a speech at a gathering of visiting Japanese booksellers—sorry about the short notice, details of the trip had only now been announced. There were calls from editors at Morrow and Harper & Row. Gordon Fields of Axel had left a message yesterday—before Max died. Two impromptu meetings had been called in the office for today, one of which she had already missed. Good. It was the rescheduled "Future Trends in Publishing" planning committee meeting—another opportunity for David Markham to parade his recently acquired business-school savvy. Amusing, maybe, but a waste of time.

Jerry had called to say he could still be available this evening, should she change her plans. There was a message from Mrs. Gonsalves—Marsha's cleaning woman—who was supposed to come three times a week.

Marsha decided to tackle Mrs. Gonsalves first because she felt guilty about the paper towels. Mrs. Gonsalves had made it abundantly clear that if she was to do her job right, she needed paper towels, and if Marsha didn't feel it was important enough to remember to buy them, Mrs. Gonsalves would not think it important to clean the bathrooms. No one picked up the phone in the apartment, which, Marsha figured, meant that Mrs. Gonsalves was a woman of her word and had packed it in for the day.

As she dialed each number on the yellow message slips she tossed them into the straw waste basket under the desk. She kept Gordon till last. On second thought, she decided to leave it today. She had an hour till the 1:00 p.m. promotion meeting, and a chance to run through a few manuscripts.

After fifteen years in the business, Marsha's idea of a good time was still the same: settling in for some quiet reading. Her office was alive with manuscripts, the desk covered at both ends, the windowsill piled to waist level. Her coffee table had no room for coffee.

Most of the typescripts had already been read by others before they came to her, and were topped by "evaluation forms," recommendations and summaries, yet she still approached each one with a sense of discovery. That hadn't changed since her year as sifter of the slush pile at Macmillan. She closed her door—normally it stayed open: she still remembered what it had felt like lingering outside an executive's door, hoping to slip by the secretary, unnoticed—settled into the beige corduroy armchair, kicked off her shoes and propped her feet up.

From here she could see down Fifth Avenue. After three years the splendor of the view still surprised her. It was a clear, cool April day and the sun glinted off the double-glazed windowpanes all along the upper floors. A few trees were beginning to show a hint of green along their branches. April fools.

She reached for her you've-come-a-long-way-baby red, blue and white presentation mug and took a couple of sips.

The first manuscript was entitled *Human Factory*, an overwhelmingly familiar title, but she would not let that put her off. It had been read by Mark Klein who was attempting to develop a line of business books, and Lynda Manning, who was notoriously good-natured and could be persuaded to give something a review overnight. Lynda's only weakness was a slavish devotion to schedules and charts. She could not tolerate even a day's delay on delivery of a manuscript to production—therefore most editors lied to her about deadlines. That made it difficult to establish publication dates in her presence.

Human Factory was true to its title: it praised the human factor in management of people for greater productivity. It cited numerous examples of successful people-management, and drew point-by-point conclusions. Well, at least it didn't suggest you had to work it all out in one minute. The author had credentials and wrote simply and coherently. Mark was recommending it for his lead next Spring, with a title change. All right, she would encourage him to present it at the editorial meeting.

Next the one she had been looking forward to for a couple of days: Geraldine Brunner's new outline and chapters. Geraldine had written some eleven books, all moderately successful, all edited by Marsha. She had followed Marsha to M & A—one of her devoted stable of authors (from time to time,

Geraldine threatened to whinny, just to prove it) and a friend. She had been struggling with this novel since December. It kept wandering off in all directions, characters changed overnight and without warning. Now she felt she had found the solution. Did Marsha agree?

Within half an hour, she was able to call Geraldine to tell her the new chapters were exactly as she had hoped. The characters had come to life and Marsha didn't want to have to wait another few weeks to find out what happened to them next. Nor would any other reader.

She grabbed a quick lunch of fruit-bottom yogurt and left for the boardroom, where the marketing people were filing in for the June titles final promotion meeting. Normally, Marsha enjoyed these meetings. She came armed with a few fresh ideas or approaches to add to the list of plans the heads of publicity and promotion had drawn up. They found her enthusiasm catching. The meetings went on longer than scheduled, but nobody minded. Nobody, that is, except David Markham. As Marsha chaired the meetings, she made a point of not allowing him a chance to shine. He did enough damage on the planning committee.

Today, however, Marsha had so little to add that when Markham remarked that she was showing no real interest in the titles discussed Marsha silently agreed.

Fred Mancuso from Publicity had also worked with Max once, and he and Lynda were in a huddle near the door. They weren't talking, merely sharing their grief.

Marsha fumbled through the Reprints and category books: Westerns, Mysteries and Science Fiction. They would all be regular releases, the plans had to be confirmed, but they had been set before. The new Romance series was probably doomed to failure; Marsha had only agreed to introduce it after pressure from Larry Shapiro. She didn't believe new angles could be applied, they'd all been tried—the Simple, the Nurse, the Gothic, the Steamy, even the Divorced Specials. The only gap left was Romance for the Elderly—for that they'd wait until the boom generation hit its sixties.

Lynda revived for the Originals—these were all new titles, not previously published by hardcover houses. Though she wasn't a wiz at promotion, Lynda did know the manuscripts and was determined to make everyone listen. Originals needed exceptional care so they wouldn't get lost on the mass-market racks. The promotion people had come well prepared. There would be generic advertising, radio campaigns in Chicago, Minneapolis and Washington. If that worked, they would expand. They had snatched $25,000 from the July genre titles budget to push a second book by a new horror story writer. Markham had made a reasonable argument that he was in the class of Stephen King, and though Marsha was sure he hadn't read the manuscript, he was, accidentally, right.

The meeting broke up at 3:00 p.m.

Soon after Marsha reached her office Margaret Stanley buzzed with a call from Judith from Toronto.

"Almost sober," Judith told Marsha, "and wondering about a manuscript Fitz & Harris lost. Or temporarily lost. Something George had and Francis can't now find." Would Marsha know someone at Axel, other than Max?

When Marsha said she knew Gordon Fields, the executive editor, Judith asked if she knew him well enough to ask about a manuscript they had acquired from George Harris.

"Why?" Marsha inquired.

Judith told her the whole unlikely story as David Parr had related it to her. Including the price tag.

"Perhaps they would even give you a copy?"

"Can't think why they would."

"You could pretend you're about to make a gigantic bid for the paperback rights."

"Sure. Without reading it."

"But Marsha, this might be the missing link. Couldn't you improvise?"

Marsha grumbled, but agreed to try.

She packed her canvas bag full of manuscripts she had put aside to read on the weekend. Axel Books was two blocks away, on the other side of Fifth Avenue, and visiting in person seemed less insensitive than phoning Gordon Fields.

Marsha hadn't been at Axel's offices in months. Usually Gordon suggested lunch when he had an important book to discuss, or he sent over manuscripts with short, witty notes telling her why they were ideal for the M & A list.

The double elevator doors opened on a pair of policemen, one with a clipboard in his hand, the other leaning over the receptionist, and using the main switchboard phone. The one with the clipboard looked up at Marsha.

"You work here?" he asked, jerking his head in the direction of the glass doors leading to the editorial department. Marsha wondered why so many New York policemen looked as if they had slept in their uniforms. This one was crumpled all over, had a day's growth of beard and dark perspiration stains under his arms and down the middle of his chest.

"No."

"What's the purpose of your visit?" He sounded like an immigration official.

"Business," Marsha said, just as automatically.

When the policeman saw she wasn't going to elaborate, his lip curled slightly in disgust.

"What kind of business?"

Valiantly, Marsha defeated the desire to say "soliciting." Cops don't like being straightmen.

"I'm going to see Gordon Fields."

"We're not allowing visitors today."

"I don't see why not," Marsha said with her best rendering of a cool Bette Davis pose. "Mr. Grafstein was a very nice man, but we all have to go on." She tried a little smile. Not much—she didn't want him to think she took Max's death lightly; but about the right amount to suggest that, uniform or not, we are all only human.

The policeman checked his clipboard.

"Gordon Fields," he repeated. He did not return Marsha's smile. "Executive editor," he added.

"Yes," Marsha said. The fellow was obviously impressed with titles and she wanted to drive home her advantage. "Mr. Fields would be very disappointed if he discovered I was here and had not been allowed to see him. Perhaps, if I can't go *in*, you could let *him* come *out*."

He lowered the clipboard and looked at his partner. Marsha could sense him weakening.

"I'm sure Mr. Fields would really appreciate that," she said as softly as she could, edging toward the reception area.

The policeman sauntered over ahead of her.

"Miss," he called to the receptionist, "could you buzz Gordon Fields and tell him there is someone here to see him..."

The receptionist gave Marsha her quizzical look.

"Marsha Hillier," Marsha said decisively.

"You been here before?" the policeman asked while the receptionist dialed Gordon's extension.

"Yes. You're investigating the murder?" she asked, hoping to occupy his attention while Gordon registered his astonishment at her sudden appearance.

"I'm not with homicide." The policeman shrugged. "Looks like a standard mugging, though...you're not a reporter, are you?"

"No. I work with books," Marsha reassured him. "If you're not with homicide, why are you here?"

"Burglary," he said.

"When?"

"Last night." The policeman pointed at the set of red plastic-covered chairs and couch in the reception area. "You can wait for him there." He turned on his heel and went back to the elevators.

Gordon came flying through the door just as Marsha was about to sit.

"Marsha *darling*, how good of you to come by!" he shouted in his disarming falsetto voice. His arm went around Marsha's waist and he folded the two of them into the couch. "These are terrible terrible times. So tragic. Max with a whole life still ahead of him." Gordon shook his head. A thin tuft of sandy hair trembled on his forehead. "We're all in shock, you know. Every one of us."

Marsha patted his knee encouragingly.

"So horrible. Ugly. You should have seen it this morning. How someone could do that…"

"You mean the burglary?" Marsha asked.

"My dear, it's not a *simple* burglary," Gordon's voice rose again. "It's vandalism—of the most brutal kind. Everything's been turned upside down. Wrecked. Desecrated. Manuscripts strewn about like confetti. It's impossible." He gestured weakly with his hand. "We'll *never* be able to sort it out. Never!"

"Did they take anything?" Marsha asked.

"Who knows? How will we *ever* tell? In that dreadful mess…and the smell. My dear, the smell! This morning—you know I'm here at 7:00—the smell was the first thing that hit me. How someone could do that?" He shook his head again. "And why? Why?"

"What you do mean 'the smell'?"

"Someone had…they relieved themselves all over the papers. And the walls. Everywhere. The police even took a sample." His eyes brightened for a moment. "In a glass vial, would you believe."

"And I thought they only kept fingerprints," Marsha said.

Gordon chuckled a little, then composed his features into the original expression of agitated grief.

"Why don't you all go home?" Marsha asked.

"The police. They're questioning everybody about where they were last night. As if we were *all* suspects. Personally, I don't believe anyone who works here would do a thing like that. They might have tried to burn the place, that's possible. Heaven knows I've thought about burning it myself from time to time. But not piss all over it. Not literally, anyway." He allowed himself another tiny hrumph of amusement.

"Poor Max. It's a good thing he didn't have to suffer through *this* degradation. His office was the worst, you know." Gordon clasped his hands over his chest, sighed and lowered his eyelids over his pale blue eyes. "All his drawers dumped on the floor. His confidential files. His little bar turned upside down. All that broken glass." He hissed the last words through pursed lips. "They broke open the safe. His collection of old books and original manuscripts was ransacked. We can't tell whether we're dealing with a thief or a maniac. May have been some guy whose work we turned down. Lots of those around. A nut with a few of his buddies. Chances are," he jerked his thumb toward the two policemen, "we'll never know. Anyway, my dear, what brings you here? Sympathy?"

Marsha told him she was hoping to find a manuscript sent to Max from Fitzgibbon & Harris, Toronto. She admitted she knew very little about it, except that Max had mentioned a big sum of money. Over $100,000.

"What's it to you?" Gordon asked, suddenly businesslike.

"We're looking for a major paperback deal in Canada," Marsha improvised. "For September, and we haven't much time left. I thought it would be quicker to pick up a copy here." Then she had to admit she couldn't remember either the author's name or the title. But how many lead titles would Max pick up in a year from Canada? Shouldn't be hard to find.

Gordon said he'd ask around but couldn't promise much. Not the way it was now. Marsha should at least get the details.

"Max was," Gordon said, looking mournfully back through the glass partition, "rather secretive about his own special projects. He liked to surprise."

They exchanged some Max stories—affectionate, but entertaining—and Gordon said he'd call if he found what she was seeking.

Twelve

THE CHILDREN TOOK IT WELL until Judith told them they were going to spend the weekend at their grandmother's. At sixteen, Anne thought she was perfectly capable of taking care both of herself and of her brother, and Jimmy didn't want to be taken care of by anybody. Least of all Granny, who was never satisfied with anything he did.

"She has the tact of a hippo," Anne agreed, and made it quite clear she wouldn't sing after dinner. Her grandmother was bound to sit at the piano and expect to accompany Anne in a golden oldie she'd taught her.

Judith offered to make their favorite meal of spaghetti and meatballs, but they felt too surly to be cheered by that. Next Judith tried for sympathy. The trip was a birthday present, and how could she have a good time in New York if she worried about them. They had to understand how much it meant to her to know they were safe, even if it wasn't much fun at Granny's.

"You're still going to have tonight on your own," Judith said to their united backs as they lined up on the couch in front of the TV set. They were riveted to a Big Mac commercial, absorbing every juicy word. Rigid. Unforgiving. That's what you get for running a democratic household, Judith thought. *Charming.*

She packed elaborately, for all weather conditions and occasions, grabbed her notes, her copy of the unfinished Harris and Nuclear Madness articles, a couple of paperbacks for the road and an umbrella to ensure it wasn't going to rain.

There was little point in trying to force them to accept her position, so she just ruffled the back of Jimmy's hair, rough and springy like his father's, kissed them both lightly on the forehead, deposited two twenty-dollar bills on the coffee table and left.

All the way to the Allen Expressway she was swearing under her breath at their lack of understanding, and at why anyone sensible would have kids. Going past Yorkdale, she remembered bringing them here shopping for specials in kids' clothes and toys, and how they had ice cream cones and chips, and how she always forgot where they had left the car. And she remembered the first night after James left, when she was discovering how large and foreign the house had grown around her, Anne coming down the stairs in her white flannel nightgown and wrapping her arms around her mother's waist, saying, "Don't worry, Mum, I'll take care of you. I truly will, you'll see."

By the Airport Road exit, she was already beginning to miss them.

She had asked for an aisle seat in the nonsmoking section, figuring she should manage without cigarettes during the short flight to New York; she had forged her way through half a pack already today. She tried putting the finishing touches to her Nuclear Madness story, but as soon as the no-smoking lights went off she was lining up at the back for a smoke. She chatted with a friendly stewardess about the difficulties of quitting bad habits and ordered herself a spicy Bloody Mary mix.

When she returned, there was a small yellow envelope on her seat cushion. She stared at it for a moment, then bent over for a closer look. It had her name on it, neatly scripted in green felt pen. She picked it up between thumb and forefinger and turned it over: an ordinary yellow envelope.

The stewardess, attempting to squeeze by with a sandwich tray, implored her to sit down.

She opened the envelope along the glue line and found a piece of yellow notepaper, serrated along one edge where it had been torn out of a book. There were four even lines in the same neat, green felt pen, centered on the page:

I know who you are and what you want.
You need help from here on. I can help you.
Meet me at F.A.O. Schwarz second floor
3:00 p.m. Saturday. Near the trains.

Judith turned the paper over in her hand. The other side was blank. She rose and swiveled toward the back of the plane. People were reading, eating, drinking, airplane style. The man in the seat immediately behind hers tried a half-hearted smile, then returned to his *Globe and Mail*. She went up the aisle, wheeled around at the toilets and walked back the length of the plane, peering at each passenger as she passed. No one was familiar and no one showed much interest.

Cautiously she examined the woman next to her. She was so engrossed in her book, hunched forward, her face close to the page that she wouldn't have noticed anything short of an electric storm. It was worth a try, though.

"Excuse me," Judith said, then again louder: "Pardon me."

The woman looked at her blankly.

"Did you happen to see who put this," indicating the envelope, "on my seat?"

"No," the woman replied, and buried her face in the book again. Anyone who had fought her way through more than one thousand pages of *War and Remembrance* deserved to be left alone.

She asked the navy-blue, sailing-away blazer across the aisle, but he hadn't noticed anyone either. Of course both of them could have been lying, but why?

She re-read the note. One place she rarely missed on her visits to New York was F.A.O. Schwarz. No question she'd be there at 3:00 p.m. tomorrow.

After they landed at La Guardia, she looked around again. No one paid any attention to her.

She dragged her suitcase down to the taxi stand. Ridiculous. Here she was carrying three suits, four dresses, two pairs of slacks, a coat. Even if she decided to change three times a day, she had brought too many clothes. Her wardrobe had grown as a direct result of the argument with the kids. Arguments made her feel insecure and insecurity made her feel uncomfortable. Multiple choice would at least afford her the chance to feel uncomfortable in a full range of outfits.

She heaved the bag into the front seat next to the driver—why don't New York cabbies help with your luggage?—and turned for a glance at the people in the line-up. Second from last, there was a man who looked vaguely familiar. He was about forty, wearing a rumpled raincoat under a rumpled face, a face that had started out with too much skin. Creased, but friendly. She hadn't seen him on the plane. But she had seen him somewhere before. She waved at him, and slid into the cab.

Then she remembered. It was the man from the Roof Lounge of the Park Plaza. He had been sitting at the next table when she had martinis with Max. And he had seemed familiar even then.

Thirteen

FOR JUDITH, MARSHA'S apartment held all the fascination of a Bloomingdale's window for a Sudbury housewife. It reflected a perfectly cool, composed vision of all her aspirations to glamour. Every piece—and in Marsha's apartment, there were pieces, not furniture—fitted into its own niche, and yet belonged with all the other pieces, polished, expensive.

Marsha had a fondness both for antiques and for the ultra-modern. The living room had two Louis Quatorze straight-back armchairs and a marble-top table, English from the same period. Judith had coveted the two turn-of-the-century Tiffany lamps ever since Marsha received them as a gift from her turn-of-the-century Russian lover. The curtains were blue and gold China silk, a recent acquisition from a publishers' conference in Hong Kong. There were Persian rugs on the hardwood floor. Marsha had never liked the wall-to-wall broadloom look, it didn't allow for variety. Nor would it have allowed for her frequent changes of mind.

The couch was a semicircular creation by Igor. It had been built to fit around three sides of Marsha's living room and to offer a fair view over the sumptuous trees of Gramercy Park.

The paintings were originals. None of the prints was numbered above fifty. She had Andy Warhol in the bedroom, Andrew Wyeth in the study, a signed Ansel Adams in the bathroom, and a Hopper house-in-landscape in the living room.

She had started out with a few good pieces twenty years ago when she moved to New York, and added to them each year. The Hopper, though, had come from daddy Hillier, as had the beginnings of the glass-elephant collection that Marsha kept in the eighteenth-century bow-legged glass cabinet in the dining room.

There were, Judith concluded once again, some advantages to having started with money. The relative squalor of her own quarters could not be attributed solely to the bad habits of a misspent youth and the price she had paid for them, in children and other indiscretions.

When Marsha let Judith into the apartment the comforting glow of the Tiffany lamps was complemented by the smell of Wiener schnitzel frying in lemon butter.

She took Judith's suitcase.

"Jeez, you're staying for a year?" she exclaimed and led her, one arm around her waist, to the couch. "Kick off your shoes. You must be exhausted after carrying *that* thing around." She shoved Judith's bag into the study. "Martini?" she asked.

"Great," Judith said as she eased into the soft cushions. She lit a Rothmans, she was entitled to it, put her head back and closed her eyes. "Glad to be here."

It was like old times. Returning from summer holidays, best friends at school; the stored memories bubbled to the surface. She gazed at Marsha's smiling face as she lifted her glass. Still the full lips, the long tapered nose, deep blue eyes, the light curved eyebrows, high forehead framed by soft wisps of blonde hair which curled around her face and clung to the back of her neck where the hair had been pulled up into a loosely-formed chignon. There were a few white strands, more like highlights, and some faint surface lines had crept in under her eyes and around her mouth but, in this light, she hadn't changed much since they boarded at Bishop Strachan. Then Marsha had looked older than her years. Now she had grown into her body.

"Was it hard getting away?" Marsha asked.

"Like pulling teeth. The kids loathe spending the weekend with my mother. I can't altogether blame them."

"Aren't they old enough to be left to their own devices?"

"Probably. But I don't feel comfortable when they're alone. I worry."

"Don't you worry when you leave them with your mother?"

"No. I came through all right, didn't I?" Judith said with a shrug.

"Did you?"

Marsha laughed her deep resonant laugh and changed the subject. "How was your trip?"

"Strange," Judith said as she dug in her purse for the small yellow envelope. "I got a message on the plane." She handed it over.

Marsha read the four green lines carefully.

"From whom?" she asked.

"I don't know." She told Marsha about her search.

"You think you looked like an ass wandering about the plane, you should have seen me trying to explain to poor Gordon Fields what I was doing at Axel the day after Max died, with the whole house turned upside down—they'd had a burglary—and me trying to locate a manuscript I couldn't describe."

Judith told her Alice's theory. Not impossible Max would have been looking for an acquisition. Axel had the energy and the resources. And Francis wouldn't want the prospect marred by scandal.

Marsha brought out a brass tray with two plates of herring in sour cream served on lettuce and two small glasses of Bols gin to drink with the herring, Dutch style.

"I hope you still like this," she said.

"You remembered," Judith said, surprised.

"It's not hard to remember. You're the only person I know who likes the slimy things. Besides, two years ago we went hunting for them together at a succession of restaurants that serve food after midnight. You had a terrible longing for them. I was afraid you were pregnant."

As they started dinner, Judith told Marsha all about David Parr's visit. Marsha recognized the look on Judith's face.

"You don't mean to tell me that you're actually falling in love with a policeman?" The way Marsha said "policeman" made the word sound like a nasty tropical disease.

Judith was surprised. She hadn't thought she was falling in love. Now, she was rather pleased at the possibility.

"Maybe I am," she said cheerfully. "He *is* rather special."

"They've all been special," Marsha said.

"The schnitzel is perfect," Judith answered, pouring herself another glass of wine.

Marsha didn't give up easily.

"Let me know when you find out, and please, this time, don't rush." She reminded Judith of her first meeting with Allan and of her later disappointment. Once, Judith had fallen in love with a pilot and discovered two weeks later he was gay but confident she'd help him over it and into the elusive joys of heterosexuality, disgusting as they appeared to him. Then there had been the Chilean guerrilla who needed a home, and the doctor who dabbled in real estate and women...

"And there was James," Judith added.

"Yes. There was James," Marsha repeated with a sigh. "But at least he *did* love you. Once. In his way."

"The only trouble with taking risks is the risks," Judith said. "I wouldn't want to stop taking them. And as I grow older, I want more risks—they prove that I'm still ready to learn and to feel."

"There are other ways of proving you're alive," Marsha said quietly.

Perhaps it was their differences that had kept the friendship alive. Marsha tried to predict the variables, to control her emotions. She had grown up in a house of strangers, where each gesture to reach out was rebuffed. The emphasis was on form, on the outward signs. She and her two brothers had been sent to boarding schools as soon as they were old enough. In the summers they had had tutors and sports counselors, while their parents traveled on diplomatic assignments. Marsha's brothers, ten and twelve years older than she was, had formed their own alliance. Marsha used to ache for the day she could return to school and Judith.

Only Judith knew how unhappy Marsha was. Outwardly she maintained an image of languorous wit and wealth enjoyed. She talked of great garden parties where the rich rubbed knees with the famous. She had met senators and governors, novelists whose work their Lit. class studied, J. Edgar Hoover in his declining years, and two presidents of the United States who had come to the Hilliers' fabled parties. The one thing she had learned from her father was that a Hillier showed no weaknesses.

She had been envied for her clothes, the strange gifts and postcards her father had mailed from around the world, the gold jewelry she had received from her mother. Marsha was the first kid in their class to drive her own car, a red MGB her father sent from London for her sixteenth birthday.

On her first visit, Judith had found the Hilliers' wealth so overwhelming she grew resentful and sullen. Later she learned to ignore it, because Marsha made it easy to ignore. That summer the Hilliers had spent a few days at home. Marsha's father had played billiards with "the boys" and given them cigars after dinner. Her mother was a polished, hand-painted porcelain doll, fragile and silent. She composed lists for parties, visited her couturier, supervised the flower arrangements. It was difficult to imagine her giving birth to her children.

"About the only advantage of your informal education was that you learned to be alone. You don't need others as I do," Judith said.

"Except for you," Marsha said, and reached over to squeeze Judith's hand.

Over coffee and brandy they talked about Jimmy and Anne. Marsha was Anne's godmother, a role she addressed with grave misgivings since she had no sense of religion. She had enjoyed the pomp and circumstance around Grace Church on-the-Hill, but had never learned to pray. She had sent Anne gifts, as Marsha's godparents had sent Marsha gifts, and taken her to dinner in Toronto and once to New York when she had persuaded Judith that Anne was old enough to fly by herself.

Mellowed by the brandy, Judith passed up the opportunity of giving Jerry one more review.

Marsha was awake by 7:00 a.m. She decided not to go running because she didn't want Judith to wake up alone in the apartment. Instead, she proceeded through her Tae Kwon-Do exercise and self-defense routine, including the eight basic combination karate-judo specials the instructor had bestowed on her graduating class as the "if all else fails" moves of last resort. Her body felt strong and controlled. As she padded out to the kitchen to start the coffee, she was intensely aware of her calf-muscles tightening with every step, her stomach pulling into itself.

Waiting for the kettle to boil she thought of the rendezvous at F.A.O. Schwarz, struck a Sean Connery 007 pose, and greeted last night's dishes with a supercilious smirk.

She wondered if 007 had ever washed dishes, 'or worried about having no toilet paper for houseguests. Would he have found some effective technique of dealing with Mrs. Gonsalves's unique methods of retaliation? She had slopped water over the bathroom, trampled it to mud, discovered the lack of kitchen towels and left the grisly mess.

When the coffee was ready she brought in *The Times* and went to check if Judith was awake. Quietly she opened the guest-bedroom door.

Judith slept with her arms around the pillow, her face to the wall, knees pulled up to her chin. Her long auburn hair spread over her face. She used to sleep like that at school. Marsha remembered how much she had wished for hair like Judith's, hair that bounced back when you put a brush through it.

She stood in the doorway. Coughed. Waited. In the end, she didn't have the heart to wake her. Early mornings were not Judith's best time.

Jezebel sat in her corner of the kitchen counter, sneering at her food. Marsha had switched to Kittysnacks, for the vitamins and iron the commercial promised, but clearly Jezebel hadn't seen the commercial.

The phone rang.

"Hillier?" asked the croaky voice.

"That you, Mrs. Gonsalves?"

"Yah. Wanted to getcha before you go out. Monday my fee goes up to forty-five. Everybody charging the same now. Don' wanna be the only schmuck on the block, know what I mean? So. Will you pay?"

"Mrs. Gonsalves, you know I'm going to London on Tuesday and I was counting on you taking care of the cat while I'm gone."

"I know."

"Then I guess you know I have no choice."

"Yah. So whatcha gonna do?"

"I'll pay."

"One more t'ing: you don' forget the paper towels?"

"I'll get them tomorrow."

Marsha slammed down the receiver and glared at the cat.

"All your fault."

Jezebel ignored her.

Marsha took the coffee and the newspaper into the living room and flicked over the bad news on the first pages to the center. She still had two books on the best-seller list. They were the same ones as last month, but what the hell, it was late in the season, the listmakers were getting tired.

Fourteen

THEY HAD LATE LUNCH at the Sherry-Netherland, still home of the best steak tartare in New York, then walked down Fifth Avenue to F.A.O. Schwarz. Having chattered through lunch, reviewing old friends and new angles, they were now quiet.

Marsha was planning a Tae Kwon-Do strategy should they be attacked in the store. The note could have been written by a nut. She knew that Schwarz would be crowded—it always was on Saturdays. Anywhere else a crowd might be protection enough, but in New York you couldn't count on anybody's help but your own.

Judith was enjoying the sunshine. She loved to walk down Fifth Avenue, savoring the view of the old Plaza Hotel (she must

111

return to the Palm Court for afternoon tea and fresh strawberries), the windows of Maison Russe, Bergdorf Goodman and the throngs of people on both sides. Two kids played hopscotch at the corner of 58th.

They turned the corner. Marsha took Judith's arm, quickened the pace, pushing through the crowd of window-shoppers. They entered through the ornate glass doors, went past the small-item impulse-buy dolls, arranged by size and color, the seven-foot panda and its smaller brothers on the circular display stand, the games for all ages, and took the escalator to the second floor. The hands of the giant Miss Piggy clock had just moved to 3:00 p.m.

Judith, despite her determination to be alert, had that familiar sense of comfort she felt each time she came to F.A.O. Schwarz. At home with the toys. She wanted to touch and fondle them, wind them up, push their buttons, pull their strings, watch and hold them. Every hour she'd spent here had been wonderful, her visits ending in shopping sprees she couldn't afford. In the beginning she had told herself that the toys were only for the children, so that she could appease them after an absence. But Jimmy had seen through that when he was eight and Judith had brought home the $50 electric train set.

"Look, Anne, Mommy's bought herself a train!" he had observed. And he was right. She hadn't known how much she had wanted that train (complete with boxcars and tunnels, lights, switches, bridge) until she had set it up in Jimmy's room and watched it go through its loops and turns, sounding its tiny whistle.

The second floor had the trains. Judith led the way from the top of the staircase, past the Sesame Street sets, the Legos, to the far end where all the electronic toys lived. She was still seized with a sense of childlike wonder as she walked past the huge glass cases where the major-league trains ran, and around the shallow tanks with the battery-powered water toys. An attendant was demonstrating a blue spouting whale, some diving porpoises, a pink turtle and a bikini-clad doll that propelled itself forward with fast-twirling chubby arms.

Judith was bewitched by a large spotted green frog that kicked itself along, but she knew Marsha wasn't listening. She kept scanning the crowd, turning her head sometimes to check behind her, searching for some give-away sign.

They stopped to the right of the staircase to admire the mobile corner that today included a brown stuffed monkey working out on an overhead swing.

"I wonder how they do that," Marsha asked without a trace of interest.

"I think he must have a battery fitted into his back," Judith said. "He's driving the swing back and forth as he shifts his weight up and down."

Marsha sighed.

"What do you suppose those big parrots do?" she asked, pointing up into the branches of a potted tree.

"They don't do anything," said an elderly woman beside Marsha. "They are purely decorative."

"Oh," Marsha said and started to move away.

"You hang them on a swing from the ceiling in a child's room," the woman persisted. "They look pretty, don't you think?"

Judith nodded and smiled. Marsha said "aha" without enthusiasm. The Miss Piggy clock was pointing to 3:15.

"They thought you would bring your friend," the woman said to Judith.

Marsha stopped. Judith inclined her head toward the woman.

"I beg your pardon," she said politely.

"I said: they thought you would bring your friend along," the woman repeated slowly, for emphasis, "and, clearly, you have." Her voice was soft and unmodulated. "Perhaps we should walk along a bit. Look like we are old acquaintances and have just run into one another by accident. We are all shopping." She smiled good-naturedly.

"There are some very lovely dolls this way." She took Judith by the arm and moved forward, chatting amiably. "Your friend could follow along, since there's only room for two people side by side." She said to Marsha, "I hope you don't mind."

Marsha was too surprised to mind.

"You could try appearing a little more friendly. If someone is watching, they should think you are relaxed." Her words came slowly, evenly spaced, as if she were taking pains with a foreign language. "As you can see, there's nothing to be afraid of."

After a moment's hesitation, Marsha concurred. The woman had to be at least sixty-five. She wore an old-fashioned black sealskin coat with a fox collar, unbuttoned, and a blue-on-pink scarf pulled forward into a peak over her forehead, shading her face from the neon lights in the ceiling. It was tied into a tight knot that made a dent in her softly wrinkled second chin. Her cheeks sagged under a thick layer of too-dark rouge. A fancy pair of horn-rimmed glasses rested on a small heavily powdered nose. The tiny black eyes behind the glasses were sharp, round and friendly, like teddy-bear eyes.

"We will have to be brief. We are being watched," she said in two short bursts. They had stopped before a three-foot-high rocking horse with embroidered bridle, gilded stirrups and leather saddle. "We are interested to see that you are conducting your own investigation. That you do not fall for the obvious. That you have distinguished between what is real and what is a set-up."

"Well, I was only... I don't know what you're talking about."

"I think you do. Anyhow, we are pleased to note you are following the larger story."

"Do you mean the George Harris story?"

"If that's what you wish to call it—the George Harris story. We cannot know exactly how much he decided to tell you." She glared at Judith intently through the thick glasses.

"We had talked for some time." Judith hesitated. She thought she should pretend she knew more than she did. "In your note you said you could help me. How?"

"It depends. First, there are the preliminaries. The exchange has to have two sides. A mutuality, you might say. What, Mrs. Hayes, is your reaction to bread?"

"To what?" Judith asked.

"Bread," the woman whispered. "We have to know. Have they already contacted you?"

"They?"

"I do wish you would stop playing games," the woman said gloomily.

"They haven't yet," Judith tried.

"And you and Miss Hillier have chosen to work together. That does make the deal somewhat more attractive, though we had in mind another type of firm. Miss Hillier, I don't want you to misunderstand, or take this as a judgment of your performance in your field, but George Harris was the perfect choice. An old, distinguished company; sole owner; being in Toronto, slightly off the beaten track. He made a terrible mistake. Lack of faith, I believe. Such a pity..." She was shaking her head sadly. She pointed at the horse. "Miss Hillier, perhaps you could go over and feel the saddle. As if you were thinking about purchasing it... That's very good. Thank you."

"Excuse me," Marsha said impatiently, bending over the pony's white mane, "but could we not start at the beginning— with who the hell are you and why are we all here?"

"The manuscript," the woman said. "That's why we are all here, Miss Hillier. That, and perhaps a dash of natural curiosity on your part."

The woman turned to Judith again.

"You haven't answered me."

"I don't have all the facts yet," Judith said, groping for an answer that would keep the woman talking.

"At least you're not inclined to *Satyagraha*, that's a good beginning. You must know that they will try to prevent you from publishing. Nor can you find the whole truth without our help. Though it is there to be dug up, there are too many protective barricades. But we have all the proof. Naturally. That's why we must trust one another."

"What about George Harris?"

"The mistake Mr. Harris made was not to. Trust us, that is. He didn't even trust the evidence of his own eyes. He wanted to hedge his bets. He lacked patience. Perhaps we should stroll along again..." When they reached the Fisher-Price area, she stooped over a model of the Castle—extra-large—and examined the ramparts.

"And there isn't any point in your trying to get it from Axel," she added, looking at Marsha. "Did you really imagine they wouldn't have found it?"

"You have this manuscript with you?" Marsha cut in. There was a chance the woman was mad, but there was at least this consistent thread of the manuscript.

"That would have been foolish under the circumstances."

"You picked the circumstances."

"What I meant is, first we have to establish the terms. You must ensure simultaneous publication in the English language world-wide. We will want maximum publicity, and you are well placed to do that. And we must have guarantees... Then we will have to ensure your continued well-being."

"Guarantees?" Judith asked. She didn't want to jeopardize the unfolding of the story, but she had to ask.

"The financial guarantees," the woman said.

"How much did George Harris offer?" Marsha asked.

"He didn't tell you?" The woman looked at Judith.

"Not exactly," Judith said.

"One point two million. That figure is acceptable."

"Oh." Judith sighed.

Marsha cut in, her heart beating faster, her hand shaking over the battlements: "We could try for that, though it is a very large sum of money."

"When you have the manuscript you will have no doubts." The woman picked up a winged dragon and placed it in Judith's hand. She was smiling. "And you will have done the world a service."

"We have no trouble with the publication conditions, if it's the right property. When do we get to read it?"

"We will contact you," the woman said, and she picked up a tiny figure of a plastic knight, smiled at both Marsha and Judith and, before either of them could say anything, left to join the line-up at the checkout counter.

Marsha considered following her, but didn't.

They both stared at the dragon in Judith's hand.

"What is *Satyagraha*?" Judith asked.

"It was Gandhi's policy of nonviolent resistance to British rule in India," Marsha replied. "Do you think she's crazy?"

"No. She thinks George confided in me about all this, whatever it is, but he didn't. What do you think she meant about my attitude to bread?"

"Maybe the story has something to do with India? I'll buy you the dragon if you like... One point two million dollars would have to be a big story."

"I'd prefer a Simon, if they still have them."

Marsha grabbed Judith's arm.

"Don't turn to look, but there's a man behind those shelves on the right. I think he's been watching us for a while."

"Let's go downstairs where the Simons used to be. See if he follows."

"I desperately need a drink," Marsha said, glancing over her shoulder. She took the dragon for herself.

Judith asked for a Simon to be gift-wrapped. For the kids.

From behind the glass pillar at 58th Street, Judith and Marsha stopped for a last look at the window display and caught a glimpse of the man Marsha had seen earlier. He was just over six feet tall, gray-haired, thinning at the temples, around fifty. He was dressed for Fifth Avenue: a three-quarter-length camel-hair coat, maroon silk cravat, charcoal-gray soft wool trousers, expensive. His hands in his pockets, he browsed with exaggerated interest, half-turned again, glanced through the glass pillar, though not directly at the two women, checked his watch, waited.

"What now?" Marsha asked. "Shall we see if he makes the first move?"

"I'm not sure I'm ready for another encounter today," Judith said. "This was going to be a holiday, remember? You were going to treat me to a strawberry daiquiri at the St. Regis. *He* can buy his own."

But he didn't follow them into the hotel. He waited a few minutes outside on the red carpet, hesitated, turned and strode off.

"Oh hell," Marsha said. "Come on." She held Judith by the arm, through the revolving doors, down the stairs, out onto the sidewalk as their distinguished follower rounded the corner of Fifth Avenue and disappeared.

He walked fast, with long strides, easy gait, his old-fashioned brown suede shoes hugging the asphalt.

"Some men improve with age," Judith said. "This one's lovely to watch. Exhausting though. If I'd known we'd be running around like this, I'd have kept up my exercise routine. And worn my Adidas. You don't suppose you might have made a mistake?"

"No," Marsha said. "He watched us through our chat with the strange old bird. Hasn't had much practice—he was knocking stuff off the shelves as he peered over them. The woman knew."

To Judith's great relief, they didn't have far to go. His destination was the Upper East Side, the half-million-a-year sector, East 61st. The doorman opened the door for him with a small, significant bow. Strictly in the big-tip bracket.

"Why anyone living on the Upper East Side would want to follow us around beats me," Judith said.

"Let's find out," Marsha said and ran directly to the doorman. She put her hand over her heart and panted hard.

"Damn," she said. "I'm too late."

He stared at her. "I beg your pardon?"

"He's gone in already, and I haven't given him the message." Her voice caught in agitation. "He's gone up, hasn't he?"

The doorman surveyed Marsha for a second, glanced at Judith, who tried an encouraging smile, and looked back at Marsha who had started to dig frantically in her purse.

"Mr. MacMurty?" he asked finally.

"Yes, yes," Marsha said, digging urgently, "of course. Dammit all, where is it?"

"I should announce you, then?" The doorman shifted toward the phone.

"Wouldn't dream of disturbing him *now*," Marsha said, extracting a crumpled sheet of blank paper from her purse. She folded it in two. "Just put it in his mailbox." She handed him a twenty-dollar bill and smiled a little, though still obviously upset by her own forgetfulness. She took out her pen.

"I do have trouble with the spelling..."

"Ethan? or MacMurty?" the doorman asked.

"MacMurty."

He spelled it as she wrote the name on the piece of paper. *Ethan MacMurty.*

They went back for the strawberry daiquiris.

"What if there is a manuscript full of state secrets worth $1,200,000 and they think we know a lot about it from George? Wouldn't someone...?"

Marsha shook her head. "That's a story by Robert Ludlum," she said. "In real life, there has to be a simpler explanation."

They made a fast visit to the Frick, almost a pilgrimage for Judith since it was the home of her favorite Rembrandt, "The Polish Rider," and one of the best Titians in the world.

For dinner they went to Le Trou Normand and afterward Marsha had tickets to the revival of *A Moon for the Misbegotten*, starring, as before, Jason Robards and Colleen Dewhurst. Tickets were harder to come by than they had been for the Picasso exhibition.

On Sunday morning Jerry arrived with a large Sam's Deli bag full of fresh coffee, lox and cream cheese, warm bagels,

Danishes, a chocolate bombe for himself, and a biographical note for them.

"He is Ethan George MacMurty, Doctor of Law, Harvard Business School, previously Harvard graduate in philosophy and history. Director of twelve companies, including two in book publishing, chairman of CFT, the Boston communications giant, three TV stations, the Chicago all-news channel, *USA Now*, *Women's Voice*, Galloway and Brooks, *LaPresse* in Paris...etc."

"Ridiculous," Judith said, chewing on her bagel.

"Maybe he's after the same story we are?" Marsha conjectured.

At M & A on Monday morning, Marsha was putting final touches to her appointments for London when Gordon Fields called.

"It's been simply dreadful around here," he whispered in exhaustion. "Police swarming all over the building. Max's funeral, and I now hear there's going to be a takeover."

Marsha made appropriate sympathetic sounds.

"There's something strange about that manuscript you're hunting for..."

"Oh?"

"Francis Harris has been yelling at me to find it. He came down for the funeral. Seems they've lost the original. And it's worth a packet of money. Did you know it was *that* valuable?"

"I knew it was special..."

"And did you know George Harris died last Monday?"

"Yes," Marsha said, and listened to the silence on the line.

"You should have told me when you came looking for the thing." Gordon was offended.

"Why, for chrissakes? I didn't think you knew him."

"I didn't. But I sure know his successor now. He's hopping mad. He thinks we're trying to cheat them. Did you know *they* were looking for the manuscript?"

"It's odd they wouldn't have a copy. Surely Harris can get another from the author?"

"There's no record of his name. And that's not all. What's even weirder is that Max had requisitioned a check for $250,000, payable to Fitzgibbon & Harris against a contract that agreed to pay a further $750,000 thirty days after publication," he squawked. "Did you know that too?"

"Then you have the manuscript?"

"No. There is no manuscript. Nothing. The contract's with Fitz & Harris. The manuscript is down as Untitled. And there are no readers' reports, nothing to identify it. It's going to be hell trying to find it. So don't expect to hear from me for a while."

"Has Max ever done anything like this before?"

"Probably. But he always stuck around to explain later."

PART THREE

Toronto

Fifteen

THE CHILDREN HAD, after all, survived the weekend at their grandmother's. Anne had developed an itchy throat with sporadic attacks of deep-down cough and had been spared the command performance of after-dinner singing. Better still, although Granny had assembled a small group of close friends for Saturday evening, Anne had been urged to slip upstairs to bed early. She was allowed to read until midnight, as long as she downed some old-fashioned brew of honey, cinnamon and herb tea. It didn't taste like much, but her throat was better.

Jimmy had been less fortunate, having had to cancel roller skating because Granny's regular canasta partner back-ended her own refrigerator on Sunday morning and couldn't straighten up for the drive over. It was too late to call off the game, even if anyone had wanted to, and they knew Jimmy had learned to play canasta at gym camp in Temagami during two weeks of the last slushy summer.

That bored a hole in Jimmy's afternoon. All the more gaping because he made mistakes, just enough of them to keep Granny going with snappy remarks about lack of concentration lurking at the root of all Jimmy's problems in geography, history, sometimes English and definitely canasta. Luckily, she had forgotten his recent performance in math.

"A boy needs a firm hand. Discipline."

She had not been indelicate enough to sneak in the subject of "poor James," as she had recently taken to calling their father, though she did cast some meaningful glances at her friends and they nodded in common understanding, all the more sincere because they were winning.

It was about then that Judith had called from the airport. Jimmy abandoned the game down 600 points and bolted for the subway. Anne caught up with him at Rosedale. They were home a few minutes before Judith.

The living room looked like it had been hit by a hurricane. There were records and bent record covers all over the floor, dishes on the table, half a pizza, socks, shoes, bottles of Coke, empty beer bottles (she counted them, twenty), glasses—one broken—potato chips and lumps of soil from an overturned plant ground into the carpet. Anne was stacking the dishes, Jimmy had hauled down the vacuum cleaner, his face flushed with the unusual exercise, and, Judith hoped, some embarrassment. Anne, conveniently, had her back turned toward the door where her mother stood transfixed.

"Why don't you go on upstairs, Mum; we'll clean this up in a minute," Jimmy huffed cheerily.

"As the prime minister said after the garbage strike," Judith muttered.

"There wasn't time to clean up before we had to leave for your mother's," Anne explained truculently, over her shoulder. Judith liked the way Anne defined the relationship with her grandmother, as if it were something uniquely Judith's.

The situation demanded a show of strength, some firm words, maybe a series of prohibitions, but she was too preoccupied with the events of the past weekend. And still feeling guilty. She had never been able to shake that. Not since the first time she left them at home with a sitter while she went out to work. Jimmy had clung to her knees all the way to the door, shrieking "Mummy." She could hear his wails all the way down the street and, in her mind, still.

Anne was four then. She had started nursery school. The bus used to pick her up shortly after Judith left. She would stand in the hallway in her small blue coat and knitted mittens, her red toque pulled down over her ears, eyes clear and steady as Judith put on her own coat. Only the slight downward turn at the corners of her mouth showed her resentment that Judith wouldn't be there when she came home, and that, hard as she tried not to show it, she felt betrayed.

They had come through OK, Judith thought. Discipline be damned. She would wait and see. She cleared herself a spot in the clutter on the couch and put on her favorite Frank Sinatra record which she found in its usual place. Luckily, both the kids thought it was sentimental sop. She rested her head on the back of the couch, lit a cigarette, closed her eyes and relaxed. She stayed there until the vacuum drowned out "Send in the Clowns," finished the cigarette and went up to bed. She would unpack tomorrow.

Anne and Jimmy came into her room about an hour later. They were cleaned and in pajamas. They sat on the edge of her bed. At least Anne did. Jimmy sort of leaned, and slouched over Judith's feet.

"Sorry about the mess," he said. "It's all fixed now."

"We had some friends over. For pizza and that, you know. Janet and Marci and Hugh…"

"And Jimmy called the kid with the frizzies…"

"Jack."

"Yeah, and Jessie who's two feet taller than him. You should've seen them dance. Yech. A riot! He was sneaking around her armpits!"

"You should've seen Hugh. Has a face like a pin cushion, more zits than skin. Hey, Anne, you oughta tell him about that new stuff you've got in the bathroom for yours…"

"Shut up. We had a fight over the records so it all broke up about 11:00 and we weren't talking by then so nobody cleaned up the mess."

There had been better explanations, but this would do. Later she would raise the question of who was drinking the beer.

"How did it go in New York?" Jimmy asked.

Judith told them of the places she'd been, and unveiled Simon. Anne fitted in the batteries and they all had a try at following it through once. Nobody made it.

Anne bent over her mother and kissed her lightly on the forehead.

"We missed you," she said. Jimmy jiggled out the door looking busy all over, which meant that he was feeling emotional. Judith was glad she had foregone the lecture.

Judith was still asleep when the phone rang at nine on Monday morning, the sound so rude, sharp and persistent she almost succeeded in overcoming the Pavlovian reach for the receiver. When she heard David Parr's voice she was glad she had not defeated her reflex.

"Did I wake you?" Parr asked, recognizing the fuzziness of her hello.

"What do you think? It's only…" searching for the numbers on her watch, eyes still half-closed.

"Almost mid-morning," Parr said in his professorial tone. "I've been at my desk for over two hours and before that I was over at Union Station checking out an assault with a deadly weapon."

"Good to know you're on your toes protecting us unsuspecting slumbering innocents."

"Would you rather I called back?"

"No. Really. I have a lot to tell you." The sleep was slowly wearing off and his voice was warming, starting from somewhere near her stomach and spreading over her thighs.

A pause. "Well? What?"

Damn. "I'd rather not on the phone."

"Why not?"

"It's too public. Phones..."

He laughed so hard she had to wrench the receiver from her ear. When he stopped spluttering, he said: "You figure someone would actually waste a thousand dollars to put a bug on *your* phone?"

"You never know." She felt vaguely sheepish. Her main objective had been to get him to come over. If it didn't start falling in place now, she might have to invite him.

"You're sure you can trust *me*?" he asked innocently.

"Well, yes, but..."

"Look, how would you feel about dinner?"

"Dinner?" Bull's-eye. "Sure. When?"

"Tonight." They agreed he would come by at 7:00 for a drink, then they would go on to his neighborhood pub, The Jack Daniel.

There went her visions of his simple dwelling in Don Mills. But there was still room for the longsuffering wife and the 2.5 children. *Whose picture did he have on his desk?*

She planned her day at the kitchen table. She and Marsha had already decided they would not wait to be contacted. Judith was no longer searching for reasons why George would have killed himself. The question was what happened to the manuscript.

She would go back to the witnesses.

Andy Frieze spent Mondays at the Toronto Transit Commission building on Bathurst Street. For the benefit of an extra day off every two weeks, he did the late shift on the line Monday nights.

Judith had no difficulty tracking him down. If anything, he was rather flattered by the journalistic attention and, better yet, he remembered reading a couple of her articles in the now defunct *Weekend Magazine*. It turned out he'd been first on the scene of the accident a week ago and had talked to the six people on the platform. But he wanted to be sure Judith would honor the unwritten rule that press stories stay away from the gruesome details of subway suicides. If subway deaths were publicized, there might be a whole new spate of demented leapings in front of speeding trains. That would not help the image of the Toronto system, reputed to be the cleanest and best-run in the world.

Once Judith had convinced Frieze that she was not interested in current TTC suicide statistics, he became helpful. He was fascinated by her search for a missing manuscript, and, yes indeed, he remembered that one of the people on that platform had carried a briefcase. A brown executive-type case. It had belonged to the executive-type fellow the police questioned first. No, he had no idea of the man's name or address.

The black woman had a plastic shopping bag, big enough for a manuscript, and the teacher had a huge handbag.

Only two of the names came to mind: a Miss or Mrs. Hall, the retired schoolteacher who got a ride home with the police. He remembered her because she had remained so unflustered. Very sensible in a British sort of way, lived somewhere on Rosedale Valley Road. And there was a girl, maybe eighteen, long straight hair, name of Marlene. She looked small and scared and Frieze had been amused to find her last name was Little. She was shaking, pale. She hung onto her boyfriend all the time. He seemed like a no-future layabout. Reminded Frieze of his own daughter's boyfriend. And, like his daughter, Marlene lived in Smithstown.

Smithstown had all the trappings of another dream gone sour. It had been designed as a low-rent apartment complex for swinging singles of all ages who could meet and mingle here in comfort and cheerful proximity. But it had become a short-term stopover for transients who neither cared for nor felt comfortable in the surroundings. Paint peeled in the neon-lit lobbies, where the bright colors were only garish. The recreation area had become dangerous at night.

Judith checked in at the rental office and found a Marlene Little registered in No. 2 building, on the fourth floor. She had been there three months and was sharing with a friend, a Scott Bentley.

No. 2 right-angled into No.1. The deep slush of early April mud went through the lobby and turned the carpet in the elevators to sludge. The security system was out of order.

A swift kick on the left side, where other feet had established a pattern, opened the elevator door on the fourth floor.

Marlene Little looked exactly as described. Straight damp brown hair hung limply with a few strands over her forehead; face pulled together into a pink peak by a pointed nose; cheeks flat; eyes round and red.

"Yes?" she asked, her voice as thin as the rest of her.

Judith introduced herself with her quietest, most professional delivery. While the apartment door did open another inch or two at the mention of "journalist," the face continued to stare without a flash of interest.

"George Harris," Judith repeated. "He died in a subway accident a week ago today. You were one of the people on the platform."

"Oh," Marlene Little said with a sniff.

"I'm talking to everybody who saw him, or talked to him, on the last day of his life. I was hoping you could tell me what you saw that night."

"Oh," said Marlene, looking at her shoes. It was rather like talking to a child, but Judith was not about to give up.

After some consideration, Marlene said, "I didn't see anything. Didn't even see the train come. Nor less him." She added, as if it would explain everything: "I was with Scotty then."

"Can you tell me anything about what happened?"

"Oh, yeah. I heard a scream or something. A loud thump, like, when he fell. You know. He must'ave hit the thing hard. They come awful fast, you know." Marlene stopped studying her shoes and gazed up over Judith's left shoulder.

"You said you were with Scott that night. Perhaps he saw what happened..."

"How'd I know?" Marlene's voice rose an octave. "You can ask him yourself. If you can find 'im. I ain't seen 'im in days."

"I'm sorry," Judith said, trying to catch the right range of woman-to-woman sympathy. She must have hit the tone because Marlene went on without prompting.

"It was some my fault too, you know. I was pretty shook up that night with that guy jumping in front of that train. Horrible. Really. So we come back here and we get into a little fight. Nothing much. We'd had worse before. But he took on so and got mad and said he'd move out. I never thought he'd do it. Never. But next day I go down to get some milk and stuff—I don't have a job now and Scotty lost his in October. Anyways I come back and the place is empty. He's gone. His stuff's gone too. Everything. Even that new guitar I got 'im with my last lot of wages." Marlene sniffed again and dug into her sleeve for a scrunched-up Kleenex. She blew her nose with a squeak.

"He hasn't been back since?"

"Nah. Never even called. Nothing." Marlene wrapped her pink nylon cardigan tighter around her.

"Any idea where he might have gone?" Judith asked. She didn't have to fake the sympathy this time.

"Nah."

"Did he have any friends he might have gone to stay with? Until he comes back?"

"Only friends he had I know of were down at The Café and I went there yesterday. They never saw 'im." She shook her head slightly. "He won't come back. He's never done anything like this before. He was different, you know. Not like the others." Judith wanted to say there's bound to be someone else soon enough, but she didn't. Marlene went on, "He didn't even care much bein' outa work an' that. He had a way of getting a little bit here, a little bit there. Nothing illegal, mind you, but we was never wanting for much, like, and now… I dunno what I'm gonna do. I jus' dunno." The pink cardigan went taut around the meager shoulders, as she hugged herself tightly. Then she tilted her head up and looked at Judith. "Sorry to run off like that. An' sorry I couldn't help you either. You see he was sorta holding me when the train came. I had my face into his shoulder. That's why I didn't see nothin'."

"Then he must have been facing the train."

"Guesso."

Judith told Marlene how she could find her if Scott returned, and asked where The Café was. Maybe they could tell her something. Marlene figured Scott would have left town but gave the address down on the Danforth anyway.

Le Café, as it had been named, was a long, low-ceilinged dining area, with a 1950s jukebox in the back.

The barman was friendly, recently Greek, and, Judith could tell in an instant, fond of attractive women, even if they were nearing forty. He knew Scott Bentley but hadn't seen him in over two weeks. He said Scott hadn't been fired last October, he quit and got a new job: selling on commission. A few times he had come in and bought some drinks for the boys, so things must have been going well for him. Perhaps not idyllic, though. It turned out the police had been looking for Scott as well. They were in on Saturday asking questions. Bad for business, police coming in on a Saturday afternoon. Place was packed.

Judith thanked the barman and asked to borrow Le Café's mangled telephone book. The directory listed only one Hall on Rosedale Valley Road. W.A.—no suggestion of gender.

There was no answer. Undaunted, Judith decided to go and see for herself.

W.A. Hall lived in a large, Georgian-style mansion three stories high. A couple of fir trees in front of the bay windows, carefully plotted garden, low wrought-iron gate. Pink latticework stones paved the path that had been elevated above the garden so as to let the slush run off. The slate roof shingles, the green wooden shutters, the hand-carved brass door knocker, all said expensive. Certainly more money than a retired schoolteacher would normally scrape together, no matter how dedicated and abstemious. Either W.A. had landed in the honey pot, or it was old money, or both.

This was the kind of house Judith's mother had wanted all her life, but never got. It had taken most of her energies to keep the one she had inherited herself. It wasn't that she had married foolishly—the pedigree was faultless—yet, as it turned out, Judith's father had proffered more charm and promise than substance. He had no feel for money and perhaps it was to remedy this that he had got himself a job at the bank. Once he'd graduated to mortgage specialist, however, he had settled down to pursue the one interest he had: the business of writing poetry. They were short poems, intended to commemorate shared moments, poems to make you gasp in recognition. So he told Judith. Her mother's gasps were in frustration at the waste of time. He had started hiding them from her when Judith was not yet ten. He hadn't shown her the two slim volumes that were published the year before his death.

Would a house like this have kept him alive?

There was no response to the doorbell or to Judith's persistent hammering with the brass knocker. On the off-chance, Judith went next door.

A woman wrapped in beige mink appeared almost before the bell rang.

"Well?" she said in a tone of overt disapproval. Clearly she didn't like persistent visitors.

"I was looking for Mrs. Hall," Judith said. "I'm a relative of hers from Vancouver. It's very important that I see her. Family trouble," she confided.

"You've come in vain then," said the pink face over the mink. "She's on holidays. Said she was going to the Bahamas, or Jamaica, or one of those islands. They're all the same to me."

"Dear me," Judith said with a great display of grief, not altogether feigned. "Did she say when she'd be back?"

"Not to me, she didn't. Why don't you ask Adrian."

"Adrian?"

"Adrian," the woman said impatiently. "In Ottawa. Didn't you say you're a relative?"

"Oh yes...yes..." Judith mumbled: "Adrian Hall. Of course. Thank you." She knew of an Adrian Hall in Ottawa, a senior civil servant, very proper. She'd phoned him once to verify the Canadian government's apparent ignorance of the American invasion of Grenada.

"He's still in External?" she asked, fishing.

"Far as I know."

"Thanks." Judith stopped halfway down the path, the woman still stood in her doorway. Watching.

"Do you happen to remember when she left?" Judith asked, as an afterthought.

"Last Monday night, I think it was. Maybe early Tuesday."

"Right," Judith said as she climbed back into her car. Six witnesses; one down, two out, three to go.

She did the grocery shopping on the way home, and picked up a large can of macaroni with meatballs as an extra. *Mamma's*, for the kids' dinner tonight.

The answering service reported messages from Alice Roy and Marsha Hillier. Alice had been waiting for Judith to phone.

"Shit's hit the fan," she announced when she heard Judith's voice. "Francis, the superwimp, has reverted to form. No more fairy tales about reorganizing, refinancing, and all of us guys sticking together to see this thing through. He's been on the phone most of the day. Gladys says he's trying to make a deal with anyone who'll listen. On any terms. The only person he'll talk to around here is the comptroller and nobody ever talks to him unless it's big trouble." Alice sighed. "If there was a deal with Axel it must have fallen through with Max."

"Did Francis tell you it was Axel?"

"No. I'm assuming."

"It would be some coincidence if George was selling both the company *and* a major-league manuscript to Max at the same time."

There was a long silence at Alice's end.

"Alice? You still there?"

"How do you know about the manuscript?"

"The police were here asking questions."

"What makes you think it went to Axel?"

"Francis told the police. Has it turned up?"

"Not a sign. The wimp has had the place turned upside down and inside out. Nothing here that could deliver a measly thousand copies in sales. Another thing: no agreement of any kind in the contracts department, or among George's papers."

"Any luck at Axel?"

"No. But I *have* come across something."

Judith held her breath.

Alice asked: "Are you still working on the story?"

"There doesn't seem to be much to work on," Judith said weakly.

"So, you are. Well, this *might* interest you. It could be part of George's calculations, maybe the basis for an agreement he was going to draft. Perhaps you'd like to see it."

Judith felt the blood pumping in her armpits.

"Yes, please. I'll come and pick it up?"

"That wouldn't be smart. I doubt if Francis wants to see you again. And certainly not with me. I'll bring it over to you, on one condition: you let me see the final version of the story before you file it."

"Absolutely," Judith lied. On an occasion like this, there was no harm in a touch of dishonesty.

Marsha was at lunch, so she called Allan Goodman in Ottawa. He was frankly nonplussed by her sudden interest in Adrian Hall.

"You're not doing another piece on Foreign Affairs, are you?"

"Not exactly. I'm still working on that George Harris story."

"Harris, the publisher?"

"The ex-publisher. He's dead."

"Right. So what did he have in common with our Adrian? Far as I know they'd never clapped eyes on each other. He hasn't been working on his memoirs, has he?"

"I can't explain now. Much too complicated." It was, too.

"Try me. I've been known to wade through one or two fairly byzantine matters before. Our foreign policy for one.".

"OK, when I see you next. Right now, though, I haven't the time. Couldn't you tell me something about Adrian Hall?"

"His vital statistics are average. He's a Columbia grad. Not Harvard like the rest of us. Background: good. Some inherited dollars when his father died. Married. Two kids. Has a small black mustache…"

"Do you know his mother?"

"His mother?" Allan shrieked. "Why in the world would I know his mother?"

"Oh, hell." Judith gave up without further struggle, but not before Allan had inquired whether she didn't think it was too early in the day to start drinking. Sun wasn't over the yardarm. He'd be in town the end of the week. He had some vacation coming. Maybe she should consider taking one too? How about a few days in the Bahamas?

❊ ❊ ❊

Alice arrived in less than fifteen minutes. She was pale, her eyes red-rimmed, a cigarette in the corner of her mouth. She handed Judith a sheet of paper, neatly folded in the center.

"Narrow enough to fit into an inside pocket. That's where George used to keep his notes for meetings," she said.

It was headed: "The Dealer." That was followed by a question mark and a series of numbers:

Canada: 100,000. U.S. 1,000,000 Axel
U.K. 500,000 H.Th? Germany, France, Italy, etc: 200,000

Japan:? Serial: $500,000?
Try for buy-out:?$1,000,000. Pay 1/2 & 1/2. No royalty.
Pub 6 wks from m.s. Legals. Sooner if can do.

At the foot of the page there was a date: April 8. Last Monday, the day George died. There was a check next to Axel.

"The numbers could be dollars," Alice said.

"Ever seen one of these before?" Judith asked. The woman at Schwarz's had said $1.2 million, and that George had tried to hedge his bets.

"Yes. He used to work out his offers on paper before he met the author or agent. The numbers are different though. Rather inflated."

"Has Francis seen this?"

"Not yet. I found it in George's old legals file. It's where he kept documents about libel suits. Gladys gave me the file to weed out."

"Any idea what this could be?" Judith pointed at the words "The Dealer."

"Sounds like a title." Alice stubbed her cigarette in the ashtray. "Would George have killed himself with a property like this in the works?"

"What's H.Th.?"

Alice shook her head. "Don't know. Of course, this could be a gigantic hoax," she said. "A con game. Remember the guy who had the Howard Hughes story?"

"Clifford Irving?"

"Right. I was thinking after I found George's note: what if he gave someone a million bucks for a manuscript called *The Dealer*, and then discovered he'd been taken? That might explain it."

"It might. What do you suppose 'legals' means?"

"Drawing up a contract, maybe, I don't know. It would be quite a thing though," she mused, "having a manuscript on the premises worth a million bucks. Would do wonders for morale..."

"Will you let me know if it turns up?"

"Long as our deal stands."

The doorbell rang. Quickly, Judith stuffed George's note into her handbag. She turned, stopped. The bell kept ringing.

"Aren't you going to see who it is?" Alice asked.

Judith stared at her, motionless. Her knuckles had turned white around the strap of her handbag. The high pitch of the doorbell cut through the air.

"Shit," Alice yelled and headed for the door.

Judith grabbed her arm.

"I'll go," she said.

Alice shrugged her arm free.

"What's the matter with *you*?" she asked, surprised. Judith approached the door, slowly. With her shoulder against the wall, she peered through the side window. She thought she recognized the limp brown hair and pink, pointed nose.

"Well," she laughed with relief, "it's Marlene Little. Looks like she's got the bell stuck."

Marlene was struggling with the bell button, pushing and pulling at it.

"I'm so sorry," she said with a sniff when Judith opened the door.

Judith hit the button hard with the palm of her hand. The noise stopped abruptly.

"There. It always gets stuck when it's damp."

Marlene giggled.

"I've got to run now," Alice said, side-stepping the introductions. She ran down the path, toward her car.

"Thanks," Judith yelled after her.

"I tried to phone you, but you were out, then the line was busy," Marlene said.

"Would you like to come in?" Judith asked.

Marlene shook her head.

"He called after you left, Scott did. I've been trying to get you ever since. He was asking if I'd like to go where he is an' he said it was awful pretty there, sunny and everything year around. Not like here..."

She was studying her shoes intently, turning up her sole to get a better look.

"He said he'd take care of the plane fare and everything. He said he'd struck it awful lucky. We'd never have to worry about 'im having a job again or me having to go to work. It'd be like a long holiday, 'cept it'd go on forever."

"Maybe you'd like a cup of coffee?" Judith suggested.

Marlene edged into the doorway but kept her eyes on her shoes.

"So, I asked 'im where he was. And he says he's in Argentina."

Marlene pronounced "Argentina" as if she'd been practicing for a geography exam.

"Argentina? Are you sure?"

"Wouldn't make up a thing like that now, would I? I mean I 'ardly knew where it was. So I said to 'im, why hadn't he called before and what in hell was he doing down there. South America it's in. An' he says he'd explain everything when I get there an' I'm to pack my stuff... Not to bring much, ya know, 'cause he'd buy me everything I needed, an' if I wanted I could have the dog I'd always been goin' on about. *And* we could even get married. He'd never mentioned getting married before. Never..."

Marlene pulled a fresh bit of Kleenex out of her sleeve and blew.

"So I thought to myself, jeez, he wants me to come and get married. Then he says he can't tell me where he is exactly, that I'm to get the ticket, one-way mind you, and he'll phone again tonight so I could tell him when I'm coming an' he'd pick me up at the other end. So I tell him I haven't any money. An' *then* he says I got to look in the fridge, at the back of the freezer. An' sure enough there is this whopping wad of bills. Never seen so much cash in all my life. Look..." She pulled a big bundle wrapped in toilet paper out of her purse and shoved it at Judith.

Judith pulled Marlene into the house and shut the door behind her. She took the bundle from Marlene's outstretched hand and unwrapped a tight roll of hundred-dollar bills.

"So, I got thinking," Marlene went on. "It doesn't look right all this money an' he's down there somewhere in Argentina and can't give me an address or a phone number. But I didn't tell the police when they came around asking questions. That didn't seem right neither."

"The police were there?"

Marlene nodded.

"I thought about it, but I didn't. After all, Scott was pretty good to me... If he's done something he shouldn' 'ave, that's his business." She took a deep breath. "So I come here."

"Let's go in the kitchen and have that cup of coffee," Judith said. "I think better on coffee."

They sat at the kitchen table, the money between them, waiting for the kettle to boil. Marlene huddled in her raincoat, pulling it tight around her.

What did Scott Bentley do to earn that much money all of a sudden?

"Seems to me you need a few days to think," Judith said, "maybe talk to a relative or somebody, ask their advice. I mean it would be a big move, wouldn't it?"

"Ten hours on an airplane he said and how would I get back if I didn't like it? An' shots I'd have to have and a visa." She looked miserable. "No. I don't have any friends here and my mother, she hasn't talked to me for a long time. She's...well... I couldn't call her. Anyways," she said addressing the money, "if he's that rich, what would he want with me? I mean later? He'd get sick of me an' I'd be stuck down there in bloody Argentina. Don't they speak Spanish down there? I don't know any Spanish..."

"Not Portuguese?" Judith asked lamely.

Marlene shook her head.

"Not that it makes a difference, I don't speak Portuguese either..." She sniffed again, then she started to snicker. "Never thought I'd need to."

"Guess not." Judith laughed.

"What would *you* do?" Marlene asked, wiping her eyes with the crumpled Kleenex.

"For one thing, I'd probably go for the visa. There's no harm in having one even if you don't go. And when he calls tonight, I'd try to find out how he got all that money. I'd stall for time."

"Helluva lot of money, eh?" Marlene giggled again. "Never had more 'n a hundred bucks before. I mean at one time."

"Have you counted it?" Judith was reluctant to touch it again.

"Six thousand."

"Whew." Judith lit a Rothmans. And she wasn't going to smoke today. "Know what? If you decide to go, don't take all that cash with you. Stick some in a bank account." She wished she'd had as much sense when James sold the house in Leaside.

Marlene was nodding.

"I could use some to pay the rent. Would that be all right, you think?"

"I guess so," Judith said uncertainly. She might be using incriminating evidence to pay her rent.

"I'll phone you later," Marlene said, stuffing the bills into her handbag and relieving Judith of her growing concern that David would arrive early and find the two of them and the money. She would feel like a rat.

Sixteen

SHE HADN'T KNOWN how nervous she was about dinner with David until now. The realization came with a bang. Searching for something suitable to wear, she tripped over a casually misplaced handbag and fell, head first, into her walk-in clothes closet. Right through the neat array of hanging dresses and into the back wall. Sprawled over the shoe rack like a beached carp.

The ruckus disrupted Jimmy's personal rendering of "Thriller" and brought him bursting into the bedroom just in time to discover his mother with one foot caught in her handbag, trying to wriggle out of the clothes closet. Jimmy grabbed her from behind and tugged. That valiant effort brought Judith's complete set of winter clothes tumbling down on her head. It took her five minutes to thrash out of the closet, and twenty more to put her clothes back on the hangers. A wonderful beginning to the evening.

A further side effect of admitted nervousness: she didn't know what to wear. Not in the pleasant sense of deciding what suited best, but in the miserable sense of not looking quite right in anything. There were bulges and lumps she had not seen since the last time she had gone into a department store to buy clothes. She looked shorter from the waist down than she had remembered. The hems of the new dresses were too long (squat calves) or too short (flabby knees), necklines too high or too low, respectively, belts curling around the front. And the left heel-pad was missing from her dark brown slingback shoes.

At 7:00 she was standing in the bathroom wearing nothing but a pair of panties and taupe tights with a run in the back of one leg. She was examining a small red rash which had crept up from her jaw over her right cheek when the doorbell rang.

"Jimmy?" she yelled.

"Yeah." He had been sitting on the edge of her bed picking at his face. As usual, he had also been helpful, noting the occasional imperfection that had somehow escaped Judith's attention.

"Can you open the door, please. Let him in. His name is David Parr."

"OK." Grudgingly.

"And Jimmy…"

"Yeah."

"Please come back upstairs and tell me what he's wearing."

By the time Jimmy slouched back, Judith had smeared half a tube of cover-all make-up over the offending rash, and over the rest of her face in case the rash decided to spread.

"He's wearing blue jeans, a jacket and a brown turtle-neck," Jimmy said with a sneer. Jimmy's general response to all men Judith chose to spend time with was, at best, polite dismissal. "He looks like a cop all duded up for a date. Where are you going?"

Judith told him.

"Eating and drinking again, no wonder you have to go on diets all the time."

Judith pulled on a pair of tailored jeans, a loose-fitting pink angora sweater, and topped it off with her suede jacket. She brushed her hair rapidly, swung the offending handbag over her shoulder, took a deep breath, then practiced smiling all the way downstairs.

"Hello, David." With a light touch.

He was standing by Anne's record collection, tilting his head to read the titles on the spines.

"Lovely as ever," he said. His eyes scanned her body as if he were trying to commit her to memory.

Judith was glad she hadn't put much lighting in the living room and attempted to lounge casually in her angora sweater (should I have worn a bra?). She fixed him a tall Scotch and water. Soda for herself, no overindulgence tonight. Then she put on Anne's favorite Rolling Stones, progressive but not lurid, and examined David from the safe confines of the coffee-stained blue armchair by the fireplace. He had the casual grace of a frequent visitor. The shabby room had grown soft and cozy around him.

"You don't look half bad yourself," she said warmly.

"Now, that's a surprise!" David said. "I've come right from the scene of a compact little assault and battery. A schoolteacher found his wife in bed with the cabdriver who'd delivered her home from the supermarket. So he bumped the cabbie over the head with the standing lamp—old-fashioned wrought iron, the only decent piece of furniture in the apartment—then punctured him with the kitchen knife. Awful mess. Then he got his wife in the back as she was running out to get help. A small guy, too. You wouldn't have thought he had so much strength. Poor bastard was curled up on the floor whining by the time we got there."

"What's going to happen to him?"

"He'll get five to six if he's lucky. Cabdriver may survive. Wife should be all right. The knife didn't go in very far. I shaved in the car on the way here and picked up the turtleneck from Levine's. I figured it was better to arrive on time than to try to dazzle you with my appearance."

"You must be tired," she said, searching for conversation.

David shook his head.

"I'm used to it. What about you? How can you seem so all-together after the kind of day you've had?"

"What do you mean?"

"Tracking down those witnesses. Such tenacity, such endurance..."

"You had me trailed?" she yelled, indignant.

"Relax. Coincidence—we were following the same routes, that's all. We're still searching for the manuscript. And not finding anything. Did you?"

It flashed through her mind that he knew more than he let on, but she didn't like the idea. He had settled into the sofa, one arm draped over the back, the other cradling his glass. Comfortable, reassuring. Any thought of duplicity jarred with the pose.

"Did you?" David repeated the question. He hadn't noticed her hesitation.

"Not much," she said. Then again, he might have had her followed for her own protection. What was it the woman had said: *continued well-being?*

"Have you found the guy with the briefcase?"

"Muller? No."

"That's Muller. Then there was the cabdriver you mentioned, Scott Bentley, and Mrs. Hall. Don't you think it's strange that four out of six have vanished?"

"I do." Parr took a big gulp of his Scotch, then coughed, apparently unused to gulping Scotch. "What do you make of Marlene Little?"

"She was looking the other way," Judith said quickly.

"You believe her?"

"Yes. And I've done of lot of interviewing—I can usually tell when people are lying." No. She was not going to give this one away. She'd tell him everything else she knew, but not this. She wouldn't betray Marlene's trust.

David nodded.

"I believed her too."

"What about the black woman with the big shopping bag?"

"Yes. We found her," David said. He walked over to the kitchen counter and poured himself a refill. He swirled the Scotch around in his glass as he came back into the living room, but stopped in the doorway.

"She's dead," he said quietly.

"No! I don't believe it! How?"

"Suicide. She was from Jamaica. An illegal. Cleaning in Forest Hill and Rosedale. Cheap labor for your waxed hardwood floors. Each year there are more of them. You see them between 7:00 and 8:00 in the morning, heading up the rich streets in waves. But they have their dues to pay. Protection money to buy guaranteed silence, anonymous contacts who find them jobs where there are no tax forms to fill out. Sometimes they get squeezed so hard there's nothing left for the family they support back home. Those who dare, leave and start again in some other city. The weak ones often collapse."

"How did it happen?"

"She took an overdose of sleeping pills. Or so it seems."

Judith looked at him quizzically. He hunched forward, his elbows leaning on his knees, his head down. A strand of sandy-brown hair dangled over his face.

"Do you believe that?"

"No." His voice was barely audible. "But I have nothing to go on yet. Not with her. Nor with the others. Take Scott Bentley, for example, a drifter, a doer of odd jobs. No reason why he shouldn't drift on. He's been moving around all his life. And Jenkins—he was a relief driver for another cabbie. Lived in a rooming house. Before that, he was in other rooming houses in Toronto, and elsewhere. We've checked him through the computer. He's been in and out of jail since he started to walk. Petty larceny. Theft. An assist in a burglary. A stint of free-lance enforcing. Check fraud. Nothing major, though you wouldn't want to run into him in an alley."

"Was Jenkins his real name?"

"He's had others. We traced him through a composite drawing."

"He wasn't carrying anything big enough to hide a manuscript. What about Muller? Have you traced him?"

"He gave us a false ID. A lot of people do when they're witnesses to an accident. Ordinary people we wouldn't have on file. They just don't want to get involved. He appeared to be a businessman. Three-piece suit. Chain-smoker. Maybe he was from out of town and worried he might have to stay for an inquest. Maybe he didn't want his name in the papers. And Mrs. Hall. Why shouldn't she take a holiday? It's nice to have a winter vacation and she could certainly afford one."

"Does her son know where she went?"

"No. He says his mother takes holidays alone and why should she consult him about her plans."

"Close family."

"But not unusual."

"No."

"That's just the point. None of the stories is unusual in itself. When you put them together... I was thinking about the two guys who caused the disturbance upstairs. Happened to be at the same time as the train was pulling into the station. It was over as soon as Harris was hit. Another coincidence?" He paced around the couch, then sat down again. "Is this what you wanted to talk to me about?"

"Yes. And no—mainly I wanted to tell you what happened in New York, and to show you this." She handed him the piece of paper Alice had given her.

Jimmy pounded down the stairs, wheeled around the bannister and swaggered into the kitchen.

"Time for my supper," he growled. "Which can should I be opening *tonight*?"

"The macaroni special—your favorite," Judith said. Why couldn't he be a touch more civil?

He came back and leaned against the doorframe.

"I'm having my ear pierced," he announced.

"You what?"

"Ear, you know, *ear*," he was pulling at his right earlobe, "pierced."

"Not tonight, OK? I'm really busy tonight. OK?"

"You're always busy," he said and turned his back. "*Sorry.* Thought you might like to know."

So it was going to be hardball. Must have learned how to play from Granny. Judith followed him into the kitchen.

"Jimmy," her voice was rising, "please. You can see I'm working. It's important. Could we talk about this stupid ear thing tomorrow?"

"Sure. Hope you'll like my earring." He was opening the *Mamma's* macaroni, slamming the can onto the counter each time he turned it.

Deep breathing. She would not allow herself to be goaded into losing her temper—not with David in the living room.

"You are not," she said evenly, "going to have your ear pierced tonight and if you keep this up—you'll never have your ear pierced."

"It won't be so long before I'm eighteen," he said, his voice cracking.

"OK. You can have your ears, and every other part of your body, pierced right after your eighteenth birthday."

They glared at each other in silence. Then Jimmy tossed the macaroni into a pot and began to stir it furiously.

When she returned to the living room, David was still examining the piece of paper, holding it up to the light near the fireplace. He looked at her expectantly.

"Alice found it among George's papers. We think it's his calculations of what a book might earn him. He used to make these before drawing up a contract. This manuscript is the one Francis is searching for. George figured it was worth $1,000,000—slightly less than the current asking price of $1.2 million."

"How do you know?" David cut in.

"From a woman Marsha and I met at F.A.O. Schwarz in New York." Judith told him how the meeting had been arranged and about the bizarre conversation over the toys. "I was already informed George had sent a copy of the manuscript to Axel Books. This note confirms it. And Max Grafstein was murdered. All right, they claim an ordinary mugging, but he had the manuscript and the woman said George had hedged his bets. She could have meant that he was going to share the asking price with Max. And it could mean—My god, I have to call Marsha..."

"Hold on now—what...?"

Judith was already dialing.

"Don't you see, there, right after Axel..."

Marsha answered on the first ring.

"Hello, kid, I want you to know you're playing havoc with my social life. Been waiting for your damned call all afternoon. You'll never guess what Gordon Fields told me about George's manuscript: they offered a whole million dollars for it. There's a contract..."

"Have they found it?"

"Hell no. Francis has been here making an awful fuss over their having lost it."

"I have an idea where it might be." Judith told her about the note and read it out. "Does H.Th. sound like a British publisher to you?"

It did.

"Hamilton Thornbush. That's where Peter Burnett is. And Eric Sandwell. I'm going to be there on Thursday..."

"Will you call them now, see if they have a manuscript from Fitzgibbon & Harris? Or are expecting one."

"OK. Tomorrow morning. I'll call Eric—and I wanted to talk to Peter anyway."

While Judith was on the phone David had poured himself some soda water, this time with ice. He swirled the cubes around in his glass, making a small jangling sound as he paced around the room.

Jimmy came by, sneered at him and ran upstairs three steps at a time. Judith hadn't noticed. When she replaced the receiver, David was rounding the sofa, a grin on his face.

"You wanted to reopen the case?" he asked cheerfully. "Well, I believe we've got ourselves a full-scale investigation."

"Why in the world are you beaming?"

"I love an interesting case," he said, rocking back on his heels as he came to an abrupt stop in front of Judith.

"And you haven't even heard about Ethan MacMurty yet."

The front door banged open. Anne marched in with two hairy friends of indeterminate sex, said "Hello," with a sideways glance at David, and stopped for a closer scrutiny.

"Aren't you the cop who came here last week?"

"Yup."

"You still trying to figure out what happened to poor old George Harris?"

"I'm working on it. As they say on *Hill Street Blues*, it's heating up."

"You going out?" Anne asked her mother.

"We were..." Judith hesitated.

"We are going to dinner," David said enthusiastically. "The first survival technique you learn in this business, my dear Ms. Hayes, is how to walk away from your work. If your mother ever tires of scribbling for a living," he said to Anne, "we'll offer her an honest job on the police force."

"She's not the type." Anne led her troops into the kitchen.

"Should I be flattered or insulted?" David asked.

Jane MacIntyre answered Eric Sandwell's direct line, as she had always done: "Mr. Sandwell's office."

"It's Marsha Hillier, Mrs. MacIntyre. May I speak to him, please?"

There was a long pause followed by a scraping sound.

"Mrs. MacIntyre, are you still there?" Sometimes the trans-Atlantic line played havoc with human voices.

"You haven't heard..." Jane MacIntyre said when she finally spoke.

"What?"

"Mr. Sandwell passed away last Thursday night. I thought Mr. Burnett might have called you—I suppose he hasn't had time what with the funeral and all the arrangements to be made."

"How did he die?"

"Heart attack. Late in the evening. They say he died very quickly—a blessing, I always say. The dreadful suffering of a slow death, at least he was spared that. Fifty-five he would have been this summer. Not an old man, Miss Hillier, and he took such good care of himself..."

"That's a terrible shock. I'm so sorry..." Marsha mumbled, her mind racing back to Harris's calculations for a contract. Harris. Grafstein. Sandwell.

"He had been so looking forward to your visit. Always such fun for him. Your dinner at The Lion's Head... I'm sure you'll want to speak to Mr. Burnett..."

"Oh yes..." Marsha was astonished to notice she was smiling. Somewhere deep down it was like a bubble bursting. Relief? *Thank God it's Eric and not Peter.*

"Hullo, Marsha," Peter boomed.

She fought for control of her voice.

"I'm very sorry, Peter."

"We'll all miss him dreadfully." Peter had such a deep, pleasant voice, without the plum-in-the-mouth "eh what" that runs rampant through British publishing. "Look, will you give us another couple of days to think about the Martin manuscript? It's been rather hectic and I just realized our option expires today. You know I wouldn't normally ask, but..."

"Of course. We'll extend..."

"Who's the agent?"

"Jelinek."

"Do you think you can handle it?"

"I'm sure he'll understand." She wasn't sure he would understand. Jelinek could use the delay to drive up the British price, but she would support Peter. Faced with a threat in the US, the agent might back off.

"Are you still coming?"

"I'll be in London in the morning."

"I hope you'll still keep your promise for dinner Thursday night."

"Yes—are you all right?"

"Not wonderful, but keeping my head above water. There's going to be a nasty battle over the succession, I think. Anthony Billingsworth-Powell is supporting me for a position on the board. Eric had insisted I join him there this year, anyhow..."

She had to ask. The manuscript could still be there.

"I'm sorry to trouble you with this now, but it's fairly important. A manuscript George Harris sent you. Perhaps the week before last. I think nonfiction and worth quite a lot. Axel was going to publish here. Seems George had estimated the British rights around half a million."

There was a long buzzing echo over the line. Marsha thought Peter would interrupt with an "of course" but he didn't. She plowed ahead.

"I was hoping you would let me see it when I'm in London."

"What's it about?"

"I don't know. I don't even know who the author is. But I gather the book is worth a bundle, and I'd like a shot at the paperback rights. Would you take a look around?"

"You're not giving me a whole lot to go on. I assume there is an excellent reason why you're not asking Axel or Fitz & Harris to send you a copy?"

"Max Grafstein died. It was going to be his acquisition." Perhaps he didn't know about George?

"I know. Horrible way to go..."

"Peter, you can't have received so many manuscripts from Fitz & Harris in the last couple of weeks. Please, would you have a look?"

"I'll do my best."

❉ ❉ ❉

Marsha sat for a while in silence, gazing out the window at the sunshine. She hadn't noticed Margaret Stanley placing the mug of coffee in front of her.

"And how is Mr. Burnett?" Margaret asked with a slight curl of her lip. She had never forgotten Peter's long letter of a couple of years ago. It had been addressed to Marsha and marked "personal." Margaret had opened it by mistake. It wasn't the first love letter she had read, but it was the first to quote extensively from *By Grand Central Station I Sat Down and Wept.*

"OK," Marsha said absently.

Margaret put a bulky package next to the coffee.

"Your schedule and airline tickets. One or two reminders. You'd promised Mr. Burnett you'd read *Hiroshima Revisited.* I've asked Mr. Mancuso to make sure he returns it to you before noon. He says he doesn't like to think about universal annihilation on an empty stomach. Don't you think Mr. Burnett's developing a morbid list of books? It's the third one from him about a nuclear holocaust since January."

"We're already publishing one of them," Marsha said, still gazing out the window.

"Is something wrong?" Margaret asked, suddenly solicitous.

"No. I mean yes. Eric Sandwell died."

"Not another one..." Margaret stood for a while not saying anything. Then she decided to leave Marsha to her thoughts.

Throughout the morning Marsha kept dialing Judith's number. It was busy.

Seventeen

JUDITH WOKE with a start. She had been drifting in and out of sleep, not wanting to wake up. The sheets, hot and clammy, clung to her body, damp hair wound around her face.

She checked her wrist for the time, then remembered she had taken her watch off during the night. It had scratched David across the shoulder as he rolled over. "Ouch," he had said, *sotto voce,* and pushed her arm over her head to feel around for what had hurt him. He had removed the watch then, while she nibbled his ear.

He hadn't said much once they had tiptoed past the children's rooms without turning on the hall light. He had left his shoes at the bottom of the stairs. She carried hers for some reason she no longer recalled. Maybe a throwback to her late teens, when she had sometimes come home after her mother was asleep.

Now, as then, she felt guilt. It ran through her body like the first stages of summer flu when you know something is irretrievably wrong, but you're not quite sure what. Why? She took stock of the possibilities.

First, there was David. Had she been too eager to go to bed with him? Could he have thought that then? And now? The evening had almost ended when he drove her home and kissed her at the door. It was she who had suggested he come inside... lightly. When he demurred, she had asked if he was frightened of her. She had said something about not being an easy woman to lay. Ugh... That had all somehow fitted the moment, then. She was even laughing. Had he laughed? She had been too anxious to make an impression on him to register what his reactions were. She was, as usual, watching herself. Her own most discerning critic. What had he thought when she asked him to have a nightcap? Some idiotic thing about having discovered a great new drink. Bailey's Irish Cream, of all things. He must have figured it was the lamest invitation he had ever had. The dumbest anyway.

But she hadn't intended to go to bed with him then. Or had she? No. She was pretty sure she hadn't.

Maybe it was the Irish Cream: three wine glasses full.

"This was meant to be sipped from brandy snifters, but I haven't had one of those in seven years. James took the snifters, I took the kids. Anyway, Bailey's too good to snift."

Asinine. Could that possibly have fitted into the mood of the evening? She'd had too much to drink. Yes, that would explain why she had let him peel off her sweater while they were still on the couch downstairs listening to Frank Sinatra, whom he hated, and Kris Kristofferson, whom he loved and collected himself.

It was easy to see why they'd had to go upstairs. "What if one of the little darlings comes down for a drink? Why don't we just...?" Yeah. Except she wasn't drunk. Perhaps he wouldn't know that.

She went to the bathroom. She had been certain she would wake up with the worst case of cystitis she'd ever had, and sure enough, here it was. How the hell could a man his age—how old was he anyway? forty-five? more?—make love three times in one night?

There was that then. She could hardly claim to have forgotten all three times. No one could be that drunk and still respond. And she had responded. Like a tornado. He'd probably think she was starved. Or that she'd been brushing up on her technique with a series of lovers…different one every week. It had all happened so easily—tiptoeing past the kids' bedrooms. Giggling.

Idiotic.

The kids. Jimmy's bedroom was right next to hers. Would he have heard? Sure, when they had last talked about sex, Jimmy had encouraged her to have an affair. But it's one thing to discuss it and quite another to listen to your mother groaning in the next room.

Judith brushed her teeth in the dark. No point in confronting herself in the mirror.

She went back to the bedroom and sat on the bed, bounced vigorously a few times and listened. Only the tiniest squeak. Probably not loud enough to hear through the wall. Unless of course he had been woken up first by the giggles, or the groaning.

She searched for her watch on the night table. David had drawn the curtains when he left. He'd said something about having to report in before 7:00. She had watched him get dressed through a haze—and scratch around under the bed trying to find his socks. She knew they must be at the foot of the bed tangled in the sheets but she couldn't tell him since she was pretending to be asleep, her arm over her face to close out the light and to prevent him seeing her with her eye make-up down both cheeks.

Judith ran her fingers over her chin. She knew she'd have a nasty beard-rash, red and sore for days. Both that and cystitis. Another long-term reminder.

There it was: 11:00. Now she knew the kids must have heard something, or they'd have called her when they left for school.

Quickly she threw back the covers, stripped the sheets, shook the pillows out of their cases, bundled the lot into a tight ball and threw it into the linen hamper. Getting rid of the evidence, it's called. She pulled out some fresh floral sheets. Leftovers from her marriage, wedding presents from his parents. Judith had kept the wedding presents. James didn't like them. Most had remained in the trunk in the basement, especially the large porcelain things, much too expensive and space-consuming to display.

How they had both hated the wedding. James had felt ridiculous in his rented tuxedo, too tight in the shoulders, too loose across the ass. The crotch hung halfway down to his knees, no time for minor alterations. He had just graduated from vet school and when he was ready to set up his practice the idea was that she would be able to help him with the decorating.

The last weeks before the wedding he had been too busy to push their eager sexual fumblings to their natural conclusion. It would have been difficult anyway in the back of his beat-up Plymouth where they had declared undying love. Judith's mother had been too concerned about "morality" to leave them alone in the house and James's house was even less inviting than Judith's. He had three brothers, all younger, all equally eager to catch him in a clutch with Judith. Better than the movies. Better even than the skin magazines they hid under their mattresses, where Mrs. Hayes was careful not to find them. James thought his mother was secretly pleased the boys were teaching themselves about sex. She most certainly wasn't going to teach them herself, and James's father never had time.

Although James had claimed otherwise, Judith was certain they were both virgins on their wedding night. What they lacked in experience, they were ready to make up for in eagerness to get on with it. For Judith, it was painful, messy and bloody—for James, little better than his furtive ejaculations in the bathroom when he was fourteen. But then his imaginary partners had disappeared right afterward. That minor miracle failed to befall Judith.

It was three days before James gave it another try. This time he expired on Judith's stomach.

Their honeymoon had been a foretaste of the marriage. They had remained rigidly unwilling to discuss their problems, or even to admit they were disappointed in each other and themselves.

In all her years of marriage Judith couldn't remember one happy night together. She had become convinced she was frigid, and so, secretly, had he. Children, she thought, might pull them together, but they didn't. What they did was fill her life with a sense of being loved and needed—a feeling, she now knew, she had been seeking for a long time. James was more comfortable handling small animals than children. So he continued fondling his pets at the clinic, while Judith hugged the babies, each in turn, until she felt quite certain they were *her* children, exclusively, and resented James picking them up. She saw it as an intrusion, and him as an intruder onto her private turf.

Judith checked the living room. Sure enough, the phone had been taken off the hook. A good sign, she thought. One of the kids must have decided to let her sleep in. They couldn't be too angry with her.

She took a hot shower, washed her hair, tidied the house more earnestly than usual, and looked over the introductory section of her *Globe Magazine* piece, but her heart wasn't in it. Mainly, she was sorting out her feelings for David and sifting the few stray bits of information she had gleaned about him.

While pondering why his wife had left him, she prepared a six-pound rump roast for supper, browning it on all sides but one, which she burned.

A man who has his daughter's framed photograph on his desk has to be able to love. Doesn't he?

She was not at all surprised that Detective Parr was in a meeting and couldn't be disturbed. She left a message and was, once more, unsurprised that he didn't call her within the next half hour. She spent it staring at her typewriter and the latest rewrite of the George Harris story. Too many unanswered questions.

She was putting her laundry through the old washer in the basement when the phone rang. She tore upstairs, tripped over the laundry basket, the hall chair and the vacuum cleaner she had brought up earlier (in case she had time). Breaking her own recent speed record, she made it on the fifth ring.

"Hello," she panted into the telephone.

"Is that Mrs. Hayes?"

"Yes. Huh...huh..." If she'd known it was not going to be David, she would have walked.

"Maybe we should let you catch your breath," the unfamiliar voice continued steadily.

"Who is this?" Judith demanded.

"It is not so very important for you to know who I am, my dear. What is very important indeed for you to understand is that I am a sensitive person." He paused as if to contemplate the sensitivity of his person, then came back again. "In the past few days you have been causing me some problems, and I am particularly sensitive to problems..."

"Is this some new kind of filthy phone call?" Judith interrupted. About all she needed now was some nut to discuss his sensitive cock and this one sounded like he had a masochistic tendency as well. "If it is, I'd just as soon you got the hell on with it so I can hang up."

"That would be most unwise, Mrs. Hayes. We have something of yours that you will want to have returned."

"You have nothing of mine."

"But we do," the voice said as if it were the most natural thing in the world. "Your children."

Judith felt the blood begin to pulse in her ears.

"And if you were to hang up now, how could we hope to negotiate the terms?"

"The terms? What terms?" Judith yelled into the telephone.

"Please stop interrupting. It would be much easier for both of us if you listened. And for them too. Lovely young people they are, and I'm as anxious to send them to you as you must be to have them back. We have not hurt them. Not yet. So you needn't worry. Though they have spent an uncomfortable night—that couldn't be avoided. And they have been most cooperative, really. Question is, will you be as obliging?"

"What do you want?... Where are they?" Judith shouted over the pounding in her ears.

"I could hardly tell you where they are, now, could I?" the voice said calmly. "But I'd be most happy to tell you what the terms are. Believe me, my dear, we're not in the habit of hurting young people, and, frankly, it's difficult to figure out what to do with them over a long period. Most difficult."

He stopped to give Judith a chance to think over the implications of what he had said, then continued, like a tour guide, taking her through a chamber of horrors. "Now. You are to stop your infernal meddling about George Harris. He is dead and gone, and no business of yours. Is that quite clear, so far?"

"Yes," Judith said hoarsely. "Yes, quite clear. What about my children?" But it wasn't clear, it was as though she were having a dizzy spell, the sound had turned hollow and distant.

"Give us a show of good faith and we will send Jimmy and Anne home. Now, *do I have your word?*"

"Yes, yes...my word...yes..."

"The implications, my dear, are simple: if you do not fulfill your end of the bargain, we will take the children again and next time there will be no bargaining. Is that clear?"

"I...yes."

"As for the show of faith... Hand in your little story. I'm certain your magazine will be relieved to see it at last. Today. Understood?"

"Yes."

"And, Mrs. Hayes, I'm afraid I must insist you keep your boyfriend out of this."

"I haven't..."

"And the rest of the police department. We wouldn't want any complications now, would we?" He hung up.

Judith held onto the phone. She didn't know when she had started shaking, but her body was bitterly cold and the hand holding the phone shook uncontrollably. The palsied hand dropped the receiver and left it dangling by the cord.

She pulled herself up, supporting herself against the wall. Feeling her way along the rough unfamiliar surface, knocking over the lamp, the couch hitting her in the shins, she made it to the foot of the stairs and stood, clutching the big round ball of the lower banister post.

That high grating sound came from her own dry throat.

A *show of good faith.* Her stomach clenched against the rising vomit. She ran upstairs to the typewriter where her story lay scattered over the desk and bed, the white pages floating in the afternoon sun. She clawed at them, sorting them into some sequence, mostly the original version, a tribute to Harris—his death an unsolved mystery—then numbered the pages in black felt pen, the ink smeared by her damp palm.

With the pages under her arm Judith raced downstairs and out the door, jumped into the car, barefoot still. The key didn't fit. She jumped out again, knocking her head on the roof, staggered onto the road, stopped.

"Get hold of yourself," she said, her voice shrill in the humming silence of the street. She leaned against the car, peeled the manuscript pages away from her body, the outside sheets wet with perspiration, laid them on the car seat, neatly, one on top of the other, and examined the car keys. "OK," she said to herself. "Steady, now, these are the right keys." She got back into the Renault, turned on the ignition, and pulled out onto the road with a jerk at the steering wheel.

She must follow instructions exactly.

She double-parked in front of the *Saturday Night* building leaving her lights flashing, ran the four flights of stairs to the top, asked the receptionist for a large envelope, inserted her story, addressed it to the managing editor, and scrawled URGENT on the outside.

PART FOUR

London

Eighteen

LONDON IN SPRINGTIME is magical. It's not only that spring comes so suddenly after a seemingly endless wait through bone-chilling dampness, though that has a lot to do with the gleaming friendliness of Londoners in April. What lends the city that quality of enchantment is the early blooming flowers. It's the crocuses in Hyde Park, the daffodils in Cadogan Square, the tulips around Westminster. They replace the soggy winter gray with crisp new light.

Marsha loved London in April. She didn't exactly take time out for the flowers, but she did stay near Hyde Park and her morning runs along the lanes lent her days a sparkle. Each year she returned at the same time.

Her day started early. She had taken the 5:00 p.m. flight from New York, so that she could count on a good sleep before her first appointment. But it hadn't worked out that way. Green's, usually eager to please its regular customers, was fully booked. Hard as they had tried to find her something close to the old-fashioned opulence they had proffered on previous visits, their best remaining space was a crowded little room near the Bond Street entrance, its window overlooking the roof of the kitchen. And it was overlooking it very closely indeed: the roof was only inches below the windowsill.

At 7:00 a.m. Marsha had been visited by several brisk, strolling pigeons. They made a great fuss of her clothes spread out on the dressing table. They cooed around the mirror admiring their own reflections, pecking at Marsha's blue and yellow silk scarf. They were cheerfully curious and a touch pushy. When Marsha tried to shoo them outside, they puffed up in indignation and fluttered deeper into the room.

As she waged the battle of the pigeons, the kitchen staff arrived and, judging by the clatter of dishes downstairs, wasted no time preparing for breakfast. Marsha gave up all pretense of catching more sleep, pulled on her navy jumpsuit, piled her hair up into a tight top-knot, and headed out toward Piccadilly.

It was a crisp, clear day, the traffic was sparse, only a few people on the street hurrying toward Green Park tube station. Marsha walked along one of the gravel paths that led to Queen Victoria and Buckingham Palace. At first she took long, loping steps, feeling her muscles stretch and come alive after the dreary flight from New York bunched up in the seat next to a talkative hairstylist from Hollywood who was taking a holiday from the stars. It had been much less comfortable back in the tourists before her promotion. She used to think that if only she could make it to first class, she could enjoy herself. Her new title, Larry had said, practically obliged her to travel first class—vice-presidents of publishing should display the wealth of their firms, it only proved the astuteness of their decisions—but she didn't like the trans-Atlantic flights any more. Lucky she had no ambitions to join the jet set; she wouldn't pass the first test.

When she reached Victoria's Memorial her breathing had adjusted to the pace, the cool air filled her lungs with the scent of flowers. She stretched her arms and her legs, loosening her muscles, then started running, slowly at first. She speeded up around St. James Park Lake, rounded The Mall, up Marlborough Road, St. James's Street, across Piccadilly and back to Green's.

She was barely out of breath when she stepped under the warm shower. She ran her hands down her hips and thighs. Firm and lean. Her buttocks were as high as they had ever been, no middle-age sag. She was lucky to have been born with good skin and small breasts, though she had never thought she would one day consider herself lucky for the latter. She remembered waiting for her breasts to sprout when she was twelve and all the other girls at BSS were beginning to show slight bulges. Later, when they had turned sixteen and their breasts bounced up and down in their tight black bathing suits on the way to the swimming pool, Marsha was still waiting. During her last summer vacation she had finally decided to join the grown-ups and purchased herself a size 32B brassiere with white lace and slight contouring. By then she'd given up hope.

She wrapped herself in a large soft white towel and lay down on the bed to dry out and prepare herself for the day.

Eric Major of Hodder was booked for lunch. She was rather hoping that he would suggest the Ritz. It was a great place for spotting publishing celebrities. That was where she had last seen Sir George Weidenfeld, and Billy Collins, Lord Harding of Penhurst. Charles Pick of Heinemann. All separate tables, of course.

She was hoping Eric would still have some manuscripts for her next Spring list. She knew Tom McCormack of St. Martin's had been in London on a buying trip a couple of weeks ago, and

Tom had an unerring instinct for "the big book" from Britain. Not even Tom's detractors could deny that, once he had run off with the James Herriot books. Who else could have predicted the public's inexhaustible interest in God's furry creatures, great and small?

At 3:00 she would see André Deutsch, at 4:30 Livia Gollancz. She hadn't seen André since Frankfurt. There would be a lot to talk about. It was comforting to know that Tom had missed Deutsch on his trip. André was the first British publisher Marsha had ever met, back in the golden days before the pound slumped, the Australians rebelled, the British houses pulled in their horns from the international scene, back when nobody in the book world had even thought of disputing British territorial rights throughout the old Empire. It was at a vast, glittering Reader's Digest party at the Hotel Intercontinental. Her very first Frankfurt Book Fair. Marsha was still low enough on the executive ladder that she thought she must impress everybody. Max Grafstein had introduced her to the legendary André Deutsch at the door. In ten minutes he had put her at ease, in another two successfully unloaded her on to the unsuspecting Livia Gollancz. But by then she was ready to start taking care of herself.

She was looking forward to seeing them both again.

Dinner was at Green's with Simon Master of Pan. Marsha had brought along a couple of manuscripts to show him. They were ideal for the Pan list and, if he was willing to make an offer for them before she returned, they could bypass some hassles. The author of one—a difficult little man with a formidable amount of talent he didn't deserve—was between agents. He had fired his first over a deal with the Book of the Month Club the agent had turned down as a ploy to force the club to up its original offer. They hadn't. The other manuscript was a thriller with a British setting. Far superior to the author's previous effort, and that had fetched close to $500,000 worldwide. Marsha thought that if she and Simon put in a joint offer now, they could get the world for the same price. If they waited, the agent would go to auction and the price might grow too high for the book.

She wished she had made Hamilton, Thornbush her first appointment. When Margaret sent out the telexes and juggled the hours to fit everyone's schedules, Marsha had thought it wise to treat Peter as just another publishing friend—and to allow herself a day to acclimatize before she faced him. Her time had already been pieced out before she learned of the Harris manuscript.

She considered calling Peter again to warn him, but decided he would think her mad. What he didn't know about the manuscript presumably couldn't harm him.

Marsha dressed in pearl-gray, a touch of color at the neck. She filled her canvas bag with papers and proofs, tucked two books under each arm and headed out toward St. James's Square.

Nineteen

ALL NIGHT JUDITH SAT BY the window, her face pressed against the cold damp glass, and waited. Her breathing was high-pitched and uneven. She watched the street, intensely aware of every movement, each car door banging, doors slamming, barking dogs, caterwauling. David had called. She claimed she was too busy to talk to him. On her way out, she had said. Around 7:00 a white van delivered a box of flowers. She had left it outside, leaning against the door.

At midnight the young couple across the street had a fight over her flirting with his boss. At 2:00 a.m. their baby cried, and cried. Neither of them picked it up. At 3:00 it had quietened, and whined itself to sleep.

Judith wrapped her arms around herself and rocked slowly from side to side. Her throat was aching dry.

At 6:00 a.m. the newspaperboy tossed rolled-up papers at the porches on the other side of the street. He kicked over a garbage can and watched the lid roll down the road with a clatter.

It had started to rain.

HIDDEN AGENDA 171

Twenty

BUT FOR A NAGGING concern about Peter's safety, Wednesday had been a perfect day for Marsha.

Lunch at the Ritz hadn't produced celebrities but it had led to one excellent author Eric was willing to let her publish, and a reciprocal deal for a string of mysteries that would find a congenial home with Eric's paperback line.

André had been courtly, though unwilling to let her purchase *The History of the Russian Revolution* without consulting his new partner. He had reminisced about early years with Eric Sandwell and the tragedy of his sudden death. Marsha wondered if André was thinking about writing his own memoirs.

Livia Gollancz hadn't wanted to join in M & A's production of *The Last of the Wild Horses*, though she loved the photographs and was, personally, a fan of horses in the wild. She thought the time of the lush illustrated book had passed. She suggested Marsha talk to Sidgwick and Jackson. Marsha had bought US rights to two of Livia's forthcoming cookbooks. Though British cooking was hardly the culinary success of the century, there was a new nostalgia in the States for old ways.

Dinner with Simon was sumptuous, and he had found the double purchase Marsha offered quite irresistible, though he hadn't read the manuscripts personally. He thought Peter was a natural for the Hamilton, Thornbush board. With the ubiquitous Anthony Billingsworth-Powell supporting him, the rest of the board would have to accept. Powell's boards included too many of the other communications giants, and his tentacles were said to range from the Upper House to the international oil companies. Publicly he was a respectable dove, a fact that made some cynics curious about Peter Burnett's swelling list of antiwar books.

Thursday had started early, with a David Higham agent's breakfast. Afterward, she decided to walk to Hamilton, Thornbush. She needed fresh air and time alone.

Number 37 South Audley Street must once have been a stately home. Now it was surrounded by ambassadorial mansions flying a variety of obscure flags from countries with Western sympathies. They were close enough to Grosvenor Square to feel the protective presence of the giant chrome and granite building fronted by the two huge iron eagles: the embassy of the United States of America.

Marsha paused by a long line of people carrying signs and slogans urging the Americans to get out of Egypt and the United Kingdom where their military bases were, decidedly, not wanted. Several of the demonstrators hauled paper bags full of ripe tomatoes.

Number 37 was four stories of red Georgian brick. The windows were protected by stout iron bars, as were the two diminutive trees and faded patches of grass on either side of the entrance. To the right of the oak door a discreet brass plaque declared that this was the home of Hamilton, Thornbush Limited, established in 1887. Inside, to the left of the central staircase, there was a small reception area with two broad armchairs and a low oak coffee table covered with magazines and carefully folded newspapers. A second brass plaque pointed an arrow toward the receptionist hidden behind a wooden partition with a small window at shoulder level.

Marsha asked to be announced to Peter Burnett, then settled into one of the armchairs to finish her reading of *The Times*. She knew from past experience that British publishers never expected anyone to appear on time, as they were rarely punctual themselves. She thought they considered it somewhat bad manners to be punctual. For Marsha it was hard to shake old habits. Besides, she rather enjoyed the club atmosphere of the Hamilton, Thornbush waiting room.

"Miss Hillier?"

Marsha looked up.

"Yes?"

The carefully coiffed hair, pulled tight at the temples and back into a bun, the straight tailored blue dress with white cotton collar buttoned high on the neck, close-set blue eyes peering over the top of the horn-rimmed half-moon glasses, the mouth set into familiar grooves of good-natured formality: Eric Sandwell's perfect secretary.

Marsha jumped up to greet her.

"Mrs. MacIntyre, how are you?"

"As well as can be expected," Jane MacIntyre said primly. Then she sighed. "These haven't been happy times for us. Not this last week since Mr. Sandwell passed away..." Her voice trailed off for a second. "I'm helping Mr. Burnett now, as you can see." There was, Marsha thought, a slight edge to her voice, though it might have been weariness. "He can certainly use the help. Suddenly he has the responsibilities of the whole house. Not easy for him. For any of us really. And so unexpected. Mr. Sandwell—you know..."

Marsha nodded. It would be particularly hard for Jane MacIntyre to adjust. She had been Eric's right hand. Marsha touched her lightly on the shoulder. She wanted her to know that she understood, even if she couldn't think of the right words to say.

Jane MacIntyre saved her from further struggle. "You're looking wonderful," she said brightly. "Not too tired from that dreadful flight?"

Marsha said she felt much better after two long runs in her favorite park.

"It's the Spring air that does it. Back home, we've hardly seen the sun yet."

"How would you, Miss Hillier, among all those skyscrapers? It's as if you New Yorkers didn't want to see anything but concrete. I just don't know how you can live there."

"Neither do I," said Marsha. "Truth is, though, I can't imagine living anywhere else."

The only time Jane MacIntyre had ventured across the Atlantic, she had run into a snowstorm in New York City, been stuck on the Triboro Bridge for five hours, hadn't been able to find a cab to take her to the Brooklyn Zoo or to The Cloisters, and had lost her handbag (she was sure it had been stolen, this was New York, after all) on the subway. Still, there had been Bloomingdale's, and Saks, and Bergdorf Goodman, and, above all, she had discovered Calvin Klein.

"I did bring you the scarf," Marsha said, handing over the small Calvin Klein bag. "I hope this is the right one."

"Well." Jane MacIntyre swallowed hard. "Well. You remembered. Thank you." She unwrapped the package and shook out the tiny silk scarf. "Absolutely perfect," she said gazing at it. "Lovely." Then, as if the emotion had been too much for her, she quickly folded the scarf back into its wrapping. "We had better be heading upstairs."

She stood aside to let Marsha into Peter's office.

"Perhaps you'll stop by later?" she said. Now quite composed, she headed down the hall.

As the door opened, Peter came striding across to meet Marsha.

She smiled fondly at his familiar loping gait, one shoulder slightly dropped like John Wayne's, and from about the same height. He was startlingly attractive. There was, perhaps, a touch more silver at the temples, but his hair was still thick and unruly. For an Englishman in the book business he looked unusually sporty, as if he had just left the football field. As ever, the top button of his shirt was undone, his tie disarmingly askew. When he reached Marsha, he held her for a moment, examining her face. Then he grinned his boyish grin—half shy, half aggressive, and kissed her on the forehead.

"My, it is good to see you, Marsha. You're absolutely splendid. As ever. Come in, come in. Here, we have made fresh coffee in your honor. Perked, not freeze-dried. And I brought you some fresh cream. Let me take your jacket. Or are you cold?" He ushered Marsha into a large leather armchair. He took her braided Dior jacket, glanced at it appreciatively—unlike most men, he knew what it was—selected a short wooden hanger from the walk-in closet between the two towering bookcases, and hung it inside.

"And you're as splendid as ever," Marsha said a little stiffly. She wanted to keep her emotions in check. "Heartthrob of every aspiring writer in the British Isles. Unfair competition, wouldn't you say?"

Peter poured coffee from the silver container perched on a silver tray on a bow-legged George III table by the door. Style. They still had the style, if not always the substance. In America, it was often hard to discern either.

"Attracting them, m'dear, is hardly the problem these days; it's how in hell we can afford to publish them that creates the difficulties. I rather think if Emily Brontë walked in with a crisply typed copy of *Wuthering Heights*, she'd have trouble getting a fair reading. There isn't enough money to go around, and, naturally, all of us are more inclined to back the sure-fire winners than bet our money on a dark horse. Your Martin manuscript, for example. Can't remember what it's called—dance of something or other, right?"

"Dance of the Marionettes."

"Right. Here's your coffee. Not too much cream? Well, then. That's your perfect example. A book that takes no risks, exposes no new theories, breaks no new ground, fits right into your Big Book Syndrome. The characters are forgettable, the story is well plotted, but nothing new—I don't recall where it takes place, it leaves you with no delusions of having had a new experience. Fits the mold."

"You don't want it, then." Marsha laughed, thinking of Jelinek's prediction. Jelinek had hung up on her in disgust when she confessed she'd fallen prey to Peter's need for an extension. "So who cares Sandwell died? Either they get off the pot, or they don't. This property is in demand. And that means hard bucks, not sweet-talk. If they don't jump first time, they'll be whimpering their way into 10 percent over their last offer. Mark my words." She knew Peter would do the best job for the book. Hamilton, Thornbush had a big brassy marketing department with a budget to match, and a formula novel destined for the best-seller list needed just such treatment.

"That's where you're wrong," said Peter. "Of course I want the book. For all the wrong reasons. And for all the right reasons—can't you see the imitation Forsyth-Ludlum hype now? It'll make a lot of money."

Marsha walked over to the window. The red-brick facade of the house opposite crowded in so close it was hard to imagine a whole street in between. Yet there was room enough for one big untidy acacia tree in front of Number 37. Amazing that someone would have planted such a messy tree between these houses. She imagined Peter looking out at this sight each day. It felt as though this shared experience brought them closer. Quickly, she turned her back on it.

"I have no innate desire to defend *Dance of the Marionettes*," she said finally, "but I cannot understand why you're so intent on doing me a favor by offering to publish." That wasn't fair, but nor was his preaching. After all, she did not create the rules.

"You're being uncharacteristically obtuse," Peter said. "Let me refresh your cup. These bloody trans-Atlantic flights play havoc with the mind. And body, in most cases. Not yours, though, thank God. Not yours." He loped over to the coffee again.

Marsha knew what was coming.

"Having suspected all along, however, that I would remain sternly unrepentant, you've had only one recourse, right?"

"Right," Peter said, grinning. He flipped open a file and extracted several long sheets of paper.

"How much?" Marsha asked.

"A little more than Jelinek expected, a little less than what we think it's worth. But then we're probably wrong. And that doesn't change my assessment of its intrinsic value, you understand?"

"Fully." Marsha took the contracts from his outstretched hand. She returned to her comfortable leather chair to read them over.

"I've been worrying about you," she said over the top of her documents.

"That's comforting. I didn't know you could afford such frivolity," he said with a quick smile. "Sorry, I didn't mean to be harsh. The past week hasn't been easy. I miss Eric dreadfully. He was more than a boss, or a colleague. He was a friend—I still can't face going into his office. I doubt I'll ever quite take his place." He turned his back on Marsha and strode over to the bookcase. He stood for a moment, studying the spines of the books, pulled one out. "Something for you," he said. "Jeremy's new novel. A very British jacket, wouldn't you say?"

It was.

Marsha had finished reading the contracts and tucked them and Jeremy's bright yellow book into her canvas bag.

"They're fine," she said. "Jelinek will like them. Next time, though, I'll be sure to send you something more soulful."

"Heaven forfend." He extracted a hefty brown parcel from the bottom drawer of his desk. "Talking about serious literature, this, I believe, is what you were seeking when you called me from New York."

"The manuscript from Fitzgibbon & Harris?" Marsha's pulse quickened.

"The same," Peter grinned. "A wonderful little story, set on a pig farm in Saskatchewan. It's magnificently written, though, and seems to have more to do with the female's natural desire to dominate the male than it does with raising pigs. Nothing personal, Marsha." This time he grinned more aggressively than boyishly, but Marsha had no interest in picking up the challenge. "But I don't think it rates half a million dollars."

"Pigs?"

"Pigs."

"Amazing," Marsha said. "Do you mind if I glance at it now?"

"Not at all," Peter said. "Take your time. It's a most rewarding read. And you never know, it may be a real find for your list."

Marsha read down the middle of the pages, as Jerry read the newspaper, looking for content, not for style. In a few minutes she concluded Peter was right. An extraordinary novel, a perceptive and talented writer, but definitely not the manuscript she was looking for.

She glanced at Peter. He had been writing something, intently, his head tilted slightly. He stopped when he felt her eyes on him.

"Finished already?" he asked regretfully. "I was becoming used to your being here."

"I don't understand," Marsha said, shaking her head. "There has to be another... Perhaps Eric took it..."

"They don't let you take manuscripts along where he went," Peter said.

"Eric *did* have a heart attack?" Marsha asked abruptly.

"I haven't a degree in medicine, Marsha, but the doctor seemed very certain. Look, for heaven's sake, will you tell me what this is all about?"

"Is this the only manuscript you've had from Harris?"

"It's the only one from Canada in some time. I was very thorough in my search, m'dear, since *you* asked."

"Was there a letter with it?"

"Yes." Peter pulled a sheet of Fitzgibbon & Harris letter-head out of his file and thrust it at Marsha. "See for yourself."

My dear Eric,

This is the manuscript we discussed on the telephone. Please read it yourself and get back to me by phone no later than April 17. You understand this could be an auction situation, but you have the opportunity of making a preemptive bid if you are willing to meet our terms.

Yours,
George

The letter was dated April 5th. It was marked "Personal and confidential."

"Impossible," she murmured.

"Right," Peter agreed. "It is quite impossible for our list. A fine piece of writing and all, but..."

"That's not what I meant," Marsha was saying, not trying to hide her disappointment. "This is not the manuscript I phoned about. There was another..."

"Well," Peter said lightly, "perhaps George Harris chose a more deserving house. There are still a few around. That brings to mind *Hiroshima Revisited*. You were my first choice. Have you reached a decision?"

"It doesn't make sense," Marsha murmured.

"On the contrary, it makes eminent sense, when you consider the alternative. Everyone should visit Hiroshima at least once, if not in person then in spirit. Only that can bring the stark and terrible facts to light. 'It's only through conscious choice and then deliberate policy that humanity can survive'— Pope John Paul II at Hiroshima four years ago. Or don't you read him either?"

"Peter. I wasn't talking about *Hiroshima*. Please. I was thinking about the Harris manuscript. I was sure it was here."

"Why?"

"He'd made a note of sending it here."

Peter shrugged.

"What about *Hiroshima*?"

"I'm afraid we decided we couldn't do it justice. There have been so many apocalyptic books recently. I can't see selling another one in the States."

"A pity," Peter said. "There are some subjects you can never overexpose." Then he laughed. "The other one being sex."

He helped her into her jacket and walked with her to the ornate front door before returning to a catalogue meeting. He would pick her up for dinner at 8:00.

She stood outside for a moment gazing at the acacia tree, wondering why in the world George Harris would have asked for an urgent response to a manuscript set on a pig farm in Saskatchewan. Why would he insist Eric read it himself in a week? Why would he talk about auctioning and preemptive bids?

She turned on her heel, opened the door again, cautiously. Peter had gone upstairs. She walked through the lobby, waved cheerily at the receptionist, and marched up the two flights of stairs, past Peter's closed door, down to the end of the hall.

Jane MacIntyre was in her office bent over her typewriter, her back to the door.

"Mrs. MacIntyre," Marsha said tentatively.

When she saw Marsha she stood up quickly, adjusting her blue dress. "I came by to say good-bye and..." Marsha hesitated for a second, then plowed right ahead. "I have a favor to ask you. I'm trying to trace a manuscript George Harris sent to Eric. It's a major property Max Grafstein was going to buy for the US. I thought perhaps you'd remember…"

"Naturally, I remember." Jane MacIntyre bristled. "But didn't you ask Mr. Burnett? He has the original."

"The original?"

"Yes. But let me just buzz Mr. Burnett for you…"

"I don't want to bother him again…" Ugh. Too lame.

"I'm sure he won't mind, seeing it's *you*." Jane MacIntyre reached for the telephone.

"No. Really." Marsha didn't quite grab the hand as it went for the receiver; the fact that their fingers touched stopped the other woman in midair. "Please."

Jane MacIntyre looked puzzled.

"Whyever not?"

"He was going into a meeting right away."

"Really, Miss Hillier…" said Jane MacIntyre, exasperated.

"I've already asked him. Only…" She had to trust her instincts now. It was the only chance she had. "… for some reason he couldn't remember it."

"He couldn't? Well…" The overt sarcasm in Jane MacIntyre's tone confirmed that Marsha's hunch was right. Peter Burnett hadn't won over Eric's exacting secretary.

"Was there anything unusual about that manuscript that you remember it so well?" Marsha pressed her advantage.

"Unusual! I'll say there was. Mr. Sandwell had been expecting it all morning. It came by courier. He was popping in and out of here asking whether it had arrived yet, as if I wouldn't have told him right away. I was to interrupt whatever he was doing and take it to him. Which I did. I hadn't seen him so excited in a long time. Soon as I opened the door, he jumped up, rushed around his desk, took it right out of my hands. Later, you know," her voice softened, "I wondered whether all that excitement might have caused what happened. He took such good care of himself otherwise."

"Oh yes," Marsha concurred. "He was in superb shape. Not a trademark of our business, on the whole. Do you recall what the manuscript was called?"

"That's the devil of it. Can you imagine, the title typed on the top page was 'Untitled'? And there was no author's name, only 'X.' It wasn't all that thick either. Not like some of the stuff we get in here—Lord, it would take a truck to cart them around. Why people will write that much with no hope of being published, I don't know."

Marsha tried to quell her excitement.

"How many pages would you say it was?"

Mrs. MacIntyre pulled out the top drawer of her desk and withdrew a stenographer's notebook.

"Two hundred and sixty-eight. Exactly," she said with justifiable pride. "I check them all in here, and I note when they are returned, which most of them are, poor things. Only Mr. Sandwell's stuff though, I *haven't* been asked to do Mr. Burnett's." She flicked back a couple of pages and lifted the book for Marsha to see. There it was in neat rounded 1930s secretarial script. *'Untitled' ms. by X. from G. Harris, F & H. Received Apr. 8. 268 pages.*

And some say the British are slipping, Marsha thought, elated. They hadn't met Mrs. MacIntyre!

"And a letter came with it?"

"Naturally. That's how I knew this was the manuscript Mr. Sandwell had been expecting."

Marsha took another chance.

"George Harris wanted a preemptive bid by April 17?" she asked.

"That's right. Never had one of *those* from Mr. Harris before. It's the agents mainly that like to play around with auctions. You know..."

Marsha nodded. She did.

"Mr. Sandwell wanted to read this right away. He closeted himself for the rest of the morning. He didn't want any calls till he was finished. Except for Mr. Burnett. I had his lunch brought up special."

"Except for Mr. Burnett, you said?"

"Well, yes. That would be different. He wanted Mr. Burnett to stand by and come and talk to him soon as he had finished reading. And that he did. About 2:00, I think. They were ever so excited. I could hear them talking and Mr. Sandwell seemed so pleased when he came out again."

"Did you hear what they were saying?"

Jane MacIntyre looked shocked.

"Miss Hillier," she said, "you don't think I would eavesdrop."

"Heavens, no," Marsha said quickly. "I thought maybe— seeing they were talking so loudly—you couldn't help overhearing..." Oh hell. "I'm sorry. It's only because this was so unusual."

Jane must have accepted her apology.

"You say unusual, well there *was* something. Before Mr. Burnett came in, right after lunch, it was, Mr. Sandwell went down to the duplicating machine and insisted on copying the first few pages of that manuscript himself. I don't remember the last time he used that machine. He had to ask me how it worked, but he went ahead and did it himself anyway." She smiled at the memory.

Twenty-odd years with a man like Eric, Marsha thought, you would grow to love him some. "There was another manuscript that came in from George Harris that week, wasn't there? Something by a young Canadian writer about pig farming?"

"Oh yes. I read some of that myself. A lovely book, but I don't think quite right for us." She checked again in her stenographer's book. "Here it is. I entered it on April 4th. *When Pigs Do Fly.* Came from Alice Roy, not Mr. Harris himself. You're publishing that?"

"Maybe," Marsha said.

Twenty-One

RICHER BY SIX NEW manuscripts she had promised to read immediately and one set of rolled galley proofs that looked as if it had done the rounds of every visiting American publisher before her, Marsha returned to the hotel.

She pulled out a file for her 5:00 meeting, straightened her blouse, fixed her hair. It seemed she had rushed through the day, constantly distracted by X's Untitled manuscript. Would X contact her? Had X been encouraged by her responses at Schwarz's? Did the woman represent X? *Was* she X?

When Marsha reached the lobby, Julian Ashby was already waiting. She was tempted to tell him about her new conspiracy theory, but he seemed pressed, checking his watch unobtrusively while she talked. Julian didn't share Marsha's enthusiasm for the manuscripts she had brought, and he had no interest in Larry's proposal for a health-care series for over-fifties: "Actually, I found the idea in rather bad taste."

Back in her room, she confronted a large pigeon sitting on the flashing light of the telephone. When Marsha reached for the receiver, it lumbered over to the windowsill with an attitude of hurt dignity.

The message was from Jerry. Call at the office. Did he think she was stupid? When had she ever called him at home?

He was lonely. He had been preparing for the trial of a client he didn't like, in front of a judge who didn't like him, against a prosecutor with a sense of mission, who was at least ten years Jerry's junior. His analyst had gone to Mexico on holiday. Kate had suggested a month in the South of France to renew their marriage. Did Marsha think he was having a crisis of confidence? Did she think he should hop on the Concorde to London?

"How in hell would you explain an unexpected business trip to Kate? And to the Partners? They would have to be primed to cover for you. You'd be indebted to all of them. Can you imagine going through life being indebted to every one of them?"

He gave in without conviction when Marsha promised to return next Wednesday night. No side trip to Paris.

Marsha was grateful when he hung up. Maybe Judith was right. She had allowed herself to be used by Jerry as a substitute for a real relationship—because that was all she could handle: mutual physical comfort, a controlled environment, the knowledge that she was needed. Just as Judith had never rid herself of the guilts bestowed on her by her mother, Marsha couldn't destroy the rigid confines of her own unloved childhood.

For a moment she stared out the window remembering Peter's big untidy acacia tree.

Over a year had passed since she had exchanged anything but publishing talk with him, but it hadn't been easy. Each time she saw him she had to remind herself to forget. And she had tried to believe that the night they had spent in her hotel room in Frankfurt had been merely casual and pleasant, though it had been neither.

Then there had been his letter.

She had fashioned a response that was cheerful, friendly, and hurriedly brisk. She had wanted to reestablish her perimeters. A long-distance love affair offered fewer consolations than an affair without love. Marsha's life was inextricably set in New York, as Peter's was in London. Though he had never acknowledged defeat, he gave up quickly enough, his letters returning to the "dictated but not signed" from his erratic handwriting.

Perhaps he had lied to her about *The Dealer* because he was competing for the world rights now that both Harris and Grafstein were dead. Perhaps he didn't know the danger. Or maybe he did and was trying to protect her?

Tonight she would tell him everything she knew. Invite him to work with her.

She dressed with a sense of occasion. Her wine-colored Guy Laroche suit, a ruffled-neck shirt with long frilled cuffs that fanned out at the ends of the jacket sleeves, her mother's old ruby-inset gold brooch a few inches below the neckline for tempered unapproachability, and wine-colored lipstick that made her feel like a foreign agent.

Peter, his tie still askew, arrived on time. He kissed her lightly on the cheek, *old friends.*

The champagne was already at the table. Sliced smoked salmon appeared as soon as they sat down. The maître d', who might have been a veteran of the Great War, all but tugged his forelock when he saw Peter.

"Such a tragedy. A man in his prime. Yes..."

"I don't know why you picked this place," Peter mumbled.

"I thought it was your spot. We came here last year. And the year before. I was being nostalgic. Why?"

"This is where Eric died."

"Shall we leave?"

"No. It would be somewhat embarrassing."

But at the end of the champagne and smoked salmon, he suggested they might try the pub next door. It lacked the old-world charm of The Lion's Head, but made up for it in ebullience.

He rewarded Marsha for her acquiescence with home-grown gossip, rumors of pending takeovers, and the newest revelations about Rupert Murdoch. He could not comprehend why the newspaper tycoon, a man known for his financial acumen, would invest in British publishing houses. Yet there he was, pitching to purchase yet another ailing old giant. He'd get no thanks for it either. The British remained tacitly unimpressed by his brash Australian aggressiveness.

What did she think of Nelson Roberts, Jr. taking over five of the UK's leading papers? A quiet, reclusive, American vegetarian millionaire, at least he had the good sense not to flash his money around Britain in person.

Peter grew more animated in the amber light, his sharp features strengthened by the shadows, leaning forward on crossed arms as he shared confidences. She loved to watch him, lithe and energetic, basking in her appreciation. She would have liked to listen all evening. And she would have liked the evening to continue into the next day, but the unasked question was beginning to take over her thoughts, until, finally, she blurted it out.

"Peter, why did you show me that lovely novel set in Saskatchewan this morning, when you knew I was looking for another manuscript?"

He took a deep breath and, leaning back in his chair, asked in a quiet voice: "What other manuscript?"

"The one Eric Sandwell had been expecting to see that day. He was so excited he called you into his office and the two of you read it and talked about it. The one which went with George Harris's letter."

"We get so many manuscripts, I might have been momentarily confused. Could you elaborate? What is it about? Who is the author? You didn't give me many clues when you phoned."

His face was now expressionless, controlled, his mouth set in a straight line, his eyes very still.

"All I know is it's nonfiction and has been referred to, variously, as *The Dealer* and as 'Untitled' by X. George Harris was going to publish it, but he died before he could get around to it. Max Grafstein read it, and *he* died. He had offered George $1 million for the US rights..."

"I was told George Harris committed suicide."

"The Toronto police department is now treating it as murder."

"Grafstein was mugged."

"True. But the same night his offices were broken into, and the manuscript vanished. I think this was the same manuscript George sent to Eric. Now Eric is dead."

Peter's glass slipped out of his hand and crashed to the table, spilling some of the beer over his pants.

"Damn. Damn." He wiped at it with his white handkerchief.

The waitress lifted their glasses and mopped up the beer. "Another one, sir?"

Marsha said yes; Peter was still too busy with his knees. The waitress offered to help and Peter accepted gladly. The tension evaporated with the stain. When he looked up again, he was his former, composed self.

"Now that the slight diversion is over, perhaps you could enlighten me some more," he said.

Marsha told him everything she knew except the part Jane MacIntyre had played.

"Quite a story," Peter said. "Mysterious old ladies, disappearing witnesses, strange notes written in green ink, high stakes, a distinguished cast. But Eric wasn't playing. He died of a heart attack. He was almost sixty. He had been driving himself too hard. And I have trouble with the rest of your suppositions—though, frankly, I like the tale."

"And that's what you really think?"

"That's what I really think. And that I almost forgot something." He pulled a small black package from his pocket and handed it to Marsha. "Last month I was in India to oversee the enthusiastic efforts of our Eastern sales force. I came across this chap."

Marsha unwrapped a padded box and, inside, an antique porcelain elephant with a tiny blue saddle and gold-painted headdress, its trunk turned upward for good fortune, its ears swept back for optimism and speed.

"Such a perfect little figure, so brave and determined, he reminded me of you," Peter said, gazing affectionately at the elephant. "Should fit right into your collection."

"It's absolutely beautiful," Marsha said, holding it in the palm of her hand, letting the amber light warm its tiny form. Suddenly she was ashamed of having suspected him of duplicity.

"Maybe we should celebrate our meeting with a touch of port. Or brandy? There is a place in Essex I'd like to show you. My own handiwork. I'd like to prove to you that I have talents other than books."

It was a crisp, clear Spring night outside—a wonderful time for a drive to the country.

There was something about the angle of his jaw that reminded Marsha of her father. Maybe it was the taut line from his ear to the corner of his mouth—the moving tension in the hollow of his cheek as his eyes dodged oncoming headlights. The narrow road curved sharply now that they had left the highway. The upper corners of his mouth puffed up, ingenuously, childlike. Her father had covered his mouth with a thick mustache.

She wondered whether it was Peter's newly acquired image of clandestine intrigue that had put her in mind of her father. A man of too many secrets, no time for explanations. She remembered him locked in his study with fat gold-colored files and graying men with tight smiles and black briefcases. Mostly she remembered his hellos and goodbyes; the gifts he brought, odd-smelling dolls in crisp costumes with tall headdresses, tiny ornate boxes full of perfumed petals, carved figurines of ivory and sandalwood—her first elephants had arrived wrapped in silk-fancy embroidered jackets and lace shirts with colored ribbons. Jewels for her mother, candleholders, furs. Sometimes grotesquely stuffed animal heads that were banished to the basement.

When Marsha and her brothers had been allowed to watch him unpack, he would tell them strange stories about faraway places where the gifts were made. She wouldn't know when he had gone again until she opened the hall closet looking for a dark place to hide, and saw that his big black suitcases were gone.

Peter stopped in front of a white farmhouse. He looked at her, waiting. She wanted him to hold her. She had resisted wanting anyone for so long. His lips were soft and faintly salty; his tongue tasted of beer. She could feel his heartbeat.

Then he was opening the car door, propelling her toward the house. He fumbled with the keys, kicked the door open, and they ran up some stairs in the dark. She saw only vague outlines of the furniture in the moonlight, the bed a large black shadow. He was pulling at the zipper on her skirt, the buttons on her blouse. His cock pressed against the hollow next to her hipbone as she lay back on the covers; her hands reached for his body as his hands and lips began to explore hers.

This was what she had wanted.

They lay listening to the grasshoppers in the farmer's field below. Then Peter whispered, "I think I'm falling in love again."

"Uhhum," Marsha said, but she was already trying to separate herself from him. She felt exposed. Too warm and comfortable as her body fitted into his. She would have to raise the barriers again, fast, before she became accustomed to needing him.

"First time's not much to go by. Usually."

"You mean Frankfurt, in my hotel room?"

"That doesn't count. I mean tonight. We'll get better with practice."

"Uhhum," Marsha said. Why did men need reassuring? "Really, it was fine."

"Fine?" he asked.

"Okay, great!" Marsha laughed.

"I'll be better as I get to know you." He was still uncertain. "Sometimes I think it would save a lot of time and grief if people exchanged simple questionnaires about what they liked the most. Everyone's different. Right?"

"Right," she said, though she hadn't wanted to think about how different they were. She didn't want to think about Jerry. Not now. "Though that would tend to destroy some of the spontaneity."

"I suppose," he chuckled.

"Marsha..." he said after a while.

"Yes?" She was glad he had stopped short of asking for her professional evaluation of his technique.

"I wish you'd stop all this nonsense about Eric."

"I know."

"It could be coincidence."

"Yes. But it isn't," Marsha said.

"You're sure of that?" he asked.

"Absolutely." Marsha stretched out on the bed, her hands locked behind her head. The cool night air fanned her still-damp stomach. She could see him looking at the outline of her body in the moonlight. It felt beautiful.

"In that case," Peter said with a sharp intake of breath, "you must try to become unsure again. Go home and forget the whole thing. While you're still guessing."

"What do you mean?" Her voice was suddenly hoarse.

"It's not like you to be so obtuse. I'm trying to tell you you're on treacherous ground. Please stop meddling. Please."

"Is that a warning?" Marsha asked. She turned to look at him but it was too dark to see his face.

"The best I can do," he said softly. "I only wish there was more."

She became aware of the smell of his body, sharp and sweet where it had mingled with her own, as they lay side by side in silence. It was cooler now, a slight breeze billowing the curtains. Marsha listened to his slow, even breathing, wanting to quell her longing to touch him. Her frustration at his warning, his decision not to level with her, slowly dissolved into anger.

She found the bathroom, filled the old-fashioned tub to the brim and lay in water up to her chin. Afterward she pulled on her crumpled clothes, adding more distance between herself and Peter, and watched him for a while to make sure he was sleeping.

His face was smooth and boyish, his mouth slightly open, soft in the corners as though, at any moment, he was ready to grin at her. His dark eyelashes fluttered in the curved hollow under his eyes: he must have been dreaming.

She watched his chest rise and fall. When she touched him lightly, he didn't respond. Marsha swallowed hard, wiped the dampness from her own eyes and turned her back on him.

She looked around the bedroom for the first time. It was wide and cavernous, but well-lit by the moon and the bathroom light. There were potted plants on the table near the windows, clothes in the walk-in closet, balls of dust and rumpled underwear under the bed. More underwear in the drawers, fat knitted sweaters, his shirts neatly folded. No hiding places for a manuscript.

Downstairs, the room was sparse and simple, the walls painted white, the oak floors polished and the broad wooden roof beams stained. No personal objects. No photographs, mementos, collectibles. Only wall-to-wall books, as in his office.

On the heavy oak round table, large enough and old enough to have served all King Arthur's knights, there was a pile of manuscripts. She skimmed some of the typed pages. Within an hour she had determined that nothing on the table could be by X, though there were a couple of stories she wouldn't have minded taking home with her.

She looked through a stack of brown folders marked, variously, *The Chicago Sentinel*, *The Boston Evening Post*, *The Dallas Journal*, *The London News*, and the names of other newspapers around the world. Each folder held a heap of clippings and tearsheets. They related to trouble spots in South America, Central America, the Middle East, Africa. There were stories about Nicaragua and the proposed withdrawal of US assistance from the contras; reports predicting defeat for the Salvadoran army when the US stopped funneling them arms and aid; stories of anti-American demonstrations in London, Berne, Beirut, Munich, Calcutta, tear gas in Ankara, bullets in Athens; lengthy interviews with nonviolent peace demonstrators.

In a separate folder there were headlines about the nuclear arms race, reports on research papers about nuclear winter, estimates of the number of dead in the case of limited nuclear warfare, related articles from various newspapers and magazines. Some lines had been underscored in yellow felt pen. "We can be safe from nuclear war only when the causes of military conflict have been removed."... "In the unending search for security, the United States and its allies have acquired the means by which the human species might well be totally destroyed..."

The bookcases testified to Peter's eclectic tastes. Czeslaw Milosz's *The Issa Valley,* Russel Hoban's *Riddley Walker, The Jerome Biblical Commentary, Eisenhower's Lieutenants, Little Gloria Happy at Last,* histories, romances, fat contemporary novels, political commentaries, a multivolume science series. On the sideboard near the couch there was a copy of Jonathan Schell's *The Abolition* and *The Cold and the Dark, The World after Nuclear War* by Ehrlich, Sagan, Kennedy and Roberts, *Survival is Not Enough* by Richard Pipes, *A Passage to Peshawar* by Reeves. The latter was lying open. She picked it up.

"Marsha."

She wheeled around. Peter stood in the doorway, one arm extended over his head, tilting against the door-frame. He wore a brown-check towel wrapped around his waist—it suited him.

"You have remarkable energy," he stated. "Quite remarkable."

"Well," Marsha said. How long had he been standing there?

"You are altogether a most remarkable woman, though a trifle stubborn, if you don't mind my saying so."

She didn't.

"Perhaps after all this," he waved his hand to include the whole room, "even you might be tired enough to wish to have a rest?"

"Are you an agent of some kind?" Marsha asked.

"A what?"

"A government agent—you know, James Bond and that sort of thing."

"Hardly. How would I have time, what with all the stuff I have to read? You do ask some strange questions for so early in the day."

"I wondered," Marsha said. "You have such an unhealthy interest in war."

"Or peace," he said. "You should check both sides of the coin."

"I guess you're right."

They stood for a while in silence.

"You're not going to explain, are you?"

"Right again," Peter said. "Shall we?" He tilted up his chin and looked in the general direction of the bedroom.

"I'm sorry, Peter..."

"Don't be," he said. "I understand. We're both sorry, really. Another time...who knows?" He spread his hands in a gesture of helplessness. "Maybe it would be simplest if you were to borrow my car. I assume you want to return to London right away?"

"Yes."

"Ah, well. The keys are in the ignition. Tomorrow, let me know where you parked it. Drive carefully," he added as an afterthought. The towel slipped from his waist as he turned and walked upstairs.

A perfect ass, Marsha thought.

Twenty-Two

THE ROOM WAS HAZY, threatening, unfamiliar. Judith walked around, forcing her stiff muscles to react, feeling her way around the bed, slowly, making every movement count. The blankets were crumpled and rolled in the center where she had left them, cold and still. On top of the tall, lopsided dresser, a row of thin gold frames from Black's camera stores—Christmas gifts from her mother. They glistened in the sunlight, drawing her closer, till she stood leaning against the dresser, her hand reaching for the nearest frame. It held four photographs of the children, mementos of a holiday in Fort Lauderdale maybe ten years ago. Anne had built giant sand animals, and was posing over a short-tailed alligator with a downward smile. Jimmy, his chubby legs spread wide around a mound of sand, ate brown ice cream from a cone. His Circus World cap had slipped to one side.

She shoved the frame back in its place and picked up another. All she could feel was a dull ache in her chest.

The phone rang. She pounced on it, wrenched the receiver from its cradle.

"Hello."

"Judith, it's Ron at *Saturday Night*. I've read your Harris piece."

Oh god, please make him say it's all right, I can't...

"Yes?" she whispered.

"Something wrong? Did I catch you at a bad time? I can call later," he offered.

"It's my throat. You were saying about the story?"

"I wondered why you rushed the ending so. It starts great, all that stuff about his early life, how he took over from his father, and the first interview with him is just fine—I never knew he was such an inveterate optimist. Then it's like you quit. No analysis. No conclusion. No final bow. I thought when we last talked you still insisted on developing a theory about his untimely death. And if not that, why not some assessment?"

"I don't know how..."

"Come on, Judith, we gave you an extension of the deadline, now we're up against it. Two good paragraphs is all we need. You can phone them in before the end of the day. Meanwhile we'll give this a light copy-edit. All right?"

"All right."

"Fine, then."

He hung up. She knelt on the floor by the phone, rested her head on the bed. Waiting. She had done as they told her. The show of faith was complete except for two paragraphs. She was afraid to turn and confront the photographs again. She picked up the phone and dialed, her hands steady but feeble, missing the numbers. Her thumb trailed blood where she had bitten the nail to a stump. Slowly, she dialed again.

Five rings and her mother answered. She sounded annoyed.

"Mother..." Judith said.

"Will you speak up, I can barely hear you." She was brisk, busy, clearly she had been interrupted at something important.

"I'm sorry..."

"Try some warm honey and lemon for your throat. Works every time. Always gave it to you when you were a child."

"Mother..."

"Perhaps you should do that now, dear, and call me later when you can talk. I'm on my way to the Gallery for a committee meeting—we have to establish the principles for the Fall fund-raising drive—and I make a point of not being late. I do wish the others were as conscientious. Some days we wait for half an hour. Are the children all right?"

"Could you come over?"

"Not today, dear. Far too busy. I can be there tomorrow, though. Now be sensible, won't you, and make that hot drink. Call me around 7:00. Sure to be finished by then. Bye, now."

❋ ❋ ❋

The phone rang as she replaced it.

"Mrs. Hayes?" The gentle, modulated tone.

"Yes," she said fast. "I've done the story... I've..."

"Yes, we know. You will find your valuables at Brunswick and Dupont. They're on their way home."

"Now?" she yelled, her voice back, jumping to her feet.

"One more thing, though. As a small precaution. I would advise, for all our sakes, you consider a holiday. A change of pace for all three of you."

"Yes." She waited till the line went dead, then ran down the stairs and out the door, her bare feet pounding along the pavement as she raced, leaped over the neighbors' angry dachshund, swerved to avoid the postman. The young woman from across the street, strolling by with her baby carriage, stopped in her path and stared. Judith ran around her, out onto the road, ignoring the cars. Her breath came in short bursts, the pain in her side made her hunch over.

Then there they were, rounding the corner, walking slowly and close together. They looked as normal as if they were on their way home from an average school day. Jeans, T-shirts half-pulled out of their pants, bomber jackets flapping off the shoulders, shoelaces trailing. When they saw her, they stood still, waiting for her to reach them. Jimmy's face was so pale and drawn that the adolescent pimples on his forehead stood out like the spots on the back of a ladybug. Anne's skin seemed almost transparent, blue-tinged around the staring eyes.

"Don't look behind us," Anne hissed.

"It's all right now," Judith said, holding onto them, feeling along their backs and shoulders, slowly coming out of her nightmare.

"They said not to," Anne insisted, her eyes filling with tears, propelling her mother to walk between them, their arms around one another.

Jimmy blew his nose in his jacket sleeve as they jostled by the baby carriage, the woman staring at them still. Once inside the house he began to cry.

Judith murmured every comforting word she knew. She had her arms around them both, as far as they would reach. She herself was crying with relief as she stroked their hair and their faces, brushed down their clothes.

"We were so frightened." Anne flopped into the couch, pulling up her knees. "I thought maybe we'd both be killed. One of them had a gun at my back. I could feel it. Did you get the police?" she asked.

Judith shook her head.

"I couldn't," she said. She drew Jimmy into the couch, next to her, cradling his shoulders, rocking him softly.

"Can we call them now?" Anne said. "They told us it was a case of mistaken identity. They were after some other kids, not us. That's what they said, this morning when they let us go. We were blindfolded in the car. They left us on the street and the woman told us not to remove the blindfolds till we counted to fifty, then to start walking slowly toward home."

"What did she look like?" Judith asked.

"We never saw her," Jimmy said, wiping his eyes. "We only saw the man when he came to the door to tell us you'd been in an accident and had been taken to the hospital. He said he'd drive us there right away."

"That's why we went with him. The woman was driving the car; she wore a hat, but we couldn't see her. Soon as we were at the car door, he held a gun to my back, told us to get in and put on the blindfolds."

Once inside, the man had threatened to kill them unless they stayed still. He had secured their blindfolds, tied their hands behind their backs, stuffed handkerchiefs into their mouths and made them lie on the car floor. They had driven for a long time, around winding roads, up and down hills, then stopped in what Anne thought must have been a garage. They had both heard a door clang shut behind them and had been hustled out of the car, up some stairs and into a bedroom, where they were allowed to take off their blindfolds once the door was shut and locked.

There had been boards on the only window. The room had two beds with matching bedcovers, and wallpaper a summery yellow-orange with white flowers, plank floors, a simple bathroom. They had been given warm milk on a tray slid through the partially open door by a man's arm. They thought it might have been drugged because they both slept after that, though Jimmy had been crying and Anne had tried to pry loose the boards. They both lay down and hadn't woken up till the next afternoon—or for all they knew the day after that. There had been dinner of hamburgers and eggs on the tray and more milk. The woman had said through the door that they shouldn't be frightened. Had they slept well?

"How did she sound?" Judith asked, thinking of the woman at F.A.O. Schwarz.

"A little like Granny. Sort of imperious," Anne said.

"English?" Jimmy asked.

"I don't think so," Anne said.

"And the man who came to the door? What did he look like?"

"About six foot, maybe taller. Balding. His face was all red. Maybe forty, maybe fifty. Older than your policeman. Wore glasses. A friendly sort of face..."

She told them she'd call David, though she wasn't sure she should yet. Let them believe the kidnapping had been a mistake. She wouldn't scare them with the truth. They were home and they were safe. It was up to her to keep them that way.

Anne wanted to have a long hot bath. She was still shivering and drowsy. Judith wrapped a blanket around Jimmy, who was asleep in moments.

Judith drew all the curtains and blinds. The house seemed like a stranger, no longer her private place. It had been defiled. She recognized the fear building inside her, cold, mean. She would get double locks on the doors and grates for the windows. Poisonous blackmailing son-of-a-bitch who could grab their lives and twist them at will, who would use the children against her.

She brushed Anne's hair, and mopped the last bit of stubborn dirt from her neck. She put cream on her chapped lips and a pair of her own woolen socks on her feet, to help stop the shivers. She tucked Anne into her own bed, and went to bring Jimmy up to join her. He was too exhausted to pull off his jeans and T-shirt. Judith helped him into his old pyjamas and cried again when she saw how short they were.

"We'll buy new ones in New York," she whispered in his ear, thinking of her bargain. New York is where Marsha would be.

Suddenly she realized that she hadn't thought much about Marsha since her own nightmare had begun. Marsha was in London trying to track that damned manuscript, and didn't know her life might be in danger. She started to tiptoe out, she'd have to phone right away.

Anne was already asleep. Jimmy half-lifted his head to see where Judith was going, smiled at her and fell back again.

"I hate pyjamas," he grumbled.

Twenty-Three

THE JAGUAR PROVED to be unlike Oldsmobiles or Pontiacs or any other car Marsha had become used to since her MG—closer to the ground and a great deal more sensitive to the touch. Fortunately, there weren't too many people about in Essex at 4:00 a.m. Several dogs, two cats and a red squirrel she had caught in the lights ran for cover with their eyes closed.

She took the wrong exit off the highway—easy enough to do even if your mind wasn't on something else. It was dawn when she maneuvered the traffic circle at Cumberland Gate, then down Park Lane, Piccadilly and up Old Bond Street, where she remembered having seen a parking lot.

The uniformed doorman she woke out of his slumbers looked her over suspiciously when he let her into the hotel, but he was too well-mannered to smirk. He handed her two messages and a large box that had been delivered by Mr. Rubinstein's office. It housed a fat, romantic family saga she had hoped to have read by the time she had lunch with Hilary that day. No chance of that now. One of the messages was from Judith. Urgent. No matter what time.

She called Judith and talked to the answering service. It was 5:00 a.m. Too late to sleep, too early to call Jane MacIntyre. She drank a large orange juice from the hotel-room bar and went for a long walk in the park. The breeze had built to a gusty wind that whipped her face with long strands of hair loosened from the chignon at the nape of her neck. The first light played around Queen Victoria's unforgiving forehead. She decided to run back—long easy strides until her shoulders relaxed and she no longer ached for Peter's touch.

Back in her room, she ordered sausages and eggs—a hearty American breakfast, ready for anything...the phone rang.

"Miss Hillier?"

"Uhhum." Chewing on the last of the toast.

"I'm sorry if I woke you. I simply had to speak with you before you went out. This is Jane MacIntyre."

"Is there something wrong, Jane?"

"Yes, well, there is rather. It's that manuscript you asked me about yesterday. I think it's caused me to be fired."

"What?"

"He called it early retirement, but it means the same thing. He said he thought I'd been working too hard and Mr. Sandwell's death had been particularly upsetting to me. Besides, he said, I wouldn't have very much to do now that Mr. Sandwell was gone. I have to agree, but I was more than willing to take on some of his work, only he hadn't asked. I have four years left before retirement, and I haven't made plans at all..."

"You're talking about Peter Burnett?"

"Of course I am... He's in charge now, you know."

"I don't understand. What does this have to do with the manuscript?"

"I'm so sorry. I should have started at the beginning. This has been rather unsettling. After you left yesterday, I became, well, somewhat concerned that I shouldn't perhaps have discussed Mr. Sandwell's business with you. Not like me to do that, but there seemed no harm in it then. To be safe, though, I went and told Mr. Burnett of your asking me questions. I explained what I'd told you, and that I'd showed you my book. He asked me to show him, and I did."

"What did he say?"

"Nothing, really. He'd had no idea I kept a record of all manuscripts coming in to Mr. Sandwell's attention. I doubt he's paid much attention to me over the years. He's a strange one, he is." She sighed. "Later on, though, he came to my office and said I should take early retirement. Just like that. I've been thinking a great deal since then. One thing I think is that you were behaving strangely when you asked me all those questions about a manuscript that shouldn't have concerned you at all. Then I found out Mr. Burnett was having dinner with you last night. You might have kept some of the questions for him. But you didn't." She paused. Then she said, "Marsha, I believe you owe me an explanation."

She was right about that, and moreover Jane MacIntyre might be an ally, so Marsha said she was convinced Eric Sandwell had been murdered and, for verisimilitude, related the tale of the other deaths—all caused, she believed, by the manuscript that Jane had innocently booked in on April 8th.

Jane MacIntyre interrupted only once. She asked why Marsha and her friend in Canada hadn't gone to the police.

"We have," Marsha said, "and in Toronto there's going to be an investigation. Here we have no evidence." That took another ten minutes to explain.

"Would the manuscript supply the evidence?"

"We think it would."

"And Mr. Burnett won't let you see it?"

"He won't."

"He's a strange one, he is," Jane MacIntyre repeated. That was as far as she allowed herself to be disloyal. "You think if you were to find that manuscript you'd be able to point the finger at whoever killed Mr. Sandwell, if he was killed as you say, God rest his soul?"

"If you would help..."

Marsha waited.

"You don't work for a man as long as I did for Mr. Sandwell and not learn a great deal about him," Jane said with some pride. "Tell you what, why don't you meet me in front of Number 37 South Audley at 7:00 a.m. I have the key. You'll be gone before anyone else arrives."

Twenty-Four

JANE MACINTYRE LOOKED as though she had been put into a doll's box overnight and taken out again in the morning, completely unruffled. Her French roll was sculpted into a flawless cone, her tailored brown dress was exactly the same pattern as the blue one she had worn the day before, even to the white cotton collar buttoned high under her chin. She stood, waiting, outside Hamilton, Thornbush's ornate front door. She held her short white lace gloves clutched in front of her, as if to ensure the formality of the occasion.

Instinctively, Marsha understood. In insane situations formality might help preserve sanity. Marsha had put on her blue running suit and jogged from the hotel. She thought it a fair diversionary tactic in case someone was following her.

To make sure she wasn't followed by car, she had taken all the one-way streets. Though she glanced over her shoulder frequently, she saw no one. As an extra precaution, she had extended to her full speed around Berkeley Square and maintained it the rest of the way. At that pace, anyone following on foot would have been obvious. Not even an Olympic hurdler could dodge in and out of doorways that fast.

"The editorial department," Jane MacIntyre was saying much too precisely, "is located on the first two stories. Our system is rather different from yours, in that our editors deal with the whole book. The entire process. They do not delegate to a copy department, or even to proofreaders. They do everything themselves. We think this gives them a feeling of direct responsibility for every word."

Wonderful, Marsha thought—a lecture in British-style editing while your skin crawls with anxiety in case one of the editors is so overwhelmed by a sense of responsibility that she can't wait till the office opens.

"When do they usually come in?" Marsha asked, peering down the stairs behind her as they rounded the corner toward Peter's office.

"Not before 8:30. That gives us well over an hour. This is the first place to search," said Jane. She walked directly into Peter Burnett's office. "I think he took the manuscript with him." She headed over to the side table near the desk where Peter's incoming manuscripts lay. She sorted through them, careful to replace everything she touched.

Marsha lingered in the doorway, reluctant to invade his territory again. She remembered the last time she was here, the look of sheer delight on his face when he first saw her.

"You could help, Marsha," Jane said over her shoulder. "Too late to change your mind now." She pointed at Peter's desk. "Why don't you see what he has in the drawers?"

Some felt-tipped pens, the kind Marsha used herself, an assortment of memos, press releases, an old-fashioned letter opener, a comb. On the desk, near the telephone, a number of file folders with newspaper clippings of the kind she had found in his house, and a Washington study surveying how a random sampling of schoolchildren felt about the threat of nuclear war; a *Time* magazine story entitled "The Darkening War Clouds"; another study reporting on the possible use of the president's Star Wars weaponry, and its lack of effectiveness in case of attack on the United States.

"What is he doing with these?" Marsha asked.

Jane MacIntyre peered at the clippings.

"He must be planning a book," she said. "We've published a lot on nuclear war. He has a morbid preoccupation." Quickly, she surveyed the bookshelves. When she was satisfied "Untitled" wasn't there, she led the way to the end of the corridor, next to her own office. She inserted a key into a polished wooden door.

"Mr. Sandwell's office," she whispered deferentially as she entered the spacious, carpeted room, all antique wooden furniture, wide-backed club chairs. The windows were closed and the room smelled of yellowing papers and old cigars.

Mrs. MacIntyre headed over to the small, ornate safe in the far corner and began to turn the dial. The door opened almost as soon as she touched it.

"The executors must have been through all this," she said. "Over the weekend, I suppose. Without asking me. Nothing here now of interest." She made sure her prediction was correct, then turned her attention to the desk. "Here," she said, "I'll check on this side, you go through the other side. Too obvious, but one must be thorough."

There was a file folder marked "Progress Reports Sydney" that seemed to relate to some market test Eric had been running in Australia. There were a series of different prices, book lengths, manufacturing estimates, sales figures by month and cumulatively. All in Eric's own precise handwriting, filling several sheets of graph paper. As if to make up for this old-world zeal, there were also some fat computer printouts of sales by title and territory that, on another day, Marsha would have found riveting. There was an empty folder marked "Expenses, personal." There were sheets of staff salary recommendations, memos about future remainders, parking tickets, and a copy of Stephen King's *The Stand*. Marsha would never have guessed Eric had been a closet Stephen King fan.

There were two manuscripts, neither by X.

They checked the bookshelves, looking behind the books individually. Jane began from the floor up, getting down on her haunches after smoothing her skirt across the backs of her thighs. Marsha, being a good five inches taller, started from the top.

"He had some special places for very important manuscripts," Jane said. "This was one of them. I suppose over the years you all develop different work habits..."

"Yes." Marsha thought fondly of her bathroom cabinet where sometimes she put manuscripts she specially liked, for relaxed bathtub reading.

They checked the coffee table and its drawers, the top of the bar, under the couch, the magazine stand and the two lopsided wicker waste baskets. Nothing.

"I was so sure it would be in here," Jane said. "Why else would he have made a copy for himself except to read it?"

"For safekeeping?" Marsha asked.

"Worth trying," Jane said. She led the way to the top floor, past sales and marketing on the second and legal, accounting and administration on the third. At the end of the passageway there was a black fireproof door, some kind of metal, hand-painted with blue and yellow birds, and the numbers, "1887."

"This has been here since Mr. Hamilton and Mr. Thornbush started the firm," she said with pride. "We still use it for some legal documents, first editions, a few of the original manuscripts—they're worth a fortune now. Naturally, we wouldn't dream of selling them, but Mr. Sandwell wanted to give some to the museum before he died. I hope he put it in his will."

She unlocked the door and turned on the light to reveal a huge cavern of a safe full of shelves with black boxes, cartons on the floor, two filing cabinets, and a greenish-purple portrait of Eric.

"He hated that picture, but couldn't bring himself to throw it out. One never knew when the royal artist might come to visit, and he would have to haul it out and put it up on his wall again."

She started a systematic search in one corner of the room and instructed Marsha to do the same at the other.

"The confidential papers are all at this end. You needn't worry about what you may come across down there. That's the ancient books and manuscripts section."

It was almost 8:05 when they finished. Marsha was covered in dust, her fingertips dry, her face coated in dirt. She had stopped close to Jane, so close she could smell the Madame Rochas hairspray and hear her quick, even breathing.

"Nothing here," Marsha said. "Do you need a rest?"

"No time for that." Jane shook her head. "We've come this far and I'm stubborn. The trick is to think the way he did, to imagine what must have crossed his mind, why he copied the manuscript for himself."

"Had he felt threatened, what would he have done?"

"Threatened?"

"Maybe if he thought he was in some danger..."

"You don't imagine Mr. Sandwell was suspecting Mr. Burnett?"

"I don't think so." Peter's face soft in the moonlight, his long eyelashes fluttering in sleep. "But he may have."

Jane stared at the green portrait.

"He trusted Mr. Burnett. The man most likely to succeed him. Never believed in leaving the firm to the family. Funny. He thought the children, though grown, would never forgive him. Nasty business, this."

Marsha put a hand on her shoulder. The brown cloth felt cool to the touch, smooth like an eggshell, and very still.

Suddenly Jane straightened up, then ran down the corridor, the three flights of stairs, back to Eric's office. She shouted something as she took off, but Marsha hadn't understood. She flung the door open to Eric's office and ran inside. Marsha followed, but stopped in the doorway and waited till Jane was ready to talk to her. The other woman was lying on the floor, tugging at a tiny handle on the surface of the wood under the main bookcase in the room.

Slowly, a long narrow drawer appeared.

"It's where he kept his personal letters…hadn't had many of these in the last several years. Some pictures…" As Marsha came closer Jane shielded the contents with her body. "Please, these are personal."

"I'm sorry." Marsha backed away.

"Too late for that. Too damned late." Jane wiped her eyes on the back of her sleeve, pulled out a small sheaf of papers, and looked at them.

"Here," she said. "Not everything you're after, but some of it. Here, Marsha, for God's sake do him justice."

Jane handed over the sheaf of papers.

For a moment Marsha hesitated. Now the chase was over, was she still sure she wanted to read what was written here?

Then she glanced down at the top of the page of the faint but readable Xerox: "Untitled, by X." And she knew she had no choice.

Twenty-Five

THREE CALLS LATER and Marsha was still not picking up the phone. Judith had pleaded with the receptionist at Green's and succeeded in having her go to Marsha's room. Later, she had convinced the bell captain that her friend was an occasional epileptic and persuaded him to check whether she was lying unconscious on the floor or had fainted in her bed. The dreadful truth was that Marsha had not returned to her room all night.

At 11:30 p.m., Toronto time, 4:30 a.m. in London, Marsha should have been in bed. Judith prowled around the house pondering the possibilities. The people who had kidnapped her children would have little hope of blackmailing Marsha into submission. But they might harm her directly. She would not allow herself to imagine that Marsha might even now be dead.

She had to marshal whatever strength she still possessed to find a way to help Marsha, at least warn her.

Judith peered through the narrow window next to the door. The street was dark and still, as it had been last night. The amber light of the streetlamp glinted off the tops of cars parked across the street.

To the right of the door, the box of flowers had been left unattended. David. She had pretended she was busy, already late for appointments each time he had called. They had warned her not to talk to her "friend."

She had been too distraught to respond to the hurt in his voice.

Now she opened the door just wide enough to reach the tall box and draw it inside. She opened it: twelve red roses surrounded by flat green fern. The card said, "Thinking of you, David."

Gently, Judith lifted them out of the box. Their heads drooped, the petals had started to brown. She found an old vase in the kitchen, filled it with water and left it on the coffee table in the living room looking forlorn.

David. If only she could talk to David, he would know how to reach Marsha, perhaps even how to protect her.

She ran upstairs. In the dark, she changed into a black sweater and jeans, pulled on black socks and Anne's black ballet slippers, tied her hair into a navy blue scarf she hadn't worn in years, found some dark-brown summer make-up by feeling her way around the unfamiliar summer-holidays drawer, and spread it on her face. Her black gloves were in the hall closet.

She turned off the light in the living room and waited for her eyes to become accustomed to complete darkness.

Once more she checked that all the blinds were down, the curtains drawn, then she pinned a towel to the top of the little window by the door. No one could see in, now.

She checked the children were asleep in her bed, their even breathing the only sound in the house, then tiptoed to the bathroom and shut the door behind her. The window led to a ledge that had once shadowed a back porch.

Very quietly she squeezed out the window and onto the ledge. She listened. Again, the baby was crying across the street. In the distance, the steady hum of traffic. Softly she dropped into the neighbor's flowerbed. Her feet sank into the mud. The dachshund barked, half-heartedly, for a minute—more like a complaint than an attempt to wake his owners—then stopped.

Judith walked around the back of the neighbor's house, through the patch of early grass, over the low picket fence and into the next yard, and the next, circumnavigating electric barbeques, climbing over sandboxes and wooden fences, working around the elevated swimming pool four houses down. She climbed six sets of link fences and a hedge, and thanked her good luck she had not met another dog before she reached the end of the street. No one watching her house could have seen her. Waiting for two cars to pass, she climbed over the last fence—this one of stylish wrought iron with useful gaps for her toes.

She crossed over into Sibelius Park, where the dogs barked, but not particularly at her. They wagged their tails as she made her way to the phone booth under the big Norway maple. With its door open, the booth was dark. She didn't risk shutting the door and dialed by counting the numbers, glad she had memorized them well.

"David?" she asked quietly.

"Yes," came the sleepy reply. *Thank God he's home.*

"It's Judith. I have to see you right away."

"Judith!" Suddenly he sounded cheerful and wide awake. "I'm so glad you called. I couldn't imagine what I'd..."

"Can you please come and meet me in Sibelius Park, now. The telephone booth."

"Anywhere you say, Judith, but can't it wait till tomorrow? I've had a lousy day and..."

"No it can't. Please come now."

"If you say so... I'll be there in twenty minutes."

"Fine," Judith said and hung up. She wasn't going to waste precious time explaining on the phone. She was already risking too much by calling him.

The expedition through the neighbors' back yards had lasted fifteen minutes. Now she couldn't return to the house before David came. Judith walked around the park, across the street and to the corner of Brunswick. From here she could see the cars parked on the street, but she couldn't see her house. A man and a woman strolled by on the other side of the park, laughing and talking. They didn't notice her, or if they did, they paid no attention. She stood in the shadow of the big Norway maple and waited. No cars stopped on Brunswick. At this time of night there wasn't much traffic in the neighborhood.

She waited.

One car drove by, its radio blaring country music. Two men walked past her house; neither stopped.

In one of the parked cars near the house there was a flicker of light, perhaps somebody striking a match. She was too far away to identify the make of car: something long with a slanting back. She was almost relieved to be able to focus on the car as the enemy. Already certain they were watching the house, now she thought she knew where they were.

It was half an hour since she had called David and her hands and her feet were numb from the cold. She snuggled closer to the tree.

Another car came up Brunswick. It slowed as it drew parallel with the house, crawling by so slowly she thought it was going to stop. But it speeded up again and headed in her direction. Once it rounded the corner, it slowed again, stopped, the door opened on the passenger side. It was David. She recognized him only after he turned to lean back into the car, the door still open. He said something to the other person, shut the door quietly and began to walk into the park. The car moved toward her.

Judith could see into the driver's side as it passed. For a second the light from the street lamp caught the driver's face. She recognized it instantly—the friendly, rumpled face of the man she had seen in the rooftop lounge of the Park Plaza when she drank martinis with Max Grafstein; the man she had seen at La Guardia; she was sure he had also been at George's funeral.

Oh, David.

The car crawled up Brunswick toward Dupont, pulled up at the curb before the main street, turned off its lights.

David was walking through the park, his hands in his pockets, kicking at something in his path, casual, as though he was out for a late-night stroll. He approached the telephone booth, walked around it, looked inside leaning forward from the waist with a motion of exaggerated interest, then turned and made for the closest park bench and wandered around that too before strolling back toward the swings. Judith watched him as though she was seeing him for the first time.

He had known where she went the day she had tracked the witnesses. She had thought then he'd had her trailed, but she hadn't wanted to believe it. And she had been under surveillance before then. That man could even have been on the plane to New York. Had he planted the green-ink note on her seat? And David had seemed so surprised when she showed it to him.

David.

Judith rubbed her hands up and down her arms for warmth as she walked over to the playground.

David was sitting on one of the swings, swaying back and forth, his head almost touching the horizontal bar. He jumped up when he saw Judith approaching and strode quickly toward her, his arms encircling her shoulders. Her face brushed against the rough cloth of his jacket. She swallowed hard.

"Judith," he whispered, his hands on her shoulders still. He stepped back from her and looked into her face. "Will you please tell me what's happening. What's wrong?"

She composed her face into a welcoming smile.

"Wrong?" she asked ingenuously. "Why should *anything* be wrong?"

"You called me down here in the middle of the night...you wanted to see me urgently...didn't you?"

"I *did* want to see you. Of course I wanted to see you. I haven't talked to you since you left in such a hurry you didn't even collect your socks."

Was he going to tell her about the other man in the car?

"But why now?" He was peering into her face. "There must be some reason... And why here? There's something the matter, isn't there? You're scared? You think your house is being watched? For God's sake tell me what's going on."

She was grateful for the pale light and the dark summer make-up. He wouldn't notice she hadn't slept in two nights.

"And why the weird outfit? Are you trying to blend into the dark? Are you hiding from someone?" He surveyed the park. Nothing stirred.

"I guess I've been worrying about the witnesses. I thought it would be safer to meet you here. In case someone's watching the house. I didn't want to take chances..."

Could David have known about the kidnapping? *How much did he know?*

"OK, but why now?"

"I was worried, couldn't sleep. I didn't want to phone you from the house, I think there may be a bug on the phone. Then it seemed this would be a good place to meet."

He shook his head.

"No," he said. "That's not it. You wouldn't call me like that..."

"I couldn't sleep. That's all. Really."

He held her around the waist and walked her to the bench.

"You're freezing," he said. "You're not wearing a coat. And why this dreadful scarf?" He tugged at it till it came away in his hand. Judith shook her hair free.

"That's better," he said, running his fingers through her hair. "I told you before you mustn't worry about Harris any longer. Now the case has been reopened, we'll take care of it. You're a terrific detective, but you do have another profession. This one happens to be mine. In fact just this afternoon we got a lead on one of the two young punks who were fighting at the top of the station. And in New York they've started to investigate the missing manuscript at Axel. Any word from Marsha?" he asked suddenly.

"No," Judith said too quickly. "She had a very busy schedule in London. Wouldn't have time to follow up on this."

"I thought she was going to Hamilton, Thornbush?"

"She had to cancel that."

"She did? Why?"

"Some auction she was to attend..." Judith lied fluently, not wanting him to think Marsha was still trying to find the manuscript.

"I've been in touch with London, but there's no news yet." His eyes traveled up the street to where his friend's car had disappeared.

"I haven't thanked you for the flowers. They're beautiful."

He drew her closer. "You had me worried," he said. "I thought there was some emergency..."

"There isn't." She looked at her watch, tilting her wrist so that it caught the light. "I must run back now. I have a story to finish by tomorrow. If I keep going all night..."

"The Harris story?"

"No. The Nuclear Madness story. I promised it by the end of the day."

Again he peered closely at her face.

"Have you been working on that for long?"

"Couple of weeks."

"Strange..."

"Why?"

He didn't explain, but kissed her hard on the lips and held her until she was beginning to feel warm again.

"I'll see you home."

"No," she protested. "I'd like to walk home alone."

"Call me tomorrow." He let go of her suddenly and set off in the direction of Dupont.

Judith waited until he was out of sight, then started for home over the fences, as she had come. She found a gap between the buildings and took a look at the car the light had flashed from. It was still there, two doors up from her house. A Ford station wagon, standard with a white line on the sides.

She put on the scarf to cover her head again and crept alongside the thorny hedge on her hands and knees. When she was close to the car, she straightened up, her back to the hedge, the tiny branches catching threads from her sweater. She covered her face with her black-gloved hands so that only her eyes showed.

There was a man in the front of the car, smoking a cigarette. He had a young face, she couldn't tell his coloring, but the hair seemed dark. His coat had a fur collar. Scattered on the sidewalk next to the car there were several cigarette butts, all within sight of his window.

Behind her, up in the hedge, a raccoon started to chatter.

Twenty-Six

IF THERE WAS an unobtrusive way of carrying the manuscript, Marsha couldn't find it. All she had brought with her from the hotel was a tiny purse concealed in the back of her jogging suit. Both she and Jane MacIntyre had been too excited about finding "Untitled" to think of looking for a bag, and it didn't fit into her sleeve or a pocket. In the end, she decided to roll it up and carry it in one hand, casually, as if it were a short stick.

She headed down Hill Street, then around Berkeley Square. As she began to jog down Berkeley Street she kept imagining cars screeching in pursuit, and started to run full out. A few minutes later she was inside the hotel entrance, one hand pressed into her stomach, the other clutching the manuscript tight to her chest.

"You all right, miss?" the doorman asked solicitously. He was examining her with barely disguised curiosity. He shuffled over slowly. "May I get you something, miss? Perhaps a glass of water?"

Marsha shook her head. She allowed the doorman to walk her to the padded bench near the front desk. She sat down hard.

"Can't say as I hold with all that jogging, miss," he said, standing over her. "People can get hurt."

He's right about that, Marsha thought, straightening up. She pulled a damp coin from her pocket and gave it to him.

"Thanks," she said, glad she could speak again. "I'll be all right now." She wanted to be in the safety of her room.

"Anything I can do for you, miss?" The doorman was still there, hesitating.

"Perhaps you could ask them to send me some coffee," Marsha asked.

"Right you are," he said, brightly. "Continental breakfast?"

"Only coffee," Marsha said. She took a deep breath and headed down the hall. The desk clerk stopped her.

"Miss, there's a message for you." It was from Judith.

She fidgeted with the key, her hand still shaking slightly. She felt better once she had locked the door behind her and slipped the chain into place.

The window was open, but this time the cooing pigeons were outside on the ledge. Marsha held the manuscript wedged under her arm and turned on the bedside lamp; she wouldn't even take a shower until she had read it.

She felt rather than heard the sound behind her. Soft scraping of cloth against cloth. A hand snaked around her mouth and clamped shut, pressing her lips into her teeth, another forced her arms tight against her sides. The manuscript dug into her armpit.

No fear. No panic. Only anger. She tightened all her arm and shoulder muscles and breathed in deeply, expanding her chest as far as she could, under the encircling arm.

"Keep still," the male voice behind her commanded. "You won't get hurt."

The voice was American. Young. His lips were almost touching her ear.

Suddenly she collapsed her shoulders forward, pulled her arms together, grabbed his hand away from her mouth using both her hands and pulled hard as she dropped down, wedged her shoulder into his solar plexus and heaved his body up over her shoulder and onto the floor. Hard. She twisted his arm around his back, forcing him face down on the floor, his left arm useless underneath him. She wrenched his right arm up almost to the point of breaking. He grunted in pain. Her fingers pressed into his palm, thumbs on the back of his hand, twisting still, forcing the arm up even higher till she heard him whimper. She knelt heavily into the small of his back, keeping him pinned under her, immobile.

"Do you have a gun?" she asked him.

"Uh huh..." he grunted.

"Where?" Marsha was elated, surprised at her own prowess. Sure, she had practiced all the moves before, but never on a real target.

"If...you'd move...a little..." he exhaled painfully, then sucked in his breath sharply, through his teeth.

"Where?" Marsha repeated. She tugged on his arm.

"Under my arm...the one you're trying to break..." he said, gulping air.

She shifted slightly, kept his arm up with her right hand, and reached with the left under his soft, worsted suit-jacket for the gun. His jacket had the fashionable splits up the back. Had he not been lying on his stomach with her knee wedged into his back, she could easily have mistaken him for a college student. Even from this angle, he couldn't have been much over twenty. Blond, short-cropped hair, no creases in his neck or the side of his face. Blond eyelashes, barely visible.

The gun was a heavy thing, almost too big to fit into her palm. It felt rather like her father's Beretta, but newer, shiny, like a toy. She lifted it by the handle, gently; it slid into her palm. Could she fire it if she had to? Would she? Her forefinger closed on the trigger. Her thumb cocked the gun.

"Don't move," she said evenly

She looked around for the manuscript. It had fallen near the bed, the pages fanned out. Then she yelled: "Help!" her voice amazingly deep and steady. "Help! Help! Help!"

Only the pigeons stirred. Too much clatter from the kitchen. She tried again: "Help!" at her loudest.

"They can't hear you," he whimpered.

"I know," she said. She would have to get to the phone.

"What we are going to do," she said firmly, "is this. First, I'm going to get off your back, and let your arm go. Then, you're going to stand up slowly. No sudden moves." (1950s western.) "I have a gun in my hand. It's loaded, and I won't hesitate to shoot." (Starring John Wayne. Lone guitar in background. Fade to:)

"OK," the young man said and lay still. "You're the boss." Chatty little bastard, considering the trouble he was in.

Marsha eased off his back and carefully retreated to the chair near the window, keeping an eye on him all the way. Once she had sat down, she said: "Get up now. *Slowly.*"

Nursing the arm Marsha had been holding, he pulled himself to his hands and knees, then straightened so slowly Marsha wondered if he would ever make it. Standing up, he looked even younger than he had lying down.

"Put your hands over your head. Yes. That's fine." Marsha was aiming the gun directly at his stomach. He had a pained expression on his face, smooth as a bun. His eyes under the almost hairless lids searched all around the room, as if he was expecting someone to come to his rescue. When no one did, he focused on Marsha, his eyebrows knitted in apparent consternation.

"Guess you caught me in the act," he said. "You surely did." His pained expression deepened.

"In the act of what? Exactly?" Marsha asked.

"It was purely in the line of business, you understand. Nothing personal," he said. "I was foraging around for something to find, your window was open, so I came in here. Over the roof, that is." He motioned with his hand toward the window.

"Keep still!" Marsha barked.

"Yes, ma'am."

"Foraging for what?"

"I'm not particular. Money, jewelry, traveler's checks, anything I can carry."

"You mean you're a regular, middle-of-the-road, average thief, who just *happened* to come into *this* room by coincidence? That's what you're telling me?"

He nodded but was careful not to move his hands.

"Your window was open," he repeated.

"Bullshit," Marsha said.

He looked up, his eyes going wide in surprise.

"You don't believe me?"

"I don't," Marsha said.

"Well, it's the truth," he said defiantly. "I staked the hotel out yesterday. Yours is the only open window I could reach."

Marsha stood holding the gun at the same level, very steady.

"I want you to turn around and face the wall. I will shoot if I have to. I really will.

"Pull your jacket up over your shoulders. Keep your hands in sight. That's right. All the way up. Steady... Now, pull it over your head and drop it behind you. Good. Turn around. Slowly. Right."

"I don't have another weapon," he said.

Maybe not. But she had to make sure.

"Lower one hand...one only...to your belt buckle. Very slowly. Right. Undo it."

"Ma'am?" he asked plaintively.

"Undo it and let your pants drop." It took him a while to fiddle with the belt, but he succeeded in the end and his pants sagged around his ankles. He wore navy-blue knee-highs, white jockey shorts and a thin-blade knife strapped around his calf in a shiny leather holster. Neat.

"Step out of them. Very very slowly," Marsha said. "Right. Now back up. Enough. Keep your hands steady. Don't move a muscle." (Efrem Zimbalist Jr. A scene from *The Untouchables*.)

Marsha edged forward until she could reach his clothes with her feet. Without taking her eyes off him, she drew the clothes back toward her. When they were out of his way, she told him to walk sideways, one step at a time, into the bathroom and shut the door. She pushed a chair up against the handle.

Marsha felt so calm, it was alarming. Still aiming the gun at the bathroom door, she dialed the front desk.

"Send someone fast—there's a man in my room."

"I beg your pardon?"

"There's a man in my room!" she shouted. She picked up the manuscript and slipped it under her pillow. Then, with one hand, she started to go through his pockets, methodically.

There was a plastic cardholder with Blue Cross, American Express, BankAmericard and driver's license. All in the name of Arnold Bukowski. The driver's license gave his date of birth as July 10, 1960, it was issued at Fountain Valley, Colorado. He had come by the slight Western drawl honestly.

There was a knock on the bathroom door. Faint and polite.

"Hey," the voice said familiarly. "That stuff in my pockets. It's not mine, you know. Lifted it from the guy upstairs."

Oh yeah. Sure. There was a set of car keys. Volkswagen. A key to room 205. A billfold with some ten-pound notes, and a set of American Express traveler's checks in $100 denominations. In his inside top pocket there was a piece of folded paper, hotel stationery. It was addressed to Ms. Marsha Hillier. The message was typed:

> Please meet me at the National Gallery, 10:00. Let's discuss terms of publication and delivery of the final manuscript.

> The Dealer

"Bukowski," she yelled at the bathroom door. "Who the hell are you? What kind of game are you playing? Why won't you, or whoever you answer to, just tell me what's going on?" She hadn't been expecting a reply, and in any case there wasn't time for one because the front door fell in.

Two men rushed past her, one in London bobby uniform, stick at the ready, the other in hotel uniform with a handgun. They stopped running when they were a couple of feet away from Marsha. Both looked puzzled.

"He's in there." Marsha pointed with the gun in her hand. They opened the bathroom door.

Arnold Bukowski was sitting on the toilet seat looking quite dejected.

"Are you all right, miss?" the security guard asked, glancing back and forth between Marsha and Bukowski.

"That's him?" the policeman asked with overt disbelief.

Marsha explained. When she got to the end and handed over Bukowski's belongings the policeman still seemed a little puzzled, but he made Bukowski put his pants back on and handcuffed him.

"How did you remove his clothing?" he asked Marsha.

"I didn't. He did. It's tough to reach for a hidden weapon with your clothes off. Not too many hiding places left. Besides, it makes them feel defenseless."

"I see," said the policeman. He was looking away. The security guard grinned. They were obviously both classifying her as a pervert.

"You have to come down to the station to sign the forms," said the policeman. "You *are* laying charges?"

"Of course I'm laying charges." Marsha was losing patience with him.

"Quite sure this isn't just a lovers' spat?"

"I want to see the hotel manager." She had lost patience.

The security guard sprang to attention.

"I'll get him."

"I'm sorry, madam." The policeman attempted a more formal approach. "I hope you understand: when I saw him… it seemed…" Suddenly gruff, he turned to Bukowski. "Name?"

Bukowski said nothing.

"He's American," the policeman said, riffling through the papers and credit cards. He said it as though being American would somehow explain why Bukowski was in Marsha's room. After all, she, too, was American.

Marsha slipped the typewritten message into her purse.

"I have an important appointment right now and don't wish to be late," she said, watching Bukowski for some reaction. There was none. "I'll come to the police station afterward."

The hotel manager arrived, on the run, full of outrage and profuse apologies. Nothing like this had ever happened before—not in his twenty years with the hotel. They would move Marsha to another room on one of the upper floors right away. He would pack all her clothes, personally, unless of course there were some private things she would prefer... No? That was fine then, he would take care of the move right away.

Marsha was glad to endure his unctuous chatter. She didn't want to be alone. While he rid her of the curious policeman and his charge, delivered the coffee, poured her a small brandy and packed her suitcases, Marsha called Judith.

It was 4:40 a.m. in Toronto, but Judith was awake, she answered on the first ring. She had been waiting by the phone since her expedition to the park.

"Thank God, it's you," Judith said. "I thought maybe something had happened. I've been calling all night. Where were you?"

Marsha explained she had spent the night with Peter, but before she could tell Judith any more, Judith poured out the story of the kidnapping, the threats, David with the creased-faced man, the Ford wagon that had been set up to spy on her movements. She would have to follow their instructions and take a holiday. She couldn't risk the children.

"And, Marsha, please leave the damned manuscript alone. These people don't play games..."

"Are the kids all right?" Marsha asked, switching away from discussion of the manuscript.

"Sleeping. They're both in shock. I haven't told them about the threats. They think they were picked up by mistake. It's what the kidnappers said. For now, they believe that, but they may not for long. And I can't even call the police for help..."

"Do you think your phone is bugged?"

"I don't know. It could be..."

"Why don't you take them to New York? They have every reason to need a holiday. So do you. Call Jerry for the keys. Go see the Statue of Liberty, hang out in Central Park, do some shopping. Try the galleries. There's an exhibition of primitive art at the Guggenheim, you've never been to the Bronx Zoo..."

"Right. That's exactly what I was thinking of. But what about you?"

"I'm going to be fine," Marsha said, far less certainly than she had intended. "I'll phone you later. I must run now. There's a 7:00 a.m. flight. I'll be your first call in New York."

Marsha didn't want to be late for her appointment. The manager informed her the new room was ready. Was there anything else he could do for her? Yes, there was; she packed the manuscript into her canvas bag and asked the manager if he would accompany her to the National Gallery. She was afraid to go alone.

Twenty-Seven

MARSHA ALLOWED THE MANAGER to leave her only when they reached the Italian Seventeenth Century. The gallery was full, the paintings well guarded. In Room 32 she found a comfortable place to wait. Now it was up to "The Dealer" to find her.

Sitting on one of the soft leather settees opposite Philippe de Champaigne's resplendent portrait of Richelieu, she pulled out "Untitled" and placed it carefully on her knee.

The twenty-five pages Eric Sandwell had copied were headed *A Note to the Publisher*, and began by appealing to the publisher's sense of self-importance.

"Every once in a while a publisher of worth and reputation will come across a manuscript that has to be published, no matter how great the risk. *The Pentagon Papers* was such a publication. The transcript of Richard Nixon's White House tapes was another. Those books had a profound influence on public opinion, and, therefore, on history." It went on to list other influential books, including *QB VII, Black Like Me, Cry the Beloved Country,* even *Mein Kampf* and *Das Kapital.*

"The manuscript you hold in your hand is as explosive and as daring as its predecessors, and its publication requires courage, speed and the conviction that the end, however noble, cannot justify the means.

"It is the story of three men who have set themselves the unenviable task of saving the world. When you consider how frequently this same virtuous impulse had catapulted the world into disaster, you will recognize the urgency of this book. Think about Hitler's plan for an Aryan Utopia, Lenin's for the Marxist solution, Mohammed's of a holy empire, ready for the feet of God, the Ayatollah Khomeini's dream of a land cleansed of sinners..."

Marsha looked up from the manuscript but saw only gallery-goers stopping at one painting or another. The guards had lost interest in her.

"These three men are ideologues, all the more dangerous because they are sincere. Their equipment is persuasion. Their strength, as Hitler's was, is words.

"They first met at Harvard in 1965. They were the same age, had similar homes, had been pampered as children, spent years in the best private schools and would each inherit substantial fortunes. They all had expectations of wielding considerable personal power and financial influence once they graduated. All three had excelled in philosophy and history. They had read a lot and experienced very little.

"It was the middle of the Sixties. They became interested in politics, particularly the politics of our polarized world—the Western democracies against the Soviet bloc. They studied the options and concluded that a third world war was inevitable. They jointly wrote a paper on nuclear war and its all-too-obvious consequences. Naturally, they became involved in the peace movement.

"Much to the discomfort of their prominent parents they took part in peace demonstrations, marches, campus rallies (not at Harvard) and set up a fund for the defense of draft dodgers.

"They were twenty-five years old, enrolled at the graduate school to learn to be leaders, to gain the knowledge necessary to manage their inherited wealth. Their parents threatened to cut them loose if they continued to indulge their passion for the peace movement, and they heeded the threat. What had been a relatively harmless expression of their shared frustration at the possibility of nuclear war and their own inability to prevent it, now took a carefully planned, if clandestine, form. They resolved to find a way to prevent the coming destruction.

"They studied both armed camps, their strengths and weaknesses. They concluded that of the two, the West was more vulnerable, more capable of changing course. Their study of the East bloc characterized the USSR as a machine in a state of permanent military mobilization since 1945, fueled by a party hierarchy that held its power as closely as any feudal monarchy and declared its objective as the victory of universal communism. Nothing short of a successful internal revolution would steer the hierarchy from its chosen path.

"The Western democracies were more vulnerable to change precisely because they were democracies. Their destiny is, in the final analysis, determined by the opinion of their people. Their governments are installed and rejected by their people. In an era of mass communications public opinion can be influenced.

"The BREAD manifesto was born out of these two assessments. It is a brilliant and coherent piece of work, bearing witness to the considerable abilities of the three men.

"Strangely, BREAD is signed in blood. Though over twenty years have passed, the three signatures are plainly legible.

"BREAD is a symbol for the Savior. It is also the biblical rite of passage to eternal life. Bread and water maintain mankind. It is the simple means for survival. It is universal. It has mythical and healing qualities. It is also short for 'Better Red than Dead.'"

Bread. The word the woman at F.A.O. Schwarz had used. Marsha realized with a start just how much the woman had thought she and Judith already knew.

The room had grown noisy around her. A group of American tourists were focusing on "The Adoration of the Golden Calf," as their leader finished his impassioned plea for them to remember the classical movements of the figures until they reached Room 9 on the other side. That would enable him to demonstrate to them how Titian had influenced Poussin. The group moved on to block Marsha's view of Richelieu, and she thought it was time to move.

She settled in Room 38, partly because she admired Tiepolo, but mainly because she liked the room's two exits, one of which led directly past three uniformed guards into the crowded gallery shop. She assumed there were too many witnesses here for an attack.

X's *Note to the Publisher* contained a short excerpt from the BREAD manifesto. It was intensely serious. It stated that the survival of the human race as a principle took precedence over the preservation of the principles of democracy, and that a man, if given the option, should sacrifice freedom for life, since without life there were no freedoms.

"The three men agreed to mobilize all their means in the service of BREAD. They would gladly exchange the inheritance of their children for an assurance of their lives. They called it 'their heritage of life' and agreed to give up their own lives, if necessary, to procure it.

"Their plan was boldly simple. They would effect major changes in public opinion in the West, changes that would lead to unilateral disarmament. Having set the target, they had several interim steps to take.

"They had to erode public awareness of the values that divide the totalitarian system of the Communist world from the pluralistic systems of the West. They would have to convince the majority of people that these differences were slight enough to be overlooked and that they *should* be overlooked in the interest of avoiding a nuclear confrontation.

"Nuclear war itself had to be brought into public consciousness as an ever-present threat; it had to be seen as the ultimate evil. People would have to be forced into recurrent and endless visions of a world devastated by nuclear explosions, flames raging through ruined cities, thousands and millions dead, of a few survivors stumbling about in toxic darkness envying the dead.

"Equally important, the public had to be distanced from its old-style politicians and its military had to be presented as the enemy.

"The United States had to be isolated from its allies. The most powerful of the Western nations, it would have to be seen as belligerent, expansionist and irresponsible, its military simultaneously blind to the realities and trigger-happy. In 1965, with the Vietnam War escalating, it was not difficult to see how such a picture might take shape.

"Yet Kennedy was still a national hero cut down in his prime and the Missile Crisis was still seen by many as a confrontation won rather than as a close encounter with the end of the world. The three idealists had a long way to go.

"The last of their interim objectives was a public relations face-lift for the USSR if being ruled by it was to be presented to people in the West as a viable alternative to annihilation.

"Like most grand gestures, the manifesto should have been doomed to failure, but these men were not ordinary men. They had the money and the determination to put their plan into action.

"To influence public opinion, they would use the media in all its manifestations. Systematically, they would buy newspapers, magazine and publishing houses, television stations, radio stations and news agencies. They would finance films and support studies pertaining to the aftereffects of nuclear war.

"The reason for this book is that they have succeeded admirably and are poised for the last stage of their objective.

"Today these three men own or control one hundred and twenty-one US, seven British, three Australian, two Canadian and fifteen European daily newspapers, three news agencies, forty-two radio stations, four television stations, four book publishing houses, and the Boston communications giant CFT.

"Their newspapers include many of the largest in circulation and many of the most influential. Their combined readership tops 245 million.

"One of the three recently purchased the Chicago all-news channel CGB, and added to his holdings *USA Now,* the weekly newsmagazine, and *Women's Voice.* He owns two New York publishing conglomerates: Galloway and Brooks, the multinational educational and reference book publisher, and McTavish and Company, the mass-market paperback house, number three in the US rankings of paperback houses. In 1980 he purchased *La Presse* in Paris and a six-paper German chain from Droer G.

"He has fulfilled his mandate as set forth in the records of BREAD's annual review meetings. This year he is to expand into Italy. His name is Ethan George MacMurty and he is running for governor of Massachusetts.

"The second man branched into the United Kingdom. His holdings include *The Manchester Telegraph, The London News, The Glasgow Enquirer* and *The Liverpool Daily News.* With his board of directors, he has majority ownership of three British radio stations as well as *News Only.* In June of 1984 he added to his growing portfolio the former Thompson showpiece, *The Sydney Gleaner.* With it, he purchased *Australia Today* magazine, two Melbourne radio stations, and FIGMENT, the Australian News Agency.

"He is Nelson Roberts Jr., the reclusive Wyoming millionaire, founder of the Benevolent Society for Helping the Poor of America, occasional SPCA benefactor, renowned patron of the arts, and chief supporter of a host of charities. Last year, Mr. Roberts set up the Roberts Foundation, to be administered by the Des Moines Archdiocese of the Roman Catholic Church of America. Its chief mandate is to support scientific studies of the post-nuclear-war planet. They are presently involved in a $6 million study of 'nuclear winter' and plan to offer assistance to the US government's five-year study series of the same subject.

"The group of three is completed by Anthony Billingsworth-Powell, his father an august member of the British House of Lords and himself much admired for his forthright opinions on labor's entrenched right to strike, at no matter what cost to the public. It is Mr. Billingsworth-Powell's US company that took control of *The Miami Sun, The Baltimore Register, The Orlando News* and twenty other papers when they made their bid for the struggling Teasdale chain in June of 1980. Cinworld, one of his offshore holding companies, established itself as the head of the BAND conglomerate. In addition to being America's largest manufacturer of sugary breakfast cereal, BAND also owns five radio stations, CHEX in Los Angeles and MUTV in Detroit.

"Sir George Billingsworth-Powell is seventy-five years old. His son, Anthony, may soon inherit his seat in the House of Lords.

"Through all these years, they have never tired of their quest. At annual meetings, they drew up plans of action and specific goals. They reviewed their progress and examined their combined portfolio.

"This book traces how they have affected public opinion on subjects as apparently diverse as NATO, missile testing in Canada, CIA activities in Central and South America, US involvement in Cambodia and the subsequent downplaying of the genocide by the Khmer Rouge, US deployment of a space-based defense system against USSR missiles. It is a measure of their success that public opinion put an end to the president's budget for Star Wars weapons (a favorite phrase of BREAD media). They wanted minimal coverage of the Soviet-directed pacification of Lebanon and Afghanistan. Their efforts to present the US as warmongering in Central America have caused public outcry against further aid to the contras of Nicaragua and the Salvadoran army. No one will mourn the passing of democracy in El Salvador.

"In Egypt the United States is to be seen as the immoral aggressor, blindly supporting the excesses of the Saudis and of

Israel, sowing the seeds of suspicion among Arabs. An Egyptian ship had been attacked by F-100s and set afire. The planes were crudely disguised as Libyan—they were sure to be recognized as American.

"An attempt on Castro's life was to have been presented as another CIA plot, a final attempt to put the Bay of Pigs right. As the situation in the Philippines grew tenser, the United States' presence on the side of the oppressor was to be seen as blatant, uncontrolled CIA meddling. Would the Senate stand by while the CIA once more interfered in the internal politics of a nation where democracy had become a Yankee joke?

"In Europe and the United Kingdom, the United States is to be seen as an irresponsible cowboy, ready to sling Pershing IIs at the well-mannered Soviets. And no matter who fires first, the Europeans must know they are hostage to what happens next.

"Through a careful choice of publishers, editors, managers, producers, presidents, directors and other staff—puppets mostly, unaware they are dancing to anyone else's tune—these three men have been able to determine how news will be covered and what news will be picked for coverage. On the agenda of discussion groups and among articles in the popular press there are questions no one would have raised even five years ago. Questions such as: 'Should the United States defend Western Europe?' 'Should NATO be disbanded?' 'Can CIA subversion in Cuba be stopped?'

"There have been films, books, articles, series on the effects of a nuclear holocaust too terrifying to contemplate, and audiences, still in a state of shock, are now being treated to interview shows and learned panel discussions on the relatively unimportant differences between our world view and that of the Soviets, and the obvious advantages of unilateral disarmament.

"Hence the urgency of this publication.

"If these men are to be stopped, their methods must be understood. Their chosen public arena must be accepted. After the appearance of this book, the other media, not now controlled, will rally. Those who read will read, those who do not will be treated to entertaining pieces of the story on television. They will have a choice whether to listen or not. Ultimately the decision rests with the people."

"Isn't it simply wonderful?" said the voice over Marsha's shoulder. "No question, the Venetians had it over everybody when it came to painting. Maybe it has something to do with living in a crumbling city. It reminds one constantly of mortality."

Quickly Marsha slipped the manuscript into her carrier bag and stood up.

"Look at this one. Here is Venus handing over a child to winged Time. The baby is already marked for death: there is a deep sadness in the eyes. I think maybe you will remember me from Schwarz's. Yes?" The voice, flat, mechanical, precise. The same pink and blue scarf over her head. In deference, however, to London's spring, she must have left the sealskin coat behind.

"You are an extraordinarily resourceful young woman. And enterprising. Far beyond anyone's expectations." She put the emphasis on "anyone's" and stretched out the word so as to make sure she herself was included in the wonder at Marsha's enterprise. The teddy bear eyes behind the elaborate horn-rimmed glasses remained fixed on Tiepolo's "Allegory with Venus and Time." The expression was pleasantly benign.

"Delighted to gain your approval," Marsha said, implying that she wasn't. "But isn't it perhaps time you stopped talking in riddles and told me who the hell you are?"

"Showing your claws a bit, my dear?"

"If you want something, say it now, or I'm going to call that guard over there and tell him..."

"Tell him what? That this little old lady is molesting you? However, you are right. The time has come to stop playing games. The Dealer is ready to meet you. You have something that belongs to him."

"I do?"

"In that bag, Miss Hillier." She sighed. "I thought you were tired of games. Now, if you will come with me, I shall take you to him. Do not worry about the two men following us; they are here to protect you. You've given them a lot of work already."

Marsha looked around. She saw a stocky, dark-haired man nearby, his back to her. He appeared to be absorbed in a close study of Longhi's rhinoceros.

The woman led the way back through Room 39, skirted the outside of the Gallery Shop, through Room 31, around the leather settee in Room 29 where a small battalion of tourists was pushing toward the Vermeers. She held Marsha back while another broad man in a tan raincoat hurried past and joined the tourist group. When they had gone, he reappeared and waited in the doorway for them to follow into the Rembrandt room.

The two men in raincoats looked so much alike they could have been brothers. Both had black hair, thinning on top, long sideburns, flat square faces with prominent, muscular jaws, long arms that reached down past where most people's arms end, and short legs tucked into even shorter trousers that left a good two-inch gap between where they stopped and the wide, chocolate-colored brogues began. They were dressed rather like refugees from Eastern Europe.

By contrast, the man they now approached appeared to have been dressed on Savile Row, his suit the perfect casual cut worn by men who spend their lives in expensive environments. He carried a briefcase too thin to be of much use.

He was tall, at least 6'2", broad-shouldered and erect. His hair was gray, turning white at the temples, coarse enough to challenge his expensively careful layer-cut. His long narrow face was tanned a light golden brown, and lined deeply around the eyes only—they were large, watery-black, sentimental eyes that reminded Marsha of Omar Sharif playing Doctor Zhivago in the latter part of that movie. His eyebrows were prominent, darker than his hair. They kept his eyes in shadow. He had a long aquiline nose, tapered at the nostrils. His chin was wide and dimpled, his mouth finely sculpted. Smiling as he turned to Marsha, he flashed even white teeth.

"Already, I feel as if we have met," he said. His voice was soft and deep. There was a trace of an accent in the way he pronounced each word. Like the woman's, too precise. "In preparation for this occasion, I have taken time to learn something about you." His movements were lithe and smooth; he walked from the center of his back, the European way, not from the shoulders, as Americans do.

Before she had even formed an appropriate response, Marsha found herself smiling politely at him. His theatrical courtliness was contagious.

"I am delighted that you have almost finished your reading. I chose the Gallery because it is my favorite place in London. Almost a second home. It is entirely appropriate that we should meet here. And this room," he indicated the small room behind him, "is my special choice for the occasion. Rembrandt, you see, is my favorite artist. The master. I have admired him all my life. Like Kenneth Clark, I have tried to reproduce his drawings, to learn to understand the deftness of his touch, the feeling he must have had each time he drew a line. How, with a few short strokes of his pen, he could capture the whole of a man's soul. Here, let me show you something." He held Marsha gently by the elbow and led her into the room.

"Come into my parlor, said the spider to the fly" was the line that came to Marsha's mind, but what she said was: "I presume you are The Dealer?"

"F-e-r-e-n-c," he said. "The last 'c' is soft, almost like an 's.' Please call me that. You will, I hope, allow me to call you Marsha. It is a lovely name. Your father's choice, I believe. A charming man. Great pity he did not take time to learn to know his daughter better. He would have been most proud of you. He was too busy, devoted to his ambitions, as I have been, all my life, to mine.

"Look at this portrait of Rembrandt"—he steered Marsha forward, "—painted in 1640, when he was thirty-four. Self-possessed, self-satisfied, in control of his own destiny. His eyes, curious and unafraid, his mouth turning into a small suggestion of amusement as he gazes at you. And over here"—he indicated the far wall "—this one was painted in the year of his death twenty-nine years later. The change in the expression is even more startling than the way his features have submitted to age. The tragedies and disappointments those eyes have seen." He stared into Rembrandt's face. "He is no longer amused at your looking in on him, he is amused at himself. He looks inward now, and how he dismisses as unimportant what he finds there..."

Marsha was growing impatient.

"The Dealer, then, is some kind of code name?"

"It's more of a..." he seemed to be searching for the right word "...an epithet. An entirely appropriate one at that, because that's what I've been all these many years—a dealer. Strangely, the Arabs gave me the name, and it stuck."

"What exactly do you deal in?"

"The most important commodity of all: information. I buy and I sell, I trade and I solicit at the right time, from the right people and for the right people."

"And you knew my father?"

"That would be overstating our brief acquaintance. I was pleased to be of service to him once. A small matter." He waved his hand as though to dismiss the topic. "I only mentioned him because you reminded me of him. Something about the chin, jaunty and determined. Or perhaps it's the gait..." He looked at her intently. "You're not frightened, are you?"

"Considering all I've been through to read your manuscript, I'm managing fairly well, but I still..."

"I've kept an eye on you since you arrived. If I've been less than diligent...well, you've been somewhat unpredictable."

"You didn't expect me to capture your messenger?"

"My messenger?" He looked over at the woman, still guarding the door.

"Arnold Bukowski. He brought your note to invite me here. What I don't know is why he attacked me."

"I still don't understand."

Marsha explained.

"Frequently they have resorted to using young idealists with no training," Ferenc said. "People who don't know their names, only the cause. If they are caught, they have no information leading to the three men. Mr. Bukowski fits the mold. He must have found my note inside the door. That's where *my* messenger had left it. Now Bukowski will have a difficult time at the police station, but eventually, as you will not appear to prefer charges, they will let him go."

"I will not?"

"He will tell his contact of our meeting." He ignored her question. "This does rather limit your options, doesn't it? Seems you are already committed."

"And my friend Judith Hayes in Toronto? Will they leave her alone?"

"She has nothing they want. You have the manuscript. Now, tell me, what do you think of it?"

"It's terrifying. It's also incredible. I haven't had a chance yet to think about it, but if it's true, you have a fantastic news story..."

"*If* it's true? My dear Marsha, please don't mock me. Would I come out into the light, when it's in my best personal interest to stay in the shadows, to reveal a story if it wasn't true? Would I give away what I have spent decades to build if I didn't feel it is of the utmost importance the world be informed of the pending catastrophe? I abhor acts of heroism, as I abhor all pretensions, but this time I have to come to the verge of perpetrating a heroic act. Don't you see, I believe I'm about to save democracy—at least for the next generation." His vast black eyes had become ever more watery, his voice deepened to a whisper, but the words remained measured, evenly emphasized.

"Yes," Marsha said quickly. "Yes, I suppose you do. Still—" she had to come to the point sooner or later "—one does have to have considerable proof...and documents...perhaps then..."

Ferenc laughed, his teeth flashed white. It was an affable, amused laugh, inconsistent with his tempered speech.

"Is that all? Easy. We have the manuscript for you and, of course, it comes with all the proof anyone should require. Immaculately legal. Not one loose end. For a moment I thought you were going to get cold feet. It would have been most disappointing."

Inside the soft blue running-shoes, Marsha curled down her toes. It was perhaps in response to what he had said, but there was no doubt they were icy cold. She shivered involuntarily.

"Well," she said, "there was Harris, and probably Max Grafstein and Eric Sandwell..."

"Most regrettable." Ferenc shook his head again. "Most regrettable. Harris was the cause of the whole disaster, poor chap, I'm sure he meant no harm."

When she was sure he wasn't going to continue, Marsha prodded again.

"What happened to him?"

"I had assumed you knew." He looked at her curiously. "Harris, unlucky man, started the ball rolling. Not intentionally. Not in the least intentionally. Though I had given him my personal reassurance, he didn't wait for the documents. He consulted his lawyer. The lawyer, an unimaginative citizen with utmost faith in law and order, consulted the Royal Canadian Mounted Police. The Horsemen—a delightful name for them, don't you think?—are riddled with informers of every stripe and, since they've been taken over by the Ottawa civil servants, no one in his right mind would trust them with real information. I know that. The CIA knows that. Even MI5 knows that. My old associate and adversary, Boris Andreevich of the KGB's North American branch, was most proud of the fact that he knew more irrelevant bits about the private lives of Canadian politicians than anyone in the world. But Harris's lawyer didn't know. Harris was given a chance to back off. When he wouldn't, he was eliminated."

"They made it look like suicide."

"Not very successful, I am told. A reasonably simple procedure. Requires one organizer and a number of hirelings. They have several organizers in Canada. Most have never met them. The hirelings are paid off—one-time service, usually."

"And the manuscript?"

"It was taken from Harris before they stuck him under the train. The fool brought it with him. He was expecting to meet me at the station."

"And where does Detective Inspector David Parr fit in? Who does he work for?"

Ferenc shrugged.

"Small potatoes—local city cop. Reports to the Horsemen. He may be useful to us later."

"And how did Grafstein and Sandwell get involved?"

Ferenc closed his eyes and exhaled loudly. "Harris sent copies to Grafstein and Sandwell early to protect his investment. The $1.2 million I wanted seemed too high a risk for him..."

"Predictably," Marsha said, her mind pausing over the numbers. She would have to contact Larry to approve the funds *if*... Would she take the risk?

"Do you think so?" His accent thickened with sarcasm.

"What I meant is, Harris didn't have too much cash in the kitty." That hadn't been what she had meant at all, but it served the purpose. Ferenc went on.

"He should have taken my advice and waited. I would have guaranteed his safety. I would have guaranteed the others'. When Grafstein went to Harris's funeral in Toronto he was ready to make a deal with the son. That's hearsay. The facts are that he was murdered because he wouldn't tell them where the manuscript was. His office was ransacked. They set it up to seem like random vandalism. Very imaginative: urinating over the entire editorial department." Ferenc chuckled. "Of course, they found the manuscript and destroyed it."

"And Eric Sandwell?"

"He was poisoned."

Her throat was dry, her palms clammy. She rubbed them against her thighs to restore the feeling in the fingers.

"Old-fashioned cyanide in his Coquilles St. Jacques. I never eat anything spicy. The strong flavor covers secret ingredients."

He smiled at his joke. "The effect of cyanide will frequently simulate heart failure. Please. I think we should start moving on." He took her elbow again and began to steer her around the corner past the huge Van Dyck portrait of Charles I on horseback. Marsha shuddered as his hand touched her.

"Where are we going?" she asked, knowing she would now have to see it through.

"A change of scenery. We have business to conclude."

"You haven't told me what happened to the manuscript Eric read?"

"Don't you know?" The Dealer stopped and stared at her. "Didn't your friend tell you?"

"Peter Burnett?"

"A pleasant young man, but not quite right for you. You are rather exceptional. A man would have to do you justice."

Marsha was relieved when he resumed their progress.

"I think you were about to tell me about the manuscript," she said coldly.

"Mr. Burnett protected his own interests. You may have noticed that his interests coincide rather directly with those of the peace-loving threesome. He was recruited by Anthony Billingsworth-Powell while he was still at Oxford—a close friend of the great man's son. Or didn't he tell you who nominated him for the Hamilton, Thornbush board?"

Marsha was concentrating on keeping up with him. She didn't answer.

"I see. He did tell you."

"He would have had no part in the killing."

"What difference does it make? He knew Sandwell didn't die of a heart attack." Ferenc clucked appreciatively as they went by the fulsome women of a Rubens painting. "And he did return the manuscript to Billingsworth-Powell."

"Did you know Eric Sandwell had copied some of the initial pages?"

"Only when I was told you emerged with them from Hamilton, Thornbush this morning."

Marsha was flanked by the shorter of the two men in rain-coats. The woman and the other man led the way. Among the crowds of visitors from all over the globe, no one gave their odd group a second glance.

They descended two flights of stairs to the basement. The man who led the way opened a brown, unmarked door and disappeared. Ferenc had his arm through Marsha's, holding her close. They waited.

Marsha had a strange sense of remoteness, as though she had inadvertently entered a drama on an unfamiliar stage. "Where does this lead?" she asked.

"Specifically, through the storage rooms and a restoration area," Ferenc explained. "In general, however, it leads to one of my offices. I rarely use the same office twice."

The door was opened from the inside. The room they entered was badly lit with a few neon runners in the ceiling. There were long tables with small lamps bending over them, and canvases of all sizes. They weaved around the tables, side-stepping jars of liquid and paint. The odor was like that of a hospital bathroom.

"Thanks to the fervor of the British unions, this place is always empty at noon," Ferenc said. "We have some sixty minutes to decide how we will proceed with the publication." He opened his thin briefcase and took out a pile of papers. He switched on one of the overhead lamps and deposited the pages in front of Marsha.

"An hour?" Marsha protested.

"Slightly less. But it will have to do," he said. "Time enough to establish to your own satisfaction that the material is as explosive as I say it is, that it is publishable, and that it contains the requisite amount of proof. Use your own judgment. You will want to have it lawyered later. You'll pick some safe lawyers. For our purposes, remember truth is still an adequate defense against libel suits. I will leave you alone."

Ferenc walked softly away from her. He wandered through the tables examining the paintings being repaired. Then he sat in the far corner, in the shadows, and watched Marsha read. She was uncomfortably aware of his attention, as she was aware of his three companions near the exits, their faces immobile, listening.

She forced herself to concentrate.

The manuscript called itself *Better Red Than Dead?* It was a clearly-written narrative that began with the backgrounds of MacMurty, Roberts and Billingsworth-Powell, continued with their Harvard resolution and traced their goals, acquisitions, reviews of achievements, their positions today.

There were detailed accounts of their activities in business, through charities and foundations. Profiles of their associates and senior employees. Their criteria for hiring and firing were included, in the form of a four-page typed list, signed by the three, dated June 1, 1967.

There were minutes of their regular meetings, one per year, with different datelines: Paris, London, New York, Sydney, Toronto. The minutes reviewed progress and set new goals. There were detailed plans for such actions as bringing the US before the International Court of Justice in The Hague over its clandestine activities in Nicaragua and Nigeria, and the subsequent media coverage of the Court's rebuke, resulting in many European demonstrations and the burning of the US embassy in Brussels. There was a battle plan for the establishment of the Russian gas pipeline into Europe, a proposal that had initially met with vociferous opposition from the public. Through the careful manipulation of public opinion, Roberts had soon switched the positions of Italy, Germany and France. The diehards in Scandinavia could be ignored for a while. The pipeline was under construction, paid for by the European financial community.

The anti-NATO plan was proving successful. Two post-nuclear films had swept the United States into a furor against the President's military budget, severe cutbacks were certain at the US end of the arms race. The CIA had put its controversial director on trial for supporting right-wing regimes in South

America. US withdrawal from Egypt was maybe a couple of months away. Israel was to be left to its own devices.

Ethan MacMurty had been experiencing difficulties in battling the powerful Jewish lobby in the Senate, but he was sure of victory if they could now implement plans for "gentile liberation." The latter was a forty-eight-point project involving all the media at their disposal. The purpose: to fan the fires of anti-Semitism throughout the United States. It was MacMurty's assumption that, if properly frightened, the Jewish lobby would crumble. Minutes of the eighteenth meeting recorded that all three pacifists regretted such methods, that not one of them was an anti-Semite and that, once their objectives had been achieved, they would do all they could to repair the damage. Meanwhile, the end would justify the means.

The manuscript contained a complete list of their holdings; a selection of photographs; a copy of the BREAD Manifesto; their early studies of the Soviet Union and of the Western powers; lists of acquisition targets, by country; memoranda detailing latest news from each in relation to specific targets; and some excerpts from Roberts's diaries.

Minutes of the most recent meeting were dated March 15, Nassau. On that day, it was agreed that they would authorize an approach to the USSR with a proposition: if they were to guarantee a continuation of their efforts, would the Soviet Union, given a free hand in Western Europe, guarantee, in return, a safe, though isolated, United States?

"Well?" Ferenc inquired.

"I haven't read it all yet," Marsha said.

"Of course you haven't," Ferenc said. "But you've read enough to know that it's worth the money I'm asking."

"Yes," Marsha said. Sure, there would be some legal questions, some more documents to produce, but the story had to be published. There were still some strong newspapers left that would run with it, there would be major TV coverage, people would listen. The three men would be exposed. "But the last three publishers who said yes to this manuscript all died."

"Please, Marsha, I'm an expert at survival. I assure you, had I known what Harris was up to, he and the others would still be alive."

He had emerged from the shadows and stood over her.

"Trust me. You have nothing to fear, as long as you follow my instructions."

"How did you get all these documents?"

He put his slim index finger in front of his mouth for quiet and said, "Trade secrets, my dear. We all have them."

"And if our legal people need more?"

"I will provide whatever they need, though I think you will find them satisfied with this."

"It could have been faked."

"It could. But then you wouldn't have to pay the money. Such are the terms—all in your favor." He smiled. "You will have five hours to read it more carefully on your way home. First, though, in the interests of your personal safety, you have three telephone calls to make."

He waved his hand at his assistants, who instantly came to life. One unplugged a telephone near the entrance and brought it to Marsha. He lifted the underside of the phone, inserted a small black device, put the cover back on, then plugged the phone into a nearby jack.

Ferenc lifted the receiver, listened, and replaced it. Marsha waited.

"You are going to phone Judith Hayes, Larry Shapiro, and Peter Burnett. The first with a message for the RCMP to guarantee your safety, the second for the contract, the third to ensure our friends believe you are staying in London."

PART FIVE

New York

Twenty-Eight

JUDITH WOKE with her arms around Jezebel and the telephone. The series of locks on Marsha's door had seemed, finally, comforting.

On the way to the airport in Toronto there had been a Ford wagon keeping pace with them through the traffic, all the way to the airport. Judith had made no attempt to shake it. They had wanted her to take a holiday—she was following instructions.

Once on the 401, as the road opened up on all sides, she had managed to glance at his face in the rearview mirror. He had shiny black hair, small busy eyes, a pale expressionless face, unlined. He might have been in his early thirties. The fur collar was rolled up close around his thin neck—he must have been chilled after an all-night vigil in the car.

Now ensconced in Marsha's apartment, she rubbed her cheek where it had pushed against the antique pattern on the dining room table. It had left a soft damp mark on the polished top. Jezebel stretched with a shiver, her open claws sliding into the crystal ashtray full of Rothmans butts. Judith stared at the white phone, hazy in the April light, and tried to remember everything Marsha had said this morning on the phone from London, the exact arrangement of her words. Marsha had asked her to repeat her instructions in the specific order she had chosen; her voice had been flat and unemotional. The essence of her message was that both she and Judith were in danger unless her instructions were followed. She would not engage in conversation, except to ask how the children were coping with the trip to New York. She sounded as though she had rehearsed her end of the dialogue and would not veer from the prepared text. Even her one small joke about shopping had been carefully phrased. Judith would have to think about that.

Meanwhile, if it was precision Marsha wanted, it was precision she would get. Any hidden agenda could wait.

She plugged in the kettle, ladled out Jezebel's foul-smelling fishy rations, checked the street through the window, the door for signs of attempted entry, the children, her map of the New York City underground, her American cash and two credit cards.

After the second cup of coffee she was ready to call David. At 12:05, the police receptionist had claimed, Detective Inspector Parr would be at his desk.

He seemed delighted to hear her voice.

"God, woman, where the hell have you been?" he shouted. "I was beginning to think I'd gone mad. Only imagined you were real. I've scoured the whole damned city looking for you. Your answering service doesn't even ask who's calling any more—we've become buddies."

"I'm sorry, David. I left rather suddenly."

"Suddenly? You mean like a bloody mirage. Now you see me, now you don't. You might at least have given me a tiny hint."

"There wasn't time." Her script hadn't suggested she wait for him to explain about his loose-skinned driver, but she gave him a second anyway.

"There wasn't?" he yelled, ignoring his opportunity. "Why?"

Was he testing her to see if, despite their warning, she would tell?

"Marsha called. I had to be in her apartment by 4:00. She's arranged for the walls to be ripped out, and she can't be here to supervise. In New York you never leave your walls in the hands of strangers. She couldn't come herself. You see, she's found the manuscript. The one everyone else has been after. She's staying in London while it's set in type, and printed. When you consider what happened to the other publishers..."

"What's in it?" he interrupted.

"The manuscript?"

"Yes, goddammit. What's in the manuscript?"

"The story of three guys who want to save the world, so they trade it to the Russians."

Pause.

"You're kidding."

"No. That's the story. Marsha says it'll be the instant-book sensation of the year. She's worked out the mechanics; even had copies of the script lodged with six separate lawyers for her own protection. In another day the presses roll and she'll come out of hiding."

"Who *are* these guys?"

"She wouldn't say."

"Did she say how the hell she got the thing?"

"From the man who wrote it."

"You're being rather tight-lipped, aren't you? Remember we were partners? That was your idea, *right*? Now who the hell wrote it?"

"He calls himself The Dealer. That's all I know."

"You're going to need some protection. I'll get the RCMP to help. It's their case now. They took me off today. Loud noises from Ottawa. Security and all that stuff. Apparently they knew about Harris all along, but there have been bigger fish to fry... I had to drop the investigation. And only this morning we caught up with Marlene Little. She was on her way to Argentina to meet her boyfriend. Seems he left her with a wad of money."

"What are the charges?"

"We have her in for questioning, that's all. How long will you stay down there?"

"I don't know. A few days. While the walls come down and go back up. We'll do the sights..."

"Are you all right, Judith?"

"I'm fine. Really." She had practiced saying that.

"You sound so remote."

"I've been worried about Marsha," Judith said, lighting another cigarette.

"And I worry about *you*. I want you where I can keep an eye on you myself."

"Why?" Judith asked suspiciously.

"What do you mean why, stupid? Haven't I told you already?"

That was all she needed for the tears to start.

"Must run now..."

"Judith?"

"Uhhum."

"Your address and phone number. Can't have you drop out of sight again."

Judith struggled through the number, choked goodbye and hung up. She hurried to the kitchen for a refill of coffee, and more tears—long wet sobs.

When the phone rang a few minutes later, she didn't reach for it.

She rinsed her face with cold water and let it run over her hands for a while. She would have to pull herself together. There were three people relying on her judgment and ingenuity—Anne, Jimmy and Marsha, the people she loved the most. And so she would focus on the immediate, the practical: she needed someone she could trust, who would make Toronto safe again, and she needed cash.

She phoned Allan Goodman in Ottawa. She didn't let herself be put off by the secretary.

"An urgent personal matter," she had told her. "Untie him." And Allan made it easy. When she told him she needed money, he offered to wire her a loan. "Same day, low interest," he joked. When she told him why she was in New York and why she hadn't asked the police for help, he listened. When she told him about The Dealer's manuscript and what Marsha said it contained he didn't laugh. He knew who The Dealer was. He would go through the Minister of Justice's department and cash in some favors with the RCMP. "Then I'll come straight to New York. I haven't seen a Broadway show in years."

Judith went into Marsha's guest room. The children were sleeping—still exhausted by their ordeal, and this morning's early start.

"Perfect timing for their school," her mother had intoned. "I suppose you worked out what you're going to do when Jimmy flunks his examinations and has to repeat the year?"

Judith hadn't.

Jimmy lay on his back, his arms flung over his head, wrists crossed, fingers curved gently, graceful as a dancer. A lock of hair fell softly across his face. His lips opened to reveal a set of perfect teeth, the orthodontist's masterpiece. Three years of all their savings, but it had been worth it.

Anne slept curled around her pillow like a cat. Her long thick hair spread out behind her in a dark cloud. The slim line of her hip still betrayed the child she had barely left behind.

With a sense of parental usefulness, Judith pulled their sheets up to cover them. She drew the curtains across the open window, then sat on the woven rope rug between the two beds. For a long, long time she listened to them breathe.

Twenty-Nine

MARSHA FOUND SHE had been booked on the 3:00 p.m. Concorde under the name of Angela Schwarz. The choice of name attested to Ferenc's strange sense of humor. The adventure had begun at F.A.O. Schwarz.

"The black angel," he explained, "was the brightest and best of all his tribe. He was a natural leader, and a gambler. Or haven't you read Milton?"

"Wouldn't you say he took one too many chances?"

"Depends on your version of what's in Paradise. Harp music is an acquired taste."

The passport was American and carried her own birthdate. Place of birth: Brooklyn—eyes and hair black. The photograph was definitely herself, though she would not have given it a second glance in a line-up. The shiny shoulder-length hair and fringe framed a face reminiscent of the early Elizabeth Taylor.

"Who is this?" Marsha had asked.

"Angela Schwarz. We used your old passport photo, some skillful retouching, and a couple of props." The woman pulled a black wig from her coat, began to brush it. Ferenc gave Marsha a small plastic container with soft, dark-colored contact lenses. "It would generally take days to become accustomed to these, but you won't have to wear them more than twice. Just in the airport and when you leave the plane. On the plane itself you can switch to these glasses." He handed her a blue, pearl-embroidered spectacles case. They were plain glass, tinted to a fashionable dark gray.

To complete the disguise she would be traveling with a matching set of Samsonite luggage, small, elegant and filled with clothes, toilet articles, a couple of inexpensive mementos from Littlewoods. The clothes were worn. All labels had been removed.

"You've been fairly confident we would go along with your proposition," Marsha remarked.

"You've shown unusual tenacity in your pursuit of the manu-script. The financial details you've known since Schwarz's. If M & A had the money, it was only a question of delivering the article."

Marsha had been amazed at Larry's reaction to The Dealer's proposition. She had expected him to protest about the amount, and the need to trust Marsha's judgment that the property was indeed worth $1.2 million. She had given him only a sketchy outline of what the manuscript contained, without the names of the three protagonists (Ferenc had insisted on that). He had agreed to have the first check prepared and the contracts drafted. They would be deposited at the First City Bank, after Larry had seen the manuscript himself. The check could not be cashed until Ferenc Jozsef had signed the contracts and returned them. As Larry saw it, he wasn't taking much of a chance. He'd had a slow week, several boring execu-tive meetings, and he was enjoying the intrigue.

Everything would be ready for Marsha at 4:00 p.m. the next day, and he would tell no one she was coming back early. He agreed to circulate a memorandum saying she would be staying in London another week. He would gear up the machine to produce an instant book and alert both company lawyers to stand by. If all went according to plan, they would have books distributed by the end of next week—a day longer than Stevenson's Entebbe book had taken, but Bantam had been able to solicit advance orders. M & A would have to forgo telling bookstores and wholesalers what the book was about. They would distribute the first 200,000 copies without orders and prepare for a massive demand on the reprint. A first printing of only 200,000 wouldn't arouse suspicion in the plant—unless someone was expecting the book to surface in New York.

The calls to Judith and Peter, Ferenc said, ensured that BREAD's agents would be looking for her in London. They would be watching lawyers' offices, typesetting houses, plants with fast-moving web presses.

"Once you have published," Ferenc said, "it will serve no purpose to kill you. They are not interested in revenge. They are murderers by necessity, not persuasion."

They had left the National Gallery through a basement door, and were now traveling by car, a black sedan with glass between the driver and the passengers. The two men in trench coats sat in front, one of them openly displaying a handgun on his lap.

The woman crouched opposite Marsha on a low, pull-out seat. She had removed her horn-rimmed glasses and her tiny eyes darted from side to side, watching the street, paying attention to every car. When she was satisfied the wig had been brushed to perfection, she rested it on her knee. Her other hand reached, once more, inside her coat. Marsha wondered if she too carried a gun.

"And you?" Marsha asked Ferenc. "Do you kill by persuasion?"

"Good god, no," he laughed. "I am strictly a professional. I operate a system based on supply and demand, purely pragmatic.

I subscribe to no ideologies. I abhor nationalism, communism, idealism of any kind. It's the zealots you have to beware of. I am a businessman. My product, information, is easily transportable, requires little space, cuts across national boundaries. Its value does not rise and fall with the Dow Jones, or with depression, inflation and monetary crisis. Its value increases with the level of insecurity felt by the buyer. I deal with banks, international corporations, oil companies, commodity traders, and some intelligence agencies."

"Why didn't you sell this information to one of them?"

"Because I want to see it published. The agencies would pay but they would not publish. They would use the information, but the poison would continue to spread. The Western world deserves a chance to make its own decisions—good or bad."

Something didn't add up. Though Marsha had grown accustomed to his florid manner of speaking, the explanation seemed too elaborate. She glanced to see if he was smiling his mocking half-smile. He wasn't. He stared out the one-way window, relaxed but completely serious, his thin mouth slightly open.

His tanned hand rested on Marsha's arm. Slim fingers, long simian thumb, tiny tufts of black hair. His nails were flat ovals. The thin signet ring on his middle finger displayed a round green stone. Marsha leaned closer to see what its markings were.

"It is rather old-fashioned," he said. "The lion in the center signifies power, the snake around his feet cunning. The scythe around the lion's head warns of the proximity of death."

"Very cheerful," Marsha said. "Did you have it engraved?"

"No. I inherited it from my mother. She, in turn, removed it from the finger of a sleeping nobleman. Rampant lions were customary rewards for sons of the nobility who relished fighting in wars. My family tradition does not run to wars or to causes. We were...wanderers." He gazed at Marsha. "Your father was a great believer in causes. A man of honor and distinction."

As they neared Heathrow, he once more reassured her that her own belongings would be packed and moved out of Green's. The bill would be paid. The suitcases, with her name on them, would fly to New York the end of the week. By then it should be safe for her to collect them. Her remaining London appointments would be canceled. The two bodyguards would accompany her onto the plane and to the hotel they had booked in her new name near La Guardia. They would stay with her throughout the next six days.

Fortunately, he had agreed that she could buy a couple of decent dresses to survive the week. Whoever her new wardrobe had belonged to, she said she had no desire to wear the clothes.

The wig was loose but not uncomfortable. She could hold it in place with two of her own hairpins. The contact lenses were more of a problem. Several times she dropped them, before managing to insert them into tear-filled eyes. The woman gave her a box of tissues.

"You could pretend you have a bad cold. A lot of people do in April." That was the first time she had spoken since she had ushered Marsha into her master's presence.

"Please," Ferenc said, as they pulled into the airport, "you must not worry. Everything has been taken care of." The two men emerged from the front seat and unloaded her fake luggage. One of them held the door for her. "Next time, perhaps, we shall meet in a more relaxed atmosphere," Ferenc said as he lifted Marsha's hand to his lips and kissed it.

The gesture fitted the absurdity of the situation.

"Just one more thing," he said. "You will please remember that you have chosen yourself as the publisher. It was you who pursued the manuscript."

"I know," Marsha said.

"Ah, but what a wonderful choice you have turned out to be."

When he said "wonderful," he sounded exactly like Bela Lugosi.

Thirty

PLAYING THE DEDICATED tourist was easy. Judith had planned the day with earnest precision. At 9:15 they took the subway to The Battery and boarded the Staten Island ferry at 10:00. The Statue of Liberty came out of the rising fog, on cue, as the ferry passed. The sun caught the last of the soft cloud around its feet and all across the bay; the clammy morning drizzle gave way to a gaudy rainbow. Anne exposed two rolls of film uninterrupted by Judith's cautionary tales about the cost. Jimmy hurled invective at the curious gulls.

Anne had loved the subway graffiti, the hard slate-gray seats, the torn posters, the seedy peeling walls—a world away from Toronto's squeaky-clean, cheerful subway cars.

For lunch they bought sloppy hamburgers to eat in Central Park. There were jugglers and mime artists, sidewalk painters, a clown, crowds of roller skaters, ponies, a pet monkey collecting money into a battered hat.

"Is someone following us?" Anne asked once.

"No, why?"

"You're looking over your shoulder again."

"Nervous habit I picked up the day before yesterday."

From time to time they brought up the kidnapping, but no one wanted to spoil the day and Judith had reassured them the police department was searching for the kidnappers. The children were easily distracted.

They returned to the apartment at 2:00. Anne had a headache, Jimmy was happy to rest. Judith said she had to run an errand for Marsha. While she was away, they were not to answer the phone or open the door for anyone.

Judith listened outside while they triple-locked the door, and tipped the doorman ten dollars to allow no one into Miss Hillier's apartment: not even deliveries.

Carefree, she thought, affecting a jaunty walk around the rim of Gramercy Park. Then a quick cab ride uptown to Saks Fifth Avenue. She went directly to the Chloé counter and purchased a scented hand cream; up the escalator for a brisk browse in women's fashions, down again through scarves and hosiery. Frequently she found herself ducking behind mannequins, to see if someone had followed her. A quick tour of some of the best costume jewelry in the world, then outside and into a passing cab.

"Bloomingdale's, please," she said once they were moving.

She went directly to the second floor and selected two Céline summer dresses, fresh from Paris with matching prices. Watching over her shoulder, she walked to the changing rooms. They were still on the right of the counter, thank god, near the Ladies' Powder Room.

Room two was empty.

Marsha had brought Judith here on her birthday three years ago and invited her to select a dress she liked. There had been one condition: Judith was not to check the price tag. The black and beige silk Chanel had transformed her into a woman of slick social grace. She could still hear Marsha's deep-throated laugh as she surveyed her in her new finery. Judith had called the outfit her "armor." It gave her confidence in unfriendly situations.

Inside the dressing room Judith told the solicitous attendant she preferred to undress alone. She stood gazing encouragingly at her own gently-lit reflection in the full-length mirror, and waited.

All day she had been puzzling over Marsha's instructions about what she had to tell David and how. Judith had derived the strong impression that David was a pipeline of information to those who had directed the killers. Then Marsha had suggested Judith play the tourist quite openly and added that Judith should consider a shopping spree: "Perhaps another *suit of armor* to fend off your amorous policeman. Only three hundred dollars at today's prices."

At BSS they had often met after curfew outside the school walls. It had been fun making secret arrangements during dinner. They had used dollars to indicate the time and special references to things they had done together to mark the place.

She had been sure Marsha had been trying to tell her something she didn't want others to hear. As soon as she recognized the code for the time, she had only to remember the elegant suit of armor and where it had come from.

Judith held up one of the dresses and surveyed herself in the mirror. The mauve frills clashed with her hair. The other was simpler, gray, but not her style. She regretted she hadn't taken a closer look—if she was going to stand around in this room, she might as well try them on.

There was a rustling sound outside, a footstep.

"Judith?"

Marsha's voice, in a soft whisper. Judith whipped the curtain aside and stared at the unfamiliar black-haired woman outside.

"Marsha?" she said uncertainly, trying to discern the eyes behind the dark glasses.

"Thank god you came," Marsha whispered, pushing past her into the dressing room. She dropped the armful of clothes she had been carrying, pulled the curtain shut behind her, took off her glasses, and embraced Judith.

"I was afraid you wouldn't understand. And even if you did, I couldn't be sure you'd come...all you've been through with the kids..."

"Of course I came," Judith said into the soft wig. "It took a while to figure out what you meant..."

"I made it up on the spur of the moment... Back then I didn't even know why I wanted you to come. Now I need your help."

"What's happened?"

"Far too much to explain. We have four or five minutes left. After that I expect they'll come in here to see why I'm taking so long."

"Who will?"

"Two men The Dealer sent to look after me."

"What?"

"They haven't left my side. They were on the plane yesterday and we spent last night in a hotel room, all three of us. They've given me ten minutes alone to change and right now I should be trying on a dress." Marsha started to slough off her crumpled jogging suit. "Did anyone follow you?"

"No. At least I don't think so."

"Good. But you'll have to be doubly careful now. Take a number of cabs. Better start going downtown, then double back." Marsha was wriggling into a beige dress.

"I've had some practice recently. But why am I playing hide-and-seek again?"

"You'll be carrying part of The Dealer's manuscript with you. Can you zip up the back?"

"I don't think I want to," Judith said, zipping up the dress. "If you want to publish it—OK, but..."

"The manuscript contains irrefutable proof that two influential citizens of this country, together with an Englishman, are conspiring to change the course of history. They have decided on our behalf that the world cannot afford democracy and are perilously close to achieving their target." Marsha was trying on another dress. The beige one had a plunging neckline that revealed all there was of her small breasts.

"Why don't you leave this to the CIA or MI5?"

"There isn't time. And I believe The Dealer when he says the agencies wouldn't let this material be published."

"What do you want me to do?"

Marsha tightened her new belt. The black silk dress suited her new hair.

"It'll have to do," she said, glaring at her own reflection, before taking a thin portion of the manuscript out of her blue canvas bag. "I sorted this on the airplane. Take it to 77 East 61st Street. Leave it with the receptionist on the fourth floor for Mr. Sankey. Ask her to give you an envelope and address it. S-A-N-K-E-Y."

Judith was still reluctant.

"Who's Sankey?"

"A writer—reporter, really. He's a possible solution. Or at least a kind of insurance."

Judith took the manuscript and began to read the first page. Marsha adjusted her hair, put on the glasses and her raincoat.

"At 3:45, meet me in front of the New York Restaurant on 54th, east of Fifth. I'll be loitering outside."

"Why?"

"We're going to M & A with the rest of the damned manuscript."

"And if you don't show up?"

"I will," Marsha said with conviction. "Those two guys are professionals." She turned to hug Judith again. "Wait at least five minutes till I'm gone. I'll have to go to the shoe department with the guards. Can't wear Adidas with the dress."

"Be careful," Judith said, sitting on the low stool. She began to read the minutes of BREAD's fifteenth meeting at which they had resolved to remove the last vestiges of US influence in the Middle East. As she scanned the detailed plans for defeating the Jewish lobby, a number of photographs slipped out from between the pages.

"May I be of some assistance?" the polite voice asked from the other side of the curtain.

Quickly, Judith gathered up the manuscript and pictures.

"Thank you. No. Thank you."

She stuffed the manuscript into her shirt and pants, put on her coat and left, holding her purse close to her chest. She apologized to the attendants for not purchasing anything, while making sure Marsha and her escort were nowhere in sight.

She took a cab to Madison and 28th. She took another to Times Square; another to 5th and 62nd. She walked two blocks in the wrong direction, ducked into a drugstore, bought a copy of *Life* and some cigarettes, doubled back on the other side of the street to 61st. Once she was in the elevator she extracted the package and placed it between the middle pages of *Life*.

Sankey's bored receptionist grudgingly handed her an envelope. Judith stuffed the manuscript inside and left it, with a note taped to the top: "Mr. Sankey: top priority."

She reached the corner of 54th with a minute to spare, but Marsha was already there, flapping her hands in an old-fashioned wave. *So now she's trying to draw attention to herself?*

"Where are they?" Judith asked when she drew up to Marsha.

"Gone," Marsha said. "I think their mission is completed. Did you reach Sankey?"

"Not in person. But I delivered the package. How is this mission completed if the book isn't published?"

"Come on," Marsha said, her voice higher than usual. She put her arm through Judith's and started to walk rapidly toward Fifth Avenue.

"It's almost over, or I've got it all wrong."

They entered the lobby through the side doors at the corner of Fifth, hurried past the stores and into an elevator.

"I sure hope you're right," Judith said. "Much more of this and I'm going to need a therapist."

Marsha took off her wig, shook loose her long blonde hair and stretched.

"Maybe they'll give us group rates. And one more thing: next time you come across a big story, would you please call somebody else?"

On the twentieth floor the receptionist greeted Marsha with a broad grin.

"Himself will be a little surprised to see you so soon," she said. "Only yesterday he sent a memo around saying you'd be in London another week." She looked quizzically at Judith.

"She's with me," said Marsha. "We're going to see Larry."

"He's got someone with him." But they were already on their way, past the accounting department, marketing, the plants decorating the door to the boardroom.

"Are you sure you want me to come along?" Judith asked, hanging back.

"All the way," Marsha said. "Or don't you want to meet the incomparable Mr. Shapiro?"

Larry's secretary was on the phone when they entered. She looked up, smiled, and cupped the receiver with one hand.

"So early?" she asked. "He's been anxious about you."

Larry's office was larger than Judith's house and a lot brighter, with a comforting wall-to-wall green plush carpet, low bookshelves, framed book-jackets and plaques for excellence in design on the walls. On a side table, a framed *Time* cover.

Larry sat behind his solid oak desk, leaning on his elbows, listening with exaggerated attention to the motionless man who sat facing him. Larry jumped to his feet.

"Well," he said, glancing at his watch, "punctual as ever. No. Actually, you're a touch early. I've been trying to reach you. We've been calling your hotel. And there's no one at your apartment." His shiny head bobbed up and down in excitement. "I was hoping to talk to you alone...before..." Then he noticed Judith. "Who's this?"

Marsha introduced them.

"What does she have to do with..." Larry hesitated "... all this." He indicated the chair, whose occupant hadn't moved. But now he stood up. A slender, elegant figure in cool charcoal gray, he turned and surveyed the two women with an expression of grave interest. He took a step toward them, hesitated, leaning on the back of his chair with one hand, then, drawing his shoulders up with obvious effort, he advanced again.

"I should like to introduce," Larry said with overwhelming formality, "Mr. Ethan George MacMurty, the next governor of Massachusetts." He looked at Marsha, then at MacMurty, then again at Marsha.

He was taller than Marsha remembered, and grayer, his hair almost white at the temples, his long sideburns completely white. His eyes were warm brown ovals, the skin on his face sallow.

"Miss Hillier...Mrs. Hayes, I'm glad to meet you." He stretched out a big, friendly hand, the kind Judith had always trusted. His palm was hard and dry, his fingers encircled Judith's hand completely.

"Do you still take an interest in toys?" she asked.

"Alas, my dear," MacMurty said, sadly, "I no longer have time to play. The world around us has turned far too serious— wouldn't you say, Miss Hillier?" His voice was deep and resonant, with a slight Boston twang that reminded Judith of the Kennedys.

"And rather dangerous," Marsha said. "Especially for publishers. You and your friends have been thorough."

"Apparently not," he said. "Since I am here as a supplicant."

"Perhaps we should all sit down," Larry said, attempting to take charge. "Then we can review our options." He was fussing with the broad leather chairs around his checkerboard coffee table. "Mr. MacMurty has explained to me some of the implications..."

"Did you know when I would be back?" Marsha interrupted, turning to MacMurty.

"No. I wasn't expecting you till later. I assumed you had unfinished business in London. Lawyers…"

Larry tried to usher Judith into one of the chairs. She wondered why Marsha looked so pleased at the mention of lawyers. That was part of the information she had given David. *Why* would David have agreed to work for them? Money?

Marsha sat with her blue canvas bag on her knees, waiting.

"Lawyers usually take such a long time," MacMurty sat, heavily, next to Judith.

"What implications?" Marsha asked.

"I don't think we have time to review all the details, Miss Hillier. I have explained our position to Mr. Shapiro. Our lawyers have drawn up the documents to prevent you from publishing this libelous material—and libelous it is, I think you will agree. I also have reason to believe you will have great difficulty proving the veracity of your 'author.'" He said the word with disgust. "I have told Mr. Shapiro some of the known facts about this 'author' of yours—a vicious, reptilic creature not likely to desert his natural habitat to be a witness in your libel action…"

"His name?" Larry asked Marsha.

"Ferenc Jozsef," she said.

"How much did you learn about him?" MacMurty asked, his brown eyes small pinpoints.

"We were not there to discuss him," Marsha said.

"I would have thought, Miss Hillier, that one of the primary rules of your profession is to check the credibility of a source. Perhaps this one would not have mentioned *his* primary profession, which is blackmail and murder? Did he tell you about his gang of assassins? About his personal responsibility for several hundred deaths?"

Marsha held her bag closer. She had already guessed Ferenc was prepared to trade in whatever came his way.

"Human life," MacMurty went on, "is of no importance to him. Mine isn't, yours isn't. Karen Poole's wasn't, and she had been an associate of his. Her mangled body was found under the Northern Express. Did he tell you about Floud and Oleg Lyalin, Herbert Norman, Alfred Johnson and Leonid Zaitsev? I expect not, or you might have backed away from him. And perhaps he didn't mention that his modest share of the international arms trade is worth $40 million? That he thrives on others' hardships? That he has supplied tanks and handguns to the Iraqis, French military equipment to the Argentines, F-4 fighters to Iran? Peace is bad for his business." MacMurty's finger stabbed at the air, emphasizing each word.

"Yes," Marsha said after a moment. "Yes, that could all be true, but it wouldn't change the substance of the manuscript."

"Don't you see he is using you, that you have become one of his pawns? That the publication of this pack of contrived lies would serve his ends and his alone?"

Marsha shook her head.

"He is counting on your natural gullibility, and, forgive me for saying so, your greed. Surely you are not going to believe what a rabid warmongering son-of-a-bitch tells you? You are not going to publish that garbage?"

"We have hardly had time to review this..." Larry said. "We haven't even..."

"He has proof," Marsha said, quietly. "You know that. You have collected up the other copies of the manuscript..."

"And killed in order to do so," Judith said. "Whatever your purpose is, you cannot justify that. And you kidnapped..."

"We have not harmed you," MacMurty said with a sigh, "I made sure of that. We are not violent men, not killers. That's the point, Mrs. Hayes. We are men of peace." He sounded tired.

"The question is," said Marsha, waving aside his protestations, "not who wrote the manuscript, but whether the information it contains is accurate, and, if it is, whether it should be published. And I believe the only effective way to fight you and your friends is the one The Dealer has chosen: publication. People have the right to know they have been manipulated. They have the right to choose."

"Even if they choose their own destruction?"

"Even then."

"And you are fool enough to believe that the political-military complex would actually allow them a choice? Has there ever been a plebiscite to determine whether people consider personal liberty to be worth the risk of extinction? Were we asked our opinion before our leaders wired our planet for destruction? That one brutal, absurd fact is ample justification for what we are doing. We are righting the balance, don't you see? Giving the world another chance. For a few hundred thousand dollars in profit you want to sacrifice our work for universal peace?"

"The price of your peace is too high," Marsha said very softly. "And I am not infallible enough to want to join you in playing God."

"That's your last word?" MacMurty asked.

MacMurty rose slowly. He walked to the center of the room, turned and looked at Marsha.

"Yes," she said.

"There are several ways of playing God, Miss Hillier. The United States might have avoided the role and sat out the last war. Roosevelt might have struck the Japanese before they struck Pearl Harbor. Or we might have bombed the Khmer Rouge before they committed genocide. Each act of intervention has its own consequences, as does each act of acquiescence. We are responsible for what we don't do as much as for what we do. Please remember that."

Without a backward glance, his shoulders bent, eyes fixed on the floor ahead, MacMurty strode from the room.

"Well," Larry said gruffly. "I think I have been excessively patient. Now perhaps you'll reward me with an explanation?"

Marsha took the manuscript from her bag.

"It's all in the top ten pages. A summary," she said wearily. Two nights without sleep were starting to take their toll.

"Fantastic," Larry said after a while. "Our legal department will have a bird."

"Call them in—and production, warehouse, marketing. Let's set the machine in motion, though I doubt we'll ever get far enough to need them. Is the contract ready?"

"Sure." Larry was still reading. "What do you mean you doubt..."

"The check?"

"Uhhum. It's incredible they would..."

"Do you still have that school pal at the CIA? The one who promised you his memoirs?"

"Yes."

"Call him. Tell him to come right over. Bring some of his colleagues. Whatever they do when something big comes up."

"My god, the details. Marsha, you *do* have the documents?"

"I know where they are. Larry, will you call?"

"Shit, Marsha, we'll have it on the street by Wednesday next. It will make *The Pentagon Papers* look like a Literary Guild Alternate. Millions of copies. Serial rights. International..."

"I know," Marsha said. "But we won't live till next Wednesday if you don't call the CIA and get them over here. That's the mistake the others made: thinking they were indestructible."

Larry picked up the phone and dialed.

"It used to be such a genteel business," he said.

Marsha grinned.

"You don't know the half of it." She perched on the edge of Larry's desk and looked over the contract. Judith went back to reading the manuscript.

Larry was still on the phone explaining, when Jane knocked.

"An envelope for Miss Hillier," she said, advancing on Marsha. "A man brought it to reception. He was insistent you would want to see it right away. He is waiting downstairs."

Marsha tore open the yellow envelope. There was a piece of yellow lined notepaper inside.

"Damn," Marsha yelled. "He's nothing if not consistent." She pushed the paper, with its pretty rounded handwriting, toward Judith.

My dear Marsha,

After much thought, I have decided to withdraw my manuscript and all publishing rights from your esteemed Company. Fact is, I've had a better offer.

Yours,

The Dealer

Thirty-One

PETER BURNETT HAD BEEN waiting anxiously in the telephone booth for ten minutes, reading names in the directories, pen at the ready, presenting an appearance of frustrated determination. He had never before been kept so long.

As soon as the call came, he flung open the door and walked briskly toward Marble Arch, picked up a newspaper from the corner vendor and headed for the Underground. At Oxford Circus he switched to the Bakerloo line, heading south to Waterloo Station, the route he always took.

Anthony's chauffeur met him on the steps. He had been standing by the kiosk eating a chocolate bar, wearing slacks and a sweater, not his uniform. The Rolls, its rear curtains drawn, was parked around the corner from the old Union Jack Club.

"I'm very sorry about the delay, Peter," Anthony Billingsworth-Powell said when Peter eased into the back seat next to him. "An unusually hectic day, the meeting ran late, and I must be on my way to Heathrow. I believe you will find all of this in order." He extracted a file from his briefcase and handed it to Peter. "I have signed agreements from nine. The four others will come along, but I don't believe you'll need them. The resolution from the Executive Committee will go forward to the Board next Friday. You will note that I neither moved nor seconded the motion for your nomination."

He knocked on the window and the Rolls pulled away from the curb, heading toward Blackfriars Road.

"Thank you," said Peter quietly, as he leafed through the sheaf of papers. A sheet near the top reported that it had been duly moved by Frank Russell and seconded by Anthony Billingsworth-Powell.

AND RESOLVED
THAT on behalf of all members of the Hamilton, Thornbush Corporation, the Directors record their great sorrow at the death of Mr. Eric Sandwell, a member of this Board and managing director of the Company. Mr. Sandwell was at the helm of the Company through a period which saw the Company grow spectacularly and mature to the important and diversified organization it is today.

As well as for his achievements in publishing, he will be remembered for his personal qualities. He was a man of consummate integrity...

"I am deeply sorry about Eric Sandwell," Anthony said quickly.

Peter closed the folder, resting his hand over it as the car accelerated. He was staring out the window.

"You will assume the title of managing director after the meeting, and be responsible for the complete operation. As well,

I have drawn another hundred shares for you from my personal portfolio. They are numbered, and not identified in any manner that would connect them directly with me. They were delivered to your lawyer's office this afternoon."

"There was no need for that," Peter said, still gazing out the window.

"I know. I am also not unaware of your reluctance to benefit in this way. However, I felt it important to give you more voting power than the office itself will bestow. There isn't much time, we're coming back to the station. Please listen carefully."

For the first time since entering the car, Peter faced Anthony. It wasn't easy to force himself to look him in the eye.

Anthony leaned forward and turned toward Peter.

"You have worked with me for ten years now, and I know you understand the importance of our effort. Should we, for any reason whatever, be unable to continue, I want you to carry on for me here, make contact with your counterparts in other countries and rebuild whatever may have been destroyed. I have placed a book in a locker at Waterloo Station. It is self-explanatory and will give you all the information you'll require. This is the key to the locker." He handed Peter a small, round-headed key. "I hope you will not need it..."

Thirty-Two

THE BREAD MANIFESTO made the front page of the *New York Times* on April 23. It ran with a page-width headline, right under the banner, and it occupied more than half the page. There were photographs of Ethan MacMurty, Nelson Roberts Jr., and Anthony Billingsworth-Powell at Harvard, class of 1965; at Nassau, Ocean View, March 1984; in London 1972; and at the locations of three other reunions. There was a recent photograph of the MacMurty family celebrating the announcement of Ethan's candidacy for governor of Massachusetts. The story turned to page two subheaded "Peace without Honor," and again to section two with more photographs. The Manifesto was reproduced, small but legible, as were copies of the staff hiring criteria drawn up on June 1,

1967, and the resolution of March 15, setting the terms for the proposal to the USSR Supreme Soviet.

None of the principals was available for comment. Anthony Billingsworth-Powell was on a business trip to Prague. His office claimed he had gone to Czechoslovakia to purchase pulp for his European papers. Sir George, his father, interviewed on the steps of the Upper Chamber, said he considered the allegations preposterous, their origins probably linked to his son's competitors in the United States.

Nelson Roberts Jr. was at his ranch in Wyoming. A spokesman for Mr. Roberts had informed the reporter that Mr. Roberts would be taking legal action against the paper. An injunction was being sought to bar the London *Times* from running the story.

There was a photograph of Ethan MacMurty entering his Central Park South condominium building at midnight last night, holding up a folded newspaper to shield his face from the camera.

The byline was Anthony Sankey's.

"It makes a hell of a story," Judith said wistfully. "Though I could have made it more exciting. It lacks flesh and blood—and sympathy."

"It would've made a hell of a book, too," Marsha said, her arm over Judith's shoulder. "But you've got to give them credit for speed. Tony wouldn't have picked up the package till 3:30 p.m. on Monday. He enjoys long lunches. After the initial shock, he would have talked to his editor, his lawyer, the research department to check known facts, teamed up with his colleagues for a review, met with the editor-in-chief and the publisher, more lawyers, more checkers. It takes a lot of courage to run a story like this one; everyone would be in on the decision. And once he was given the green light, he still had to write it. All that in less than two days."

They had been sitting around the dining room table in Marsha's apartment eating a breakfast of scrambled eggs and toast, waiting for *The Times* to be delivered. The children were still asleep, as was the young man called Bob whom Larry's CIA friend had assigned to stay close to them while the Agency's people mulled over the information they now had. The Dealer's man had demanded the manuscript back, and without a contract to publish, they couldn't hold it. Without the supporting documents, they had no proof.

Marsha had expected Ferenc to send for the rest of his property, but she hadn't heard from him.

"He thrives on never doing the expected," Bob had said. "Nurtures his own aura of mystery. And if he has sold out elsewhere, you can be sure he's already collected his fee and moved to a new location. He never stays in the same place longer than a week."

She hadn't told them where the documents were. Though she was sure the CIA would use them to remove Roberts, MacMurty and Billingsworth-Powell from their positions of influence, she did not believe they would cause the information to be published. And if there was one opinion she shared with Ferenc, it was his assessment that the Agency would find other uses for the documents.

"I guess this will put them back on regular duty, whatever that is for the CIA," Judith said. She was shaking the young man on the couch to wake him.

"I think you'll want to read this," she said, when he sat up.

Bob stared at the front page of the paper in disbelief.

"The boss isn't going to like this much. No, sir," he said, shaking his head.

As it turned out, Marsha's boss didn't like it any better: Larry phoned in a rage.

"You," he yelled at Marsha, "what the hell gives you the right to make a decision like that? You set me up like an idiot. Not once, but twice. First you harass me to publish some goddamn book you already know isn't ever going to be published. Then you use me to involve the CIA and you don't even level with them. What kind of game are you playing?"

He didn't really listen to her explanation. In the middle, he hung up.

"Perhaps you could write it out for him," Judith suggested. "He didn't sound like he was taking it in."

The next call was for Bob. He said yes about a dozen times, then handed the phone to Marsha.

"Like I told you—he's not happy. He wants to speak to you," he said.

"How," asked the voice, "did you get that stuff to Sankey?" Marsha told him.

"You must have known, then, long before you saw his note, that The Dealer wasn't going to let you publish."

"I didn't know. I suspected."

"Why?"

"Instinct, I guess. It was the fulsome way he went on talking about democracy—as though he had just converted to a new religion. And there was something about his signet ring. I started to think about whether lions ever change their true nature. He enjoyed calling himself The Dealer—that was his true nature. He'd be looking for the best deal. I began to suspect he was using me as a lever. As he had used the other publishers. None of them had been intended to publish either."

"Looks like he may have the last laugh, though. He has already collected $5 million from Billingsworth-Powell, and $2 million from MacMurty. *And* he's got the story published. Score one, net two. He *is* consistent. It's you that worries me."

"When did he get paid?"

"As far as we can tell, while MacMurty was in Larry's office. He must have known he couldn't change your mind. Still, it was worth a try."

The doorman buzzed to announce that a Mr. Allan Goodman was downstairs, hoping to be let in.

"It's all right," Judith told the young agent. "A friend from Toronto, and he's almost like one of you. He works for the government."

Anne and Jimmy came out of the guest room. Since they had discovered their role in the story, they had become too excited to sleep. Jimmy was particularly fond of their protection.

"I've always wanted to meet a real live agent," he told Bob. "What's it like crossing swords with the KGB all the time?"

"Gets kinda boring after a while," Bob said. He turned to Marsha who had now put the phone down. "I guess he didn't give you a rough time, after all. He likes people with guts."

Judith found it encouraging to see Allan standing in the doorway. He looked bright and cheerful in his dapper brown suit, his neat polished shoes, the beige handkerchief tucked into his jacket pocket, his air of having been firmly planted on the planet for a purpose. She had needed some reminder that not so long ago she had been leading a normal life.

"I see the whole gang is here," he said scanning the room. "And who is that?" he asked, raising his eyebrows toward Bob, who had held the door open with one hand, palming his holstered gun with the other.

Marsha told him. It didn't dampen his spirits when Bob insisted on searching him for weapons.

"It's the patting down I really like," he said, but Bob didn't laugh. He'd probably heard that one already.

"You two have had yourselves quite a day." Allan waved his folded copy of *The New York Times*. "All that's missing is the proper credits. Why didn't they quote the sources?"

"They didn't know," Marsha said.

"Wise."

Allan asked for coffee and toast.

"They don't serve you breakfast on the red-eye special from Toronto anymore."

Anne and Jimmy were still devouring the newspaper and Marsha had turned up the television to hear what the newsmen were making of the story. Allan joined Judith in the kitchen, where she was boiling water for coffee.

"It's wonderful to see you," Judith said.

"Glad to be of service. Not too many opportunities left for short errant knights in armor to polish up their tricks." He patted her hand gently. "You've been through a lot." He wanted to know everything she could tell him about the manuscript, The Dealer, why Marsha hadn't published the book. "Soon enough," he said, "it'll probably become classified information."

"I don't suppose this is just personal interest?" Judith asked suspiciously.

"It isn't," he said. "Though it started out as that. I wanted to make sure it was safe for you to come home again. After all, I can't afford to keep you in New York forever—not on my salary."

"I'll pay you back," Judith protested.

"Only kidding."

"And *is* it safe for me to come home?"

"It should be. After you called I went to see the Attorney General for Ontario. It seems he's known about the manuscript for some two weeks. George Harris's lawyer sent a copy to the RCMP the Friday before you last saw George. He wanted confirmation of its authenticity, I think, though he now says his motives were those of a good citizen. The RCMP didn't pay a whole lot of attention till Harris died. Then they began their own investigation, running more or less parallel with yours. One of their men was even assigned to watch over you, a sort of guardian angel."

"Where was he when I needed him?"

"That one night he thought it safe to leave you unattended. You may have forgotten since, my dear, but that Monday night you spent in the company of one of Toronto's finest—a Detective Inspector Parr, who professes to have some personal interest of his own in your affairs."

"You've talked to David?"

"Not directly. Policemen are several departments below mine—no offense, still kidding. The good Detective Inspector didn't know about the RCMP involvement till he began his own investigation and literally ran into them while tracking Adrian Hall's mom. Then they ordered him off the case. Too many cooks, and all that."

"Does he know about the kidnapping?"

Allan shrugged.

"He knows something's screwy because the RCMP have asked him a lot of questions about you. They were expecting trouble. In fact, the night you apparently called him from

Sibelius Park he came with an RCMP chap, in case you were about to reveal something the RCMP ought to know…"

"The same man who'd shadowed me before?" Judith interrupted, thinking of the creased face behind the wheel of the sedan.

"Your guardian angel—and a damned sight more experienced than the young CIA man out there. Still, he hadn't expected the kidnapping. It was you they were concerned for, not the children."

"Do they know who kidnapped them?"

"Yes and no. They arrested the man who followed you to the airport. He hasn't admitted anything, but the police know he was also at the Rosedale subway station the night Harris was killed."

"Which one was he?"

"Muller. Parr knew him instantly. He chain-smokes. The other kidnapper was Mrs. Hall. Embarrassing as it has proved for my colleague, Adrian, his mother has been MacMurty's cat's-paw in Canada. She's been a prominent peacenik since Hiroshima—met MacMurty around 1970 and has worked for him ever since. Adrian knew she was deeply involved in the peace movement, but he thought she'd joined some version of Moral Rearmament. All along she probably believed she was acting in the public good."

"When she kidnapped my children?"

"They weren't harmed."

"When she killed Harris, then?"

"We don't think she actually pushed him. But she did organize the group on the platform. All but the young girl—she was cover. The police have had her in for questioning and let her go."

"Who *did* push him?"

"They think Muller. Does it matter? Mrs. Hall put them up to it. She paid off two of them; two others work for her; the girl was incidental."

"And the Jamaican woman? Did Mrs. Hall arrange that too?"

"That's the assumption. Though there is no proof. No witnesses have volunteered yet."

Marsha came in, flapping her arms and waving at the living room. "It's all over CBS. Don't you want to see it? You two have been cooped up in here for ages. What's going on?"

"Don't you feel just a little bit guilty?" Allan asked her lightly.

Marsha hovered uncertainly for a moment.

"Yes," she said. "They may have meant well, but I didn't feel I had a choice."

Allan nodded.

"Why didn't David tell me he was with an RCMP man? I thought..." Judith was still struggling to accept what she had heard.

"I suppose because you didn't ask," Allan said.

Judith turned to Marsha.

"Wait a minute. Didn't you tell me The Dealer was using the RCMP to leak information to MacMurty and the others?"

"He said they were the thinnest security service in the world. But he said a lot of things..."

"Isn't that how MacMurty knew you had left copies of the documents in London?" Judith persisted. "That was the information I passed to David, which he was to convey to the Mounties..."

"The Dealer had so many ways to let them know. I think he set that up to make me think I was safer than I was. The six copies of the manuscript were never delivered to those lawyers. Does it matter, now?"

"It would to the Justice Department," Allan ventured, "but as for me, I'd rather have the toast you promised, and jam if you can spare some."

"Me, too," Jimmy said, slouching in the doorway in his tough-guy pose. "Or don't we rate breakfast today?"

Thirty-Three

"COVER ONE IS, primarily, a selling surface. An attention-grabber. There's no point trying to force it to tell the story. It's a waste of effort. It is most effective when it has nothing whatso-ever to do with the story. Content is not a serious consideration. Content will only interfere with what we are trying to do here. Our job is to sell the book. This cover will be up there among a wallfull of paperbacks. It will occupy only one pocket out of five hundred. What will make it stand out?

"The casual browser sure as hell isn't going to pick a book up because the author has a way with words. I don't want to hear that the author's prose is 'breathtaking, spare, witty, delightful.' Let the reviewers do that. I want a cover which will leap off that wall and land in your hands."

David Markham looked around the room. He had been addressing one of Marsha's new recruits, a fiction editor fresh out of Farrar, Straus who had taken her editorial training seriously. She still believed in stories.

"Cover four," Markham went on, "is a horse of a different color. By the time the buyer has turned the book around to see what it's about, you've got his attention. Now, sell him! Tell him it's the best read he'll ever have. Tell him to grab it and run. But don't tell the goddam story. If you tell him the story now, why would he layout $3.95 to read it?"

Marsha searched the room for signs of life. There were sixteen people around the small boardroom table. At least ten, including the copy chief, the art director, the man from production and the guys from the wholesale division, had heard this speech half a dozen times. Marsha knew that Lynda Manning, who seemed to pay rapt attention to every word, could do a lively imitation of Markham delivering it. Yet nobody interrupted. No one told him to shove it. The two weeks Marsha had been away were apparently long enough for Markham to have been appointed VP, but surely not long enough for him to be taken seriously.

"What I'm telling you, Jaquie," Markham went on enthusiastically, "is that you're wasting our time with all this bullshit about what the author's intent was and how brilliant the book is. Plot summaries, dear, are purely for Eng. Lit. courses. This," he waved his arm around to include everyone, "is a cover conference."

Marsha took a deep breath. If she was to retain the remnants of her power and rebuild the edifice, she would have to challenge the little bastard. It couldn't wait until tomorrow. She had already lost too much ground.

"For example," Markham continued, "if I were to present this book..."

"Point is, though, you're not." Marsha jumped in with both feet. She'd work on her strategy as she went. "And *I* want to hear the end of the story."

"What?" Markham flashed.

"I said I want to hear the end of the story. Your cover theories I've heard before. The story is new, so let her tell it, will you?"

"With due respect, Marsha, I don't see how that will help us find a cover. We need to establish the market, the angle, the audience..."

"Listening to the story might help."

"Trouble is we ought to know all that before we buy. Not try to figure it out at cover conferences."

Marsha sighed theatrically.

"I believe I'm still in charge of the buying and your job is to sell. Or are you planning to join the editorial department?"

Markham threw his pencil down in disgust but didn't say anything. Marsha turned to the young editor from Farrar.

"Let's get on with it, Jaquie," she said softly.

Lynda Manning grinned. The art director made vigorous strokes with his broad-tipped felt marker. Fred Mancuso blew his nose loudly. Round one to Hillier.

Jaquie finished her presentation. They decided on a *French Lieutenant's Woman* type of approach, a cover painting. A serious woman's novel—"so we might as well go to the heart of the market and evoke an all-around classic," Marsha summed up. "Next one on the list is *The Mission Conspiracy*. Is that title firm?"

The editor shook his head in despair.

"I tried to change it, but the author wouldn't. Says his mother likes it. Really."

"There's been a glut of conspiracy books," Marsha said. "Don't you think people are getting tired of being threatened?"

Markham joined in again.

"I think it's got something," he mused. "Mission has a religious note, brings in a whole different perspective."

Marsha tuned out. She was still recovering from a major bout of conspiracies. She had been debriefed and briefed by a host of self-proclaimed guardians of US society, dogmatic and humorless, each in turn satisfied by the rich array of justification for his growing paranoia about the media and Soviet intervention in America.

Earlier this morning Bob had finally left, though Marsha still felt watched and followed, no doubt with reason.

There was to be a Senate investigation into all the activities of Nelson Roberts Jr. and Ethan MacMurty. A law regarding ownership boundaries in communications had been hastily drawn up. The Committee wanted to call Ferenc Jozsef but could not find him. There was talk of a big public trial for treason that would center the debate on what the three had done and why. There had been more stories, photographs, editorials and arguments by learned and ignorant panelists.

Nelson Roberts's application to enjoin further publication of excerpts from the Manifesto, the minutes of meetings and the diary had not been granted.

BREAD jokes were in at fashionable parties.

Anthony Billingsworth-Powell had not returned from Prague. In a televised interview with a stringer from the Associated Press he had expressed only grief that he couldn't. He declared loyalty to his country and its people. He hoped that his wife and grown children would be able to visit him in Czechoslovakia while he made plans for his own future.

Marsha's name had not been linked with the revelations surrounding BREAD, but Judith had asked if the two of them could spend a few days in Eleuthera in early May and discuss the possibility of Judith's writing a long magazine piece out of the story. As usual, Judith was short of money, and this time she wanted a real holiday without borrowed provisions. "Has sudden fame ever harmed a woman of my age?" she had asked Marsha.

Romance had certainly been healthy for her. David Parr had arrived in New York the same day Allan Goodman left.

Judith reported that Jimmy was about to start talking to him. The accumulated bribes of badges, earrings, bubblegum and tickets to the last Stones concert were beginning to take their toll. Now it was Anne who was putting up resistance. She thought it dishonest for David to buy Jimmy's tolerance.

Marsha herself thought Allan a more suitable companion for Judith. He was friendly, funny and realistic about himself. But the past few weeks had suggested to her that she, herself, was a mediocre judge of men's potential.

Marsha had not yet returned Jerry's keys to her apartment. Maybe she never would.

There had been a letter from Peter Burnett. It came with the package Marsha had inadvertently left at his house the night she drove back to London: the tiny porcelain elephant. She had made it the centerpiece of her collection, even though its happy, turned-up trunk had not yet brought her luck.

"You'll be glad to know," Peter said in his letter, "that Jane MacIntyre has decided not to take advantage of her early retirement privileges. She has returned on a part-time basis..."

About the manuscript he said that, on reflection, he regretted not having told her more. He had thought she would abandon the project once the leads ran dry. While he understood what she had done, he would have chosen, and indeed did choose, a different path. There was no evil comparable to the evil of global nuclear war...

Marsha had never mentioned Peter's involvement to her various questioners. Let the CIA track him down for themselves, if they had to find the London connection.

Fitzgibbon & Harris, together with the feisty Alice Roy, had been sold to Douglas & McIntyre.

Marsha's mother had sent a note and an invitation to her annual May 3 garden party in Boston. To make sure she had focused Marsha's attention, she hinted that Jerzy Kosinski and John Irving were both expected, as well as the crème de la crème of Boston society, several senators, and an assembly of congressmen. Maybe the president would make it this year.

Marsha should buy a new outfit—something outrageously expensive but understated.

Eleuthera with Judith sounded much more attractive.

"Marsha," David Markham said loudly. Then, again: "Marsha," in a voice as sweet as molasses, "perhaps you could tell us what *you* think."

Damn. There was nothing on the table to give her a hint of what they had been talking about. No leads propped up against the window. She tried to see the art director's pad, but it was too far away. Everyone was looking at her—some expectantly, a few sympathetically, but mainly they looked embarrassed. No doubt the son-of-a-bitch knew she hadn't been listening. Question was: would she admit it or should she try to bluff her way through and risk a fatal mistake?

While she pretended to consider the problem at hand—whatever it was—she noticed that the young editor from Farrar, Straus had half-cupped one hand in front of her mouth and placed the index and middle fingers of her other hand inside it. Her eyes fixed on Marsha with grave intensity.

What the hell, Marsha thought, she'd take a chance.

"You know very well, David, I pick number two. That's the only way to go."

There was a tiny sound, like a communal sigh of relief. Markham grinned with gritted teeth and held up two cover roughs that had been lying face-down in front of him. *Fools' Game* was the title. One of the covers was an imitation Ruth Rendell; the other showed a single black spider against a white background, with the title splashed blood-red across the top.

"For once, I must agree," Markham said, and tossed the one with the spider at the art director. "That's it. Next?"

Marsha smiled at Jaquie. Smart kid, she would go places.

The phone next to Marsha's elbow rang.

"Miss Hillier?" asked the switchboard.

"Yes," said Marsha curtly. Cover conferences were not to be interrupted by phone calls except in emergencies.

"There's a man on the phone, insists he must speak with you now. I told him you were in a meeting, but he says it's imperative..."

"What's his name?"

"He says it's *Mister* Joseph. Should I put him through?"

She had been expecting him. She had been hoping he was far away manipulating some eager new quarry, yet she had known all along he would contact her. No sense trying to avoid it now.

"Yes."

Click.

"Marsha?" The unmistakable accent, transforming her name into that of a romantic heroine direct from the steppes.

"Hello," she said, tentatively.

"A thousand pardons for the interruption. I am told you are in the midst of a most important meeting. Yet I had confidence you wouldn't object since, as you know, we have still some unfinished business."

"We have?" Marsha whispered, her throat suddenly dry, the air thin around her.

"The trouble with unfinished business, my dear Marsha, is that it renders one rather nervous, edgy. Wouldn't you say?"

"Yes. Well..." "Edgy" didn't do justice to Marsha's constant sense of foreboding since she had not returned the documents to The Dealer's messenger.

"In the beginning I had misgivings about you, but you already know that. You do remember, I stressed that you were your own choice, not mine. Yet, contrary to my expectations, you have played your role to the limit and beyond. Your remarkable tenacity is surpassed only by your ingenuity when faced with a difficult problem. It was a gamble worth taking and we have both won."

"We have?"

"I have more than I had bargained for and you...you must admit you have been substantially more fortunate than your fellow publishers who were granted the dubious pleasure of reading *Better Red Than Dead?*"

Marsha remained silent.

"You will find a small token of my appreciation in the top drawer of your desk. And that, as they say, concludes our business. Until next time..." The Dealer hung up.

His gift was a small brown ink-and-wash sketch, study for a 1669 Rembrandt Self-Portrait. Or so it appeared.

Craving more
Anna Porter?

Read on for the first chapters
of her new thriller,
The Appraisal

available now from
ECW Press

ECWPress.com

THE APPRAISAL

ANNA PORTER

"A deftly written novel abounding with intrigue."
—PUBLISHERS WEEKLY *on* MORTAL SINS

He HAD BEEN COMING to the Gerbeaud for thirty years, but he never tired of it. During the summer he liked to sit under its wide, grey umbrellas on Vörösmarty Square, enjoying snippets of conversation at adjoining tables and watching life go by. It was a cozy respite from the nastiness of work. He didn't much care whether the service was slow, the chrome tabletop wiped clean, or his espresso lukewarm, he loved the tangy black coffee oozing across his tongue and the reassuring normalcy of unfolding the daily paper on its wooden holder. He savoured the familiarity.

Although pretty much everything in Hungary had changed since the advent of the "market economy," the Gerbeaud's sole concession to the winds of capitalism had been a steady increase in prices. The new owners had left the rest of it alone. He could still sit here as long as he wished, nursing the single espresso that cost him a quarter of a good day's wages, and the waitresses never pushed him to reorder.

There had been a time when the manager, sleek as a young trout in her fitted black dress, had refilled his delicate china cup and hadn't charged for it, but she had long gone to greater fortunes in the States. Her name was Klari, now probably changed to Claire, or maybe Clara to preserve a touch of the Continent. She would have discovered by now that it cost a damned sight more than an occasional refill of coffee to buy a policeman in the so-called home of the free. Even in Budapest, bribery was no longer a bargain.

At the table beside his, a young man wearing Gucci wraparound sunglasses, a gold Tissot watch, a collarless white shirt, and beige calf-leather pants was reading the *Wall Street Journal*. He was sucking on a split of champagne, surreptitiously checking his watch. Someone was keeping him waiting. He didn't like it, but he wasn't going to betray any anxiety. A man in Gucci wraparound glasses couldn't admit to being kept waiting. He seemed familiar. A long-ago police lineup? Judging from his attire, his career had blossomed since then.

It didn't matter. The real target of Attila's interest was near the first wide window, her back to the pastries counter and across from a frothy-haired man who also looked vaguely familiar. Her elbows were on the table and her long blond hair was dangling over an open blue file folder placed between them. Sheets of paper dropped so fast from her fingers, he presumed she was speed-reading until she came to the last sheet, which she stared at for several minutes. She closed the folder, pushed it toward her companion, and leaned forward as she talked. He listened, then produced something from his breast pocket. A picture? A passport? It was small, dark, and oblong. She palmed it so quickly that had Attila not been watching he would have missed the movement.

He scanned the room, pretending to pay equal attention to all the customers. He was pleased that neither the woman nor her companion had once looked at him.

The waitress, a country girl with short henna-red hair, was asking the *Wall Street Journal* man if she could take his spare chair. A group of German tourists was next in line for a table with not enough chairs. She asked in Hungarian, her hand on the chair, her meaning fairly clear, but he pretended not to understand. Playing for time, Attila thought, time to decide whether to reveal he had been waiting for someone. Without relinquishing her hold on the chair, the waitress — he must find out her name — asked, "Okay?" For emphasis, she jiggled the back of the chair, clattering its metal legs on the asphalt.

The fellow nodded without enthusiasm, swivelling his head toward the group of tourists. One of them waved and shouted "Vielen Dank." The Habsburg Empire had self-destructed some ninety years ago, but German speakers still viewed Budapest as an anachronistic piece of Austrian territory.

At the table behind Attila's, three elderly Hungarian women were debating the relative merits of the chestnut purée — sweet, traditional, brandy-basted — and the kugel loaf — historically more interesting, but less tasty. In the centre of the square, under the seated bronze statue of Mihály Vörösmarty, Hungary's beloved poet, three young men in faded blue jeans were making a small drug deal. Vörösmarty was looking down as if observing the activities of the young men. The vendor pulled a plastic bag from his pocket and offered a taste. Hardly worth the effort, it was no more than ten ounces. "Be faithful to your land forever, oh Hungarian . . ." The great poet's words ran around the pedestal, where a bronze phalanx of fellow Hungarians formed Vörösmarty's adoring public. The buyer finger-tasted the coke and nodded to his companion, who would be carrying the cash. Street value of maybe a couple of thousand dollars. Small-time dealer. Attila assumed he worked the hotels on the Pest side and some of the classy apartments along the tramline. A couple of years ago Attila would have been bearing down on them. But back then they'd have already spotted him for a cop and moved the trade somewhere else. What was it about him that had changed so much in only two years?

Attila had been hunched over his table, a broad-shoul-dered, greying man, balding on top, overweight, ham-fisted, thick-necked, his shirt collar and jacket both too tight. He straightened his back when the young dealer glanced at him, mildly suspicious, but then the dealer palmed the money and handed over the merchandise without a second look at Attila.

The man with the *Wall Street Journal* examined his bill, counted some forints into the tray, and stood up to leave. His pants, caught in the wedge of his ass, stuck to his thighs. He must have gained weight since he bought them, Attila thought with some satisfaction. Anyway, it was too warm for leather pants.

His attention was caught by a young woman, her red hair flying, her light-blue summer dress swinging, and her slender white heels flying over the paving stones as she ran toward the Gerbeaud. She lifted her long legs over the silk rope barrier, straddling it for a second, her cotton skirt billowing around her, offering a glimpse of her white cotton panties, then she was wrapping her arms around the sweaty young man with the calf skin caught between his buttocks. "Jancsi," she called him, her voice soft as the inside of her thighs.

"Where the hell have you been?" he demanded. Obviously, although the days of swooning over Westerners were long gone, he still thought it stylish to sound foreign.

The woman by the window glanced at the gilt-framed mirror above her companion's head. She adjusted her silk scarf, flicked her hair over her shoulder, then made that little moue that some women make when they are checking their makeup. She stood up with her weight on her palms flat against the table. Attila figured she was probably still exhausted from her flight and the long drive from Vienna, but she recovered quickly and walked out fast, her dress clinging to her legs, a leather handbag dangling from her arm. She was pretty, although a little older than pretty warranted, and her bare arms and long legs showed the kind of muscle earned by regular workouts. Her erstwhile companion stayed at the table, sipping coffee and digging into the large serving of chestnut purée that had sat there ignored for the past twenty minutes. He was no longer only vaguely familiar. The narrow forehead under the froth of hair. He ran a posh art shop on Váci Street. Attila had paid him a visit about ten years ago. The man had been caught with some stolen primitive art. Indian. He couldn't remember what the outcome was, except that this man had somehow got away with it.

Attila laid his change on the tray and followed her across the square, past Vörösmarty's statue, the McCafé, the Hard Rock Café, the exorbitantly expensive clothing stores, down to the Danube, where his quarry was marching past the souvenir vendors with only an occasional glance at the river. Although she did pause for a moment to survey Gellért Hill in all its spring glory, she was not behaving like a tourist. A tourist would have stopped at the Shakespeare statue outside the Marriot Hotel and read the words on the brass plaque.

He kept at a distance as she crossed to Buda over the Szabadság Bridge and walked around the periphery of a small square (why the hell was it under construction again?) to the Gellért Hotel.

2

SHE HAD CHOSEN THE Gellért less for its old-world charm than for its several entrances. She preferred the small rooms at the back. They didn't offer the view of the Danube for which the hotel was known, but they were adequate. A single bed, a narrow desk, a phone, two shelves, a hanger for clothes, and a safe. She preferred no fuss and not too much cleaning. Maids came only early in the morning for light cleaning and bed making. The view was of the side of Gellért Hill where, late at night, noise makers cavorted and played music and lovers had open-air sex.

Helena had been here before but with different hair, a different name, and a man she had liked more than she wanted to. He had booked a suite at the front of the hotel, ordered flowers, and they had danced to lackadaisical gypsy music in the dining room. She didn't like dancing to gypsy music, but that was not the reason they broke up. She had not been ready for a long-term relationship. She was struggling with too much unresolved anger and a couple of persistent ghosts. The ghosts still refused to go quietly, but she had almost managed to master her rage. But Robert was no longer waiting.

She opened her black canvas holdall and arranged her clothes over the bedcover: black pants, a grey woollen sweater, black T-shirt, a black hoodie, faded black Nike running shoes, thin skin-coloured pantyhose, a short white cardigan, a small-brimmed foldable hat, five cell phones, black leather gloves, dark-rimmed glasses, a long pearl-grey linen jacket with a high collar, a raincoat, a cross-strapped navy bathing suit, four passports, a clear plastic bag containing a black wig with a fringe and a light-brown one, a small Revlon makeup case, a vial of face cream, the photograph Kis had given her, a foldable flashlight, wire cutters, a pocketbook, a Nikon Coolpix 16MP, a suede sheath containing a long-handled straight knife with a thin blade, a snub-nosed SwissMiniGun with six bullets.

She put the wigs and passports into the safe.

She slipped out of her dress, untied the blue silk scarf, placed the slingback shoes next to the door, and pulled on the black pants, the T-shirt, and the hoodie. She removed her blond wig and laid it, its tendrils trailing, on one pillow and pushed the second pillow lengthwise under the covers. From a short distance, it looked like a figure lying knees up, face to the wall.

Her own hair was light brown with a few grey streaks, cut short and soft on the sides, bristly on top. She used a dollop of gel to make it lie flat. Standing in front of the mirror, she removed the blue eyeshadow and thick lashes and peeled off the thin plastic strip over her upper lip. She selected a dark purple lipstick from her collection of makeup pencils and dabbed it on her lips. Her reflection showed an almost middle-aged woman who didn't much care about her appearance. She packed the flashlight, the handgun, the wire cutters, and the camera into her backpack and pulled on the pair of frayed running shoes.

She picked up the slingbacks and left the room, dropping the shoes at the last moment as she pulled the door closed so they would be just inside the door. She hung the "Do Not Disturb" sign on the door handle.

She took the back stairs next to the wrought-iron elevator that ferried guests down to the hotel's famous Turkish baths. She showed her plastic key-card to the attendant, went through the baths' exit between the two stone Grecian figures, and walked down toward the river.

The tall heavy-set man she'd noticed in the Gerbeaud was standing at the tram stop, leaning against the ticket machine, frequently glancing into a paperback book while observing the Gellért's main entrance. He looked at her for only a fraction of a second as she stepped over the tram tracks. She was sure he had not recognized her. He didn't seem very committed to his task. Perhaps he was a retired policeman. She had seen dozens of them all over Prague, Bratislava, and Berlin, even in Warsaw, although not so many there. Most of the old Polish police and security men had long gone to villages where they would be harder to identify. She had tracked one of them a few years ago. It had not been easy. He was now farming potatoes near Częstochowa. Back in the 1980s, he had been high up in the Ministry of Public Works. He had taken a ten-by-twelve-cm Leonardo da Vinci drawing as payment for keeping an informer out of jail. Her job had been to recover it.

The Poles were less forgiving than the Czechs, Slovaks, and the Hungarians. In Budapest, beneficiaries of the Communist era didn't need to hide. That made it easy to find people. Unless they were dead.

Géza Márton had left here in 1956 after the failed Hungarian Revolution. Had he returned recently, he would know whom the system still protected and who could still do him harm. But then he wouldn't need her services.

She ran along the river, taking long strides, pumping her arms, and slowly settling into her usual energetic jog. Although the sun had almost set, it was light enough to see the street signs, and the air was warm. In Toronto, there had still been snow on the ground, it was getting dark at 7:30 p.m., and the few early birds perched in the desolate trees in the Mártons' garden had seemed stunned. The house was on a low hill, with the garden sloping down to more trees and bushes in the valley below. Géza was proud of his Georgian red-brick house with its tall bay windows, its white pillars flanking the entrance, and delighted with his young white oaks, his sugar maples, his spectacularly green rhododendrons, and his long sloping lawn — still brownish in April — that ended at the ravine.

He had been pleased to show off his paintings, the nine quasi-Impressionists, a couple of almost Picassos, a possible Max Ernst, and a Watteau. Over the wide wooden staircase to the second floor, there had been a Rubens drawing of a nude, a Cellini, a Degas, and there were more paintings in the study, although Géza had saved the best for the master bedroom: an early Van Gogh, which he may have bought from her father, Simon. At their initial meeting, he had insisted she see it.

Géza Márton had made most of his money in Vaughan, a town just north of Toronto, but he didn't want to live there. Rosedale was a sedate, leafy, midtown neighbourhood, a long way from the subdivisions of Vaughan, where immigrant families lived cheek by jowl with their fellows and could hear every altercation, every lovemaking, child's cry, and dog bark on either side of their new homes.

He said this place reminded him of his family's old home in the Buda Hills and that walking through the front door made him feel that he was entering his own small country. Helena had wondered whether his English wife had added her own touches to the décor or just allowed him to recreate a childhood dream.

At Bem József Square, she turned up Fekete Sas Street and started to climb Rózsadomb. She was relieved to find that there were few cameras on the hydro poles on this street, the surveillance that was so ubiquitous on the Pest side seemed lax in the Buda neighbourhoods. She walked on, savouring the smell of the early acacia blossoms, the broad chestnut trees with their candle-like flowers, the shaded garden homes of the wealthy burghers and politicians who had managed to make money and keep it.

She found the house easily. It was set back from the street; a low stone wall enclosed the front garden. Roses climbed over its wrought-iron gate. The single camera on the nearest utility pole was angled to survey the other side of the street. A tall stone fountain stood in a pond at the centre of a grassy knoll to the left of the driveway, and four white-painted, wrought-iron chairs and a table were arranged near it. The house was dark except for one bevelled window with wooden foldout shutters near the front door. Two tall ceramic pots flanked the oak door. To the side, the garage door was open, and inside was a turquoise 2014 S-Class Mercedes Benz sedan with white wheel rims and grey-tinted windows. Its body shone. A camera positioned under the roof overhang was aimed at the garage entrance. Easy to avoid if you were not interested in the Benz.

From where she stood, she could see the electrical box on the inside wall of the garage, next to a door to the house.

Pretending to look for street numbers, she waited for a noisy couple to pass. They were competing with each other to finish a story that made them both hiccup with laughter. When was the last time she had laughed like that?

The stone wall was easy to step over. Keeping low to the grass, she crossed the yard and stopped behind the fountain to look into the lighted room. Even from this distance, she could see tall bookcases, a wide desk facing the garden, a straight-backed, unpadded chair. As she crept closer, she saw a thick rug running the length of the room and a man with his back to her, talking to someone through an inner door.

He had a strong voice. Through the open window, she could hear his tone, if not the words themselves. Imperious. Annoyed. Demanding.

He turned to a bookcase, picked up a book, and stood it upright with the others. He half-turned to the window. He was tall, broad-shouldered, erect, with short white hair, a long neck, a protruding chin, and a high forehead. All he seemed to have in common with the man in the photograph Géza Márton had shown her was his bearing. The rest must have changed with age. Márton had guessed that the man would be in his late eighties, and he could have lost much of his brawn and his bull neck. Certainly his hair would have turned white. Or this was not the right man. Yet Géza had been so certain.

A woman entered the room, carrying a round tray with an open decanter and one glass. She could be a servant, but that was unlikely because she was dressed in a well-cut blue suit with large golden buttons, a frilled blouse showing at the neck. He must have married again in the years since Gertrude had left. Perhaps it had not occurred to the Mártons that such a man would marry twice. Still, they do. And the women seem not to mind that their men are monsters. Even Lavrentiy Beria had a wife. The infamous head of Stalin's secret police was not only a murderer, he was also a sexual sadist, yet his Nina stayed faithful. She enjoyed the material rewards he offered: the Georgian silver, the antique jewels, the purloined Rembrandts and huge Tintoretto that had graced their living room. She had been reluctant to part with any of it.

The man poured from the decanter as he riffled through papers on his desk, casually, distracted, as if he was making sure something was there but was not interested in reading it. He played with the point of a silver letter opener, then replaced it exactly where it had been, an inch to the right of his leather-bound diary. His hands were thin with long fingers, not the massive meat-hooks Géza had mentioned.

The phone rang, a clear metallic tone. He pressed a button on the receiver and listened. His lips did not seem to move, and she did not hear what he said.

It was 7 p.m. They would be gone in less than an hour.

She stepped back over the wall and continued up Fekete Sas Street, past a block of flats and other sizable houses, to a tiny park. There were a couple of benches, a sandbox, and some downtrodden grass. She sat on a bench and watched the small children playing with their mothers, the dogs cavorting on the grass near the one-way entrance, then took out her well-thumbed copy of the *Aeneid*.

The Benz rounded the corner a little too fast, tires whining as it turned onto Margit Boulevard, on its way to the Margit Bridge and on to Pest and the Hungarian State Opera House.

She waited another five minutes, glancing up from the book at cars passing, in case they had forgotten something and returned. At 8 p.m., she pulled the hood over her head, covered her mouth with the scarf, and returned to the house. The shutters were closed. She scanned the wall with her flashlight, once, then edged her way to the garage, keeping to the side closest to the house. Just outside the camera's range, she unlocked the garage door with a twist of the knife, then cut the four electrical cables with the wire cutters and pried the connecting door open with her knife. It was too easy. Inside, she disconnected the alarm just as it began its loud whine.

She had calculated that it would take a car fifteen minutes to get here from the Pest police station. She would hear the siren. She had to be fast.

She examined the windows for separate alarms and found none. She wedged open the door to his office and surveyed the tidy desk, the letter opener, the orderly bookcases, the round tray still there on the round side table, his crystal tumbler with a trace of his evening drink. His study opened onto a hallway lined with sepia photographs of men and women in formal dress, the women wearing gloves and cradling bouquets. There was a framed portrait of the man in a dark suit, hat sitting low on his head, the rim shading his forehead, dark glasses, hands folded in front, still the long, thin neck and long fingers. There were a few small paintings: an early Poussin, a Raphael with angels and a blue Madonna, something that looked like an Arshile Gorky — a sad-eyed women with scarf — a large, early Monet of boats in shimmering water, and an early Picasso drawing. A dark Velázquez of two overdressed, expressionless children in a chocolate-coloured frame hung above the bar in the dining room. On either side of the door, there were four small paintings by Lajos Kassák that she recognized only because she had seen a collection of his forgettable abstracts at a recent Museum of Modern Art exhibition of Hungarian artists banned during the Communist years.

The painting Géza Márton had described was in the living room, hanging over a long, florid sofa. It was six feet long and four feet high. She felt its presence even before her flashlight found Christ's face. It was the sheer size of the gilded frame and the figures blending into the dark resin background. The small grey donkey in the centre left seemed to have been outlined with a brush handle or a sharp palette knife. There were dabs of white and yellow on the faces of the figures looking up at the man on the donkey. The paint was laid on thick and heavy, the artist having used both a palette knife and his fingers where the figures blended into the sombre background. It was a very physical painting, with its big figures, his style freed from his times' constraint of mirroring every detail. Palma il Giovane had talked of Titian's vigorous underpainting, the reds, blacks, and yellows, and of his predilection for using a palette knife.

Thin shafts of blue and white emanating from a magenta cloud lit up the back of Christ's head. His face was just a suggestion of browns and ochres and his eyes were deep holes. His muddy, sandalled feet were scraping the ground. There were splashes of red on his neck and ankles, as if to prefigure the Crucifixion. In contrast to Christ's purple robe, the ones worn by the men following him were dirty white. Some were holding their arms aloft, their faces shiny with sweat and anticipation. Two women were laying palm fronds on the uneven path in front of the donkey. Mary Magdalene, walking ahead in her signature green gown, looked out of the painting. Her bright eyes and pink-and-white face made her seem at once beatific and accusatory. Another upturned face and a dash of blue by the donkey's flank depicted the Virgin Mary. Incongruously, two small spaniels in the bottom right-hand corner gazed upward, as if expecting treats. The artist had taken great care in detailing their fur.

It could be a late work, perhaps as late as 1570, when Titian was well into his eighties. There was a hurried, sketchy quality to some of the figures. It was reminiscent of *The Death of Actaeon*, but the stormy sky may have been finished by one of his workshop students, perhaps Polidoro da Lanciano, although she doubted Polidoro would have completed any of the late works. Titian hadn't finished putting on the varnish, but in his final years he often left the varnish off parts of his paintings.

Alternatively, it could be a study for an early work, a mere sketch, something intended for Philip II, who liked both religious paintings and detailed nudes posing as naiads or some other mythological women who cavort about naked.

There was no signature.

Without the right equipment, it was hard for her to tell whether it was a Titian or a good forgery. She had used chromatography and a spectrometer to analyze the paint of a Rubens in St. Petersburg and had determined that it was a late copy. Another time, she had established that a beautifully executed Raphael at the Borghese was an exquisite reinterpretation by the Dutch master-forger, Han van Meegeren. That man could redefine genius. He could imitate the style of any artist, and it would take years of technical examination to identify which paintings were his. She had studied Titian and read all extant documents about his work. There was no mention of this particular painting.

She took photos from all angles, then close-ups of details, shining her flashlight on each part of the painting.

When she was done, she knocked over the bottle of whisky and the glasses on the sideboard, tucked the silver cigar box under her arm, broke the window by the front door, pulled the hood over her face, and left.

It had taken her eleven minutes.

No serious police officer would be convinced by her efforts to stage a break-in, but the smashed window and missing box would offer an easy diagnosis, and experience told her that one should never overestimate the police.

She walked back to the little park, dropped the cigar box in the garbage bin next to a man sleeping on a bench, listened to the sirens of police cars climbing the hill from the river, did a few stretches against the other bench, then loped back to the hotel.

3

ATTILA WAVED CASUALLY at the overdressed doorman, entered the Gellért Hotel by the revolving door, and walked across the marble lobby with the purposeful steps of a guest. No one even looked at him. The stairway led up to the third floor. A "Do Not Disturb" sign hung from the brass handle of the door to Helena Marsh's room. It took him a full minute to open the electronic lock; less time than an old-fashioned keyed lock would have taken. She hadn't used the chain. It was dark inside the room. The few lights flickering outside the window illuminated her long blond hair spread out on the pillow. Obviously, she had decided to have a nap. Whatever she was up to, it couldn't have been much — or she had astonishing sang-froid. Why hadn't she put the chain across the door?

He went back down and sat in the bar, which gave him a clear view of both the elevators and the marble stairway. He ordered a Vilmos brandy with a beer chaser.

He hadn't intended to wait till nearly 11, but the barman had been telling him a long, episodic story fitted between serving other guests, and Attila's drinks after the first two had been free. The barman had once been a junior lawyer in the justice department, mostly petty crime but there had been one case of a journalist who had written for a Western paper and was caught, prosecuted, and jailed. He was lucky even to have had a trial. Now, after the advent of democracy, the journalist was a member of parliament and the lawyer was serving Attila Czech beer.

At 10:45 p.m. he took the tram home to Rákóczi Avenue. The street had been spared some of the 1990s' construction boom, and, while many old apartment blocks had been destroyed and replaced by condominiums, Attila's hundred-year-old building, with its small wrought-iron elevator that rarely moved, had remained in its pre-war state. It featured peeling paint, crumbling brick, and uneven floors and was just the way he liked it. His apartment's tall windows, high ceilings, and balcony made up for the street noise. Most of the year, except in the depth of winter, he could leave the balcony door open for Gustav, about the only thing his ex had allowed him to keep from their marriage. A miniature long-haired dachshund mix, Gustav had an uneven temperament but a keen nose for quality food, and, unlike the ex, he was always pleased to see Attila.

After a short walk around the block, they shared a couple of salami sandwiches and settled in to watch the latest episode of an American series about a teacher who turns into a drug dealer. Another advantage of democracy was the plethora of utterly mindless television options. This was better than most. There were times he felt nostalgic for the heavy-handed Soviet propaganda films of the 1970s and the occasional cheap Hungarian tragedies of that time, with their disguised messages of protest or exasperation with the system.

The phone rang at around 1 a.m.

"What the fuck happened to you?"

"Huh?"

"Remember you had a job? You didn't do it. Fell asleep at the bar? Went to a movie? What the hell?" The voice was rough, spittingly breathy, as if he was holding the phone too close to his mouth.

"István?"

"Captain dammit, Detective Tóth to you, never mind the István, and where the hell were you?"

"Waiting," Attila said. "She never came out of her room."

"Bloody funny, that," Tóth shouted. "She was in a house on Fekete Sas Street at eight thirty, walking about like she owned the place. She knew the real owners would be out all evening. She knew the opera schedule. No hurry at all. Took her time. The client is not happy."

"Impossible. I checked her room and she was lying in bed. Sleeping. I watched the elevators and the staircase till 11 p.m. She never came down."

"So, it must have been her ghost." Tóth harrumphed into his cell phone.

"Were there no alarms?"

"She cut the wires."

"How do you know it was her?"

Tóth laughed too loudly. "It was a woman in a black hoodie. About her height and shape."

"It could have been another woman."

"Don't be an ass."

"Cameras?"

"One, hidden, by a big painting in the living room. She didn't try to steal the painting, but that may be because it would be hard to hustle a thing that's about two metres long with a thick gilt frame out of a house in a residential area."

"Did the camera pick up her face?"

"No. Like I said, she was wearing a hoodie."

"Do they have anything else worth stealing?"

"He may have a couple of other paintings. And he has a safe, but it was not disturbed. He's retired and thought they had nothing to worry about. Or didn't. Till now."

"Oh." Even if the guy had nothing to hide, why not install some outside security cameras, just in case a couple of neighbourhood kids decided to relieve him of a few household items? There were more cameras throughout this city than parking meters.

"No valuables?" Attila asked, nonplussed. Everyone had valuables, even if it was only bits of rock from a holiday. Anyone living on Rózsadomb would have valuables; it was an elite part of the city.

Their address defined them. That so many former Communists and their fellow travellers had held onto their homes here was, he thought, an indication of capitalism's victory over memory.

"Anything missing?" he asked.

"Only a cigar box. Silver. And they do have security," Tóth said. "Us."

"Last night?"

"You were on the job, last night," Tóth yelled. "Your job was to check if she went anywhere. You were hired to follow her." He must have lighted a cigarette, Attila heard the match scrape the phone, then Tóth let out a long breath, as if exhaling smoke. "Tomorrow morning at eight," he said and disconnected.

"Son of a bitch," Attila murmured after he put the phone down. Eight a.m. was just four hours away, and his mouth felt like a pigsty. What did those Czechs put in their beer? It used to taste better in the 1980s, but that might be his age.

The dog lay on his back at the end of the bed, paws in the air, farting. Salami might not be the best thing to eat just before going to sleep. Too much red pepper.

If the woman had left the hotel, it must have been through the baths' exit. He couldn't see it from the bar, but he had stood on the tram island till after 9 p.m. and had not seen her. What about her blond head lying on the pillow? Was it a set-up? How the hell could she have been on Fekete Sas Street at 8:30?

He made himself an espresso. The machine had been a gift from a grateful store owner on Váci Street after Attila had ended a two-year protection racket that had each of the high-end stores paying into a "beautify the city" fund that existed only in the imagination of the Albanian gang that had failed to pay its own dues to the local police. The gang had learned its lesson and was now happily beautifying Vienna.

He lay down on the sofa — not nearly as comfortable as the squishy corduroy one that had exited with the wife — and tried to read an old Jack Reacher novel, waiting for the machine to heat up. The ex had decided to leave his collection of detective fiction but took most of the quality stuff, along with the bookcases. His remaining books were still in cardboard boxes piled high next to the kitchen. He was too tired to read. Too tired to make coffee, but he persevered till 7 a.m., when Gustav insisted on his morning crap. It was barely daylight, and there was just enough rain to dissuade the dog from going outside. He hunkered down in the long passageway between the elevator and the entrance. Attila kicked the tidy cigarillo of dog turd into the darkest part of the passageway and led the disconsolate Gustav back to the apartment.

At 8 a.m., Attila was at the Police Palace (which is what everyone called the police headquarters after the government added the tall tower), showing his ID to the fat woman who had been on security long enough to know him even in the dark. As usual, she made a big production of examining his photo, looking at him, examining the photo again. Then she waved him through the X-ray machine, minus his holster and wallet. The building had become even more of a mindless fortress since he left.

Naturally, Tóth was not yet in his office, and the young uniform who guarded the second floor didn't know enough to let Attila wait in one of the empty interrogation rooms, so he sat on the bench for petty criminals awaiting questioning. A couple of young offenders wearing American pants with crotches at their knees made room for him. They were discussing why they had been picked up and, coming up empty, focused on a girl they had both tried to take home the night before. He could have told them the reason they had been hauled in was their pants, but decided it was pointless. Most of the policemen (and sole policewoman) looked like they were at the end of a night shift, rather than starting the day. They were slow-moving, damp, bleary-eyed, and smelly.

Tóth arrived close to 9 a.m. He was eating some kind of sugary pastry that left white powder on his thin mustache — the only thin part of the man — and down his ample front. His shirt barely fit across his belly. One button had already popped, and the day had barely begun. On the other hand, his dung-coloured jacket was just-out-of-the-box new. But why, Attila wondered, had he chosen that shade of brown?

Tóth grunted when he saw Attila and motioned with his chin toward his corner office. Since Attila's last visit, the small fringed rug and the colour photo of the smiling woman at the edge of the desk — the same desk Attila had used when this had been his office — had both disappeared. Tóth finished the pastry before he looked at his former boss and, even then, he seemed reluctant to start the conversation.

"So," he said, at last. He sat with knees wide apart, hands clasped. "She has been on the phone all morning. We have a man with binoculars on the path up Gellért Hill and he has a perfect view of her room. She is using her own phone, not the hotel's. We can't get a fix on the number. She must have one of those cheap disposables you can pick up anywhere. She has a rental car, due back in Vienna in three days. The Ukrainians want her gone before then."

Attila shook his head. "The Ukrainians? What do they have to do with her?"

"Don't know. But they are anxious to have her out of the country. As is Mr. Krestin, the guy whose house she broke into, and he has some influence with the government. The government runs the police, in case you've forgotten." He rubbed his palms together, looked at them, wiped them on his knees. "Your job is to not lose sight of her again."

Attila sighed.

"Is that simple enough?" Tóth asked.

"Krestin?" Attila refused to be baited.

"János Krestin."

"Guy who used to own a studio making utterly dreadful movies?"

"Him."

"And he owned the Lipótváros football team?"

"His house is not in Lipótváros, and it's his house that she couldn't have been in because she was asleep in her bed."

"If he owned Lipótváros, he has some valuables. Did you say nothing was missing?" Attila didn't know a whole lot about János Krestin, but he did know that the man had accumulated a fortune, and some of it might have come from the bribes he collected before 1989. Rumour had it that if you were accused of petty crimes against the state, Krestin could get the state to forget about them. Or he could ensure fewer years in jail.

Most former functionaries had fitted seamlessly into the new system. Many of them had the advantages of knowing other languages, and most had done well since 1989. Back then, ordinary people were still too busy trying to repair their lives to pay much attention to the successes of others. That didn't last.

"I said nothing was stolen except the cigar case."

"So, what was she doing there?"

Tóth shrugged.

"Perhaps she was looking for something but didn't find it?"

Tóth shrugged again.

"And she cut the security system. So, she is a professional?"

"Not exactly," Tóth said, chewing on his thumbnail.

"Do you have some information about her that you are not sharing?" Attila asked. "Something that explains her connection to Krestin? You told me this Helena Marsh hasn't been here for seven years, and, even then, no one knew what she was looking for until after she left. You remember the Bauers and their Rembrandts?"

"Vaguely. Two pictures their neighbours had appropriated during the war. She had nothing to do with that."

"In the end, the Bauers got their Rembrandts back, and the Szilágyis decided not to prefer charges, although they told me at first that their paintings had been stolen."

Tóth shook his head. "Irrelevant."

"It's not irrelevant if that's what she does. She spent time in Germany and Holland, tracking art stolen from Jews during the war. She is some kind of expert. Is that why she is here?"

"This is not about stolen art," Tóth said. "And Krestin was never a Nazi. He was a card-carrying party member. At least for a while."

"A while?"

"There were no card-carrying Communists after '90."

Some guys, Attila thought, could easily have been both Nazi and Communist, or Nazi and then Communist. A willingness to dole out physical violence would have been an advantage after the war. A man could go a long way with those credentials. Not that Krestin had ever been accused of that publicly, but one could never be sure with men of a certain age.

"But she is, as you put it, some kind of expert on art. And if you could encourage her to leave the country, I would be very grateful," Tóth said.

"As would the Ukrainians?"

Tóth didn't answer.

They sat in silence for a while, Attila trying to estimate just how grateful everybody — especially the Ukrainians — would be and how much extra he could charge if he persuaded the woman to go home. Then he got to his feet, buttoned his jacket, and left. Simple enough.

He was halfway across the Szabadság Bridge when he saw her. She was wearing the same dress as yesterday but she had added a summery cotton hat and a tight-waisted white cardigan. The blue scarf was tied into a knot at her neck. She was heading to the Pest side. Striding fast, her skirt fanning out in the wind off the river, she looked like a tourism commercial: cheerful, carefree, her blond hair swept back. She glanced at him without much interest when they came face to face, but he caught the hint of a smile at the corner of her mouth. Close up, she seemed older than yesterday and older than the photo in his breast pocket. But the blond hair, the slim hips, the confident way she carried herself all added up to fortyish and foreign. Women in Hungary hadn't walked like that for years, not since the economy tanked.

He waited for her to reach the baroque church in Ferenciek Square before he began to follow her. It was ridiculous to imagine she would not notice or that she wouldn't remember swinging past him on the bridge, but he had agreed not to lose sight of her, and he was not about to let her disappear again.

She turned onto Dob Street and stopped outside a dull little café. Attila knew it; sometimes he dropped in for a cream scone. The black-clad Garda louts who had been strolling this neighbourhood for the past few months were across the street, smoking and glaring. Atilla had seen them patrolling this street and had heard that they occasionally tripped some elderly Jew on his way to the grocery shop or, better still, on his way back. Then he would be likely to drop his eggs and milk on the sidewalk. The louts would chortle and would declare that had people been more vigilant in '44, there wouldn't be a "Jew problem" now.

The trouble with allowing free speech, Attila thought, was that this sort of thing could go on unchecked. But then, according to the government, there was no problem. And, according to the government, the Garda had been banned. But here they were, as usual, although only half a dozen of them, unlike the past Sunday when they held a rally on Hösök Square. In the past, when Attila had arrested members of the Garda, they would be out in an hour or less. Hardly worth the effort. Tóth said the Jews and the gypsies could take care of themselves. It wasn't entirely true, but it did save a lot of time and trouble with lawyers and foreign reporters who wanted to know why the Garda was still marching. (Local journalists knew better than to cover Garda events; the government's media council could yank their licences.) The Garda had changed their uniforms, but they were still black, their flags were even more in-your-face patriotic, and they carried on.

Helena stayed at the café take-out window for a moment, examining the aging pastries in the glass case and checking her phone. She ordered an espresso in a Styrofoam cup, looked up and down the street (no doubt spotting him on the other side, talking to himself on his cell phone), and strolled on to number twenty-two. The lads made piggy noises but didn't bother to cross the street.

She pressed the bell to one of the apartments. The door was opened immediately by an elderly man with thin, bent shoulders. He must have been waiting for her. It was murky inside, the only light a flash of sunshine far beyond the door. Attila took a photo with his phone but expected that it would show only the shadows.

The man let her inside and shut the door.